THE
STAR OF
KAZAN

Also by Eva Ibbotson

THE
STAR OF
KAZAN

Eva Ibbotson

MACMILLAN CHILDREN'S BOOKS

First published 2004 by Macmillan Children's Books
a division of Macmillan Publishers Limited
20 New Wharf Road, London N1 9RR
Basingstoke and Oxford
www.panmacmillan.com

Associated companies throughout the world

ISBN 1 405 02054 7

1 3 5 7 9 8 6 4 2

A CIP catalogue record for this book is available from
the British Library.

Typeset by Intype Libra Ltd
Printed and bound in Great Britain by Mackays of Chatham plc, Kent

For Rowan

CONTENTS

CONTENTS

CHAPTER ONE

A PERSON IS FOUND

Ellie had gone into the church because of her feet. This is not the best reason for entering a church, but Ellie was plump and middle-aged and her feet were hurting her. They were hurting her badly.

It was a beautiful sunny day in June and Ellie and her friend Sigrid (who was as thin as Ellie was portly) had set out early from Vienna in the little train which took them to the mountains, so that they could climb up to the top of a peak called the Dorfelspitze.

They went to the mountains on the last Sunday of every month, which was their day off, changing their aprons for dirndls and filling their rucksacks with salami sandwiches and slices of plum cake, so that when they got to the top they could admire the view without getting hungry. It was how they refreshed their souls after the hard work they did all week, cleaning and cooking and shopping and scrubbing for the professors who employed them, and who were fussy about how things were done. Ellie was the cook and Sigrid was the housemaid and they had been friends for many years.

But on this particular Sunday, Ellie was wearing new boots, which is a silly thing to do when you are going on a long excursion. They were about halfway up the mountain when they came to a flower-filled meadow and on the far side of it, standing quite by itself, a small white church with an onion dome.

Ellie stopped.

'You know, Sigrid, I think I'd like to say a prayer for my mother. I had a dream about her last night. Why don't you go on and I'll catch you up.'

Sigrid snorted.

'I told you not to wear new boots.'

But she agreed to go ahead slowly, and Ellie crossed the wooden bridge over a little stream, and went into the church.

It was a lovely church – one of those places which look as though God might be about to give a marvellous party. There was a painted ceiling full of angels and golden stars and a picture of St Ursula holding out her arms, which made Ellie's feet feel better straight away. The holy relic wasn't something worrying like a toe bone or a withered hand but a lock of the saint's hair in a glass dome decorated with pearls, and though the church stood all by itself away from the village, someone had put a bunch of fresh alpenroses in a vase at the Virgin's feet.

Ellie slipped into a pew and loosened her shoelaces. She

said a prayer for her mother, who had passed on many years ago . . . and closed her eyes.

She only slept for a few minutes. When she awoke the church was still empty, but she thought she had been woken by a noise of some sort. She looked round carefully, but she could find nothing. Then, peering over the edge of the pew, she saw, lying on the crimson carpet at the foot of the altar steps – a parcel.

It was about the size of a vegetable marrow – quite a large one – and Ellie's first thought was that someone had left it there as a harvest offering. But harvest festivals happen in September not in June. And now, to Ellie's amazement, the marrow made a noise. A small, mewing noise . . .

A kitten . . . a puppy?

Ellie did up her shoelaces and went over to look.

But it was worse than a kitten or a puppy.

'Oh dear,' said Ellie. 'Oh dear, dear, dear!'

Sigrid had reached the top of the mountain. She had admired the view, she had eaten a salami sandwich and she had breathed deeply several times, but there was still no sign of Ellie.

Sigrid was annoyed. When you are on top of a mountain admiring a view you want somebody to do it *with*. She waited a while longer, then she packed the rucksack and made her way back down the rocky slope, through the pine woods, till she came to the meadow with the little church.

Ellie was still inside, sitting in the front pew – but she was holding something and she looked bewildered, and flushed, and strange . . .

'Someone left this,' she said.

Ellie pushed back the edge of the shawl and Sigrid bent down to look.

'Good heavens!'

The baby was very, very young, not more than a few days old, but it was quite amazingly ... alive. Warmth came from it; it steamed like a fresh-baked loaf, its legs worked under the shawl – and when Sigrid stretched out a bony forefinger to touch its cheek, it opened its eyes, and there, gazing up at them, was a *person*.

'There was a note pinned to her shawl,' said Ellie.

On a piece of paper, smudged with tears, were the words: 'Please be good to my little daughter and take her to Vienna to the nuns.'

'What are we going to do?' asked Sigrid.

She was upset. Neither she nor Ellie was married; they knew nothing about babies.

'Take her to Vienna to the nuns, like it says in the note. What else can we do?'

It took them an hour to carry the baby down to the little village of Pettelsdorf. No one there knew anything about a baby, no one had seen anyone go into the church.

'She'll have come up from the other side, over the pass,' they said.

A peasant woman gave them a bottle and some diluted milk from her cow, and they trudged on to the small lakeside station to wait for the train back to Vienna.

It was late by the time they arrived in the city with their damp and fretful bundle, and they were very tired. The only convent that they knew of which took in foundlings was a long way from the house of the professors, where they lived and worked, and they didn't have the money for a cab.

So they took the tram, and though it was one of the new electric ones it was almost dark as they walked up the drive to the Convent of the Sacred Heart.

The wrought-iron gates were shut; from the low white building came the sound of singing.

'She'll be all right in there,' said Ellie, touching the baby's head.

Sigrid pulled the bell rope. They heard the bell pealing inside, but nobody came.

She pulled it again, and they waited. Then at last an elderly nun came hurrying across the courtyard.

'What is it?' she asked, peering into the dusk.

'We've brought you a foundling, Sister,' said Sigrid. 'She was left in a church in the mountains.'

'No, no, NO!' The nun threw up her hands. She seemed to be horrified. 'Take her away, don't stay for a minute; you shouldn't have come! We're in quarantine for typhus. Three of the sisters have got it and it's spreading to the children.'

'Typhus!' Ellie shivered. It was a terrible disease, everyone knew that.

'Take her away quickly, quickly,' said the nun, and she began to flap with her arms as though she were shooing away geese.

'But where can we take her?' began Sigrid. 'There must be somewhere else.'

'No one in Vienna will take in children while the epidemic lasts,' she said. 'It'll be six weeks at least.'

Left outside, the friends stared at each other.

'We'll have to take her back with us and try again tomorrow.'

'What will the professors say?'

5

'They needn't know,' said Ellie. 'We'll keep her below stairs. They never come down to the kitchen.'

But there she was wrong.

The three professors had lived in the same house since they were born.

It was on the south side of a small square in the oldest part of the town, not far from the emperor's palace and the Spanish Riding School. If you leaned out of the upstairs windows you could see the pigeons wheeling round the spires of St Stephen's Cathedral, which stood at the very heart of the city and therefore (to the people who lived in it) of the world.

But though one could walk from the square to all the important places, it was as quiet and contained as a room. In the centre of the cobbles was a statue of General Brenner riding a bronze charger, which pleased the children who lived there because there is a lot you can do with the statue of a horse: pretend to ride it, pat it, shelter under it when it rains. The general had been a hero and fought against Napoleon, and because of this the square was named after him: Brenner Square.

Next to the general on his horse, there was a fountain with a shallow basin and a wide stone rim, and sometimes there were goldfish swimming in it because the children who won fish at the funfair in the Prater, a park in the north-east of the city, tipped them in on the way home.

The west side of the square was taken up by a church named after St Florian, who was the patron saint of fire engines. It was a pretty church with a grassy graveyard where wild flowers had seeded themselves, and on the opposite side to the church was a row of chestnut trees in iron corsets, which sheltered the square from the bustle of the street that led into the centre of the town. There was also a small bookshop on one corner, and a cafe with a striped awning on the other, so really the square had everything a person could need.

The house the professors lived in was in the middle of the row. It was the largest and the nicest and had a wrought-iron balcony on the first floor and window boxes and a door knocker shaped like the head of an owl.

Professor Julius was the oldest. He had a pointed grey beard and was tall and serious. Once many years ago he had very nearly got married, but the bride he had chosen had died a week before her wedding day, and since then Professor Julius had become solemn and stern. He was a scientist – a geologist – and lectured in the university, where he told the students about fluorspar and granite and how to hit rocks with a hammer so that they did not get splinters in their eyes.

His brother, Professor Emil, was quite different. He was small and round and had almost no hair, and when he went upstairs he wheezed a little, but he was a cheerful man. His subject was art history and he could tell just by looking at the toes of a painted angel whether the picture was by Tintoretto or by Titian.

The third professor was a woman, their sister and the youngest of the three. Her name was Gertrude and what she knew about was music. She gave lectures on harmony and counterpoint and she played the harp in the City Orchestra. Having a harp is rather like having a large and wayward child who has to be carried about and kept from draughts and helped into carriages, and Professor

7

Gertrude – like many harpists – often looked worried and dismayed.

Needless to say, none of the three had ever in their lives boiled an egg or washed a pair of socks or made their beds, and when Ellie and Sigrid had their day off they always left a cold lunch laid out. But by evening, the professors needed help again. Professor Julius had a whisky and soda brought to his room to help him sleep; Professor Emil, who had a delicate stomach, needed a glass of warm milk and honey; and Professor Gertrude suffered from cold feet and always had a hot-water bottle brought to her before she got between the sheets. So now they waited for their servants to return. Sigrid and Ellie were always back by nine o'clock – but not today.

'What shall we do?' asked Professor Julius, putting his head round the door of his room.

'I suppose we had better go down and investigate,' said his brother.

So they made their way downstairs, past the drawing room and the library, to the thick green-baize-covered door that separated the house from the kitchen.

Carefully they opened it. The wooden table was scrubbed white, the fender was polished, the stove had stayed alight.

But where were Ellie and Sigrid?

And where were the whisky and the warm milk and the hot-water bottle?

Just at this moment the back door was opened and the two women came in. Sigrid's hat was crooked, Ellie's hair was coming down – and she carried something in her arms.

Silence fell.

'What . . . is . . . that?' enquired Professor Julius, pointing his long finger at the bundle.

'It's a baby, sir. We found her in a church; she'd been left,' said Sigrid.

'We tried to take her to the nuns,' said Ellie, 'but they were in quarantine for typhus.'

The baby turned its head and snuffled. Professor Emil looked at it in amazement. He was used to pictures of the baby Jesus lying stiff and silent in his mother's arms, but this was different.

'It's absolutely out of the question that we should allow a baby to stay in this house,' said Professor Julius. 'Even for a day.'

Professor Emil nodded. 'The noise . . .'

'The disturbance,' said Professor Gertrude. 'Not to mention what happens to them . . . at the far end.'

'It would only be till the quarantine is over,' said Ellie. 'A few weeks . . .'

Professor Julius shook his head. 'Certainly not. I forbid it.'

'Very well, sir,' said Ellie listlessly. 'We'll take her to the police station in the morning. They'll have somewhere to put unwanted babies.'

'The police station?' said Professor Emil.

The child stirred and opened her eyes. Then she did that thing that even tiny babies do. She *looked*.

'Good heavens!' said Professor Julius.

It was not the look of somebody who belonged in a police station along with criminals and drunks.

Professor Julius cleared his throat.

'She must be kept out of our sight. Absolutely,' he said.

'She must make no sound,' said Emil.

'Our work must not be disturbed even for a minute,' said Gertrude.

'And the day the quarantine is over she goes to the convent. Now where is my whisky?'

'And my warm milk?'

'And my hot-water bottle?'

The professors were in bed. The baby lay in a borrowed nappy on a folded blanket in a drawer which had been emptied of table mats.

'She ought to have a name, even if we can't keep her,' said Sigrid.

'I'd like to call her by my mother's name,' said Ellie.

'What was that?'

'Annika.'

Sigrid nodded. 'Annika. Yes, that will do.'

CHAPTER TWO

THE GOLDEN CITY

The city of Vienna, at the time that Ellie and Sigrid brought their bundle home, was the capital of the Austro-Hungarian Empire, which took in thirteen different countries spread over the heart of Europe.

The empire was ruled by one old man, the Emperor Franz Joseph, who had a winter palace in the centre of the city and a summer palace out in the suburbs, where the air was always fresh. He was a lonely person because his wife had been assassinated by an anarchist and his son had shot himself, but he worked hard at his job, getting up at five o'clock every morning to read state papers, and sleeping on an iron bed like his soldiers. He even washed the feet of twelve needy men who were brought to him on the Thursday before Easter because he wanted to be good.

Because he was so old, bad things happened to him.

Little girls would present him with bunches of flowers and when he bent down to take them, his back would seize up and his aides would have to come and straighten him. Or the school children of Vienna would make pink paper tissue hearts and throw them over him as he rode by, and they would get into his moustache, and up his nose, and make him sneeze.

All the same, the people of Vienna loved him. They liked his obstinacy and the way he would never get into a motor car though they had been invented a few years earlier, but always drove through the streets in a carriage with golden wheels and waved to anyone who greeted him. They liked the firework display he ordered on his birthday, and the military uniforms into which he struggled whenever there was a procession or a party: the pink trousers and blue tunic of the Hussars . . . the silver green of the Tyrolean Rifles . . . and with them a great helmet with gigantic plumes.

Every school in Vienna had a picture of him on the wall, and his face, with its mutton-chop whiskers and bald head, was as familiar to the children as the faces of their grandfathers.

As well as the emperor and his court, Vienna was known for its music. Almost every famous composer who had ever lived had worked in Vienna: Mozart and Schubert and Beethoven and Strauss. Music poured out of the houses, waltzes were played in every cafe and by the barrel organs in the street – and in the richly decorated opera house, large sopranos sang their hearts out every night.

Then there was the food. The Viennese really liked to eat. Wonderful cooking smells wafted through the streets – vanilla and freshly ground coffee; cinnamon and sauerkraut. Even cucumber salad, which in other cities hardly smelt at all, had its own scent in Vienna.

In the sweet shops you could buy tiny marzipan beetles and spotted ladybirds and snails curled snugly in their shells. There were sugar mice so beautifully made that the children who bought them could scarcely bear to bite off their heads, and gingerbread houses complete with terrible witches made of nougat, with hats of liquorice. The cake shops sold seven kinds of chocolate cake, and tarts made of vanilla wafers layered with hazelnut cream, and pastry boats filled with the succulent berries that grow in the Austrian countryside: wild strawberries so bright that they seem to be lit up from the inside, and blueberries, each one a perfect globe.

There were other things which made Vienna a splendid town to live in: the Prater, a royal park shaded by ancient trees where everyone could walk or ride, and the Prater funfair, where the highest Giant Wheel in Europe had just been built. There was the River Danube, which curled round the north of the city; from a landing stage on the quay you could take a paddle steamer and go all the way up to Germany or down to Budapest in Hungary. And there were the mountains, which could be reached in an hour on the train.

But Vienna's greatest pride was in the dancing white horses which performed in the Spanish Riding School. The Spanish Riding School was not in Spain but adjoined the emperor's palace in the middle of the old town, and with its vaulted ceiling and rows of columns it was certainly the most beautiful arena in the world. The horses which could be seen there – the Lipizzaner stallions – were bred especially in a village called Lipizza in the south of the empire and only a few, the very best, were sent to the emperor in Vienna. The chosen horses were stabled in what had once been the arcaded palace of a prince. They fed from marble troughs, and spent four years learning to perform to music the movements which had once been so important in war. Incredible movements with resounding names: caprioles and courbettes and levades . . .

When visitors came to Vienna and were asked what they wanted to see most, the answer was usually: 'The Lipizzaner horses. The dancing white stallions. Could we please see those?'

CHAPTER THREE

THE SINKING OF THE *MEDUSA*

As soon as she woke, Annika opened her attic window and looked out at the square. She did this every morning; she liked to see that everything was in order and today it was. The pigeons were still roosting on General Brenner's head, the fountain had been turned on, and Josef was putting the cafe tables out on the pavement, which meant it was going to be a fine day. A door opened in the ramshackle little house on the opposite corner and her friend Stefan came out and set off across the cobbles with a can to fetch the milk. He was the middle one of five flaxen-haired boys and his mother, Frau Bodek, was expecting a sixth child any day. She had said that if it was another boy she was going to give it away.

Now a solitary dog came sauntering between the chestnut trees, from the street. It was a dog she did not know and Annika looked out eagerly – perhaps it was a stray and ownerless and if it was, Ellie couldn't refuse to let her keep it, surely? After all Ellie had taken her in when she was ownerless; she'd been a sort of stray left in a church.

But behind the dog now came a lady carrying a lead, so that was no good. The church clock struck seven and Annika turned from the window to get dressed. No school today – it was Saturday, so she could leave her hair unbraided and put away her pinafore – but there was still a lot of work to do before she could go out and find her friends.

Nearly twelve years had passed since Annika had been carried into the kitchen of the professors' house. When the typhus epidemic had come to an end, and the Convent of the Sacred Heart had sent word that they were out of quarantine, Ellie had bundled up the baby, and she and Sigrid had gone upstairs to seek out their employers.

'We've come to say goodbye,' they'd said. 'We'll find some way of providing for her, but we can't give her up.'

The professors were deeply offended. They were puzzled. They were hurt.

'Have we complained about the baby?' said Professor Julius stuffily.

'Have we made any objections?' asked Professor Emil.

'I'm sure I never said a word,' said Professor Gertrude, blinking and looking stricken.

Sigrid and Ellie had looked at each other.

'You mean she can stay?'

Professor Julius bent his head.

'We shall of course expect her to be *useful*,' he said.

'Oh, she will be,' cried Ellie. 'She'll be the best-trained child in Vienna.'

And she was. By the time she was seven, Annika could bake and ice a three-tiered chocolate cake, and bring a roast to the table. At nine she could cut cucumbers so thinly that you could read a newspaper through the slices, and when she was sent to do the marketing, the stall-holders brought out their best vegetables and fruit because the little girl was famous for her eagle eyes. Sigrid had taught her how to polish the parquet floors by sliding over them with dusters tied to her feet, and how to clean silver, and how to crochet and knit and sew – and from both women she learned that work was something that had to be done, and how you *felt* had absolutely nothing to do with it.

But neither Ellie nor Sigrid had taught the child how to dream. The ability to disappear into her own head had come from the unknown parents who had abandoned her.

Ellie was grinding coffee and putting the bread rolls to warm in the oven when Annika came down, but she turned to give her adopted daughter a hug. She had stopped expecting to hear a knock at the door at any minute and see a strange woman standing there, claiming the child – but all the same, every morning when Annika came down from her attic, Ellie gave thanks.

'Have you washed behind your ears?'

Annika nodded and extracted an ear for inspection. She was a sturdy child with heavy corn-coloured hair, thought-ful grey eyes under level brows, and a wide mouth. There were many such pleasing, clear-eyed girls at work in the Austrian countryside – goose girls and dairy maids and girls who took the cattle to the high pastures in the summer – but not many with Annika's look of eager

17

intelligence. More than that, she was a child who comforted others; she had done so from the start.

Now Annika, returning Ellie's hug, drank in the scent of green soap and fresh bread that clung to the cook's white apron, and wrinkled her nose with pleasure, because coming into the kitchen was coming home. Nothing changed here: the table was always scrubbed to whiteness, the emperor's picture hung above the stove, the calender sent each year by the Bavarian Sausage Company stood on the window sill beside Ellie's pots of herbs – and on a sacred shelf beside the dresser lay the worn black recipe book that had been Ellie's mother's and her mother's mother's before her.

But it was time to start work.

Annika put out the apricot jam for Professor Julius and the raspberry jam for Professor Emil and the honey for Professor Gertrude and carried them upstairs to the dining room. Then she laid out the napkins, saw that the sugar bowl was filled and came down again to fetch a jug of hot water for Professor Julius to wash in, and down again to fetch another one for Professor Emil.

By this time Sigrid had swept the downstairs rooms and tidied them and she and Ellie and Annika had their own breakfast at the kitchen table. Then the bell rang from Professor Gertrude's room and Sigrid went to fetch the black-silk skirt she had ironed and from which she had removed a small piece of cheese that had got stuck to the hem, and gave it to Annika to take upstairs. Gertude was playing the harp in a lunchtime recital and it was always necessary to clean her up before she left.

And now the bell rang again and it was Professor Emil, who had lost his cravat, followed by Profesor Julius, who gave her ten kreutzer and asked her to go and buy a copy of *Vienna Today* from the newsagent round the corner.

'That idiot Jacobson has published a piece about the origin of volcanic rock which is absolute rubbish,' he said. 'I had to write a letter – they should have printed it.'

So Annika ran across the square and through the chestnut trees into the Keller Strasse, hoping that they *had* printed it, because when they didn't print his letters he got very upset.

The lady in the newspaper shop was a friend of Annika's and she had already seen that the professor's letter had been put in.

'So he'll be in a good mood,' she said. And then, 'I hear the Bodek baby is due any minute.'

Annika nodded. 'If it's a boy she's going to give it away.'

When she got back with the paper she was sent out again to the flower seller who sat with her basket beside the fountain. It had become Annika's job to choose the flowers that Professor Julius put every Saturday in front of the picture of his Beloved – the one who had died before her wedding day. Today, with summer on its way, Annika bought gentians and edelweiss from the mountains and took them to the professor's study, where he was reading the letter he had sent to the paper for the third time.

His Beloved, whose name had been Adele Fischl, lived on a table near the window, and as she arranged the flowers, Annika thought again how sad it was that she had died. She was a serious-looking woman with a strong nose, and Annika was sure that she and the professor would have suited each other very well.

After this Sigrid put her to polishing the silver candlesticks and then it was time for her elevenses – a glass of frothy milk and a golden vanilla kipfel straight out of the oven which she took out to the cobbled yard behind the house.

Annika loved the yard with its vine-covered door to the back lane. The wash house was there and the clothes line and the woodshed, and the old stables which were no longer used for a horse and carriage but acted as a storeroom. Ellie grew tubs of geraniums and petunias there, and in a sunny corner by the house was a blue bench on which the servants liked to sit when they had a minute to themselves.

Today though there was no lingering in the sun. The washing had to be taken out of the copper and hung up to dry and the carpets beaten and the peas shelled for lunch. And then Annika ran out to chose a suitable cab for Professor Gertrude from the row of hansoms drawn up on the far side of the Keller Strasse – one that was tall enough for the harp to fit inside but had a peaceful-looking horse which would not rattle the instrument.

Then back into the kitchen to help Ellie with the lunch – and lunch on Saturday was a big meal: today there was pea soup and stewed beef with dumplings, and pancakes filled with cherry jam, all carried up and down from the kitchen to the dining room and back again for the two professors, who sat with their napkins tucked into their collars and ate with a hearty appetite.

Then Sigrid and Annika and Ellie sat down to their lunch in the kitchen, and after that came the washing up – masses and masses of washing up.

But on Saturday afternoon Annika was free.

She went first to the bookshop on the corner. It was an antiquarian bookshop, which meant that the books that were sold in it were old ones. It also meant that not many people came into the shop. No one quite knew how Herr Koblitz, who owned it, made a living. He was not a sociable man and whenever anyone tried to buy a book he hadn't finished reading, he became grumpy and annoyed.

Today he was reading a book about mummies – the kind that are embalmed.

'Has Pauline finished?' asked Annika.

Pauline was Herr Koblitz's granddaughter. She lived with him because her mother was a ward sister in Berlin and had to sleep in the hospital. Like Annika, Pauline had to help with the chores, dusting the shelves, sweeping the floor, stacking the books.

Herr Koblitz nodded.

'She's in the back.'

Pauline too was reading. She was a thin girl with frizzy black hair and black eyes. Pauline was clever; she seemed to remember everything she came across in the books she devoured and she kept a scrapbook into which she pasted important articles that she had cut out of the newspapers. These were about the courageous deeds that had been done by people even if they only had one leg or couldn't see or had been dropped on their heads when they were babies.

'It's to make me brave,' she'd explained to Annika, but Annika said it was silly to want to be brave *and* clever.

'You're perfectly all right as you are,' she'd told Pauline – but Pauline was nervous of the outside world and did not agree. She found it difficult to leave the bookshop on her own; open spaces and strange people frightened her, and she knew she would have to do something about this if she was going to put right the many things she did not approve of, like rich people having everything and poor people having nothing.

Now she closed the book, which was a story about the sinking in the Atlantic of a ship called the *Medusa*, and followed Annika out into the street. 'I think we could do it,' she said. 'It's exciting, with all the people crowded on a raft and getting swallowed by the sea.'

Annika nodded. 'Tell us when we get there so Stefan can hear.'

Stefan's family, the Bodeks, lived in the bottom half of the smallest house in the square.

They were very poor. Herr Bodek worked as a grounds-man in the funfair at the Prater and Frau Bodek took in washing, but with five boys to feed there was never any money to spare.

All the same, it was Frau Bodek who had come round to the professors' house on the night that Annika was found, bringing a pile of freshly boiled nappies and some baby clothes for the foundling. Stefan, the middle boy, was exactly the same age as Annika; the two had grown up together, sharing their few toys, learning to crawl in each other's kitchens. All the Bodek boys were friendly and cheerful, but Stefan was special. Annika would have trusted him with her life.

'I can't stay long,' he said now. 'The baby's definitely on the way and they'll want me to take messages.'

But he put on his cap and together the three children ran down the alleyway beside the church, along a cobbled lane – and paused by a crumbling wall covered with ivy.

Mostly the wall was high and fairly solid, but in one place, if you pushed aside the ivy, you could see a hole. They crawled through it – and then they were in the garden.

Each time they straightened themselves and looked round they felt a shiver of relief – for the garden was doomed; they knew that. It belonged to the city council and they were going to build offices on it. Any day the diggers and shovellers would come and the destruction would begin.

But not yet. Butterflies still hovered over the long grass, thistles and dandelions blew in the breeze, the great cedar spread its branches. At the top of a flight of cracked stone steps, a statue of Venus with missing arms stared quietly out at what had once been a fountain; and in the pond, the water lilies still flowered among the weeds.

The garden belonged to the ruined house of an Austrian nobleman who had come to Vienna more than a hundred years ago to serve the emperor and make his fortune.

And he *had* made it. Unfortunately he was a gambler and soon he lost all the money he had made, and the beautiful house he had built had to be sold, and sold again. Then it stood empty, and a fire had broken out . . . and now the villa was just a heap of fallen pillars and broken stones.

But the garden had survived. The garden was better than ever: wild and tangled and mysterious.

'We won't try and tidy anything . . . we won't even weed the flower beds,' Annika had decided, and the others agreed.

But there was one place which they did tidy and care for and even scrub. In the middle of a shrubbery, overgrown with lilacs and laburnums, stood a green-painted hut. It had once been a tool shed, and unlike the house, the hut was undamaged. The roof was sound, the windows were unbroken, the door could be properly closed.

The hut was their headquarters; they had borrowed a blanket for the floor, and some mugs, and stuck a candle in a sauce bottle and Stefan had found a padlock for the door.

When they first came to the garden they had kept house in the hut, found nuts and berries for food, pretended it was time to go to bed and get up. But now they were older, the hut had become the springboard from which they planned their games. It might be the barracks in Mafeking besieged by the Boers, or a tomb in the Valley of the Kings threatened by robbers. Last week it had been the tower in which Mary Queen of Scots had been imprisoned.

It was usually Pauline who found the stories in the books she read, and once they had decided on a story they were off, doubling roles, being now soldiers, now the people that the soldiers shot. It was half playing, half acting and while they were doing it they were lost to the world.

Today Pauline told them about the *Medusa* – a slave ship run by a corrupt and incompetent captain who ran her aground on a reef off the coast of Africa.

'All the rich people saved themselves in lifeboats and left the slaves to look after themselves. So the slaves made a huge raft and kept it afloat for days and days, but gradually they began to die of thirst or get washed overboard or go mad. They even ate the flesh of the people who had died – and when a rescue ship found them, only fifteen people out of more than a hundred were still alive.'

Annika nodded. 'The hut can be the *Medusa* and we'll put the blanket in the middle of the lawn; that'll be the raft, and the grass all around is the sea. Stefan can be eaten and his remains thrown overboard – and then he can be the captain of the rescue ship.'

She frequently altered the story so as to make it more dramatic and fairer, giving each of them a chance to drown or be shot or run into the hut under a hail of arrows.

For a couple of hours they suffered shipwreck, thirst, terror and cannibalism. Then suddenly it was over. They ate their sandwiches – Pauline and Annika sharing theirs with Stefan, whose mother never had any extra food to give him. When the clock struck six, they came out of their private world, tidied the hut, padlocked the door and crawled back through the hole in the wall.

In the square they separated and became their ordinary selves again.

Later that evening, when Annika was sitting in the kitchen dunking strips of bread into her eggs-in-a-glass, there was a knock at the back door and Stefan came in.

'It's come,' he said. 'The baby.'

Everybody waited.

'It's a boy,' said Stefan.

Annika pushed back her glass. 'Will she give it away then?'

Stefan grinned. 'Not her. She's holding it and petting it and telling us what a lovely baby it is. She even thinks it's got hair.'

Ellie got up and fetched a shawl she been knitting for the baby and a bonnet Sigrid had crocheted.

'Are you sure she won't give it away?' asked Annika a little anxiously after Stefan had gone.

'Not her,' said Ellie. 'Mothers don't give away their

babies,' she began – and broke off, seeing Annika's face. She laid her hand over Annika's. 'Your mother would have kept you if she could, you know that, don't you?'

And Annika did know. When she was in bed in her attic and had put out her lamp, she told herself the story she told herself night after night.

It began with the ringing of the door bell – the *front* door bell – and a woman stepped out of a carriage. She had thick auburn hair under her velvet hat; her eyes were almost the same colour as her hair, a rich warm brown; and she was tall and beautifully dressed, like the woman in the painting Professor Emil had in his room, which was called *The Lady of Shalott*. She swept into the house, saying, 'Where is she? Where is my long-lost daughter? Oh, take me to her,' and then she gathered Annika into her arms.

'My darling, my beloved child,' she said, and she explained why she'd had to leave Annika in the church. The explanation was complicated and it varied as Annika told herself the story, but tonight she was very tired so she skipped that part and went on to where her mother turned back to the carriage and a dog leaped out – a golden retriever with soft moist eyes . . .

'I brought him for you,' her mother said. 'I was sure you'd like a dog.'

And Annika was asleep.

CHAPTER FOUR

WHITE HORSES

There was only one child in the square whom Annika couldn't stand. Her name was Loremarie Egghart and she lived in a big house opposite the house of the professors.

The Eggharts were extremely rich because Loremarie's grandfather had been a manufacturer of soft furnishings and in particular of duvets and pillows. These were stuffed with goose down from the plains of Hungary, where the poor birds were rounded up and plucked naked, but the Eggharts did not worry about the geese, only about the money.

Loremarie's father still took money from the factory, but he had become an important councillor and went each day, with a flower in his buttonhole, to sit at a large desk overlooking the Parliament Building, where he helped to make boring laws and shouted at the people who worked for him in his foghorn of a voice.

What he wanted more than anything was to become a statue. Not a statue on horseback, he knew that was unlikely, but a proper statue on a plinth just the same. There were many such statues in Vienna: statues of aldermen and councillors and politicians, and Herr Egghart thought that if he could become one too, his life would have been worthwhile.

Loremarie's mother, Frau Egghart, spent her time spoiling her daughter, shopping, gossiping and looking down on her neighbours, particularily the Bodeks, who, she felt, should be rehoused somewhere else. She was driven everywhere in her husband's brand-new canary-yellow motor with its outsize brass lamps and its bulbous horn that could be heard three streets away, and she didn't just have maids from the country to work in the house, but also kept a snooty manservant called Leopold, who walked behind Loremarie carrying her satchel when she went to school.

Needless to say, Loremarie was not allowed to play with a 'kitchen child' like Annika, so it was easy enough to keep out of her way.

But on Sunday morning after church Annika liked to catch up with what was happening in the city, and she did this by walking carefully round a large red pillar covered in notices and advertisements which stood on the pavement on the other side of the chestnut trees.

On this pillar were notices of the plays being performed and what was showing at the opera. There were notices of military parades, visiting circuses, special matinees at the theatre, and receptions given by the old emperor at whatever palace he was staying at.

And of course there were advertisements for stomach pills and for ointments to cure baldness, and a picture of a man with huge muscles, which he had got by eating a particular kind of liver sausage.

Today there was a new notice; a big one, with a picture of a snow-white horse with golden reins and a gold-and-crimson saddle, sitting back on his haunches with his forelegs tucked under him. A man in a bicorne hat and a brown cutaway coat was riding him – and Annika, like any child in Vienna, knew that it was one of the famous Lipizzaner stallions doing a levade. And not any stallion but Maestoso Fantasia, the oldest and strongest of the horses and a great favourite with the emperor.

The notice said:

GALA PERFORMANCE AT
THE SPANISH RIDING SCHOOL
14 JUNE 1908
in honour of His Majesty King Edward VII
of Great Britain
and in the presence of His Imperial Majesty,
The Emperor Franz Joseph.
The Band of the Austrian Grenadiers will play.
(A limited number of tickets are available to
the General Public.)

Annika stared at the poster for a long time. She walked past the Lipizzaners' stables often, she had even been allowed inside because Stefan's uncle was the blacksmith who shod the horses, but she had never seen a proper performance in the Spanish Riding School.

She would have loved to go, but the tickets would be incredibly expensive; there was no hope that Ellie and Sigrid could afford to take her; she would not even ask.

She was still looking at the notice rather wistfully, when she heard a high and bossy voice behind her.

'*We're* going to the gala, aren't we, Miss Smith?'

Loremarie was with her English governess, a tall sad-looking woman. Loremarie had had a lot of governesses – English ones and French ones and German ones. Some of them had been thin and some of them had been fat, some of them had been strict and some of them had been gentle – but all of them, after a few months with Loremarie, had looked sad.

'We're going in the front row on the first tier,' bragged Loremarie.

She was wearing a pleated tartan skirt and a tartan tam-o'-shanter, although the Eggharts were not known for their Scottish blood. Her small dark eyes were set very deep in her pale cheeks and she had a particular way of walking, with her behind thrust out, as though she wanted people to know that her backside, like her front, was important.

'It costs a lot of money to go,' said Loremarie, who loved to taunt Annika for being poor – and then the sad governess led her away to her dancing lesson.

Since no one knew exactly when Annika had been born, Ellie and Sigrid did not celebrate her birthday, they celebrated her 'Found Day', the day on which they had discovered her on the altar steps at Pettelsdorf.

They did this by leaving Vienna very early and taking the same train into the mountains as they had taken then, to give thanks in the little church and to pray. At first they had walked through the village in fear and trembling, waiting for someone to tell them that an unknown woman had been seen asking questions, but as the years passed and nothing was heard, they relaxed. It really seemed as though the woman who had left her daughter on the altar steps had vanished from the face of the earth. When Annika was a baby they had left her with the Bodeks when they went to the mountains, but as soon as she could walk they took her along. It always seemed to be fine on the twelfth of June. The scent of the pines blew softly from the slopes, the stream sparkled – and the fortunate cows grazed contentedly on salads of clover and primulas and harebells which studded the rich grass.

'I'd rather have been found here than born in a boring hospital,' Annika would say.

Inside the church, though, she always felt bewildered and cross. 'It was me you were giving away,' she wanted to say to her absent mother. 'It wasn't just anybody, it was me.'

And then of course she felt guilty, and that night, when she told herself the story of her mother's arrival, the love between them knew no bounds.

But the important part of the celebrations came on the Saturday after Found Day, when the professors let her choose a treat, something to which all the household could go. The year before they had gone on a paddle steamer down the Danube to Durnstein, where Richard the Lionheart had been imprisoned, and the year before that they had gone to the opera to see *Hansel and Gretel*.

This year Annika plucked up courage and asked if they could go to the gala to see the Lipizzaners dance for the English king. She was tired of Loremarie's taunts.

'If it's not too expensive?' she asked.

It was expensive, very expensive, and the professors were not entirely pleased with her choice because they thought that the emperor spent too much money on his beautiful white horses – money which could be better spent on making the university bigger, especially the parts of it in which they worked. Sigrid too did not really approve of the Lipizzaners.

'They could build new hospitals all over the city with what those animals cost,' she said.

But the professors gave in – and bought tickets not only for the household but for Pauline and Stefan, whom Annika always wanted to invite.

Treats which involved the professors always started off with rather a lot of education. Before they went to Durnstein, Professor Julius had told her about the depth of the river at that point, the speed of the current and the kind of sandstone from which the castle had been built, and Professor Gertrude had played on her harp the tune that Richard's rescuers had played under his castle window.

'We've learned a lot about the horses at school,' Annika said now, thinking she might get away without too many lectures.

She already knew that the horses were bred in Lipizza, near Trieste, from Arab and Berber strains brought from Spain and that the Archduke Charles had brought the first ones to Vienna 300 years before. She knew that the horses did not start off white but dark brown or black, in the same way as Dalmatian puppies are born without spots, and that each stallion had his own rider who stayed with him all through his life in the riding school.

But Professor Julius was not satisfied. He took Annika up to his room and got out a map of Karst, the plateau on which Lipizza was situated.

'The soil is sparse and there are rocks close to the surface, so that the horses learn to pick up their feet and this helps to form their high-stepping gait. All the area is limestone, which is very porous . . .' And he was off, because he was after all a geologist, and very fond of limestone – and it was an hour before Annika could get away.

Professor Emil took her and Pauline to the art museum. Both girls knew it well, with its marble floors and the pictures of half-dressed ladies with dimpled knees. Now, though, Emil led them to the seventeenth-century Spanish artists who had painted huge battle scenes with rearing horses and dying soldiers and blood dripping from swords.

'You see the way those forelegs are poised over the enemy soldier,' he said, pointing to a grey stallion with flaring nostrils and wild eyes, 'that's a courbade, and when he brings his hoofs down, he'll crush the man to pulp. And over there, the Duke of Milan's horse – the one that seems to be flying – he's doing a capriole. See how he's kicking out with his hind legs!'

And he explained that the most famous of the movements that the Lipizzaners performed, the 'airs above the ground', were originally developed in battle, where they could help a rider to escape, or kill his foe.

By the time they set off in two hansom cabs, with the professors and Annika in the first, and Sigrid, Ellie, Pauline and Stefan in the second, Annika was almost wishing she had chosen a different treat. As soon as she knew that Loremarie would be at the gala, Sigrid had decided that Annika needed a new dress and had gone out for a roll of sea-green silk. She was a superb needlewoman, the dress was a triumph; Annika's hair was brushed out and taken back with a band of matching silk. All the same, she felt rather as though she was going to a lecture given by horses instead of people.

But when they went up the stairs and came out in the riding school itself, everything changed.

It was like being in a ballroom: the crystal chandeliers blazing with light, the white walls, the red velvet on the banquettes, the huge portrait of Charles VI on his charger. The band played soft music, and below her, the russet sand was raked into swirls like the sea.

Loremarie was at the other end of the row, wriggling and showing off, but Annika had forgotten her.

The band broke into the national anthem, everyone rose to their feet; the emperor in a blue-and-silver uniform came in, with his guest – the portly English king – and Ellie sighed with pleasure. She dearly loved the emperor, who was so old, so alone and so pig-headedly dutiful. Then everyone sat down again, the band started to play the *Radetzky March*, the great double doors opened – and two dozen snow-white horses came into the ring.

They came like conquerors, in perfect formation and in perfect time to the music, lifting their legs high, bringing them down exactly on the beat, and as they came level with the place where the emperor sat, they stopped as one and the riders swept off their cockaded hats in homage.

Then they began. They started with the simpler movements: the passage, which is a kind of floating trot, the piaffe, where the horse trots on the spot, the flying changes, the turn on the forelegs . . . The tall riders in their white buckskin breeches sat silent, guiding the horses with movements so small they could not be noticed – or even just with their thoughts. The understanding between the stallions and the men who rode them had been built up during the long years of training. There was no need any longer for commands.

Now the younger horses left the ring, the band played a Boccherini minuet and three of the most highly trained stallions did a pas de trois: weaving the earlier steps into an intricate and faultless dance.

'They're so beautiful,' whispered Annika. Light poured from their white skins, their manes and tails tossed like silk, they held their heads like princes.

The three stallions disappeared through the huge double doors. The horses which came in now were rider-less; their riding masters walked behind them, holding them only on the long reign. These were the most experienced horses, who could do the steps on their own – the one in the lead was the emperor's favourite, Maestoso Fantasia, the horse Annika had seen on the poster.

If Annika had chosen to come to the horses to get even with Loremarie, she had long forgotten it. Beside her Pauline, who was always doubtful about horses – the way they tossed their heads and stamped their feet – was hanging eagerly over the balustrade.

And after the interval, the climax of all those years of training, the famous 'airs above the ground', with the riders riding without stirrups as they took their mounts through the levade, known to Vienna's children because of the many statues where the horses sit back on their haunches and lift their legs into the air ... and the courbette, where the horses don't just rear up but jump forward on their hind legs and one can see their muscles bunched and rippling with the effort . . . And the most difficult of all, the dazzling 'leap of the goat', the capriole, where the horse really seems to be flying, and Annika, along with most of the spectators, let out her breath in an 'Oh' of wonder.

The show ended with the famous quadrille, 'The ballet of the white stallions', in which all the horses took part.

Unlike the other children in the audience, Loremarie had found it impossible to sit still. She fidgeted and fussed and dropped her purse and picked it up again . . . Now she stood up and pointed at one horse in the centre of the row of stallions weaving faultlessly between the pillars.

'That horse is the wrong colour,' she said loudly. 'He's brown; he isn't white. He shouldn't be there!'

She was hushed not by her doting parents but by an old gentleman in the row behind who told her to sit down and be quiet.

'You had better study the traditions of the Imperial Spanish Riding School before you come here again,' he said sternly.

Loremarie shrugged and sat down, and the dance went on.

Then once more the riders raised their hats to the emperor, the horses' ears came forward, acknowledging the thunderous applause – and it was over.

'It makes you proud to be Austrian,' said Ellie as they stood up to go, and nothing more was said about the money being better spent on new buildings for the university.

The Eggharts hurried Loremarie away without speaking and were driven home in their enormous yellow motor, but the professors now led the way to Sacher's restaurant, where they had booked a table, for on Found Days they were very democratic and ate with their servants.

And at the end of the meal, they had something important to say to Annika.

'We have decided that from now on you do not have to call us "Professor". You may call us "Uncle",' said Professor Julius. 'Not Professor Julius but Uncle Julius.'

'And not Professor Emil, but Uncle Emil,' said Professor Emil.

And they smiled and nodded, very pleased with this gesture. Professor Gertrude did not say that she could be called 'Aunt' because she had wandered off inside her head, where she was composing a sonata for the harp, but she too nodded and smiled.

So all in all it was a splendid evening and as they got off the tram in the Keller Strasse and turned into the square, the party was in an excellent mood, singing and telling jokes.

Then suddenly they stopped.

In front of the Eggharts' house a white motorized van with high windows was parked. There was a red cross painted on the side and the words 'Mission of Mercy' written above it.

Had there been an accident? No one liked the Eggharts, but that did not mean they wanted them to be hurt.

The door of the van opened, and two nurses in navy-blue uniforms got out. Then they turned back to the van and fetched something – a bundle of shawls and blankets. One nurse took hold of one end of the bundle and the other nurse took hold of the other end and they began to carry it towards the house.

'What is it?' whispered Annika – for the bundle seemed to weigh more than one would expect from a pile of blankets.

At this point the bundle twitched and said something. It gave a jerk and a nightcap with a ribbon fell out on to the pavement. Not a bundle then, a person. And a person who was not pleased.

Meanwhile, the driver of the van had got out and rung the Eggharts' bell. A maid came and seemed to be giving instructions, pointing upwards. There was no sign of the Eggharts, though Annika saw the curtains of the drawing room twitch.

Then the manservant, the snooty Leopold, came out and opened the back of the van and took out a battered-looking trunk, which he carried into the house. When he had done that he returned and pulled out two wooden boxes and these too he carried in.

Presently the door opened once again, and the two nurses got back into the van, the driver returned, and the van drove away.

As the birthday party crossed the square to their own houses, they were very quiet. No one sang now or told jokes.

It had been a strange arrival. Was it really a person who had been delivered so carelessly? And if so, what did it mean?

CHAPTER FIVE

THE COUNTESS OF
MONTE CRISTO

For a few days after the bundle, looking like a pile of unwanted clothes, had been carried into the Eggharts' house nothing more was heard. The Eggharts didn't speak to anyone and of course rumours flew round the square. The bundle was a madwoman like Mrs Rochester in *Jane Eyre*, who laughed hideously and would set the place on fire . . . or she had bubonic plague and had to be sealed up and quarantined.

Then Pauline read a book called *The Count of Monte Cristo* about a man who had been wrongfully imprisoned in a dungeon in a castle on an island in the middle of the sea.

'That's what she's like. She's a Countess of Monte Cristo,' Pauline said. 'They've walled her up and she can't get out.'

It was Annika who found out that the 'countess' lived not in a dungeon but in an attic. It exactly faced the attic where Annika slept, across the square, and on the third day she saw something carried to the chair beside the window. Then the window was opened, and the old lady was aired – like the washing, thought Annika – before the window was closed again and she was carried back to bed.

It was not until the beginning of the second week that Mitzi, one of the Eggharts' maids, was able to slip into Ellie's kitchen for a cup of coffee and tell them what was going on.

The old lady was Herr Egghart's great-aunt. She was ninety-four years old and sometimes wandered in her mind, and the Eggharts had done everything they could to find a hospital or old people's home where she could be looked after.

'They put her in the asylum – the one they're going to pull down, behind the infirmary,' said Mitzi, 'but the man who ran it found she was related to the Eggharts and he said she wasn't mad and they should take her in. She's very frail and he said she wouldn't live long. There was quite a fuss, but the Eggharts were afraid of what people would say so they agreed. She has a nurse in the morning and evening to tidy her up, but she can't get downstairs and most of the time she just lies in bed. She'll go soon; old people know when they aren't wanted.'

'Poor soul,' said Ellie, stirring her coffee. 'It's hard to be old.'

This annoyed Annika, who was sitting on her stool in the corner, stringing beans. 'No it isn't. It won't be for you because I shall buy a house in the mountains and look after you – and Sigrid too.'

40

'Mind you, she can be a handful, the old lady,' Mitzi went on. 'She didn't get on with her family and when she was fifteen she went her own way and the family lost touch with her.'

The Eggharts had been forced to take in their great-aunt but that was all. They never mentioned her to visitors who came to the house, they never took her out. It was as though they were pretending to themselves that she wasn't there.

What happened next was odd and Annika couldn't make sense of it. Loremarie stopped to speak to her when she met her in the street – and not to sneer or to show off. She was polite, almost friendly, and though she still stuck out her behind, the black eyes, sunk so deep in her face, did not seem quite so baleful.

The first time Loremarie came up to her was when Annika was wheeling out the new Bodek baby in his ancient, rickety pram. Usually Loremarie walked past all the Bodeks with her nose in the air, but now she forced herself to look under the hood and even asked how old he was.

The second time, Annika was returning from the shops with a basket of new potatoes and this time Loremarie actually crossed the street to speak to her.

But it wasn't till she found Annika leaning over the rim of the fountain, crumbling bread into the water for the goldfish, that the reason for Loremarie's friendliness became clear. She wanted something from Annika and it was the last thing that Annika expected.

'You know you're poor,' she began, 'aren't you?'

Annika shrugged. She was worried about the goldfish – one of them had fungus on his fins – and though it would have been nice to hit Loremarie, there was always a fuss at home when she hit people.

'So would you like to earn some money?' Loremarie went on, looking back at the windows of her house to make sure her mother wasn't watching.

Annika crumbled the last of the bread into the water.

'How much money?'

'Quite a lot. Twenty kreutzers. Each time you go.'

'Each time I go where?'

Loremarie looked round again furtively. 'Go and read to my great-aunt. Sit with her. I'm supposed to do it for half an hour every afternoon. The doctor told my mother that she was lonely – the old woman. But I can't. I tried once and it was awful. She dribbles and her head wobbles and suddenly she goes to sleep and her mouth falls open.' Loremarie shuddered. 'It made me feel sick.'

'Yes, but how could I do it instead of you? Your mother would know.'

'No, she wouldn't. I go up between tea and supper when she rests. Anyway, even if she did find out she probably wouldn't mind as long as it keeps the old woman quiet. The doctor is horrid to us. He says we'll be old one day and we should be kind to her. But we won't – not like that . . . poor and mad and dribbly . . .'

Annika was thinking, wringing the water from the ends of her hair. 'I can't come till next week when school breaks up and even then I have jobs to do. But I'll come when I can. Only you must give me twenty-five kreutzers. Twenty isn't enough.'

If she could stick it out a few times she'd have enough money to buy a proper birthday present for Ellie.

'All right. I'll leave the money on the window sill in the scullery, in an envelope. You'll come in by the back door, of course, being a kitchen child, so you'll see it.'

Annika nodded. It was odd how people thought she *wanted* to come in by the front door instead of straight into the nice, warm, friendly kitchen of whatever house she visited.

School had finished; exams were over and so was the tidying up, which was almost worse. Pauline had come top in everything except gymnastics, in which she got a very low mark indeed, and this set her worrying about a man called Ferdinand Haytor, who had become wrestling champion of Lower Austria even though he had been born with his left foot the wrong way round.

'I don't know why I can't be like him,' she said.

Annika was still very busy. Ellie had decided that she was old enough to make a proper apple strudel entirely by herself.

Making an apple strudel on your own is a bit like climbing Everest without oxygen. Only one very special type of flour will do, the dough has to be teased out to be paper-thin and laid over a tablecloth, and the apple slices and melted butter and nuts and spices have to be poured on without making a single hole, before it is rolled into a dachshund shape and baked.

Annika managed it, but it was a mixed blessing because Ellie then said it was time she started working with aspic.

'Quails' eggs in aspic – now there's a dish!' she said.

In the holidays, too, Professor Emil liked to take Annika behind the scenes in the art museum, to the restoration room, where men in baize aprons were at work cleaning old paintings.

'Look at that!' he would say as the halo of some tortured saint turned from grubby brown to shining gold under the restorer's hand. 'Isn't that splendid? And that idiot Harteisen actually thinks pictures shouldn't be cleaned! The darker and dirtier they are, the better he is pleased.'

But on Saturday the children still escaped to their deserted garden. Stefan's older brother Ernst came too and they acted the whole of *The Count of Monte Cristo* with the hut as the dungeon on the island and the steps of the ruined house as the palace of the villain who had plotted the count's downfall.

In the story the count escaped and vengeance was done. But in the Eggharts' attic, the other prisoner still lay unvisited and alone.

The first time Annika went to sit with the Eggharts' great-aunt, Loremarie was waiting to show her the way. As she tiptoed after her up the stairs, Annika's feet sank deep into the patterned carpet; Chinese vases stood on pedestals, there was a smell of hothouse lilies.

After the third flight of stairs they came to a landing with a wooden partition and a door. This led to a last flight of stairs, but these were very different: narrow and bare and airless, and instead of the scent of lilies it was the smell of disinfectant that drifted towards them.

Here were the two attics where the servants slept, and a third one, which now housed the unwanted old lady.

Loremarie turned the handle, pushed Annika into the room, and closed the door again.

The room looked like a lumber room. The trunk and the two wooden boxes that had come in the ambulance were stacked in the corner; nothing seemed to have been unpacked. In the middle of the floor was a narrow bed with a chair beside it. On a bedside table was a jug of water, a glass and a pile of books. No flowers, no fruit, nothing that was usual in the bedrooms of the sick.

The Eggharts' great-aunt was snoring, small snuffling snores like the snores of a pug dog; and her mouth hung open, just as Loremarie had said.

Annika walked to the window. It was strange seeing her own house and her attic from the other side of the square.

Behind her, the snoring had stopped. She turned.

The old lady was so small and wizened that she scarcely made a hump in the bedclothes. Her white hair was so sparse that you could see the scalp through it. She might have been dead already.

But not when she opened her eyes. They were very blue and her gaze was steady.

'You're not Loremarie,' she said.

Annika came over to the bed. 'No.'

The old lady gave a grunt of satisfaction. 'Well, that's a good thing anyway,' she said.

Annika smiled. She knew she shouldn't but she did. 'Would you like me to read to you?'

The great-aunt sighed. 'Not really. Not from those dreadful books.'

Annika picked up the top book on the pile. It was the colour of bile and the title was *Meditations of a Working*

Bishop. The one below that was called *The Evening of Life by One Who Has Suffered*.

'They're not exactly *cheerful* books, are they?' said Annika.

'No. No indeed. But then the Eggharts are not exactly a cheerful family. That's why—' She was stopped by a fit of coughing.

'Would you like some water?'

'Yes. You'll have . . . to help . . . me to . . . sit up.'

She was so light and bony and frail, it was like propping up a bird.

'So . . . who are you if you're not Loremarie?' she said when she could speak again.

'I'm Annika. I live across the square. And I'm a foundling.'

'Ah, that explains it.'

'What does it explain?'

The old lady lay back on her pillows. 'Foundlings make their own lives.' For a while she was silent and Annika was wondering if she should go, when she said, 'We could *tell* stories instead of reading them.'

'Yes. I'd like that,' said Annika. 'I know a lot of stories because my friend Pauline works in a bookshop, and we act them.'

'Ah, acting. Do you like that?'

'Yes, very much. I don't know that it's proper acting though; we only do it for ourselves.'

'Of course . . . Of course . . .'

Annika waited, sitting on the chair with folded hands. 'Will you start?' she said.

'All right then . . . Once upon a time . . . there was a girl who lived in a very pompous, silly family in a very

46

pompous, silly town. Her mother and father were stuffy and her brothers and sisters were stuffy – they used to take two hours to finish their breakfast and then it was time to start laying the table again for lunch: salt cellars, pepper-mills, mustard pots . . . on and on and on.'

Annika nodded. She knew about meals that went on and on.

'The girl wanted to see the world – and she wanted to dance and act and sing, properly – in a theatre. But no one in her family danced or sang – dear me, no. Dancing was not respectable. So they looked about for a husband for her and they found an alderman with a big stomach and a watch chain across it, and when the girl saw him she decided to run away.'

'Properly?' breathed Annika. 'With a ladder and knotted sheets?'

The old lady nodded. 'More or less. She escaped at night and she had a little bit of money saved and she went to Paris. You know about Paris? So free . . . so beauti-ful . . . She found someone who ran a theatre and she begged him for work – any work, so that she could learn and watch – but he only laughed at her. He said he had a hundred girls who wanted to dance and sing, for every place he had.

'So the girl became very poor and very hungry; she scrubbed floors and worked as a waitress, but she didn't give up. Then one day she found a theatre manager who said she could stand at the back of the stage and pretend to milk a cow – it was a musical comedy set on a farm. So for many months she milked cows and sang songs about springtime, but all the time she watched and practised and learned.

47

'And then one day something happened. A new designer came and he had made a swing that rose up very, very high above the stage, and swayed back and forwards, and on the swing was a great basket of flowers – and they wanted a girl to go up on the swing and strew the flowers.'

Annika thought she knew what came next.

'And everybody was frightened except this girl?'

'That's right. Mind you, they were right to be frightened – it was a dangerous contraption. But the girl said she would do it. She was not afraid of heights and she liked the idea of strewing flowers – even paper flowers. She liked it very much. So they combed out her hair – she had lots of hair; pretty hair like yours – and they hauled her up and up and up, and she strewed and smiled and everyone clapped and cheered. And that was the beginning . . .'

The old lady's voice died away.

But Annika wanted to be sure. She put her hand over the wrinkled one lying on the counterpane.

'It was you, wasn't it? The girl on the swing was you?'

The lids fluttered; the blue eyes opened. She smiled.

'Yes,' she said. 'It was me.'

When Annika got back she found Pauline hunched in the wicker chair in the corner of the kitchen. She was eating a cheese straw, which Ellie had given her before she went to the shops, and she looked angry and most unusually clean. Pauline's hair had been washed and stood up in a frizzy mass round her head, her fringe had been ruthlessly cut and she wore a starched dress with a glaringly white collar.

'Your mother's come?' asked Annika.

'Yes. For a whole week. She's scrubbing her way round the shop at the moment. Grandfather's gone to bed with a book about the Galapagos Islands, but it won't help him. She's going to turn out the bedrooms next. Really, Annika, I don't know why you're so interested in mothers.'

Pauline's mother wasn't just a nurse, she was a very high-ranking one, and the way Pauline and her grandfather lived filled her with despair. Whenever she had a holiday from her hospital she came from Berlin and washed and scoured and scrubbed and polished, while they tried to keep out of her way and became cleaner and gloomier by the minute.

'The trouble is, by the time she goes, I've sort of got used to her and I almost miss her. You really can't win with mothers.'

But of course her mother wouldn't be like that at all, thought Annika. She would step out of her carriage in her lovely clothes, smelling of French perfume and hold out her arms. Scrubbing and cleaning simply wouldn't come into it.

The next time Annika went to visit the Eggharts' great-aunt, Loremarie let her go up alone. There seemed to be nobody about and she was glad of it, because she had brought a sprig of jasmine from the bush growing against the courtyard wall.

'And Ellie baked some honey cakes, but we didn't know if—'

The old lady shook her head. 'I don't get hungry. But the jasmine . . .' She put it to her nose. 'I can still smell it. Just.'

She was drowsy today, but she had not forgotten that it was Annika's turn to tell a story.

49

'But not "Gunga Din" or Stanley and Livingstone. Your story. How you were found.'

So Annika told her about the church in the mountains and about Ellie and Sigrid, who had taken her in and brought her up.

'Ellie is soft and comfortable like a mother and Sigrid is strong and busy like an aunt – and the professors are good to me. But sometimes . . . I dream about my real mother coming. Often I dream it – that she's looked and looked for me and at last she's found me. Do you think it's wrong to keep dreaming that?'

'How could it be wrong?'

'Well, when Ellie and Sigrid look after me so well.'

'Dreams don't work like that, Annika.'

She was still holding the spray of jasmine to her face and her eyes were shut, but Annika didn't go away. She wanted the rest of the story.

'Last time you said it was the beginning,' she said. 'Being on the swing.'

'Yes. I was a success. People called me La Rondine – it means a swallow in Italian – and they put me on to clouds and into hot-air balloons and gondolas, but always high, high over the stage and always I strewed something. Flowers mostly; but sometimes autumn leaves or golden coins or gingerbread hearts . . . And once, in Russia, I strewed snow!'

'Snow! But how . . . ?'

'Well, of course it was tissue-paper snow, but it looked wonderful. We were touring Moscow and St Petersburg and I was the Spirit of Winter. The Russians stamped and shouted and cheered. They love it when it begins to snow – it makes the streets so quiet, the horses' hoofs are muffled and there are sledges everywhere. A count who lived in a wooden palace in the middle of a forest gave a great banquet for us. He was mad but so generous – he gave me an emerald pendant, which had belonged to his grandmother. The Star of Kazan, it was called.'

'Were there wolves?'

'We didn't see any, but we heard them – and when we arrived it was dusk and there was a whole line of the count's servants with lighted flares to lead us up the drive and welcome us.'

Her eyes closed. She began to snore, and her mouth went slack, but it didn't matter any more. Annika was looking at a friend.

Then she woke as suddenly as she had slept.

'The world was so beautiful in those days, Annika. The music, the flowers, the scent of the pines . . .'

'It still is,' said Annika. 'Honestly, it still is.'

CHAPTER SIX

THE STAR OF KAZAN

Summer was now well under way. The geraniums in Ellie's window boxes had to be watered twice a day, the cats lay in the shade of the cafe awning, and were shooed away, and came back . . .

At the opera, the season was nearly over, and Annika was sent out to buy the roses that Uncle Emil always sent, at the last performance, to a lady in the chorus called Cornelia Otter, whom he had admired for many years.

Professor Julius was relabelling the collection of rocks in his study, helped by Sigrid, who stood beside him with a duster looking sour, because it is not at all easy to dust rocks. Professor Gertrude was having trouble with her harp sonata and kept to her room, dabbing lavender water on to her temples to help her think.

But when she went to visit the Eggharts' great-aunt in her stuffy attic, Annika was in a different world.

'I was La Rondine for several years. The Little Swallow. There were pictures of me everywhere and people gave me such presents . . . Once a posy of flowers was brought on to the stage for me, and when I took it it seemed to be covered with drops of dew. But they weren't drops of dew, they were diamonds . . . A banker sent them, just to say thank you. And a marquis gave me a priceless brooch in the shape of a butterfly. People were like that in those days; so generous – and so rich. My jewels were famous. I could have bought horses and carriages and mansions if I'd sold them, but they were friends, I loved them.' She turned her head. 'It's true what I'm telling you,' she said anxiously.

'Of course it's true.'

'Anyway I was too busy – with my work . . .'

'With strewing,' said Annika, who liked that word particularly.

'Yes. Not only, of course. I danced and sang too, but every time at the end of the show there had to be a number where I was hoisted up high and scattered things. The stage hands used to get quite cross, sweeping up roses, sweeping up daffodils, but the audience insisted. We toured all the big cities . . . we even went to London.' She paused and stretched out her hand for the glass of water and Annika helped her to drink.

'And then something happened,' she went on.

Annika put her hand over her mouth. 'You fell?'

'I fell all right, but not off the swing. I fell in love. Oh my goodness how I fell! He was a wonderful man . . . a

53

painter . . . and when he smiled . . . Ah well, you'll know one day.'

'Did you get married?'

'No. But I gave up the stage. I gave up everything and went to live with him in the most beautiful place in the world.'

'Where's that?

'It's called Merano. It's a village in the South Tyrol, in the Dolomites; it's where the mountains come down to shelter the valley. There are vineyards everywhere and flowers, and orchards full of fruit – and when you look up there are the great peaks, which turn to rose when the sun sets.'

'Yes, I know about that. It's called *Alpengluhen*.'

She nodded. 'Yes. His house was a little yellow villa halfway up the mountain, smothered in wisteria and jasmine, with a blue balcony where we had our meals. You must go there one day. You'll know it because it has a tiny clock tower with a weathervane shaped like a crowing cock.'

She groped for her handkerchief, then shook her head impatiently. 'I'm not sad. It's good to remember. We lived there for ten years and I was so happy. Not famous now . . . but my goodness, so happy! Then he was killed in a climbing accident. He was trying to help someone who was trapped on an ice ledge.'

She stopped and Annika got up from her chair.

'You'll want to rest now.'

'No, not yet. Then the vampires came. Six huge vampires. Harpies with fangs and claws. His relatives. Two sisters, an aunt, three cousins . . . They turned me out of the house – they wanted to sell it at once and get the money. So I went back to Paris. I tried to get back to work, but ten years is too long to be away from the theatre and I wasn't so young and pretty any more. It was a difficult time. But I still had my jewels – the harpies couldn't take them away from me. I'll tell you about my . . . jewels when you . . . come again.'

And almost at once she was asleep.

The weather now became very hot and all the important people left Vienna to go on their summer holidays.

The most important person of course was the emperor, who put away his military uniforms and the helmets he wore to attend to his duties and went off to his villa in the mountains, where he put on lederhosen and embroidered braces and pretended to be a peasant.

Ellie was always pleased when he went away.

'The poor old man: all those parades and processions and him with his bad back.'

When the emperor left Vienna, so did the courtiers and the civil servants and the bankers and the opera singers.

And so did the Lipizzaners – who were most certainly important – who went off to the high pastures to rest and grow strong on the rich grass. Their grooms led them through the quiet streets at daybreak, to the special train that was kept for them, and the Viennese heard them and smiled because it meant that the holidays had begun.

The professors too went away. They always went to the same place, a quiet hotel in Switzerland, where they swam up and down a dark-green lake and read their books. Though the holiday was not a complicated one, getting them off safely was hard work. Annika's job was to search their long woollen bathing costumes for moth holes, through which somebody might see pieces of their skin, while Ellie oiled their boots and Sigrid ironed Professor

Gertrude's dirndls, which were of the stately kind, with black aprons and many pleats.

And the Eggharts left in their canary-yellow motor car, which was quite a performance because Loremarie and her mother had to wrap their heads in layers of veiling to protect them from the dust, and Herr Egghart had to find his gauntlets and his goggles and his leather driving coat, and poop the horn loudly to make sure everyone would get out of the way before he even got in. They had rented a house in Bad Haxenfeld, a famous spa in Germany where sulphurous water gushed out of the rocks and people sat in mud baths up to their necks and were massaged and pummelled and put on diets.

'I feel absolutely exhausted, having that old woman in my house,' Frau Egghart told her friends before they left. Actually all she had done was to go up to the attic once a week and stand by the door with her handkerchief over her mouth as though old age was catching – but her friends were very sympathetic.

Because they had rented a house, the Eggharts took all their servants except the youngest of the maids, who was left in sole charge of their great-aunt. The people in the square were shocked by this, but for Annika it was a relief. She could go over when she liked and stay as long as she wanted. Loremarie had not left any money for the holidays, but Annika had almost forgotten that she was ever paid.

Ellie had taken a pot of her scented geraniums and some fruit to the old lady, and she tried to warn Annika.

'You mustn't be sad when she goes,' Ellie told her. 'She's very tired and she'll be glad to slip away.'

'No, she won't,' said Annika furiously. 'She's only tired because the weather's so hot. When it gets cooler she'll be better again; she's NOT going to die!'

And Ellie shook her head because it was impossible to convince Annika that she was not in charge of the world.

Meanwhile, in her attic, the old lady was coming near the end of her story.

'I went to live in a little room on the Left Bank and I was all right. I bought a dog.'

'What kind of dog?' asked Annika eagerly.

'A little schnauzer. I would have liked a big one, but not in the middle of town.'

'Yes, schnauzers are good,' said Annika and sighed, for her quest for a dog of her own was not making any progress.

'So I was all right. I still had my jewels you see. I still had the Star of Kazan and the butterfly brooch and the diamond tiara and the rings . . . I used to look at them, when I was alone. They were so beautiful. And while I had them I was still rich – very, very rich. But of course one by one I had to sell them to buy food and pay the rent.'

'Were you very sad?'

'Yes, I was. But I had a friend – such a good friend. He was really a saint, that man; he was a hunchback and he was a brilliant jeweller – he built up one of the most famous jewellery businesses in Paris: Fabrice, he was called. He remembered me from when I was famous and he helped me. Whenever I needed money, I would take him a piece of jewellery and he would sell it for me at the best possible price. But – this is what was so special – every time he sold a piece for me he had it copied in glass or paste so that it looked almost exactly like the original. He sold my Star of Kazan and copied it, and my butterfly brooch and my cluster rings . . . and after a while I got just as fond of the copies as the originals. I thought they were just as beautiful even though they weren't worth anything at all. Wasn't that kind of him?'

'Yes, it was. It was very kind.'

'And so I managed for twenty years. I suppose I could have saved some money, but I didn't and there were other people as badly off as me whom I wanted to help. Perhaps I had got into the habit of strewing. Then the day came when I didn't have anything left to sell, and just about this time my jeweller friend died.'

Annika leaned forward. 'What did you do?'

'What everybody does when their luck runs out. I was old by then. I got what work I could, cleaning the streets . . . scrubbing . . . There were quite a few of us – people who'd been on the stage or in the music world. And there were soup kitchens . . . I managed. Then I decided to come home to Austria. I suppose I wanted to die here, or perhaps I thought my family would . . . and you see in the end they did take me in, though I don't know why.'

Annika did know why. It was because Herr Egghart wanted to become a statue and you can't become a statue if you leave your aunt to die in an asylum – but of course she said nothing.

'Anyway I'm glad I did,' the old lady went on, 'because I made a new friend and not many people make friends at ninety-four.' And she stretched out her hand and laid it for a moment on Annika's arm.

*

Ellie was right about the Eggharts' great-aunt. She was getting very weak. Sometimes now when Annika came she would do no more than smile at her before she drifted off to sleep, and when she spoke it might be just a few words, which did not always make sense.

'A rose garden in the sky,' she said once, and the maid who had come to straighten the bed said, 'Poor old thing, she's wandering in her mind.'

But just a week before the Eggharts were due to return, Annika found the old lady alert and excited with a mischievous look in her eye.

'I'll show you something,' she said. 'If you can open the trunk. It's locked, but I wouldn't let them keep the key. I made them give it back and then I forgot where I'd hidden it, but now I've found it. It was in my other bedsocks.'

The trunk was a big one, banded in rings of wood, but Annika found she could pull it over to the bed.

The key turned easily in the lock and Annika lifted the lid.

Inside were dresses in gauze and satin, wisps of muslin, a wreath of daisies, silver gloves . . . The clothes were very old; some were a little torn, here and there were splashes of powder still clinging to the material, or dabs of greasepaint. It was like opening a door on to a theatre dressing room.

'Now take off the top shelf . . .'

The trunk was separated into two parts, like a box of chocolates. Annika took off the top – and found herself looking at a large number of parcels wrapped in newspaper.

'Go on. Unwrap them.'

59

Annika took out a packet wrapped in paper so old that it was beginning to crumble, and unwrapped it.

'Oh!' she said. 'Oh, how beautiful!'

She was holding a necklace of rubies, the jewels seeming to flash fire against the setting of gold.

'The stones came from a special mine in Burma. I was given it after I was an Eastern Princess and strewed lotus blossoms. I think it was lotus blossoms . . . You wouldn't know the stones aren't real, would you?'

'No. And anyway it doesn't matter – they couldn't be more splendid.'

'Go on; unwrap them all. I'd like to see them once again.'

The next parcel was a butterfly brooch in sapphires – the stones as blue as the famous morphos of the Amazon. The wings were outlined in tiny diamonds and the antennae trembled with filigree gold.

'I wore that when we were presented to the Duc d'Orléans. And those earrings were brought round after I was Cupid and strewed pink-paper hearts. The diamonds were eighteen carats – if I still had the real ones you could have bought a castle with them. But you can see what a craftsman that jeweller was. You'd have to know a lot about jewels to tell the difference.'

One by one Annika unpacked the parcels and laid them on the bed, till the old lady seemed to be floating on an ocean of colour: the piercing blue of the sapphires, the warm glow of the rubies . . . and the brilliance of the Star of Kazan from the country of dark firs and glittering snow . . .

Right at the bottom was a small parcel, wrapped not in newspaper but in a piece of black velvet. Inside was a box which opened to show a picture of a man and a woman standing in front of a house – a woman with thick, light hair, a man with a lean, intelligent face. It must have been one of the earliest photos ever taken, but Annika knew at once who they were.

'That's you and your painter, isn't it? You look so happy.'

The old lady took the photo in its wooden frame, and as she cupped the picture in both hands, the jewels heaped on the bedspread were forgotten. 'So happy . . .' she said softly. 'So very, very happy . . .'

'You see,' said Annika, when she got back home, 'I told you she would get better.'

But the next day the old lady asked for a lawyer, though she had no money to leave, and for a priest. That evening the doctor's carriage was seen in front of the Eggharts' house. It was still there two hours later – and then the young maid was seen running wild-eyed towards the post office.

CHAPTER SEVEN

A SWALLOW SET FREE

Although the Eggharts had been sorry to cut their holiday short, the funeral which they gave their great-aunt was a very respectable affair.

'No one can say we have not done all we should have done,' said Herr Egghart as he pulled on the trousers of his funeral suit and fixed a black rosette into his buttonhole.

'No indeed,' said his wife. She had bought a new black-silk suit and her hat was veiled in yards of black netting. 'In fact I'm not sure you haven't overdone it a bit. With the church so near we could have had the coffin carried over by hand.'

'Well, a bit of show doesn't hurt,' said her husband and he looked out of the window at the four black horses with their mourning headdresses of jet feathers. The coffin was just being loaded on to the hearse, and the horses would pull it across the square so that everybody could see that they had not stinted on the old lady's funeral. 'After all, she was an Egghart,' he said.

And really it was tactful of his great-aunt to die after only a few months in their attic. He had been afraid that the mess and the expense would be long drawn out.

'How do I look, Mummy?' asked Loremarie, coming into the bedroom. She too had acquired a whole new outfit for the funeral: a purple velvet dress with lace round the collar, and black kid gloves.

The hearse set off for the short journey across the square. The Eggharts followed with bowed heads, and after them at a respectful distance came the Eggharts' maids and their manservant, the snooty Leopold.

As they made their way to the front pew, the Eggharts noticed that quite ordinary and unimportant people had come to pay their respects to the old lady. There were three of the Bodek boys, the old bookseller and his grand-daughter . . . and sitting with the professors, as though they had a right to be there, their servants, Ellie and Sigrid, and their adopted daughter, Annika. It is not possible to turn people out of a church during a funeral, but the Eggharts were not pleased. Fortunately the head of the asylum, a very eminent doctor, had also come, and two councillors from Herr Egghart's office, as well as the manager of his bank.

Ellie and Sigrid had mourning dresses; so many of their elderly relations had died. Annika only had the black shawl that Sigrid wore to mass over her Sunday dress, and Loremarie turned round to throw her a contemptuous glance.

Annika didn't even see her. She had watched the coffin carried up the aisle and, though she had promised herself not to cry any more, she couldn't stop the tears coming, because La Rondine shouldn't have been shut up in a box – no one should, but certainly not someone who had flown high over the stages of the world.

I should have gone to see her more often, thought Annika. I should have brought her more flowers, and stayed longer; she was so lonely.

Beside her, Ellie squeezed her arm.

'She was glad to go, love,' she whispered. 'You know that. She was so tired.'

'But I'm not glad,' sobbed Annika. 'I didn't want her to die.'

The organ pealed out, the service began. Annika, not wanting to be seen in tears, wrapped herself in Sigrid's shawl.

The Latin words of the service were dark and frightening. Though the priest spoke about resurrection, he seemed to spend more time on the yawning grave and the dust to dust. The incense swept through the church like smoke.

Annika heard the old lady's voice: 'The world was so beautiful in those days, Annika.' And her own reply: 'Honestly, it still is.'

She'd been wrong. The world was not beautiful. People you were fond of died, and got shovelled into holes.

The congregation rose for the last hymn. Annika let slip her enveloping shawl and lifted her head, to look up at the roof of the church.

And then for a moment she saw her! Not the exhausted old lady – but the girl on the swing. Higher she went, and higher, in time to the music; there were flowers in her hair and she was strewing the beams of light from the stained-glass windows.

As they filed out, Loremarie turned and hissed at her. 'You smiled. I saw you. You smiled because my poor great-aunt is dead.'

Annika looked at her.

'Yes,' she said. 'I smiled.'

The funeral tea, like the funeral, was a most dignified affair. The maids had set out slices of Sachertorte and various kinds of strudel, and open sandwiches spread with fish roe, which might well have been caviar – though actually it wasn't. Needless to say, the servants from the professors' house were not invited back, nor the Bodeks, nor the old bookseller and his daughter, but the head of the asylum stayed, and the councillors and the manager of the bank.

'We will miss her dreadfully,' Frau Egghart told her guests, dabbing her perfectly dry eyes with a handkerchief. 'And Loremarie was so fond of her, weren't you, dear?'

'What?' said Loremarie, turning round with her mouth full of cake.

'Weren't you so fond of your great-aunt,' shouted Frau Egghart above the noise of the conversation.

'Yes,' said Loremarie, letting some crumbs fall from her mouth, and turned back to reach for another slice of chocolate cake.

Then, as soon as the last guest had gone, the maids were sent up to the attic with buckets of hot water and scrubbing brushes and mops and bottles of disinfectant. Frau Egghart came with them and saw that the work was done properly: the bed stripped and the bed linen steeped in Lysol, every window pane squirted, every floorboard scoured.

'That's better,' she said when it was done and all traces of the old lady had been removed. 'That's much, much better.'

After that Leopold came with another man, to take the great-aunt's trunk and boxes down to the cellar for the dustcart to take away.

'I could use the things in the trunk for dressing up,' Loremarie said. 'All those funny turbans and jewels and things.'

'Don't be silly, dear,' her mother said. 'Everything in there is full of germs. And you can't use vulgar rubbish like that, even to dress up. You'd look like a circus horse.'

So the trunk and the wooden boxes were taken down to the cellar and that was that.

But the following morning two men in dark coats arrived and presented their cards. 'Gerhart and Funkel,' they said. 'We work for the firm in the Karntner Strasse. The old lady's lawyers. She left a will and we have to take all her possessions into safekeeping. Here are the papers.'

Frau Egghart pursed her lips. 'She hasn't got any possessions. She was penniless.'

'It says here a large tin trunk and two wooden boxes.'

'That's all rubbish. It's in the cellar waiting to be carted away.'

'Nevertheless we would like to take charge of it.'

'I tell you it's all vulgar rubbish.'

'But perhaps not to her,' said the lawyer's clerk quietly. And then, 'Have it brought up please.'

CHAPTER EIGHT

THE CHRISTMAS CARP

Annika used to love October almost best of all the months: the smell of chestnuts roasting everywhere on street corners, the school outing to the Vienna Woods to collect mushrooms and berries, the drift of blue smoke from garden bonfires . . .

But this year she saw autumn not just as beautiful but as sad. She missed the old lady and for the first time she wondered about her own future.

Stefan too seemed less settled. He still carried his younger brothers about, delivered the washing for his mother, ran errands . . . But once, in the hut, he put it into words: 'I don't want to end up spearing rubbish with a stick like my father,' he told Annika and Pauline.

'Yes, but what do you want to do?'

Stefan blushed. 'I want to be an engineer. I'd like to build bridges.'

'Well, what's wrong with that?'

'Everything. Even if I got into the technical school, I couldn't spend long training. My parents need the money I'll bring in when I start work.'

Because she felt restless, Annika's daydreams about her mother became longer and more detailed. She came now not in a carriage but in one of the new motors like the Eggharts', except that it wasn't a garish yellow but a soft and tasteful grey. She wore a hat with a plume and carried a sable muff, and the dog she brought had become grander too: a Russian borzoi, white and brown and black, with a silken tail. But the words with which she entered the house were always the same:

'Where is she, my long-lost daughter? Take me to her please – take me to my child!'

But when the first snow fell, Annika cheered up; and in no time, she and Ellie and Sigrid were off to the market to buy the Christmas tree.

This was a serious business. The tree could not be big; it had to fit into a particular corner of the dining room – but it had to be perfect.

And it always was.

As they came out of the market, carrying the tree, they saw Leopold with one of the stallholders, loading an absolutely enormous fir tree on to a cart. Beside him stood Loremarie looking smug.

'It's the biggest there was,' she said with a smirk. 'It's probably the biggest in the whole of Vienna.'

Annika stopped for a moment and felt a pang of envy. What would it be like to have a tree that would fill a whole room with its scent and its beauty. She imagined candle-light from the floor to the ceiling, the shimmer of silver and gold . . .

But that night, Mitzi, the Eggharts' maid, came round to see them.

'Guess what?' she said. 'The tree's too big! They had to cut the top off and Loremarie's having a tantrum because there's nowhere to hang the star!'

After the tree, Ellie and Annika began to make the gingerbread house. By this time the professors had realized that Christmas was near and started to think about presents. On the grounds that the best presents are those one would like to have oneself, Professor Julius bought Annika the new edition of *Kloezberger's Mesozoic Fossils*, and Professor Emil bought her *The Encyclopedia of Eighteenth-Century Painting*, which they gave to Sigrid to wrap up. Professor Gertrude took the advice of the lady in the shop and bought her a manicure set that included tweezers for removing facial hair.

Then Sigrid brought down the decorations from the attic. They had been made over the years from scraps of silk, ribbons, fir cones painted silver and gold – but each year they made new things, and each year the sweets had to be wrapped in silver paper and hung on the lower branches so that the younger Bodeks could reach them when the time came.

In Vienna Christmas is celebrated on the twenty-fourth – on Holy Night. But it is not a goose or a turkey that is roasted on this night of nights. No one on Holy Night would dream of eating meat. What is roasted is a fish – and not any fish but a carp, the largest and most succulent fish in Austria's rivers.

And just three days before Christmas, the carp arrived.

It arrived packed in lumps of ice from the salt mines of Hallstadt and the fishmonger had done them proud.

'It's the biggest we've ever had,' said Annika, and certainly the fish was magnificent, the kind that appears in fairy stories, rearing up out of the sea and granting wishes.

During the next day it was clear that Ellie had something on her mind. She and Sigrid talked together, and when Annika came they stopped suddenly and looked at her in a considering sort of way.

That night, just as Annika had got into bed, she heard footsteps coming up to her door and Ellie entered. She usually said goodnight downstairs – Ellie's legs were tired by the end of the day – so it was clear she had something important to say, and she had.

'We think you can do it.' Ellie's voice was solemn. 'We have made up our minds.'

'Do what?'

'Cook it entirely by yourself. Without any help.'

'Cook what?' said Annika, bewildered.

And Ellie said, 'The Christmas carp.'

Annika came downstairs the next morning looking pale, with dark smudges under her eyes. Ellie too looked as though she'd had a sleepless night.

'I'm sorry, pet, I shouldn't have suggested it. You're too young. There's ten things to go into the sauce alone, and there's the stuffing and the basting . . .'

Annika put up her chin. 'Yes, I can. I can and I will. Please will you get down The Book for me.

So Ellie lifted down her mother's worn and faded recipe

book, which contained all the wisdom of her family, and Annika found the page headed 'Christmas Carp'.

The instructions were written in crabbed handwriting in violet ink, not even by Ellie's mother, but by her grandmother, and they covered nearly three pages.

Annika began to read. The fish had to be washed four times in running cold water and the fifth time in water and lemon juice. At *least* four times, the book said. After that it had to be put to soak in a marinade – a kind of bath of white wine, chopped onions, herbs and lemon.

'It says here that Chablis is the best wine to use.'

Sigrid raised her eyebrows. 'That's the most expensive,' she said.

'But it's the best,' said Annika firmly, and Sigrid went down to the cellar without another word.

By lunchtime the fish was in its marinade, where it would stay for the rest of the day, and Annika had started to assemble the things she needed for the stuffing. She had been given the main kitchen table to work on. Ellie prepared the vegetables and the desserts at the smaller side table, but she was beginning to suffer, seeing Annika heave the enormous fish kettle about. Annika's hands were red and chafed, she had tied her hair up in an old cloth, and when anybody spoke to her she didn't hear. Something was sure to go wrong, thought Ellie, and to stop herself from interfering she took herself off to the shops.

By now the news that Annika was cooking the professors' Christmas carp entirely by herself had gone round the square. Pauline in particular was very upset and she came in after lunch bringing her scrapbook of people who had done brave and difficult things even though they were too young or too old or too ill.

'There's one here about a girl of ten who swam across the Danube to rescue her grandfather, even though she had the measles.'

But Annika did not seem to be cheered up by this. She had reached the grating stage: grating honey cake, grating lemon rind, grating horseradish, grating (but only slightly) her middle finger . . .

In the afternoon Ellie returned and sent Annika out into the crisp snow to get a newspaper, thinking some fresh air would do her good, but this turned out to be a mistake, because the lady in the paper shop told her that her mother's stuffing for the carp at Christmas had always contained chopped prunes.

Annika was unsettled by this, but then she remembered that the paper-shop lady's family had come from Czechoslovakia, where they probably ate all sorts of things, and she turned back to Ellie's book.

There was now only one more day to go, and the professors began to quarrel about the best way to stop the tree from going up in flames if the candles set it alight. Professor Julius believed in a bucket of sand to stand beside the tree. Professor Emil thought that a bucket of water was better, and Professor Gertrude favoured a large blanket with which to smother the flames. They argued about this every year and could never agree, so this year as in other years they took all three into the dining room. Sigrid polished the knives and forks, the napkin rings, the candlesticks . . . Ellie put the finishing touches to the poppy-seed strudel, the chocolate mousse, the iced and marbled gugelhupf, which is the most famous cake in Vienna.

And Annika removed the carp from its bath and patted it dry and stuffed it with truffles and chopped celery and chestnut purée and lemon rind and grated honey cake and dark plum jam, and greased the gigantic roasting tin with clarified butter and laid the carp to rest on it until the following day, when it would go into the oven. There was only the sauce to make now, but there wasn't anything 'only' about the sauce – which took up a page and a half in Ellie's mother's book.

Later that evening, Frau Bodek came over with a blouse for Annika which she had stitched in her spare time, though where she got spare time from was not easy to see. But she too unsettled Annika, for Frau Bodek's aunt in Moravia had always added chopped walnuts to the sauce.

'It gave it a lovely crunch,' Frau Bodek said.

But Annika was determined to stick to the the recipe handed down from Ellie's grandmother. Anything else would be cheating.

And yet that night, the last night before Christmas, she felt restless. A single word kept going round and round in her head, and the word was *nutmeg*.

Only why? Nutmeg was a lovely spice, but there wasn't a word about nutmeg in the instructions for the sauce. Other spices, yes, and other herbs . . . but not that.

'I mustn't,' said Annika again. 'I mustn't change anything or add anything. It's got to be the way it always was.'

The bells woke her in the dark on the morning of the twenty-fourth. She shrugged on her clothes, and then she and Ellie and Sigrid went across the square to church for early-morning mass.

When she got back she knew with a deadly certainty that lunch was going to be a failure. The carp would come apart, the sauce would curdle, the stuffing would leak. Fighting down panic, she went to the larder to fetch the fish and put it in the oven.

Then, right at the last minute, she did something she knew she would regret.

The three professors were dressed in their best clothes, their starched napkins were ready round their necks, their eyes were expectant and the table was set with the gold-rimmed Meissen plates, which were only used on very special days. Then the door opened and Annika entered with the carp.

The professors smiled benevolently. Ellie brought the vegetables and the sauce. Professor Julius began to cut the fish into slices.

'Delicious,' they said. 'Absolutely delicious. Just as always.'

But when Ellie and Sigrid and Annika sat down in the kitchen to their share of the fish, the worst happened.

Ellie put a helping of carp to her mouth. Her face clouded. Annika had seldom seen her look so angry.

'What have you *done*?' she asked, aghast. 'What have you done, Annika? My mother would turn in her grave.'

She took another mouthful. An awful silence fell.

Then Sigrid said, 'Just taste, Ellie, just taste, don't lecture.'

Ellie speared another piece of fish in its dark sauce . . . and another . . . She closed her eyes. She still did not speak, but when the first course was finished she got up and fetched the black book from the dresser and with it a pen and a bottle of ink.

Then, 'You can write it in,' she said to Annika. 'Don't smudge it.'

Annika took the pen. 'What do I write?' she asked, bewildered.

Ellie pointed to the instructions for cooking the Christmas carp. 'Here . . . Under the last line write: "A pinch of nutmeg will improve the flavour of the sauce." '

The tree did not catch fire. Sigrid had made Annika a brown velvet dress with a wide lace collar, and Ellie gave her a silver charm to add to her bracelet. Later the Bodeks came and Stefan lifted up the smaller ones to get their sugar mice and gingerbread hearts from the tree.

All in all it had been a wonderful Christmas; 'the best ever,' Annika said, as she said each year, and meant it. She had quite forgotten her doubts and sadness. Her future lay clear before her; she would learn to be the best cook in Vienna – perhaps even a famous cook who had dishes named after her. Certainly there was no better place to grow up than here in this familiar square in the most beautiful city in the world.

She opened her double windows, which she was not supposed to do, and held out a hand to catch a snowflake. Faintly, across the cobbles, there came the noise of a child screaming. Then the Eggharts' door opened and Loremarie threw her new skating boots out into the street.

'They're the wrong colour,' she yelled. 'I told you, I wanted them to be *blue*!'

And Annika, who had prayed only that morning not to think unkind thoughts, felt that this was the perfect end to the day.

CHAPTER NINE

THE GIANT WHEEL

At the end of February the funfair in the Prater, which had been closed in the winter, prepared to open once again. This meant taking the tarpaulins off the roundabouts, reassembling the shooting booths and checking the machinery of the famous Giant Wheel with its large, closed carriages.

And on the last Saturday before the fair opened officially, the men who worked there, like Stefan's father and the other groundsmen and mechanics and carpenters, were allowed to invite their family and friends to come to the Prater free.

Stefan went, but his elder brothers all had Saturday jobs, so Annika went with him. Pauline too was invited, but she knew that the day would mostly be spent on the Giant Wheel, which she found alarming and far too high, and her grandfather was expecting a new delivery of books, so she stayed at home.

Pauline was right. Annika and Stefan went round on the Giant Wheel three times, but then Stefan caught sight of the engineer who serviced it and went off to talk to him – so that the last time Annika went up, she was alone.

Perhaps it was because of this that she saw everything so vividly.

There is a moment when each carriage stops with a little click and just hangs there in space. The music ceases, one can hear the wind – and there beneath one lies the whole city. To the east, the Danube, to the north and west the Vienna Woods . . . and to the south (but one has to look very hard for this) just a glimpse of the white peaks of the Alps, where the snow is everlasting.

Everything she saw now seemed to be part of her own life. The spire of the cathedral where, on Easter Sunday, Aunt Gertrude had knelt on a dead mouse . . . The roofs of the palace where the emperor slept on his iron bed, and the Spanish Riding School where his Lipizzaners had danced for them . . .

The copper dome of the art museum where Uncle Emil had told her so many important things about the painting of human flesh, and the opera where he had picked Cornelia Otter out of a chorus of thirty well-covered village maidens and decided to adore her.

She ran from side to side, looking, looking . . . Here was the park of the Belvedere, where soon now she would go and search for the first violets . . . and the pond in the Volksgarten where they had found an injured duckling and brought it to Ellie to heal. Beyond the marshy islands on the Danube ran the great plain which stretched all the way to Budapest and – nearer again – the graveyard where Sigrid's uncle was buried after he ate twenty-seven potato dumplings in a row and fell senseless to the ground. And Annika, on a level with the clouds, thought of her friend, the Eggharts' great-aunt, who had swung and strewn high over the stages of the world – and she had a great longing to break the windows of the carriage and strew something marvellous over the city: flowers, thousands and thousands of flowers, which would land in the wintry streets to please the people who lived in Vienna and had made it beautiful.

'Oh, Stefan, we're so lucky,' she said, when she was down again. And as he looked at her puzzled she added, 'To live here, I mean. To belong.'

Afterwards it seemed strange to her that she had said those words on that particular day.

They got off the tram a stop early because the snow was almost gone at last and the sun was shining.

'Goodness,' said Annika, as they turned into the square. 'There seems to be a meeting.'

There were certainly a lot of people standing by the fountain: Josef from the cafe, with his mother wrapped in a shawl. Father Anselm from the church. The Eggharts' maid, Mitzi. Frau Bodek, with the baby in the pram and the three-year-old Hansi clinging to her skirts, and not only Pauline but Pauline's grandfather, who hadn't been seen outside his shop in months.

And in the centre of the group was the coal-man, who had been delivering bags of fuel to the professors' house, and to whom they were all listening.

'I tell you,' he was saying, 'there was Ellie slumped at the kitchen table, crying her heart out, and Sigrid looking at me as though she's never seen me before, when I've been to their house once a week for the past—'

He broke off. His listeners had turned and now everybody could see Annika and Stefan coming towards them. The coal-man fell silent. Everyone fell silent except Hansi, who wailed, 'I don't want Ellie to cry, I want her to make *buns*.'

Annika stopped.

'What is it? What's happened?'

'You must go home, Annika, they're waiting for you,' said Pauline's grandfather in a solemn voice.

Now she was very much afraid. 'What's happened?' she asked again. And as no one answered her she said, 'Will you come with me, Pauline?'

Pauline stepped forward, but her grandfather put a hand on her shoulder. 'No. Pauline, you stay here. Annika's family—' He stopped himself. 'They . . . will want to have Annika to themselves today.'

Annika was already running across the square. She threw open the kitchen door, and what the coal-man had said was true. Ellie was slumped at the kitchen table, her face was blotched and, most extraordinary of all, she wasn't doing anything. Not beating something in a bowl, not kneading dough, not slicing vegetables. Sigrid sat in the wicker chair; her hands too were empty and she seemed to be staring at something no one else could see.

'What is it – what's happened? Why will no one tell me anything?' said Annika, throwing her arms round Ellie. 'Are the professors all right? Has someone died?'

Ellie managed to shake her head. 'No one's died.' She

loosened Annika's arms. 'You're wanted in the drawing room.'

'In the drawing room?'

So something serious was the matter. The servants never went into the drawing room except to dust or clean. As a matter of fact the professors did not go into it much themselves; it was a dark and formal room, not welcoming like the other rooms in the house.

Sigrid roused herself enough to lunge at Annika's hair with the comb she kept in her overall pocket. Then she said, 'Go on; you'll do.'

Annika went through the green baize door, along the corridor, up the first flight of stairs. She knocked, entered and curtsied.

Professor Julius and Professor Emil stood on either side of the writing desk, which was covered in official-looking papers. They seemed somehow smaller than usual, and this was because, standing between them with her back to the door, was a very tall woman wearing a dark fur cloak and a hat with osprey feathers.

'Come along in,' said Professor Julius, and his voice seemed strange; a little husky. And then, 'This is Annika.'

The woman turned. She had very blue eyes, but her brows were black and the crescent of hair showing under her hat was black also. With her strong features and her height, she looked to Annika like a queen.

The woman stood absolutely still and gazed at her. She lifted up her long arms so that her cloak spread out on either side like a pair of wings, blotting out the two professors. And only then did she say the words of Annika's dream.

'My child,' said the tall woman, 'my darling, darling daughter – have I really found you at last!'

And she stepped forward and took Annika into her arms.

CHAPTER TEN

HAPPINESS

There is nothing more amazing than walking into one's own dream. Her mother was real, she had come, and Annika, from the moment she felt her mother's arms round her, was in a daze of happiness. She could hardly bear to be separated from her even by the length of a room.

Annika had imagined an elegant and confident woman, but even in her wildest dreams she had not thought that her mother might be an aristocrat – a nobly born woman with a 'von' in front of her name and a family crest – yet it was so.

Her mother's name was Edeltraut von Tannenberg and she lived in an ancient, moated house in the north of Germany which had been in her family for generations.

Not only that, but she was beautiful: tall with thick

black hair that she wore in plaits round her head; long, narrow hands and feet, and a slender neck. The way she carried herself, the way she spoke – in her deep, serious voice and in an accent so different from the lilting speech of the Viennese – held Annika spellbound. Even the scent she wore was different: a dark, musky, exotic scent that smelt as though the flowers it was made of came from an unknown land.

Frau von Tannenberg had of course brought papers to show that she was truly the woman who had left her baby on the altar steps in the church at Pettelsdorf. Among these was a document witnessed by one of Vienna's most famous lawyers, Herr Adolf Pumpelmann-Schlissinger. It was an affidavit signed by the midwife at Pettelsdorf, Amelia Plotz, swearing that she had assisted at the birth of a daughter to Frau Edeltraut von Tannenberg on the sixth of June 1896.

There could be no doubting a document witnessed by Herr Pumpelmann-Schlissinger. He was a small dapper man with a well-oiled moustache, who wore pointed shoes and purple cravats and could be seen at most fashionable gatherings in the city. The professors knew him well; he belonged to the same club as Uncle Julius, collected silver salad servers, and was often called in by the university in their disputes with the council.

'If Pumpelmann-Schlissinger's put his name to it, then that's the end of the matter,' said Professor Julian sadly, and all hope that there had been a mistake or a misunderstanding had to be abandoned.

The afternoon was spent in business matters, but as supper time drew closer there were problems. Frau von Tannenberg obviously could not eat in the kitchen. On the other hand if she dined with the professors, Annika could not be expected so suddenly to eat upstairs. So most tactfully Annika's mother invited her daughter to join her for supper at the Hotel Bristol, where she was staying, so that they could get to know each other quietly by themselves.

'My God, the Bristol,' said Ellie – and she and Sigrid pulled themselves together and washed Annika's hair and buffed her nails and dressed her in the brown velvet dress that Sigrid had made for her for Christmas . . . And they were only just ready when the doorbell rang and it was Annika's mother come to fetch her in a hansom cab.

The Bristol was Vienna's most luxurious and expensive hotel. Even royalty stayed there when they visited the city and Frau von Tannenberg was pleased with it.

And her new daughter was going to be a credit to her, she could see that. Watching Annika come towards her in the dining room, weaving her way between the tables with their starched damask and gleaming silver, seeing her smile at the waiter as he pulled out her chair, Frau von Tannenberg could only congratulate the cook and housemaid who had brought her up. She had been prepared gently to initiate Annika in to the art of managing the battery of knives and forks and showing her from which glass to drink, but there was no need. In Vienna's most splendid dining room, Annika was perfectly at home.

Because she was still trying to match up her daydream with what was happening, Annika asked about a dog. 'Did you bring one?' she asked a little foolishly.

Annika's mother shook her head. 'Are you fond of dogs?'

'Yes, I am. Very. I have always wanted one, all my life.'

'Well, there are plenty of dogs at Spittal. Plenty of animals altogether. There's a farm attached to the house.'

Annika nodded. It sounded good. But of course it did seem as though her mother was going to take her away. Well, obviously, except that in her daydream her mother had just come and then the dream had stopped. It was a dream about coming not going. No one in her dream had gone.

Annika took a deep breath. 'I kept wondering why . . . you left me.'

Her mother leaned forward and took both of Annika's hands across the table.

'Of course you wondered. Of course my poor child. And now that I've met you I know you will understand – you have such a sympathetic face. I'll tell you exactly what happened, but I'm afraid you'll have to face one thing, my dearest girl. Your father was a louse.'

Annika was startled. She knew that the aristocracy often used strong language, but it was strange to hear her father called a louse.

'So good-looking – you take after him – but a louse just the same.'

And she told Annika what had happened all those years ago when she was a young and inexperienced girl.

'I was so young – you must remember that. I was just eighteen years old. I had developed a bad cough and Spittal – my home – is very low-lying. So the doctors said I needed mountain air and they sent me – with my maid of course – to a hotel in the Alps.'

'Near Pettelsdorf,' put in Annika. Her heart was beating very fast.

'Yes, on the other side of the pass.' She paused and

86

lifted one finger in the direction of the waiter, who came at once to remove their plates.

'When I'd been there a few weeks my maid became ill and I sent her back to her home, but I didn't tell my father. He was very, very strict. I'd never been alone and I was enjoying it. But then of course I met a man.'

She gave a deep sigh and took another roll from the dish.

'My father?'

She nodded. 'You can't believe how handsome he was. The same dark gold hair as you have, and the same thoughtful eyes. He was a hussar – he wore a blue uniform with silver facings, and well . . . we fell in love.'

She paused and Annika waited. Her father in a blue uniform like the Kaiser wore . . .

'He asked me to marry him and I agreed. I was so happy. He said he would get the papers we needed – I knew nothing. I had never been away from home before. We went through a wedding ceremony in a little office somewhere – I see now that he must have bribed some clerk . . . and then we set off on our honeymoon.

'A week after that he vanished. He simply disappeared off the face of the earth. I tried to trace him through the army, but they'd never heard of him. Oh, I was desperate . . . I'd trusted him completely.'

She paused and put a hand to her throat as though she was once again living through the agony.

'And then,' she looked away for a moment, 'I found I was . . . expecting a child. I don't know if I should speak to you so frankly, but I imagine that children brought up as you have been learn things early.'

'Yes.'

'I was frantic. I knew my father would kill me if he found out . . . the disgrace and shame . . . the wedding was only a sham, you see. So I pretended I was still with my maid and taking a cure. I was quite alone when you were born, in a little chalet. The midwife only came at the last minute. Oh, the agony I went through, deciding what to do for the best – the best for you, I mean. I had found the little pilgrim church in Pettelsdorf on one of my lonely walks and I thought it was so beautiful. Such a holy place. So I wrapped you up . . . and . . . took you there . . . and laid you down beneath the altar . . . and then I went home.'

She was holding her handkerchief to her eyes – a lace-edged one with the von Tannenberg crest embroidered in one corner.

'May you never know such despair and wretchedness, my daughter. May God shield you from it.'

'And you never found my father? You never saw him again?'

'Never. I think he must be dead. It would be better if you thought him so.'

Annika was going through the story in her mind. She could imagine it all: the love and then the anger, the sorrow . . . the awful decision to be made.

'You will want to know why I have come now, so long afterwards, to claim you, and I will tell you. You see, my father died not long ago – he was a man feared everywhere – the Freiherr von Tannenberg. But Spittal now belongs to me, and anyone who does not accept my daughter will be banished from my sight.' She stretched her hand out across the table. 'We will start a new life, Annika. A new life in your family home.'

'Yes,' said Annika. 'Yes.'

So she *was* going away. Of course she would come back on visits but she was definitely going.

'You see, you haven't just found a mother,' said Frau von Tannenberg, smiling. 'You have a brother too; a half-brother all of your own.'

Annika was bewildered. 'How . . . ?'

'When I came back home, I was so lonely; so sad . . . you can imagine. But then a man came to court me. A decent man and of a good family – Franz von Unterfall. His people had an estate not far from ours. So I married him, and very quickly our son was born. Hermann. He's not much younger than you and you will love him. Everybody loves Hermann.'

Annika was trying to take all this in. 'So I have a step-father too?'

'You have, but you won't see him for a while. He's away in America, on diplomatic business, which is why I'm living in my old home. But you mustn't worry about being lonely: my sister lives very near Spittal and she has a daughter, Gudrun. She's a dear girl, your new cousin, so you see you won't be short of company.'

Annika slept very little that night. Mostly of course it was because of her great happiness – but partly too it was because she had a stomach ache. She wasn't really used to eating large meals late at night.

At two o'clock she got up and went to the lavatory and was sick. Usually when she was unwell she called Sigrid next door, or went down to Ellie in her room near the kitchen. But of course she couldn't do that now; the daughter of Edeltraut von Tannenberg couldn't wake people up just because she felt ill.

In fact, Sigrid was awake, and Ellie too. They heard Annika, and waited for her to come to them. But she did not come. Her door clicked shut again and they knew then that the old life was finally over.

After that everything happened quickly. Once Professor Julius had checked out the documents that Frau von Tannenberg had brought there was nothing to put off Annika's departure, and he called her in for a lecture on her new home.

'You will be living in Norrland, in the north-east of Germany, not far from the Baltic Sea. The soil there is clay on a bed of granite, so the land is liable to flooding and the main crop is sugar beet and other root vegetables . . .' And he went on to explain that the different German states were now one country ruled by Kaiser Wilhelm II, the Emperor of Germany, who was younger and healthier than the Austrian emperor with a bigger moustache, and was trying to build up the German army and navy so as to make Germany the most important country in Europe.

Two days before Annika was due to leave, Sigrid came into the kitchen to find Ellie holding the old black book of recipes that had belonged to her mother and her mother's mother before her.

'I wanted to give it to Annika on her next Found Day. Do you think I should give it to her now, to take away?'

Sigrid stood beside her friend, looking at the page Ellie held open: the instructions for cooking the Christmas carp and the words Annika had written underneath: 'A pinch of nutmeg will improve the flavour of the sauce.'

'Ellie, she's going to a different life. She's going to be a proper lady – a "von". She won't get much chance to cook, I'd say.'

'Well, if they don't encourage her, they're wicked,' said Ellie fiercely. 'Annika's got a proper talent. If it was for music or painting they'd see she carried on.'

But she stood looking at the book a little longer and then she put it back on the shelf.

Ellie had managed to pull herself together and was determined not to spoil Annika's joy. If she cried now, she did it at night under her pillow, and in the morning she washed her face rather longer than usual so that Annika saw nothing wrong. Sigrid too busied herself washing and ironing Annika's clothes, sewing on buttons, checking hair ribbons . . . Frau von Tannenberg was not going to buy anything for the child till they got home, she said. Spittal was not far from the spa town of Bad Haxenfeld, where the most important people in Europe went to be cured of their diseases, and the shops were splendid.

'You can imagine how much I shall enjoy dressing my little girl,' she told Sigrid. 'It's what every mother dreams of.'

And Sigrid sighed, for she too would have liked to take Annika into a dress shop and fit her out without worrying about the cost, but she said nothing.

Rather a lot of people were saying nothing, it seemed to Annika. The professors, the Bodeks, Pauline . . . it was as though they didn't understand the marvellous thing that had happened to her. Only Loremarie's family seemed impressed. Her father had looked up Spittal and found that it was mentioned in the guidebooks as an interesting fortified house of the seventeenth century. To see

Loremarie curtsying when she was introduced to her mother had given Annika a moment of pure pleasure.

Pauline had hardly come out of the bookshop since the day Frau von Tannenberg arrived, and Annika was puzzled. She couldn't believe that her friends were jealous of her, but why couldn't they share in her happiness?

Then, on the day before she was due to leave, Stefan and Pauline asked her to come to the deserted garden.

The snow had melted at last, but it was still very cold. They sat inside the hut, wrapped in a blanket; Ellie had prepared a picnic but no one felt much like eating.

Both of Annika's friends had brought farewell presents. Stefan had carved her a little wooden horse.

'To remind you of when we went to see the Lipizzaners,' he said.

'I won't need reminding,' said Annika.

Pauline had copied the best of her scrapbook collection into a special notebook that could be fastened with a ribbon. All her favourite stories were there: the one about the girl with measles swimming the Danube, the one about the champion wrestler with the back-to-front foot – and a new one about a boy who was herding his mother's cow across a frozen lake when the ice broke and the cow fell into the water.

'He held the cow by the horns and he just held on and held on till help came and his fingers were so badly frost-bitten that one had to be amputated, but the cow was saved.'

Annika took the book and thanked her warmly. It must have taken hours and hours to copy all the stories in.

'I know you don't need to be made brave because you are brave, but one never knows,' said Pauline.

But the real reason they had brought her to the hut was to tell her that whatever happened to her in her new life they would never forsake her.

'I really hate aristocrats, as you know,' said Pauline, 'always grinding the faces of the poor.'

'My mother wouldn't grind the faces of the poor,' said Annika.

All the same, she knew how Pauline felt. Last spring they had acted the story of Marie Antoinette going to the guillotine. Annika had been the doomed queen and she'd been shocked at the glee with which Pauline and Stefan had jeered at her as she bared her throat for the knife.

'On the other hand it isn't your fault that you've turned out to be a von Tannenberg,' Pauline went on. 'So if you need us, just say the word.'

'Yes,' said Stefan, nodding his blond head. 'Just say the word.'

After that the hours rushed by and suddenly her suitcase was packed and it was time for the last goodbyes.

She had said goodbye to Josef in the cafe, and his mother, to Father Anselm in the church, to the lady in the paper shop . . .

Now she went upstairs to say goodbye to the professors, who weren't professors any more but uncles, and to Aunt Gertrude, who suddenly bent down to kiss her, bumping her nose.

Then came Sigrid and Ellie . . .

They had prayed and they had practised. Now they stood dry-eyed and side by side to give Annika a cheerful send-off.

But as Annika put her arms round Ellie something horrible happened to her. It was as if she was being disembowelled – as though her insides really were being pulled apart.

'I'm coming *back*,' she cried. 'I'm coming back often and often. My mother says I can.'

Why did no one *listen*; why did no one understand that she was coming back?

'Yes, dear; of course you're coming back,' said Ellie quietly.

Then the carriage was at the door. Though Annika had already taken leave of everyone, they had all gathered in the square to wave. The same people as had been there just a few days ago, when she and Stefan had come back from the Prater. The Bodeks with the baby, Pauline and her grandfather, Josef from the cafe . . .

Annika climbed into the carriage, where her mother sat waiting. As it clattered away across the cobbles, the Bodek baby in his pram began to scream. He screamed and he screamed and he screamed long after the carriage had turned into the Keller Strasse and was out of sight.

Nobody hushed him. Instead, as he became more and more purple with sorrow and rage, they nodded their heads.

'Exactly so,' they said to each other. 'Yes, yes, exactly so.'

CHAPTER ELEVEN

JOURNEY TO NORRLAND

They had travelled all morning and for the best part of the afternoon. The train was stuffy, but when her mother opened a window the wind that blew in seemed to be full of knives.

Annika had looked out eagerly as they had crossed the Moravian hills, stopped at pretty towns with onion-domed churches and trundled over gorges cut by rushing rivers. Now, after several hours, she was getting sleepy and the landscape had changed. As they went north, and still further north, there was just a wide plain with patches of trees and pools of water circled by dark birds. Snow still lay in the hollows and the gnarled trees were bent by the wind. This was Norrland and the site of her new home.

Frau Edeltraut had said little on the journey; just smiled at Annika from time to time and reached out to pat her hand – and Annika was free to imagine what she would find . . . the farm, the dogs and horses . . . and Hermann . . . A brother: she had not dared to imagine a brother in her dreams.

They did not go to the dining car; just bought some rolls from a woman with a basket at one of the stations, and Annika remembered hearing that aristocrats did not get hungry like other people, nor did they mind being uncomfortable. The seats of the railway carriage were surprisingly hard.

The light had begun to fade by the time the train stopped at Bad Haxenfeld, and they climbed down on to the platform. It was bitterly cold and a strong smell of rotten eggs drifted over from the town. Rather a grand town it seemed to be, with big hotels and a casino, so the smell surprised Annika. Was it the drains?

'That's the sulphur you can smell,' said her mother. 'It's in the water – it gushes out of the rocks above the town and that's why people come here to take baths in it and get cured. Sulphur is good for a whole lot of diseases. I have an old uncle who lives in one of the hotels here; he has arthritis.'

Annika nodded. The Eggharts came here too, she remembered. They had been at Bad Haxenfeld when news reached them of the old lady's death.

As they crossed the platform to leave the station, a large number of men in dark suits – thirty at least – got out of the back of the train. They had badges pinned to their lapels and obviously belonged together.

'I think they must be dentists,' said Frau Edeltraut. 'Unless they're undertakers, but I believe my uncle said dentists. They come here for conferences. One month it's dentists, one month it's undertakers or locksmiths or bank managers. They stay in the hotels and take the waters and talk about teeth or coffins or whatever.'

Annika watched the men, still streaming out of the train. As they alighted, uniformed porters with the names of the hotels on their caps fetched their trunks and suitcases out of the luggage van and trundled them out of the station, and the dentists followed. Tall dentists, small dentists, fat dentists, thin dentists . . .

'I didn't know there were so many dentists in the world,' said Annika.

On the road outside the station a large closed carriage with two horses was waiting. It was painted black and on the side Annika could just make out the von Tannenberg crest – the same crest that had been on her mother's handkerchief.

The carriage was old, with a musty smell and leather seats. The coachman was old too and when he had raised his hat and nodded to Annika he fell silent. People did not seem to talk so much here in the north.

They left the town behind them and drove for more than an hour in the gathering dusk. Annika could just make out the same clumps of gnarled and wind-blown trees; the same patches of wind-ruffled water. Then it became too dark to see and she leaned back against the cushions and closed her eyes.

She was woken by the rumbling of the carriage over a stone bridge spanning a river; then came a second bridge, a smaller wooden one, over a moat, and they drove into a large courtyard. A single lantern came bobbing towards them and she remembered what the Eggharts' great-aunt had said about arriving at the home of the Russian count – the hundred flares held up to welcome them. But those were Russians. Russians were different, and it was long ago.

'Good evening, *gnädige* Frau,' said the old woman who held the lantern, and she bobbed a curtsy.

'Bertha, this is my daughter, Annika,' said Frau Edeltraut, and the old servant curtsied again to Annika. It was the first time anyone had curtsied to her and she wished it had not been someone so old whose knees were stiff.

They followed Bertha through a heavy oak door which led from the courtyard into the main part of the house, down a long stone corridor to a flight of steps.

'I think my daughter will want to go straight to bed,' said Frau Edeltraut, and Bertha nodded.

'I've put a warming pan in her bed. Shall I bring up some hot milk?'

'I expect she'll just want to go to sleep right away, won't you, dear?'

'Yes,' said Annika obediently, though she would have loved something hot to drink.

Her mother bent down and kissed her cheek. 'I am happy to have you under my roof,' she said formally.

'And I am happy to be here,' said Annika – and followed the old servant up the curving stone stairs.

In the very early hours she was woken by an explosion and for a moment she thought she was back in Vienna and it was the emperor's birthday. They always let off fireworks in the city on that day.

Then she saw the outline of the room, cavernous and strange, and got up and went to the window with its heavy iron bars. Moored on the bank of the long reedy lake that stretched away in front of the house she could just make out a flat-bottomed boat and a man crouched in it, holding a gun. A flock of birds, black against the grey sky, came over. Wild duck, she thought. There were two more bangs, and two birds fell into the water.

Annika went back to bed. When she woke again it was light and she saw the room she had slept in clearly.

She had never dreamed that she would wake in such a room and know that it was hers. The walls were covered in brocade hangings, dark and heavy, embroidered with the kind of battle scenes which Uncle Emil had shown her to explain the movements of the Lipizzaners. There were two crossed swords nailed to one wall; a table with heavy carved legs and a chair with a high leather-covered back stood in the middle of the room, and on the headboard of her enormous bed were carvings of people in helmets trampling on other people whose helmets had come off.

But there were things that surprised her. The rugs on the floor were threadbare, the curtains were frayed and the pelmets hung crooked. The tiled stove had gone out – or perhaps it had not been lit the night before; her toes as she put them to the ground curled up with cold, and there were bare discoloured patches on the wall where pictures had been removed.

She dressed quickly, washing in cold water in the basin high on its stand. The von Tannenbergs must all be tall, and clearly they were strong and hardy. They weren't pampered and spoilt as she had been in Vienna, waking in a warm room, washing in warm water.

Feeling for a moment rather desolate, she went to the window – and suddenly her mood changed, and she thought, No, it's going to be all right, it's going to be good.

For she had almost forgotten one of the best things about her new life. She had almost forgotten Hermann.

Now she saw a boy riding bareback across the fields beside the house. He was galloping, letting the black horse go full out. But what she could see even from the distance was the ease and enjoyment with which he rode.

Perhaps Hermann would teach her to ride? Perhaps – no, there was no 'perhaps' about it – she and Hermann would be the greatest of friends. Sometimes you see someone even quite far off and know he will become part of your life.

'I have a brother,' said Annika aloud – and she turned from the window and hurried down the stairs.

She found herself in a square hall with a stone-flagged floor. A heavy wooden chest stood against one wall, and above it, fixed to the walls, were a number of glass cases containing stuffed fish: stuffed pike, stuffed roach, stuffed perch . . . all carefully labelled. In one corner stood an enormous brass gong; beside it was a stand holding a broadsword, a cutlass and a battleaxe.

Several doors led off the hall. Which one should she take?

Then from a corridor on the left, she smelt coffee and, making her way along it, she opened a door.

She'd been right – the door she now opened led to the kitchen.

It was much bigger than Ellie's kitchen in Vienna, and darker, with its high, barred window, but at once she felt at home. There was a scrubbed table, an iron range, a set of copper dishes on the dresser – and it was warm! An old woman was stirring something on the stove. It was Bertha, who had let them in last night, and now in the daylight Annika could see how old and wrinkled she was, how tired. She must have begged to be allowed to stay at Spittal; there were servants who couldn't face that they had come to the end of their working life.

'Good morning,' said Annika.

Old Bertha swivelled round. 'Good heavens, miss, you mustn't come in here. This is the kitchen.'

Her Norrland dialect was hard for Annika to understand.

'Yes, I know it's the kitchen. Can I help you to take anything through into the dining room?'

'No! No! What would Frau Edeltraut say, her daughter helping in the kitchen! Go back down the corridor, and into the hall. The dining room is the second door on the right. Quickly – go, go, or I'll be in trouble.'

The dining room faced north over the lake. It was huge with a long, dark table, and pictures of a number of von Tannenbergs on the walls, but here too there were spaces where some ancestors were missing and the wallpaper was stained with damp. After the warm kitchen it seemed very cold.

Her mother was sitting at one end of the table, buttering a piece of bread. She was wearing a morning robe of green brocade, and her thick, dark hair was loose down her back. Annika, filled with pride, ran up to her for a good-morning kiss and it was only then that she really took in that there was another person in the room: a large man with red hair, a red beard, and a long scar running down his left cheek. He wore corduroy breeches and a green loden jacket, and a small feather was caught in his beard. A duck feather it seemed to be. This then must be the man she had seen in the punt.

'This is my brother-in-law, Herr von Seltzer. You may call him Uncle Oswald,' said Frau Edeltraut, and explained that he was the husband of her sister, Mathilde, who lived near by and that he came over most mornings to shoot. Then she turned to him. 'Well, this is my Annika, what do you think of her?'

'She's pretty,' he said, 'but not very much like you.'

Frau Edeltraut frowned. 'Sit down there, dear. Do you drink coffee?'

'Yes, I do, thank you.'

Breakfast was simple: black bread cut into thick slices, butter – and a single jar of a kind of jam Annika had not seen before. It was a dark-yellowish colour and tasted like turnips, but of course it couldn't have been. It had to be a special kind of fruit that grew here in the north. As Annika spread it on her bread she looked across at the fourth place laid at the table.

'Is that where Hermann sits?' she asked.

'Yes. He'll be here in a minute. Ah, I think I can hear him now.'

Footsteps . . . the door opening . . . and a boy stood on the threshold.

'This is Hermann, Annika. Your brother.'

The two children stared at each other. The boy did not come forward to shake her hand. Instead, still standing in the doorway, he bowed from the waist, clicked his heels sharply together, and said, 'Pleased to make your acquaintance.'

He was an amazingly handsome boy, with fair curly hair cut very short, his mother's dark-blue eyes, and a clear pale skin. He was neatly dressed in a cadet uniform: khaki trousers, a khaki tunic with brass buttons, and highly polished riding boots.

And he was most definitely not the boy on the horse.

CHAPTER TWELVE

THE HOUSE AT SPITTAL

After breakfast, Annika was shown round the house by her mother.

'You come too, Hermann,' she said to her son. 'Annika may be interested in your plans.' She turned to her daughter. 'When he is of age, Hermann will of course be the master here. I am just looking after Spittal for him until then.'

The house, with its massive stone walls and windows protected by iron grilles, was ancient. It had survived the Thirty Years War in which Protestants and Catholics had slaughtered each other in various gruesome ways. Even now it seemed to be a house meant for sieges and wars, with its surrounding moats, and the long lake that stretched away to the front and made it impossible to approach it from the north.

They went through the downstairs rooms first. The

drawing room, which, like the dining room, faced over the water, was grandly furnished with rich, dark hangings, and gilt-legged tables and claw-footed chairs. The vast floor was bare, which made their footsteps sound very loud, and on the walls were still more portraits of von Tannenberg ancestors, and glass cases housing – not stuffed fish as in the hall but stuffed waterbirds: ducks, geese, teal and pochard all crouching among realistic-looking reeds.

'My father shot those before he went away,' said Hermann. 'He's the best shot in Germany.'

But here too there were unexpected spaces on the walls. Which ancestors had been removed, wondered Annika, and why? Wicked great-aunts? Drunken uncles banished to the cellar? They would be my relatives too, she thought. But the truth was simpler: the pictures and tapestries, explained Frau Edeltraut, had been taken to Bad Haxenfeld to be cleaned.

'They're very valuable,' she said, 'and have to be looked after carefully.'

In the library, which looked out over the moat to the east, there were more bare patches, and a lot of the bookshelves were empty because the books, as Frau Edeltraut explained, had been taken away to be rebound. 'The leather bindings can be affected by the damp, and some of the books are priceless,' Annika was told.

Hermann didn't seem interested in the fate of the books, but he showed Annika a table on which was painted a large shield in crimson and black with two griffins rampant and a mailed fist. The motto, in gold round the edge of the shield, said: 'Stand Aside, Ye Vermin Who Oppose Us!'

'That's the family crest,' said Hermann. 'We've had it since the time of the Emperor Charlemagne.'

Annika was impressed. The room was icy like the drawing room, but the crest was splendid and for a moment she wished that Loremarie was standing by her side.

The other downstairs rooms were shuttered, and Spittal, unlike the professors' house in Vienna, did not have electric light.

'We won't fetch lamps now,' said Frau Edeltraut, and she explained that the rooms they entered were the billiard room and the music room, but that the piano had been taken away to be retuned.

'You may go into any of these rooms if you wish,' said Frau Edeltraut, and Annika thanked her mother though she was not sure how much she wished to enter these cold and echoing places. 'But there are other places which you must be careful to avoid. That door there leads down to the cellar and you must on no account go there. It is flooded at the moment and if you slipped on the steps you could be drowned. And Hermann doesn't like anyone to go into his room – he has everything carefully arranged, haven't you, dear?'

Hermann nodded. 'I've got three hundred lead soldiers lined up in battle formation. They're valuable and I count them every day.'

'Hermann is going into the army. He's waiting for a place at cadet college now, St Xavier's. He'll be off as soon as—' She broke off.

They were making their way up the stone stairs that led to the first floor. Ahead of them, her back bent and breathing heavily, was old Bertha, holding both handles of a basket piled high with logs which she was carrying up to her mistress's bedroom.

In a moment Annika had bounded up the next three steps and taken one of the handles. 'Let me help,' she said. 'It's awfully heavy.'

As she began to lift the basket, her mother's voice came from behind her.

'Annika, what on earth are you doing? Put it down at once. Bertha doesn't want to be helped.'

'No . . . no . . .' muttered the old woman. 'I can manage.'

Bewildered but obedient, Annika let go of the handle and the old woman stumbled on.

'Perhaps now is the time, dear, to make something clear to you,' said Frau Edeltraut, when they reached the landing 'I know you have been brought up to make yourself useful, but now you must promise me not to interfere with the servants in any way. For example, I don't ever want to see you go into the kitchen or the scullery or any of the rooms where the work of the house is being done. It's particularly important because of your background.' She put an arm round Annika's shoulder. 'You see, I want my daughter to take her rightful place in society, to be part of our family. If anyone found you with the servants they would think . . . well, that you were nothing better than a servant girl yourself. And that would break my heart,' she said, pulling Annika closer and dropping a kiss on her head. 'You do understand, don't you?'

Annika nodded, safe in her mother's embrace. 'Only . . . Jesus did help people—' she began, but then she realized that she was being foolish. Jesus had not been an aristocrat, he had been a carpenter.

They went on to look at the other bedrooms, the old nursery, the guest rooms . . . Everything was very large and very grand – and everywhere there were spaces on the walls where pictures or tapestries or statues were being reframed or cleaned or polished by experts in Bad Haxenfeld.

'This is my boudoir. I work here and for that I need to be alone. But of course if you want me you only have to knock and I shall come out at once. And now, dear, I will let Hermann show you the grounds – and tell you where it is safe to go. I have some tiresome papers to see to. Don't forget to be ready at half-past twelve to go to lunch with your new aunt and your cousin.'

Hermann led her out into the cobbled courtyard. The cobbles were covered in a layer of mud. There was a large stable, but some of the doors hung off their hinges, and the loose boxes were empty. Most of the outhouses were deserted; wisps of straw blew about. They passed an old cider press, a rusty ploughshare on its side. A flock of starlings flew out suddenly from under the sagging roof of the old brewery.

'I'm going to rebuild the stables and keep my carriage horses up here,' said Hermann, 'as soon as I'm of age. And build some proper kennels for the hunting dogs – Uncle Oswald keeps them at his place, but they're ours really – and a decent gunroom that can be locked properly. You can't trust people nowadays.'

'Are there any animals here now?' asked Annika.

Hermann shook his head. 'They're down at the farm, across those fields.' He led her round to the front of the house, to a terrace of paving stones which abutted the lake. On each side were drainage ditches, dark with waterweed and frogspawn.

'This is Spittal Lake. It's fifteen kilometres long and it all belongs to us.'

The lake on this cloudy morning was uniformly grey with only a few sudden bubbles of marsh gas breaking the surface. There were thick reeds growing right round the edges, and the ground surrounding the water was a muddy swamp. Wooden duckboards led to a boathouse on the eastern shore, and another walkway connected with a path over the fields which led to a huddle of farm buildings. The wind rustled in the reeds, a flock of geese flew over, honking mournfully, bitterns boomed, and in the ditch dark shapes darted through the water.

'Do you swim here in the summer? In the lake?'

Hermann shook his head. 'It's too muddy – you have to wade for ages to get into clear water.'

It was a mournful, lonely scene, yet Annika was happier here than she had been in the house. In spite of the wind it felt less dank and cold than in the unheated rooms, and there were living things. She looked curiously at the frogspawn; she had never seen so much. 'You must get an awful lot of frogs.'

'The cats mostly kill them,' said Hermann, 'but there always seem to be more. I'm going to change everything as soon as—' He broke off. 'I'm going to clean the moat and dredge the lake and fill it with trout and freshwater salmon – they give you good sport. And I'll invite all the important people to come and shoot; there used to be famous wild-fowl shoots here before—'

This sentence too he left unfinished. 'Could we go and look at the farm?' asked Annika.

Hermann sighed. 'It's time for my bayonet practice,' he said. 'I always do it at eleven.'

Annika stared at him. Surely he was joking?

'I have a straw dummy on a stand in my room. It's important to stick to the routine.'

'Would it be all right if I went alone, then? I'll be very careful and not disturb anyone.'

'There isn't anyone to disturb down there. They're just farmworkers. Tell Zed I'll want my horse saddled for three o'clock tomorrow. He's to bring him into the courtyard, to the mounting block, not hang about in the lane.'

'Who's Zed?' Annika asked.

'He's the stable boy. He's called Zedekiah because his mother was a gypsy and gypsies are all mad. Be careful of him; he steals.' Hermann was making his way back to the house, but at the door he turned. 'He stole my dog,' he said.

It was a relief to be alone. There was a high light-grey sky over the sombre lake, and she could see the yellow heads of coltsfoot just appearing on the banks. Spring was coming, even to Norrland.

All the same she was hungry. In Vienna no one had bayonet practice at eleven. What they had at eleven was a drink of milk and whatever it was that Ellie had been baking, but obviously the aristocracy did not go in for feeble things like midday snacks, and resolutely she started off down the path towards the farm.

The low buildings were made of lath and plaster and looked homelier than the main house. Being sunk in the swampy earth seemed to suit them better. As she came closer she heard the sound of lowing cattle, and stopped at the door of a shed to find three black-and-white cows tethered in their stalls, and an old man carrying a milking stool. It was the man who had driven them from the train the night before, and when she had said good morning, she asked him if his name was Zed.

He shook his head. 'I'm Wenzel. Zed's in the paddock. Go through the farm and you'll see him.'

Annika thanked him and watched for a moment before she went on.

After the cow byre came the hen-house; the chickens were scratching about outside in the mud and a handful of ducks were cleaning their feathers in a puddle in the rutted lane.

If there were chickens and ducks, thought Annika, there must be eggs. Perhaps they would have omelettes for lunch; soufflé omelettes, soft and golden and splendidly filling. She imagined herself hurrying them out of the oven, sprinkling them with chopped chives . . . and then drew in her breath as she remembered that she was never going to cook again. She would obey her mother, but it was going to be hard – harder than anybody realized. It wasn't till you were told you couldn't do something that you realized how much it had meant to you.

The door of the pigsty was closed and the pigs were inside. She walked past it, past a storage shed and the dairy . . . past the two big carriage horses that had brought her to Spittal the night before, looking over their stable door. There seemed to be a lot of empty buildings here too – deserted sheds and byres and stalls like the ones she had seen in the courtyard of the big house. The farm must have been much bigger once.

Then the path dipped into a hollow and she came to a small house. It was a very small house; a hovel really, though the checked red-and-white curtains looked clean and fresh.

But what made Annika stop and give a cry of pleasure was what was on the roof.

On a wheel fixed to the chimney was a pile of sticks – a messy and untidy pile, as though someone was going to light a bonfire. And sitting on the pile, looking very large against the smallness of the house and very pleased with themselves, were two storks.

'Storks bring luck,' Ellie had told her. 'They come back year after year if they like a place and they bless the house.'

Annika stood still for a while, her head tilted back, and the storks clattered their beaks together, making an amazing din. They did not seem to be in the least shy or bothered by her presence.

But now she had seen the paddock ahead of her – and walking towards the gate, one arm thrown round the neck of his horse, was the boy she had seen out of the window when she woke.

Annika waited till he came up to her, and introduced herself.

'I know who you are,' said the boy.

'And you're Zed?'

'Yes.'

He was taller than Hermann, and older she guessed, thirteen perhaps, and he had an unexpected sort of face. His skin was a clear olive and he had thick, dark hair that looked as though it had been cut with shears – but his brown eyes were flecked with lighter colours; with bronze and hazel and with gold.

And he was eating something, a slice of some large root with white flesh, cutting off pieces and sharing them with the horse.

Annika sighed. She had a message from Hermann and she found that she didn't really want to think about Hermann.

'Hermann said could you please bring his horse round at three o'clock tomorrow.'

The boy stopped eating. 'Really,' he said, grinning. 'Hermann said please?'

'Well, I may have put that in,' Annika admitted. 'He said bring it into the courtyard, to the mounting block, not into the lane.'

'He'll never make a soldier if he can't mount without a block,' said Zed.

'But isn't it difficult? Hermann's no bigger than me. How big is his horse?'

'This is his horse. Everything in the place belongs to Hermann, surely you know that, even if you only came last night.'

Annika was silent. She had felt sure that the horse that was resting his muzzle on the boy's shoulder belonged to him.

'Does he know he belongs to Hermann?' she asked. 'The horse, I mean?'

Zed looked at her sharply and did not answer and Annika asked him the name of the root in his hand.

'It's a mangel-wurzel. We grow them for the sheep, but they're not bad. You need to pick a small one.'

'Can I try a bit?'

Zed nodded and cut her a piece, shaving off the skin.

She chewed it carefully, then nodded. 'It's nice and crisp. Is there any more?'

'They're in the root cellar; I'll show you. You better ask me till you're used to the place; you have to make sure there's no mould on them.'

Annika smiled, and the boy looked at her, noting the way her face changed; she had seemed rather forlorn when he first saw her. 'I never thought I'd be eating the sheep's mangel-wurzels now that I'm a member of the aristocracy.'

'We all eat them down here – those of us with teeth,' he said, glancing at old Wenzel, who was shooing the cows out into the field.

He had begun to lead the horse out of the paddock and Annika walked by his side. She had been wrong about the stallion's colour; in the full light of morning he was not black but a rich chocolate colour, with a darker mane and tail. There was a white star no bigger than a coin between his eyes, which looked both gentle and intelligent.

As they passed the empty sheds and byres and stalls again she said, 'Do cows and sheep and pigs have to go away to be cleaned too? Or reframed in Bad Haxenfeld?'

Zed turned his head and saw that behind her flippant words there was anxiety.

'It used to be a big farm when the Master was alive. Everything was different then.'

'I know I'm asking a lot of questions, but who was the Master?'

'The Freiherr von Tannenberg. Your mother's father. Your grandfather, I suppose.'

The man who had been so strict and fierce that her mother had not dared to bring her baby home!

'We had some marvellous riding horses then. Rocco is the only one left.'

'Is that what he's called? Rocco?'

'Yes.' They had stopped in front of a stable with an open door. 'I'm going to groom him now,' he said.

'Can I help? Have you got more than one brush?'

Zed looked at her curiously. 'If you like.'

He handed her a brush, and showed her how to use it, moving away from the horse's head in slow, steady strokes. Then he took down a wisp of plaited straw and began to rub Rocco's flank. After a while he said, 'You've been used to work, I see.'

Annika stopped, her brush in mid-air. 'Oh no, don't say that. I'm not supposed to help. I tried to help Bertha carry a basket of logs and it's the wrong thing to do because my mother doesn't want people to know I was brought up as a servant.'

She looked so upset that Zed said, 'Well, I'm a servant too. It seems to me that servants are the only people who can actually do anything. It's who you choose to serve that matters.'

'Yes, I know . . . only I have to learn to be a von Tannenberg.' But she had taken up the brush again. 'It's going to be difficult – I'm so used to working. I'll have to be careful.'

'No one will see you down here.'

'I know. But I've only just found my mother. I don't want to disobey her even in secret.'

The went on grooming in silence for a while. Then she said, 'When I saw you riding this morning it reminded me of seeing the Lipizzaners in Vienna. I know they were white and they were dancing . . . but they seemed happy like your . . . like Rocco. Sort of light and floating . . .'

Zed had wheeled round to face her. 'You've seen the Lipizzaners? The ones in the Spanish Riding School?'

'Yes. I went for my last Found Day . . . I mean I went with the people I lived with. I don't know anything about horses, but there are things you can see . . . like the way they do everything so willingly when they must be strong enough to break away.'

'Were they using Maestoso Fantasia? Is he still the lead stallion?'

'Yes. He's old, but the Viennese love him.'

'Lipizzaners don't get old for years. What about Pluto Nobilia? He had a tie-back operation last year.'

Annika nodded. 'They used him for the "airs above the ground". When he did his caprioles everyone cheered.'

But some of Zed's eager questions were difficult to answer. Had the riders used stirrups for the quadrille? Did they use the long reign or the short reign for the piaffe at the pillars?

As she answered him she was frowning, trying to remember everything that had happened on the day of her treat. Then suddenly the remembering went wrong. She forgot the horses and felt Ellie's warm bulk beside her, and remembered the way she had stood up at the end and said, 'It makes you proud to be Austrian.' She remembered Pauline, hanging over the balustrade . . . and afterwards the meal at Sacher's, where the professors had told her that she was to call them uncle. And her eyes filled with tears, which she tried in vain to hold back.

'It's the wind,' she said angrily, and Zed agreed that it was the wind.

'There's always a wind here,' he said politely. 'Even in the stable.'

She wiped away her tears and for a while they went on working in silence while Rocco blew contentedly through his nostrils. Then Zed put down his brush and said, 'Come on. I'll show you where I live.'

Where he lived, of course, was in the house with the storks on the roof. The birds were still on their nest, managing to looking both absurd and regal.

'You're so lucky to have storks! Why aren't there any at the big house?'

'Storks go where they want,' said Zed.

He opened the door and she stepped into a tiny, dark room with a scrubbed, flagged floor, plants on the window sill – and a big tiled stove, which was alight and gave off a marvellous warmth. Round the stove was a wooden bench on which lay a neatly folded blanket.

'Bertha sleeps there,' he said. 'It's her house. I sleep out at the back on a truckle bed.'

Annika was looking round her with pleasure. The house she had thought of as a hovel was cosy and in a way familiar. Ellie too had a pot of chives on the window sill and a picture of the emperor on the wall – only this was the Emperor Wilhelm, whose expression was much fiercer than that of the Austrian ruler.

'Is Bertha your grandmother then?'

Zed shook his head. 'She's no relation. She was the Master's nurse; she came when he was a baby. The Master asked me to . . . look out for her – that's why I'm still here.'

'She seems very old to do the work she does up at the house. I suppose she doesn't want to retire?'

'She wants to all right. Sometimes when she comes back she can hardly walk, her joints are so stiff. But no one else will work up there for nothing.' He went over to the table and lifted the muslin cover from a blue jug. 'Here, drink this. We don't have much, but there's always milk.'

'Thank you.'

As she drained her glass and stood up to go, she heard the sound of barking coming from an outhouse at the back.

'That's Hector. He's woken up.'

'Could I see him?'

'No, not now. You need . . . a lot of time for that, and I've got to go and feed the pigs. Anyway, you'd better get back; they'll be wondering where you are.'

He had suddenly withdrawn and she made her way to the door, trying not to feel snubbed.

'Thank you,' she said, turning to smile at him.

'For what?'

'The mangel-wurzel, the milk . . . letting me help with Rocco.' Outside the dog stopped barking and began to whine. 'I've always wanted a dog,' she said wistfully.

'You wouldn't want this one,' said Zed.

CHAPTER THIRTEEN

LUNCH AT THE HUNTING LODGE

Annika's new-found aunt, who was married to the red-haired Uncle Oswald with the feather in his beard, lived some five kilometres from Spittal in the middle of a wood.

There were a number of such patches of woodland dotted about the great plain of Norrland, and as Uncle Oswald drove them along the lane to his house, Annika was surprised by how closely the dark pines and firs were packed together. The daylight, even now at midday, seemed to have trouble in reaching the ground; they might have been in Siberia.

Her mother's sister was called Mathilde. She was tall and dark like Edeltraut, but Annika could see that she was a very different kind of person. Where her mother was regal and dignified and stately, Aunt Mathilde was shrewish and pathetic with a whining note to her voice.

'So this is Annika,' she said. 'Well, well . . . we must just hope . . .' and broke off as she encountered her sister's raised eyebrows. She kissed Hermann, who closed his eyes and endured it, and then introduced her daughter, Gudrun.

'Gudrun has been looking forward to meeting you,' she said and the two girls shook hands.

Gudrun did not look as though she had been looking forward to meeting Annika or indeed anybody else. She was very thin and very pale and very tall, with the same light hair as her cousin Hermann, but her single plait, like Gudrun herself, seemed undernourished and ended in a discouraged-looking wisp. If one had not known that she was Gudrun Brigitta von Seltzer one would have taken her for an orphan in an institution – the kind of girl that is seen standing listlessly at the orphanage gates, not even playing with a ball.

Next to his wife and daughter, Uncle Oswald looked even pinker and ruddier than before with his shiny skin and ginger beard and the dramatic scar running down his cheek. It was a duelling scar, her mother had explained: Oswald had got it when he was a student. It was the longest scar anyone had got that year and he was very proud of it.

The von Seltzers' house, which was on the edge of the Spittal estate, was a hunting lodge set right in the thickest part of the forest. It was called Felsenheim and was built entirely of wood, with carved shutters like those of the alpine houses Annika was used to seeing in the meadows of her homeland, but there were no pots of geraniums on the window sills, no smoked hams hanging from the rafters.

What there were ... were antlers. There were antlers everywhere. Antlers on the walls and antlers making up the furniture. Some were huge and branched, some were small and sharp and spiky, and some weren't strictly antlers but simply horns.

Those antlers that were not part of the furniture still had their heads, and their glass eyes, and were nailed to the wall. The stuffing was coming out of them here and there, but no one who came to visit could doubt that this was a house devoted to the chase.

Yet here too there were those curious spaces on the wall and in the display cabinets which held antique guns and skinning knives and bullet-holders, as though many of the treasures had been removed.

'Did you bring anything?' Annika heard her Aunt Mathilde ask her mother.

'What should I bring?' her mother answered. 'Anyway Oswald brought you three of our mallards the day before yesterday. Surely you can't have eaten them all?'

Mathilde sighed. 'Gudrun is growing,' she said.

Annika, who had managed to avoid sitting on an antler chair and was perched on a stool made of deerskin stretched over two logs, was getting a little worried. It was half-past one, and they had definitely been asked to lunch, but she could smell nothing at all. Even if the kitchen was quite far away, surely there should be some smells? Onions softening in butter ... a joint roasting ... and with the serious smells of the meat a lighter smell. Vanilla, perhaps, or cloves added to simmering apples. They must have put apple rings down in the autumn to dry.

'It's the maid's day off,' said Mathilde. 'So we are having a cold collation.'

Annika did not know what a collation was, but the lunch they had was definitely cold. The dark thighs of some muscular waterbird, which arrived on a platter, were cold and so were the pellets of lead embedded in the flesh. The potatoes, sliced but without any dressing were cold. The three pickled gherkins, cut up to go round, were cold, and also slightly slimy.

There was no dessert.

All the dishes were left on the table, and Annika was frowned down by her mother for automatically starting to gather up the plates. The two sisters and Uncle Oswald now made their way to the study. It was apparently to do some business rather than to eat lunch that they had met.

Gudrun and Annika, meanwhile, were sent out for a walk.

'Only be careful not to take the path down to the spring,' Mathilde told them. 'They've dug a pit there. Not that they'll catch anything.'

Hermann refused to go with them. This was the time when he studied the maintenance of gun carriages, and he had brought his book.

'What sort of thing would they catch in a pit?' asked Annika.

'Someone saw a bear, but I don't suppose he'll come again.' Gudrun sighed. 'A bear would feed us for weeks.'

'I've never eaten bear. Is it nice?'

Gudrun shrugged. 'Meat is meat,' she said in a gloomy voice.

But it was Hermann that Gudrun wanted to talk about. Clearly she hero-worshipped her cousin.

'Don't you think he's wonderful,' she said. 'The way he goes on with his studies. He does everything he would do at St Xavier's, and at exactly the same time that they do it.'

'Bayonet practice you mean?'

'Everything. He got the prospectus with their timetable straight away when he thought he was going. He gets up at six and salutes the emperor's picture – he can't do proper reveille because he hasn't got a bugle – but then he has his cold bath and does his exercises and then he has a kit inspection. He inspects everything and if something isn't absolutely clean he polishes it. Then he does drill – all before breakfast – and then he arranges his soldiers on the carpet; he sets up a different battle every week. At the moment he's doing the campaigns of Frederick the Great . . .' She went on through her cousin's day: the fencing lesson, the horse riding, the shooting practice . . . 'And he has to do everything himself. That awful stable boy won't help him with anything though he's only allowed to stay because he looks after Hermann's horse. You must be really proud to have a brother like that. I keep offering to help, but he's very independent.'

'But why can't he go to St Xavier's if he's so keen?'

'I'm not sure . . . my mother won't talk about it. But she says it's all going to be different very soon. There's a plan, only I'm not allowed to know what it is.'

They had taken a path which led downhill from the house. Annika had expected to see clearings with patches of bilberry leaves and bubbling streams, but the forest was not like the ones she knew. It was tangled and dark and difficult to walk through; logs had fallen across the path, briars caught their skirts. It was wild and should have been beautiful but it was not.

'My father's going to get it cleared,' said Gudrun. 'When . . . when he can get the men.'

They passed a wire enclosure with a number of wooden kennels and heard the sound of excited barking.

'Can we go and see them—' began Annika, but Gudrun shook her head.

'They're hunting dogs. Papa doesn't like them to be fussed over.'

Then she stopped suddenly in the middle of the path and turned to Annika. Her face was flushed and she spoke with a kind of nervous excitement. 'Is it true that before you came here . . . that at the place where you were before . . . they treated you like a servant?'

Annika met her eyes. 'They did not *treat* me like a servant. I *was* a servant,' she said clearly.

Gudrun poked at a fir cone with her shoe.

'Then why are your clothes so nice?'

'Sigrid made my clothes. The housemaid. She was a very good needlewoman.'

'And that scarf?' She pointed to a red-and-white kerchief which Annika had knotted round her neck. 'She didn't make that?'

'No. It came from a shop in the Karntner Strasse.' Annika looked up and found that Gudrun was looking at it with a kind of desperate hunger. 'Would you like it?' she asked.

Gudrun flushed again. 'Well . . . yes, I would. I haven't had anything new to wear for ages.'

So Annika unknotted the scarf and tied it round Gudrun's neck. 'It looks very nice on you,' she said, though actually it looked rather like a distress signal – a handkerchief tied round a telegraph pole to show where someone had left the road.

Back at the house, Hermann was waiting impatiently.

'I have to move my lancers at four,' he said, opening his silver pocket watch with the von Tannenberg crest on the cover.

Fortunately just then the adults came out of the study and Annika looked up eagerly. Being away from her mother was still difficult. But she came out ahead of the rest, looking serene and resolute, and behind her came her sister, muttering, 'Well I hope you're right, Edeltraut, that's all I can say. Because if it doesn't work—'

'It will work,' said Edeltraut. She caught sight of the three children and it was to Annika she went first, not to Hermann. 'You have been waiting so patiently, dear. But it's time to go home now.'

They were climbing into the carriage when an appalling scream was heard, somewhere in the forest. The scream was followed by a string of blood-curdling oaths, which seemed to come from beneath the ground.

Someone had fallen into the bear pit – but it did not seem to be someone one could eat.

CHAPTER FOURTEEN

FINDING THE FOAL

Zed had watched the carriage, with Uncle Oswald at the reins, turn down the road to Felsenheim, and felt a pang of pity for Annika, facing her first lunch with her new aunt.

Then he saddled Rocco and rode off down the lane that skirted the lake, to the little village of Marienbau. He was still on Spittal land; the houses belonged to the von Tannenbergs and the church on the edge of the green had housed the graves of the family for generations.

Zed tied Rocco to the hitching post and made his way between the tombstones to a large sarcophagus, standing on its own. The Master had wanted a simple grave, but his daughters had insisted on this edifice of stone.

HERE LIES JOHANNES AUGUST HEINRICH
VON TANNENBERG, FREIHERR OF SPITTAL.
BORN 1844, DIED 1906.
GOD REST HIS SOUL.

Zed took off his cap and bowed his head. Then he sat
down on the turf, out of sight of the village street, with his
legs drawn up and his back against the cold stone. His
mother's people, the Romanies, liked to play music and
dance on the graves of the people they had loved, but he
could not dance on this great stone box.

'Oh, why did you have to die?' he said to the Master.

He had heard that Edeltraut's long-lost daughter was
coming to live at Spittal and thought nothing of it. The
rumours were of a timid kitchen child who would be overawed by the grandeur of her new life. In any case it had
nothing to do with him; his future lay elsewhere.

But Annika was a person. She was real and she was nice
– and she would lose the battle. They would turn her into
someone who thought she had a God-given right to rule
others. In a few weeks or months the friendly, helpful girl
would become a stuck-up little madam; she would speak
like Herman, and stamp her feet if she didn't get her way.

'And I can't help her,' said Zed to the old man who lay
beneath the stone. 'You know I can't.'

If the Master had been alive Zed could think of no better place to grow up than Spittal, but now . . .

He sat there, thinking, till Rocco whinnied and it was
time to go.

When Hermann was born, his mother was not living at
Spittal. She had married a year earlier and gone to live on

127

her husband's estate, Borwald, which was some fifty kilometres away. Mathilde too had married, and their father, the Freiherr von Tannenberg (whom everybody called the Master) ran Spittal on his own, which suited him well.

He was a huge man with broad shoulders, big hands, greying hair and very blue eyes – one of those men who never needed to raise their voice to be obeyed.

Under his rule the farm prospered, the tenants were well cared for; he was on good terms with his neighbours, as they were with him.

When his grandson, Hermann, was born, the Master was pleased and proud. He rode over to Borwald and was shown the baby. Hermann was handsome and healthy, a worthy heir for the von Tannenbergs, and as he grew into a toddler and then a sturdy little boy, the Master started to look out for a horse that the boy could grow up with, and train, and be trained by.

So he travelled by train to a famous stud farm on the edge of the Hungarian plain: a place of wind and grass and men who seemed to be born and to die in the saddle, like the Mongols of old. The plain – the puszta it is called – goes rolling on eastwards towards the steppes of Russia; gypsies travel there unhindered, as do horse-herders and aristocrats riding with their servants to feasts or hunting parties. And of course as always there are the peasants who herd their geese and tend their flocks and do the real work of the land.

The Master knew the stud, which was called Zverno. It was linked with Lipizza, near Trieste, where the white stallions were bred for Vienna, and had provided some of the best riding horses in Europe. And there he consulted a man he knew, Tibor Malakov, who had come west from Russia, buying and selling horses, and had ended up as manager of the stud.

Tibor liked the Freiherr, the Master of Spittal. He knew him to be a man of honour, and he liked the idea of finding a horse for his grandson. He took him round the paddocks, where the colts frisked and skittered, and through the big stone barns, where the mares waited for their foals. There were greys bought from Lipizza that had been crossed with Arab and Berber mares, smaller, sturdy horses from Mongolia, Irish hunters . . .

Tibor led the Freiherr on slowly, pointing out the special qualities of this animal or that and the Freiherr asked questions. Nothing was said about any particular horse.

The Freiherr had the feeling that they were waiting for something and he was right. Presently, down the straight white road which led from the village, a small figure appeared, looking even smaller under the weight of the school satchel on his back.

'My son, Zed,' said the manager. And to the child, 'Are you sure about what you told me yesterday?'

'I am sure,' said the boy, doffing his cap, shaking hands with the Freiherr.

The boy couldn't have been more than eight years old, and looked less. He was very dark – and burnt darker still by the sun, so that his strange light-flecked eyes were very noticeable.

'Then get changed quickly and take Herr von Tannenberg to see him.' And as the boy ran off, 'His mother was a gypsy . . . and you can say what you like, they're not like us. The boy has . . . I don't know what it is. An instinct . . . He had it almost as soon as he could walk.

But I don't want you to be influenced – if you disagree . . .'
He looked at the huge man standing relaxed beside the
paddock gate and broke off. To influence this old aristocrat would be difficult.

The boy came back without his satchel, dressed in a
pair of breeches and an old jersey. Without his cap he
seemed even smaller.

'You'll find me in my office,' said the manager. 'I've got
a rather good bottle of Tokay.'

Though he was so small, the child was not shy. He took
the Master's hand and led him with absolute assurance to
a part of the farm the old man had not seen before, and
into a stone barn with clean whitewashed walls and high
windows through which the sun shone on to the deep
yellow straw. About twenty mares were tethered in a line
along the walls, resting or suckling their foals. The foals
wandered freely among them; the more curious ones came
up to the Freiherr and the boy, exploring, nuzzling their
clothes.

'Watch,' said the boy.

They stood still in the middle of the barn for what
seemed to be a long time. There were foals of all colours,
dappled greys, roans, bays, some new-born, others already
confident on their long legs.

After a while the boy turned his head to look at the
Master. 'Do you see?' he said.

'There are several which—'

'No,' said the little boy, and the assurance in his voice
was almost comical. 'There is only one.'

The Master went on watching. He was beginning to see
what the boy saw but he was not yet sure. Zed waited till
the foal came closer.

Then, 'That one,' he said.

The foal was tawny with big lustrous eyes, curious and eager. There were other foals almost as curious, as eager and trembling with life. Almost, but not quite.

'He's the best,' said the child. And then, 'If your grandson is nice. His name is Rocco.'

Rocco was not ready to leave his mother, nor to make the long journey by train to Spittal. The Master left a deposit, drank a glass of Tokay and waited. In the event it was nearly six months before the colt could be sent to Spittal. The Master went to the station; the guard opened the door of the van, the groom led the horse down the ramp. In a dark corner, a pile of straw moved and a small head appeared.

'I came too,' said Zed.

'Where is your father?'

The child turned his face away.

'He died.'

The groom explained. 'He tried to stop a fight . . . there were knives.' He shrugged. They were so common, these pointless drunken fights. 'There's a woman at the stud who's happy to adopt the boy, but he wanted to come to you.'

The Master nodded. He examined the colt, shook hands with Zed.

They went home.

The first two years Zed spent at Spittal were happy ones. He lived with Bertha in a flat above the stables in the courtyard, he worked with the horses, he made himself useful on the farm and went to the village school. But often in the

131

evening the Master took him into his room, showed him his books and his maps, or told him stories between puffs on his long-stemmed pipe. Bertha looked after the boy as she had looked after the Master, but really he needed very little care.

And the colt grew and became tame and was handled, ready for Hermann.

Then everything changed. Edeltraut's husband, Franz von Unterfall, sold his estate and she brought him and her son back home to live at Spittal. When Hermann came, Zed who was two years older, thought it was his job to help and protect him, but Hermann soon made it clear that he didn't want a stable boy for a friend.

A year after Edeltraut's return, the Freiherr had a stroke. He lived for two more months, unable to speak, helpless. Bertha and Zed nursed their Master, willing him to recover, but he got steadily weaker. They were both at his bedside when he died.

After the funeral, Bertha and Zed were sent to the hut in the farmyard, allowed to work in the big house but not to sleep in it. A few weeks later, Edeltraut's husband sailed for America. From then on she dropped her married name and ran the estate on her own.

CHAPTER FIFTEEN

HECTOR

Annika had been at Spittal for a nearly a week. It was still bitterly cold, both outside the house and inside, where the only stoves that were lit in the morning were in the kitchen and her mother's boudoir. The last of the ice had thawed from the hollows, which meant that not only the fields but most of the paths were flooded, and Annika's feet were permanently wet. She had resisted all Ellie's efforts to buy her waterproof overshoes in Vienna – no one who cared how they looked could wear galoshes. But now she decided to ask her mother if they could buy a pair the next time they went to the shops.

More birds had come from Greenland – skeins of wild geese and flights of teal, for which the red-bearded Oswald waited each dawn in his punt. He was a good shot – seldom bringing in fewer than half a dozen birds, which were hung in the outside larder and cooked, sometimes still full of lead shot, by the only other servant who worked in the house, a sulky silent girl called Hanne from a village on the other side of the lake. Hanne had been taught to bang the gong in the hall loudly before each meal, but when the ear-splitting noise had died away, the food that awaited them in the dining room was always the same. The charred legs of geese, stewed duck, pieces of blackcock fried in lard, made up both lunch and dinner, sometimes with turnips and potatoes, sometimes alone.

The family from the hunting lodge came over often, usually for lunch, and ate hungrily. Mathilde still looked desperate and tried to take her sister, Edeltraut, aside to whisper in her ear.

Zed had suggested that Annika should ask her mother if she could learn to ride.

'You'd do less harm than Hermann,' he had said.

But when Annika had put the question to her mother, Edeltraut had shaken her head.

'Not at the moment, dear. There's only Hermann's horse just now and he has to be able to ride whenever he needs to so that he will be able to keep up at St Xavier's. But it will all change soon, I promise you.'

Annika had also asked if she might go out in one of the boats, if she stayed near the shore.

'I can swim,' she said, 'and I'd be very careful. Maybe Hermann would come and we could fish?'

But there were only two punts; one leaked and was dangerous, the other had to be kept free for Uncle Oswald.

Because she had fared badly over the riding and over going out in a boat, Annika had been careful not to ask if she could go to the farm. She would never have disobeyed her mother, but the days, with no school and no real occupation, were long, and down there she was happy. Zed not only did not mind her helping, he refused to let her stand about and watch with idle hands. She had taken over the egg collecting and he was teaching her to milk.

'Why does nobody go to school here?' she asked him, for she had seen children with satchels making their way down the lane towards the village.

Zed was stirring swill for the pigs. 'Hermann doesn't go to school because he's not allowed to mix with the common children, and nor is Gudrun. I don't go to school because there's no one to do my work if I go. And you don't go because you have to learn to be a stuck-up von Tannenberg instead of a servant girl.'

'My mother isn't stuck-up. She's—'

'All right, I know. You're quite right to defend your mother. I'd be the same with mine if she was still alive.'

Though he answered general questions easily enough, Zed had told her very little about himself. Now though he said, 'She was a gypsy . . . a Romany.'

So Hermann had been telling the truth.

'There are a lot of Romanies working in Vienna, mostly playing in the cafes,' said Anika. 'They're marvellous musicians.' She sighed. 'I miss music . . . not that I could play anything, but we used to sing at school, and there was always music coming out of the buildings.' She grinned. 'And of course Aunt Gertrude's harp.'

'Well, you'll hear some music next Friday. You're going into Bad Haxenfeld and there's a bandstand there.'

'Are you sure? Nobody's said anything.'

'Yes, I'm sure.'

Sometimes now, when no one was waiting for her,

Annika went back with Zed to Bertha's little house, watched by the storks, who had laid their first egg and were more wary now, but however much she asked, he wouldn't let her see the dog she heard out at the back.

As far as she could see, Zed and old Wenzel did all the work of the farm and it was unending. Not only did the animals have to be fed and mucked out and milked, but this was the time of year when fences had to be repaired and ditches cleared and logs cut and carried to the house. Zed worked without complaint, but it was when he was with Rocco that he relaxed and was happy.

He exercised the horse every morning, he saddled and bridled him for Hermann when he had to, but whenever there was a spare moment he went to talk to him, or walked with him through the lanes as one would talk and walk with a friend.

To Annika, who had only seen horses ridden formally in the Prater, the way that Rocco and Zed played together was amazing. Rocco came to Zed's whistle in an instant; he chased after Zed in the paddock like a child playing tag. When Zed rolled on his back in the grass, Rocco copied him.

'He's special, isn't he?' asked Annika.

'Yes, he's special. I know you think I'm saying that because I've looked after him all his life, but it isn't so. Some horses stand out . . . it's their action; the way they hold their heads . . . You can tell from the start. My father could . . . so could the Master; that's why he bought him.'

Zed was silent, remembering the stud at Zverno, and the foal caught in a ray of sunlight, coming so eagerly towards them.

'Horses like that want to learn things. There's nothing

136

you can't teach them if you handle them right. But they're easily spoilt, especially if they're young. If you tug at their mouths or hit them or give the kind of signals that don't make sense, you can turn the best horse into an enemy. Rocco's only just four; you have to go gently with him.'

'Is that why you don't want Hermann to ride him?' asked Annika, who had seen the change which came over Zed when he had to get the horse ready for her brother.

Zed had been scratching Rocco behind his ears. Now he stopped for a moment and the horse turned his head and looked at him reproachfully.

'Hermann's hands are bad. He hauls at his mouth and kicks much too hard – and you can't trust him with a whip. Any other horse would have thrown him.' He turned away and Annika only just caught the words he said next: 'When I take Rocco up for Hermann I feel . . . as though I'm betraying the horse.'

The next day Annika had the chance to see for herself what Zed had meant.

Hermann was in a gracious mood. 'You can watch me ride,' he told Annika after breakfast. 'The boy is bringing my horse round at ten o'clock.'

And punctually at ten Zed led Rocco to the mounting block in the courtyard. Annika had expected Zed to look sulky and sour and he did, but the change in Rocco was what surprised her. His ears were flat against his head, he walked slowly like a horse going to the slaughterhouse after a life of toil, and when Hermann, dressed like a miniature cavalry officer, got on his back, he shivered and skittered and rolled his eyes.

'I hope you've tightened the girths properly,' said Hermann. 'And where's my whip?'

'You don't need a whip,' said Zed.

Hermann glared at him, but he said nothing and dug his heels into Rocco's flank.

'Forward!' he commanded. 'Come on, you lazy brute.'

But it wasn't till Zed gave Rocco a firm slap on his rump and told him to move that he set off reluctantly towards the field where Hermann liked to practise what he called his riding drill.

Zed went back to the farm; he couldn't bear to watch, but Annika stood patiently at the edge of the field. Hermann was her brother and she wanted to be fair.

But after half an hour she too returned to the house. You did not have to know anything about riding to see that what was going on in the field was both dangerous and wrong.

The following day the first letters came from Vienna. There was one from Pauline, one from Stefan and one from Ellie, which Sigrid too had signed.

Pauline wrote that they had tried to go to the hut without her and it had been no good. Stefan had brought his brother Ernst and Pauline had found a really good story called 'Androcles and the Lion'.

It's about a lion who was put in an arena in ancient Rome to eat Christians, but when the first Christian came in the lion recognized him because he had once taken a thorn out of the lion's paw and he refused to eat him or anybody else, and the emperor was furious and there was a riot. You'd think it would have worked, wrote Pauline. *The story, I mean, but it didn't and we've decided to give up acting and just use the hut as a meeting place.*

Stefan's letter was very short. He missed her and so did

his mother. The baby was teething and cried a lot. They kept asking about her at school . . . everyone thought she should come back . . .

Then Ellie's letter. Everything was fine, and they were sure she was having a lovely time. Professor Emil had tried to give up chocolate for Lent, but the doctor had said this was a mistake because he needed the iron for his blood. Professor Gertrude had ordered a new concert-grand harp from Ernst and Kohlhart and was very excited. Loremarie's governess had said she would rather beg her bread in the streets than look after Loremarie one minute longer and had gone back to England. The flower lady said to tell Annika that the first gentians had come from the mountains . . .

She read Pauline and Stefan's letter twice and Ellie's over and over again. She had just finished when her mother came in.

'I saw you had letters from Vienna. Is everything all right there?'

'Yes, thank you.'

'They don't mention anything that has come for you? Anything that needs to be sent on?'

Annika shook her head. 'I don't think there'll be anything. Ellie got my other coat back from the cleaners just before I left.'

'No . . . I just thought . . . Well, never mind. If there is anything, be sure to let me know.'

Annika had got used to the sound of Uncle Oswald shooting at dawn, but the noise that woke her the next morning was a different one. It had rained again in the night and what she heard was the sound of drops of water plopping from the ceiling.

They were not plopping fast but they were plopping steadily, and a small puddle had formed on the floorboards by the window.

She looked about for something to catch the water and remembered a large Chinese vase which had been on a shelf inside the lacquered tallboy, but the vase had gone. It had definitely been there the day she came, but it was not there now, so she washed quickly, and carried her bowl over to the place where the crack in the ceiling had formed.

Her shoes were still wet from the day before, but she forced her feet into them and went down to the dining room, where she asked her mother if she could fetch a bucket from the scullery to take to her room.

'Oh no!' said Frau Edeltraut dramatically, passing her hand across her forehead. 'Will it never stop?'

'You know it will stop, Edeltraut,' said Uncle Oswald under his breath. 'And you know when. If you don't weaken.'

It was still raining when Annika got down to the farm. She found Zed in the little house, whittling a new bolt for the barn door, and as she came in he looked at her sharply. Her clothes were soaked – one pigtail had escaped from under her hood and turned from gold to a sodden brown. He could hear the water squelching in her shoes, and she looked tired.

'Are you all right?'

'Yes, I'm fine,' she said. 'It's just . . . I had letters from home. I mean from Vienna – and they went round a bit in my head in the night, you know how they do.'

Zed, who never got any letters, said he did know. Then he put down his knife and said, 'Come on, we'll see what sort of a mood Hector is in.'

'Hector? The Trojan warrior?'

'That's right. Hermann likes heroes. Wait here.'

He went out of the door at the back, and returned with the dog he had stolen from Hermann.

They came slowly because Hector, in spite of Zed's hand on his collar, was not certain whether he felt sociable or not. The hero of the Trojans walked with an irregular gait, a kind of lurching movement, and the reason for this was simple. He only had three legs; the back leg on his left-hand side was missing. His tail was missing too and the jagged stump which was all that remained did not, at this moment, feel inclined to wave. As he turned his head, growling softly in his throat, Annika saw that one of his eyes was useless, filmed over and completely blind.

She looked at him in silence.

Then, 'You're wrong,' she said angrily to Zed. 'You're completely wrong.'

'What do you mean?'

'You said I wouldn't want him. You said I wouldn't want a dog like that.'

Zed was stroking Hector's back. 'I didn't know you then,' he said.

The dog had stopped growling and positioned himself so that he could see Annika clearly. She put her hand up very slowly, and he allowed her to scratch his head before flopping down on the floor.

'Please tell me what happened to him,' said Annika. 'I won't say anything . . . I won't even think anything. But I'd like to know.'

141

Zed had squatted down beside the dog. When he spoke he did not look at Annika.

'Hermann wanted a dog,' so the Master went to choose one. It was his last present to Hermann before he had his stroke. He went to see a friend who bred water-spaniels – the ones that come from Ireland. They're marvellous swimmers and . . . well, they're wonderful dogs. I was there when he brought the puppy home for Hermann. He was six weeks old and he had this tight woolly coat all over and black eyes and his tail never stopped going . . . About a week later the old man had his stroke and Bertha and I were kept busy nursing him, and Hermann looked after the dog.'

Zed stopped and stared in front of him, but his hands went on rubbing Hector's back. 'At first it was all right, when the puppy was small, but then Hermann began to train him. He wanted him to be a proper army dog who wasn't afraid of gunfire – you know what he's like about being a soldier. At first he just blew up paper bags and exploded them in the puppy's ear – well, they do that sometimes to gun dogs so that they won't be gun-shy. Then he wanted him to do more and more tricks . . . and then he thought he should be trained so as not to mind explosions and . . . fire. So he waited till everyone was out and then he tied firecrackers to his tail and his leg. He thought they would just go off like ordinary fireworks, but something went wrong . . . Water-spaniels have very tufty tails; the tail caught fire and it spread down his leg and then a spark went into his eyes. Hermann threw a jug of water over him and ran away; he didn't come back till after midnight. Your mother thought we should have the dog put down, it seemed the kindest thing, and she told

142

her brother-in-law to come and shoot him, but Bertha and I brought him down here . . . and as you see, he lived. Only you can't rely on his temper. Mostly he's fine, but when he gets nervous he begins to shiver and then he bites.'

Annika was silent. Hermann was her brother; he had been much younger then, only a little boy. Boys did these things. She tried to imagine Stefan or any of his brothers tying fireworks to a dog's tail – and failed miserably.

'Can he swim still – with three legs?'

'Like a fish. And he's a marvellous beachcomber. He's got quite a collection; he's got the head of a decoy duck and half an eel trap and a sock-suspender which was washed up from the lake. He keeps them in his kennel and if anyone touches them he turns quite nasty – especially the sock-suspender. I try to see that he gets to the water for a time every day. You wouldn't notice there's anything wrong with him when he's swimming.'

Annika looked down at the dog, now lying on his side and permitting Zed to scratch his stomach.

'There isn't anything wrong with him,' said Annika staunchly. 'He's beautiful.'

Annika was on the terrace, looking at the lake, when her mother came out of the house to stand beside her. At once the wind felt gentler, the mournful stretch of water became interesting and romantic and a skein of geese flew in from the north. It was always like that when her mother stood beside her. She could turn night into day.

'I came to tell you that we're going into Bad Haxenfeld tomorrow. My uncle lives there in the Hotel Majestic and he's asked us to lunch. You'll like it; there's plenty to see.'

143

'I'm sure I will.' She hesitated. Then, 'Do you think we could get a pair of rubber overshoes when we're there? Galoshes? For the mud . . . You said—'

'Oh, I know! I know I said I was going to dress you as my daughter should be dressed! There's nothing I want to do more than make you comfortable and pretty. And it will come – all of it – everything you want!' She gathered Annika into her arms and Annika smelt the special perfume her mother always wore. 'You shall have a pony of your own, and parties, and a governess. But this is a waiting time for all of us. Trust me, Annika. Be patient and trust me and I will fulfil your wildest dreams.'

'Of course I trust you,' said Annika, blissful in her mother's embrace. 'Of course I trust you!'

As they were making their way back to the house her mother said, 'There's just something you and I have to do when we're in Bad Haxenfeld. We have to go to a lawyer and sign some papers.'

'Me too? Am I allowed to sign?'

'Yes, you are. The laws of Norrland allow children over the age of ten to sign in the presence of their guardian. It's only a formality, but I want everything to be done properly. I want to make absolutely certain that you are registered as my daughter and a von Tannenberg. And not just a von Tannenberg – that your full name is on all the documents: Annika von Tannenberg-Unterfall; my married name.' She moved closer and put an arm round Annika's shoulders. 'You see, if anything happened to Hermann, which God forbid, you would have to step into his shoes. You would have to run Spittal.' She turned her face to her daughter's. 'There have been von Tannenbergs at Spittal for 500 years

144

– and I want you, my darling child, to be properly one of us too.'

Annika was overwhelmed. Not only did her mother want her to belong to the family absolutely, but she trusted her to look after Spittal.

How could she have been so feeble as to ask for waterproof shoes?

CHAPTER SIXTEEN

HEALING WATERS

Bad Haxenfeld was one of the most famous spas in Europe. The mineral springs that gushed out of the rock at a temperature of fifty degrees Celsius were supposed to cure almost every illness in the world. Heart disease and liver failure, rheumatism and bronchitis, anaemia and dropsy and gout – all of these and many more, said the doctors at the spa, could be successfully treated.

When the hot springs had first been found, many years ago, engineers had pumped the water into pipes and conduits and fed it into pools where the patients could bathe, and into treatment rooms where they could be squirted, and into fountains and taps in the pump room where they could drink.

Things were done to people in Bad Haxenfeld which you might think people would pay *not* to have done to them. They were dipped into very hot water and very cold water, so that they turned from pink to blue and back again. They had steam blown over their bodies; they were pummelled and massaged and lowered into tubs of evil-smelling mud – and every year the doctors invented new treatments like blowing hot smoke into the patients' mouths to cure them of toothache, or fixing air pumps on their bodies to extract the rheumatism from their joints.

You might imagine therefore that people would stay away, but you would be wrong. Rich people flocked to the place. They seemed to love being bullied by the doctors, and whether they got better or not, they certainly thought they did because they had paid such an amazing amount of money.

And round the baths with their smell of hydrogen sulphide and clouds of steam, there sprang up luxury hotels and casinos and ballrooms and tennis courts and bandstands. Parks were planted with rare trees; winter gardens were built; fabulous shops and cafes opened, and at night music was played in the hotels and in the pump room, where people paid all over again to drink the water which tasted so disgusting that it had to do them good.

And it was here, in the largest and most expensive hotel of all – the Hotel Majestic – that Frau Edeltraut's old uncle, the Baron Conrad von Keppel, now lived.

Annika sat beside her mother in the carriage, with Hermann on the other side. Hermann hated missing his routine, but he wanted to practise shooting at the Bad Haxenfeld rifle range.

There had been a surprise when the carriage clattered into the courtyard to pick them up. Instead of Wenzel driving, it was Zed. He got down to open the door for Annika and her mother, but he wouldn't touch his cap to Hermann and Hermann started to grumble as soon as they were on the road.

'He ought to treat me with proper respect,' he said angrily to his mother.

'Hermann, leave it. I told you it won't be for long,' she said under her breath. And to Annika, 'Zed helps my uncle when his own servant has a day off. He wheels him to the bathhouse and he makes himself useful in the hotel.'

When they had driven for nearly an hour the country-side began to change: there were hills now, and the colours of the ground grew richer. Ten minutes later they had reached the town.

Annika turned her head from right to left and back again, taking in the large exotic trees that lined the road; the luxurious villas and stately hotels. They passed a building with a brilliantly gilded roof and a flight of steps leading up to an ornate door, but when Annika asked what it was, her mother shuddered.

'It's the casino,' she said. 'It's a dreadful place. People go there and gamble away all their money and when they lose they borrow more and start again.'

'There's a clump of trees at the back where people go to shoot themselves when they're ruined,' said Hermann gleefully.

But the people passing by in the promenade did not look at all as though they were going to shoot themselves; even the ones in wheelchairs or walking with sticks seemed to be enjoying themselves. They passed chauffeurs wash-ing limousines and a uniformed porter crossing the road to the park with five dogs of assorted sizes on a long lead. No one at Bad Haxenfeld had to walk their own dogs or look after their own motors.

Then they drove through an archway and into the courtyard of the Hotel Majestic, and while Zed saw to the horses, they made their way into the building.

Waves of warm air from the steam heating wafted towards them. There was the scent of pot pourri from porcelain bowls in the hall. An orange tree grew in a tub by the reception desk. Winter was not allowed to trouble the guests of the Majestic.

'Baron von Keppel is expecting you,' said the head porter at the desk, and clicked his fingers for an underling to take them to the lift.

The Baron did not get up when they came in; getting up was something which took him a long time because his joints were crippled and bent with arthritis, but he welcomed them jovially and insisted on kissing not only his niece, but Annika.

'Well, well, a pretty little thing, isn't she?' he said. 'You've done well, Edeltraut. Don't know why you kept her hidden all these years.'

Conrad von Keppel was the brother of Edeltraut's mother; even before he was struck down by illness he must have been smaller and slighter than the von Tannenbergs. His hair was white, he smelt strongly of toilet water and his blue eyes were keen and alert. He offered them wine and biscuits, but Frau Edeltraut said that she would go with Hermann to the rifle range and come back to the hotel in an hour to pick up Annika and take her to the lawyers.

'Don't hurry back,' said Uncle Conrad. 'Annika can

149

come with me to the baths; I like to be accompanied by pretty girls. You've brought the boy, I take it?'

'Yes. He's downstairs. But don't keep her; our appointment is at eleven.'

Zed was waiting with the wheelchair, wearing an armband with the name of the hotel on it. Though he had refused to touch his cap to Hermann he saluted the Baron respectfully, tucking a rug round his knees, and it was clear that he was used to working in the spa.

He began to push the chair along the promenade towards the big bathhouse, and Annika walked beside him. Uncle Conrad seemed to know a great many people and they stopped again and again while he was greeted by ladies in enormous hats, or men on horseback or other invalids on their way to the baths who stopped their chairs beside him.

'That was Lady Georgina Fairweather,' he said after a very tall willowy woman with a huge muff had greeted him. 'You wouldn't think it, but her kidneys are in dreadful shape – completely covered in fungus. They're putting her on to thermal effervescence. And that man there in the bowler hat, he used to be the Dutch Ambassador to the Solomon Islands, and when he was out there he got an enormous tapeworm in his gut. They're trying to draw it out with hydro-suction, but pieces keep breaking off.'

Though she was sorry about Lady Georgina's kidneys and the tapeworm, Annika looked about her with pleasure, enjoying the elegant shop windows, the well-dressed people, the hanging baskets of greenery on the lamp-posts. This was a different world to Spittal.

They were getting near the baths now and the treatment rooms. The smell of hydrogen sulphide grew stronger, more wheelchairs joined the procession. And now, coming towards them with towels round their necks, was a group of men looking very damp and clean.

As they came closer, the Baron whispered, 'Ah, the dentists, delightful people. They're going home tomorrow – I shall miss them.'

Annika too was pleased to see the dentists, who had been on the station platform when she arrived. It made her feel established, as though she belonged. Not all the dentists were there, but there were at least a dozen who had gone to the treatment rooms early and were now going into the town. They stopped by the Baron's chair, greeted him and advised him to be careful about the water in the first of the hot pools.

'The temperature's very high in there today,' said a tall dentist with a moustache. 'I'd miss that one out.'

'You wouldn't believe how much I've learned from them,' confided the Baron when the dentists had wandered on in search of coffee and cakes. 'You see, when you're in the treatment rooms there are only curtains between one cubicle and the next and you can hear everything your neighbours are saying. Apparently the Duke of Arnau bit right through the thumb of his dentist when he was doing a filling. And the new zinc treatment for gums is absolutely useless, but the patients go on begging for it.' He shook his head. 'Next week it's undertakers, so I suppose I shall learn about coffins, but it won't be the same. There's always something so fascinating about teeth.' He looked over his shoulder at Zed. 'Do you remember the jewellers who came at Christmas? Three hundred, no less – and the stories they told would make your hair stand on end. You don't have to leave Bad Haxenfeld to know everything that's going on in the world!'

They had reached the entrance to the bathhouse. Only patients and their attendants were allowed beyond the entrance. Uncle Conrad's doctor came out of his office with a piece of paper listing details of the Baron's treatment for the day, and Zed wheeled him away down the long stone corridor.

'Don't forget I'm expecting you to lunch,' Uncle Conrad called to Annika over his shoulder, and she nodded and made her way back to the hotel.

The office of Herr Bohn was comfortably furnished with a deep carpet, a large mahogany desk, a palm tree in a brass pot – and a clerk who led them in and begged them to be seated because Herr Bohn would be here in a minute.

'I was expecting him to be here already. Our appointment is for eleven o'clock.' Frau Edeltraut was not accustomed to being kept waiting and made this clear.

The clerk went into the outer office and spoke to the typist, who went away to make coffee. Even when they had drunk it there was no sign of the lawyer, and Annika saw that her mother was getting upset. The papers they were here to sign must be very important, and Annika, to reassure her, said, 'But I am a von Tannenberg already, aren't I? I am your daughter, everyone knows it.'

'Yes, yes,' said Frau Edeltraut absently. 'All the same, things must be done properly.'

They waited for another half-hour, then the phone rang in the outer office and presently the clerk came in. 'That was Herr Bohn – he is extremely sorry, but his wife has had a fit and he has had to take her to the hospital.'

'A *fit*? How extraordinary. Doesn't he have servants to look after his wife?'

'Yes, yes. But . . . He says he will be with you by two o'clock without fail.'

'I very much hope so,' said Annika's mother, 'otherwise he cannot expect to go on handling my affairs.'

Lunch in the dining room of the Majestic was very grand. Annika was put next to Uncle Conrad and he had Edeltraut on his other side. Hermann was in a bad mood; the gun they had given him at the rifle range had thrown to the left, and though he had explained this, they had refused to give him another one.

Zed was not present of course; servants did not eat in the hotel dining room. Everyone spoke very quietly and Uncle Conrad occasionally told them in a low voice what was wrong with the other guests. The lady on the next table had come in with an agonizing septic throat, which had turned out to be caused by a green bean wrapped round the root of her tongue.

'They had to give her chloroform to get it out,' he whispered.

The food was splendid: venison broth, asparagus, beef in a pastry case, lemon soufflé with whipped cream. Annika had begun to wonder if there was a famine in Norrland, but if there was it had not reached Bad Haxenfeld.

She would have enjoyed her meal more if she had not thought of Zed perhaps going hungry. Then, as the waiter came out with coffee, she had a glimpse into the busy bustling kitchen. And there, with his sleeves rolled up, was Zed, his face flushed by the heat. He was helping to load the trays and laughing at something one of the cooks had said and he did not look hungry in the least.

The lawyer was still not in his office when they returned after lunch.

His clerk was grovelling, wringing his hands.

'Herr Bohn sent word that he will personally come to Spittal tomorrow with the necessary documents. At his own expense.'

'I should hope so,' said Frau Edeltraut. 'Please tell him that I am most displeased.'

But she looked more than displeased. She looked distressed and very worried, and Annika was puzzled. Why was this document so urgent? Surely nothing was going to happen to Hermann for years, if at all?

'I shall go back to the hotel and rest,' Frau Edeltraut went on. 'If you like you can go to the pump room. There's usually a band there. It doesn't cost anything to go and watch. I'll expect you back at the hotel at four o'clock.'

Annika heard the music coming out of the pump room before she reached it: a large domed building with a flight of steps flanked by statues. Inside there was a round hall with a fountain in the middle. People came up to it, gave some money to a lady sitting there, and were given a tin cup, which they took to the fountain to fill with spa water.

The rest of the floor was filled by people parading up and down, nodding their heads to the music, greeting each other. The orchestra was an eight-piece band and they were playing the kind of music Annika had grown up with in the streets and parks of Vienna: waltzes, polkas, marches . . .

She made her way closer to the orchestra and stood listening. The violins soared sweetly, the leader smiled at her and she came closer and closer still. After a while she felt a tap on her shoulder and turned to find a white-haired gentleman with a clean-shaven face and a paunch, looking down at her.

'Would the fräulein care to dance?' he asked.

Annika was startled – no one else was dancing, and in any case one didn't dance with strangers. She was about to refuse when an elderly lady in a wheelchair propelled herself forward.

'This is my wife,' said the old gentleman. 'She saw your feet tapping and she thought you might like to waltz a little.'

The old lady nodded. 'As you see, I can't dance any more – but you should have seen us when we were young!'

Annika smiled, and held up her arms. As she and the old gentleman twirled in a waltz, the spectators smiled too, then a couple joined in, and another . . . The members of the band were delighted. When the music came to an end they played another waltz, and another . . .

Then she heard an angry voice calling her name. Zed was standing at the edge of the dancers, scowling at her.

'What on earth are you doing?' he hissed, coming up to her. 'You know you don't dance with strangers.'

Annika flushed. 'This is Herr Doktor Feldkirch,' she said angrily. 'Frau Feldkirch suggested that we might like to dance.'

But Zed was in a temper. 'I'm supposed to fetch you – it's time to go home. What will your mother say?'

'That depends on what you tell her.'

They walked back to the hotel in silence.

Then Zed said, 'It's not even proper music that they play there.'

Annika stopped and glared at him. 'What do you mean? It was lovely. It was proper Viennese music.'

Zed shrugged. 'If you like everything to be sickly and sweet. If you want real music, you should listen to the gypsies.'

'How am I supposed to do that?' she snapped. 'There aren't any gypsies anywhere near here.'

'There might be soon. They come through sometimes on the way to the Spring Fair at Stettin. If they do, I'll take you.'

It was the nearest she would get to an apology.

In the carriage on the way back, Annika was sleepy and content, which was as well since Hermann grumbled all the way home about the men in the shooting gallery.

They drove in twilight, then darkness. As the carriage went over the first bridge, Zed suddenly drew up. In the same moment he extinguished the carriage lamp.

'I think we should go back,' he said in a low voice to Frau Edeltraut. 'There are people there. Look!'

They stared up at the courtyard of the house and saw lamps being carried round the building – then heard hammering at the door.

'Come on, open up – we know you're there,' somebody shouted, and the hammering started again.

Not burglars then, as Annika had feared.

'They're from the Land Bureau, I think,' whispered Zed. 'They've come in two automobiles.'

'Turn round at once,' ordered Frau Edeltraut, but Zed had already begun to turn the carriage in the only passing place behind the bridge. 'Where can we go?'

'Felsen Woods,' said Zed over his shoulder. 'No one will find us there.'

They drove back the way they had come, past the turning to the farm, then down a narrow forest road which led away from Spittal into a dark thicket of spruce.

'I'll kill them for this,' muttered Herman. 'When my father comes back, I'll kill them.'

'They won't stay long,' said Zed. He had jumped down and gone to the horses' heads.

But they waited in the cold and silent woods for nearly two hours. To Annika the hotel, the music at the spa, now seemed a distant dream. Who were those men who had tried to storm her mother's house? What was it that ailed Spittal? Would no one tell her the truth?

CHAPTER SEVENTEEN

A SMELL OF BURNING

After Annika went away with her mother, odd things happened in the professors' house.

For example, the professors would come downstairs to the smell of burning. It might be the breakfast rolls singeing in the oven, or the soup boiling dry on the stove, but it was such an unusual thing to happen that they found it hard to believe their noses. Ellie had not burned anything since she had first gone to work as a kitchen maid twenty years ago, but she burned them now.

Then Sigrid broke a plate. It was not a particularly valuable plate but it was a nice one, with a pattern of golden stars and blue flowers. It lived on the dresser, and when Sigrid picked it up to dust it, it slipped from her hand to the floor.

Just as Ellie had not burned anything since she was

fourteen years old, so Sigrid did not let things fall from her hand. The professors trusted her with their mother's precious crystal glasses and they were right to do so. Her large, square-tipped hands picked up objects as if they were eggshells.

All the same, after Annika went she broke a plate. Sometimes if you don't let your feelings out, you do odd things instead. Ellie and Sigrid did not think it was right to cry and wail and moan because they had lost what they thought of as their daughter, but their unhappiness came out in other ways.

The professors too were not in the best of spirits. By the time she left them, they realized that Annika had done a lot of work in the house and they decided to take over some of her jobs.

This was not a success.

Professor Julius decided to buy his own flowers from the lady in the square, and to arrange them himself in a vase beneath the portrait of Adele Fischl, his beloved – but when he did so she seemed to be looking at him in a very gloomy way. Arranging flowers is not as easy as it looks, and the lilies of the valley, jammed together like a bundle of leeks, seemed to upset Adele, who had always felt things keenly.

Professor Gertrude had decided to help by choosing her own hansom cabs to take her to her concerts and this too did not end well. Cab horses were just a blur to Professor Gertrude, who was short-sighted and did not care for animals very much, and she and her harp had some very bumpy and unpleasant rides.

As for Professor Emil, he missed Annika for different reasons. Just after she went, the museum had shown him a new painting of three bare-footed ladies dancing in a meadow and asked him if he thought it was a genuine Titian. He had known at once that it was not because of the way the feet were painted – Titian never used models who were pigeon-toed. This was the kind of thing that Annika would have understood at once, and he was getting ready to hurry home and tell her before he remembered that she was gone.

The people in the square did not make things any easier. The lady in the paper shop said she was not at all sure that the climate of north Germany would suit Annika; Josef from the cafe said he did not like the way the Emperor Wilhelm was carrying on, and Frau Bodek said they could say what they liked but the baby missed her.

Then the first letters came from Spittal. Pauline and Stefan carried theirs to the hut so as to compare notes and both agreed that Annika's letters were strange.

It had been difficult to stop Annika from talking when she was excited about something, but she wrote about her new life in a careful sort of way, rather as if she was writing an essay for school.

What she made clear to both of them was that she was very happy. In Pauline's letter she had underlined the word 'very' and in Stefan's letter she said she was very happy *indeed*. She wrote about her marvellous and amazing mother, who looked after Spittal all by herself, and she wrote about Hermann, who was going into the army and did press-ups and bayonet practice in his room. She wrote about how big Spittal was and how brave the aristocracy were, not minding about being cold and never having pudding and she described the bear pit in the hunting lodge into which a drunken labourer had fallen.

Hermann showed me the family crest and the motto. It says, 'Stand Aside, Ye Vermin Who Oppose Us!' Vermin is anybody who gets in the way of the von Tannenbergs, he said.

There were some crossings-out in both letters. Something about Jesus having been a carpenter, which they couldn't read or make out properly, and a few lines about the farm, and the stable boy who looked after Hermann's horse.

After that came the questions. These flowed on in quite a different way, as though she had written them quickly without thinking. Had the baby's teeth come through? What was Pauline reading? How were the goldfish in the fountain? Had Loremarie got a new governess?

'Do you think she's all right?' asked Stefan.

'Of course she's all right,' said Pauline, sounding cross. 'Why shouldn't she be?'

Ellie and Sigrid had hoped to read their letter quietly by themselves, but the postman had spread the news that Annika had written and presently the kitchen filled with people who demanded to know what she had said. Mitzi from the Eggharts' house, Josef from the cafe, the lady from the paper shop . . .

'Well?' they asked. 'Is she happy?'

'She is very happy,' said Ellie firmly.

She knew that this was so because Annika had said so in her first paragraph, but she found the letter puzzling and wasn't quite sure what to tell them.

For Annika had found it difficult to explain certain

things to Ellie: the dead birds with pellets . . . the leaking roof . . . She asked if Ellie could send her some chilblain ointment; she described the lake, which was large, the frogs, which were hatching, and a beautiful bay horse, which belonged to Hermann but was looked after by the stable boy. Her mother had said she might soon have a pony of her own.

After that, she exploded with questions. Her questions to Pauline and Stefan took a whole page; her questions to Ellie sprawled over three. Was the geranium cutting growing? Did Uncle Emil manage his cravats? What was the flower lady selling? Had Cornelia Otter started to sing again at the opera? How many letters had Uncle Julius written to the newspaper? Was Ellie going to bake a poppy-seed strudel for the end of Lent? Had the asparagus seller come to the market yet . . . ?

And right at the end she told them once again how very much she was enjoying her new life.

A week after Annika's letters came, a serious-looking man in a dark suit, carrying a briefcase, rang the bell of the professors' house.

'I'm looking for the guardians of Annika Winter,' he said. 'I believe this is the right address?'

Sigrid, who had answered the door, turned white.

'Is she . . . has something happened? An accident?'

'No, not at all. I represent the firm of Gerhart and Funkel in the Karntner Strasse and we have some business with her. Perhaps I could come in?'

'Yes. Yes, of course, I'm sorry.'

She showed him into the drawing room and fetched the

professors, and after a short time both Sigrid and Ellie were sent for.

'I have explained to Herr Gerhart that Annika was adopted by you as a baby, and given Ellie's surname, and that I agreed to act as her guardian,' said Professor Julius. 'Also that she is no longer in our care because her real mother – her birth mother – has come forward and that Annika is now living with her. It seems that the old lady she used to visit – Fräulein Egghart – has left Annika something in her will.'

'It's nothing at all valuable,' said Herr Gerhart. 'Just a trunk with some keepsakes from the theatre – old clothes and suchlike. All the same, we shall want to check the new adoption papers. You see, the child is definitely described as living at this address.'

'She did live here,' said Ellie in a choked voice. 'She lived here all her life till two weeks ago.'

The lawyer gave her a sympathetic glance.

'It shouldn't take too long to get everything sorted out, since the professor has kept copies of the documents which Frau von Tannenberg brought. The affidavit signed by Herr Pumpelmann-Schlissinger should be decisive. When we've investigated them we will inform her and send the legacy on to her for the child.'

'Annika will like to have the trunk,' said Ellie when the lawyer had gone and they were back in the kitchen. 'She can use the things for dressing up. She's probably doing some acting with her new friends; you know how fond she was of making up plays.'

'Yes. Though she doesn't say anything about it in her letter.'

'Well, it's early days yet,' said Ellie, sighing. And then,

'Shows how fond the old lady must have been of Annika, leaving the trunk to her and not the family.'

'Well, that's nothing to wonder at,' said Sigrid gruffly, stacking plates beside the sink. 'Being fond of Annika, I mean.'

CHAPTER EIGHTEEN

ANNIKA BREAKS A PROMISE

Annika had been frightened on the evening they returned from the spa. The dark figures moving about trying to force doors to the house, shouting, had been menacing – but what had really upset her was her mother's rage and fear. In Vienna she had not seen adults afraid in this way. Professor Gertrude was nervous before concerts, Professor Julius was cross when they did not publish his letters to the newspaper, and no one spoke to Ellie when she was preparing quails' eggs in aspic. But this was different. Whoever those men had been, they had made her proud and beautiful mother lose control.

Nothing had been damaged or taken when they returned to Spittal. Annika and Hermann had been sent straight to bed, but it was a long time before Annika slept. She would have gone through fire to protect her mother from whatever it was that troubled her . . . but the next day nothing was said. There was the usual rain in the morning, the sound of Uncle Oswald's gun, the little pieces of stonework falling into the moat . . . and then a long day because Zed was taking the carriage horses to be shod and there was no one at the farm.

But on the following morning she slipped down to see him. He was taking water to the pigs, but when Annika went to help him she found that there were only two pigs left in the sty.

'What's happened to Dora?' she asked.

Dora was a huge and bristly saddleback and Annika had been fond of her.

'Sold,' said Zed. 'We're down to two pigs, three cows, half a dozen sheep and a handful of chickens. God knows what the Master would have said.'

He was in a bad mood, but Annika couldn't bear not knowing what was wrong any longer.

'Zed, who were those men the night before last? Why did we have to turn round and go back? What does it all mean?'

He shrugged. 'Why don't you ask your mother?'

'I can't,' said Annika in a low voice. 'I don't want to upset her.'

'It's not my business to tell you what's wrong with your home.'

Annika turned away so that he wouldn't see her face. But Zed had sensed her misery.

'What's wrong with Spittal isn't your mother's fault,' he said. 'Come on, we'll take Hector to the lake; he's in a good mood this morning.'

*

That afternoon the lawyer whose wife had had fits came to Spittal and Annika signed an important-looking document, which took up several pages and was not at all easy to understand.

And a few days later, Annika was called into her mother's boudoir to hear the explanation she had been hoping for.

'I know you must have been puzzled, my poor child, by those dreadful men the other night, and I can tell you now that they were bailiffs.'

'Bailiffs? Those men who take the furniture away when people can't pay their bills?'

'That's right. You can imagine how I felt – someone from a family like mine classed with common poor people who can't pay their bills.'

Annika was silent, remembering the Bodeks, to whom the bailiffs had always been a dread – yet somehow they had always managed to pay their debts in time. Frau Bodek had taken in extra washing, the boys had run errands round the clock . . .

'You see, I have not told you anything about my husband; I didn't want to upset you, but the truth is, he was no good.'

'A louse, like my father?'

She gave a wintry smile. 'Yes, dear. I'm afraid I'm not very good at choosing men. He's gone abroad, but before that . . . Well, he was a gambler. A frightful gambler. He didn't know how to stop and when he lost all his money he borrowed more and more. He gambled away my money and my sister's and then he started selling off the family paintings and jewels. My father had had a stroke by then; he couldn't do anything to stop him. Everything went . . . We became poor . . . Even buying food became difficult and we had to turn the servants away because there was no money to pay their wages. You can imagine how Hermann felt when we told him that he couldn't go to St Xavier's because we simply couldn't pay the fees. The army is his life.'

She put her arm round Annika and drew her close.

'Perhaps I shouldn't have brought you here when I had so little to offer you,' she went on. 'Perhaps you would rather not have come, but once I found you I couldn't bear not to have you by my side. Are you sorry that you came, Annika?'

'Oh no, no, no! I love being with you. Only I wish you'd let me help – I really can do things.' Annika's face was alight as she saw herself being of use. 'I can cook and sew and clean. We could save so much money if—'

Frau Edeltraut laid a finger on Annika's lips.

'My dear, don't be foolish. Don't you see, it's more important than ever that people should see you're one of us – a proper von Tannenberg. I only told you about the bailiffs because I think we may be over the worst. I had some news today which may – it just may – make everything better. I have to go to Bad Haxenfeld and look into it, and then possibly on a journey to Switzerland, and I'm afraid I can't tell you anything yet because it might all come to nothing. But if things go as I hope, the bad times will be over. And then, my darling daughter, you shall have whatever you want. You did ask me for something, didn't you?'

Annika smiled. 'Galoshes.'

'You shall have them. If matters turn out as I hope, you shall have as many pairs of galoshes as you like.'

*

'I was such an idiot,' said Annika. She had learned to clean out Rocco's hoofs and Zed was watching her critically. 'I mean, I never thought that we were just poor. I thought aristocrats were never poor like that. I knew they were always toughening themselves up to go on crusades and battles, and I suppose I thought they went on doing it. And I didn't guess, because my mother stayed at the Bristol in Vienna and that was unbelievably expensive.'

Zed was inspecting the hoof she had cleaned.

'Did she? I never knew that.'

'I keep thinking how nice it was of her to fetch me when they were so hard up. I mean, I eat quite a lot. Perhaps I could try to eat a bit less in case the business in Switzerland doesn't work out.'

'Don't be silly.'

But Annika was touched that her mother had come to fetch her even when things were so bad at Spittal. She must have wanted to find her daughter very much.

Sometimes now, Zed would throw Annika on to Rocco's back and lead her through fields invisible from the house. 'You're not riding,' he would say. 'You're just exercising the horse.'

'I wish I knew what it was about horses,' she would say as she slithered off again. 'Why does one like them so much?'

'It's been like that since there were men and horses in the same world. But make no mistake about it; it's the men who need the horses, not the other way round. Horses did fine on their own.'

The next morning Uncle Oswald came over early, but he was not dressed for shooting. He wore a dark suit and there were no feathers in his beard or any blood round his fingernails. Even his duelling scar looked as though it had been freshly scrubbed. Frau Edeltraut too was very elegant, wearing the fur cloak and feathered hat she had worn when she went to fetch Annika. They breakfasted before the children, and left for Bad Haxenfeld in the carriage, taking neither Wenzel nor Zed. Uncle Oswald took the reins and they clattered away over both the bridges almost before it got light.

It was well past midnight when they returned. Everyone in the house was fast asleep, but in the kennel behind the stork house, the three-legged dog heard a splash in the lake, stirred, and slept again.

Whatever they had found out in Bad Haxenfeld was clearly encouraging because the following week Annika's mother, her Uncle Oswald and her Aunt Mathilde all set off for Switzerland.

'We'll only be away for a few days,' Edeltraut had explained. 'Gudrun will come and stay here, and Bertha will come and sleep in the house at night, so there's nothing to worry about at all.'

But she gave some orders to Hermann. 'I don't want you to go riding till I get back – if there was an accident I would never forgive myself. And don't do your shooting practice either. Everything else you can do as usual.'

So Gudrun arrived with her suitcase and moved into the bedroom next to Annika's, and the hunting lodge was left to its antlers, and to the woodworms chomping in the rafters.

The adults drove away before dawn, to catch the first of the trains which would take them south on their long journey to Switzerland. An hour later Annika came down to breakfast in the dining room, followed by Gudrun and Hermann. Bertha brought in the dark bread and weak coffee, but she seemed flustered and preoccupied and hurried back down to the farm as soon as she had cleared away.

After breakfast Gudrun followed Annika to her room and asked if she could see her clothes. Fortunately she was too tall to wear Annika's skirts and dresses, but she sighed over two more scarves and a velvet hair ribbon, which Annika presented to her.

After that she wanted to play cards.

It was a long morning. At lunchtime there came the first sign that the domestic arrangements were not going to go smoothly. Hanne, the sulky maid who came from the village on the far side of the lake, told the children that she wasn't coming back the next day. She'd got a proper job somewhere else, she said, slapping down the platter of cold breast of teal, and the musty potatoes; the kind of job where you got paid on time.

The afternoon dragged like the morning. Hermann went to his room to 'present arms' and Gudrun wanted to stay indoors and talk about boyfriends. Since she didn't have any boyfriends and Annika only had friends who happened to be boys, conversation was slow and after a while Annika, looking longingly out of the window, agreed to play a paper-and-pencil game.

Bertha usually came up to serve supper, but today there was no sign of her – only more cold meat and bread laid out in the dining room.

'What happens if she doesn't come and spend the night here? We'll be all alone,' said Gudrun.

'Well, it wouldn't matter; there are three of us.'

'I think the way servants behave these days is disgusting,' said Hermann.

'I'll go and see what's happened to her,' said Annika.

She hurried down to the farm, gratefully drinking in the fresh air, and knocked at the door of the hut. Bertha was sitting in the rocking chair with Hector at her feet. Dozing on the bench by the stove sat an old man whom Bertha introduced as her brother.

'He's driven over from Rachegg,' she said, 'to tell me that his wife has died. My sister-in-law. He wants me to come to the funeral.'

'And will you?' Annika asked.

'I'd like to,' she said. 'It would be proper. But I promised the mistress I'd come and sleep at the house.'

At this moment the door to the outhouse opened and Zed appeared with a grey blanket slung over his shoulder.

'It's all right,' he said to Annika. 'I'll come up and sleep – there's a bed in the room behind the kitchen. Bertha needs to go.'

Zed was as good as his word. When Annika got up next morning she found Zed in the kitchen, filling the stove.

'It should burn now till lunchtime. But Bertha's gone off with her brother. She'll be away for a few days. Can you manage? I've got to go and see to the animals, but I'll be back later.'

'Of course I can manage. Thank you for doing the stove.'

Annika looked round, wondering what to do. She had promised her mother not to go into the kitchen and not to work as a servant . . . not on any account.

She had *promised*.

She put on the kettle and went upstairs to make her bed. Then she reached for the notebook Pauline had given her and untied the ribbon. All the people whom Pauline turned to when in trouble were there. The man with the back-to-front foot, the girl with the measles . . . the boy who had been stung a hundred times by bees and gone on to school to get top marks in his maths exam before he fainted . . . the cow sinking under the ice . . .

Disobeying one's mother was difficult. It was almost as difficult as holding up a sinking cow by the horns or swimming the Danube with measles. But what if it had to be done? Would her mother want Hermann to go hungry?

She closed the book and went back downstairs.

There was some bread in the bin – half a loaf – and some butter out in the dairy. The strange yellow jam had been finished the day before and there didn't seem to be any more. She put out three cups and plates on the kitchen table and made coffee.

Then she went upstairs again to wake Gudrun and Hermann.

'There's no one to help in the house today, so I've laid breakfast in the kitchen.'

'I can't eat in the kitchen,' said Hermann, 'I never have.'

'Well, that's all right, you can fetch your food and take it into the dining room.'

Gudrun too did not think she could eat in the kitchen, so she and Hermann took their slices of bread and cups of coffee through into the dining room, where they sat shivering and looking out at the grey lake.

Annika, meanwhile, took stock. It wasn't quite true that there was nothing to eat, but there was amazingly little. Hanne usually did the shopping in the village, but Hanne had gone and Annika didn't have any money to go shopping herself. She found some flour in a jar and half a jug of milk. In the vegetable rack there were a few potatoes and a turnip. In Uncle Oswald's cold larder two unplucked moorhens with blood on their beaks were hanging on hooks. She shut the door on them and went to the broom cupboard.

She would think about lunch later, but now it was necessary to start on the cleaning, for she could not cook in anything except a clean kitchen, and a clean kitchen meant a clean house. Only where to start? For a moment, as she looked at the tins of polish, the cloths and dusters and brooms, she felt overwhelmed by the task she had set herself. Then she heard Sigrid's voice as clearly as if she were standing beside her.

Yes, you can do it – you can do it all. Don't rush it, only think about the one job you're doing. And make sure to mix the beeswax properly; no one can work with lumpy polish.

She picked up the buckets, the floorcloths, the brooms and feather dusters and made her way to the dining room. Hermann and Gudrun, who had just finished their breakfast, looked at her in amazement.

'What are you doing?' said Gudrun as Annika began to sweep the floor. 'You'll get your clothes dirty.'

'Perhaps. But I'll get the house clean. Some of it. You can help me if you like.'

But Gudrun hurried from the room as though what Annika was doing might be infectious.

Annika dusted the huge carved chairs, she shook out the window curtains, she polished the oak table, and slid across the parquet floor with dusters tied round her shoes.

Presently she found that she was singing; the first time she had done so since she came to her new home.

When she had finished the dining room she started on the hall, wiping the glass cases of the beady-eyed fish, mopping down the flagstones. Then she put away the cleaning things and made her way down to the farm.

'Zed, I want some eggs. Can you spare some?'

'There are plenty of eggs – well, there are a dozen, but they're supposed to be taken into the village and bartered for Hermann's ammunition.'

Annika stared at him. 'Is that why there are never any eggs?'

'Yes. The eggs go so that he can shoot, and the pigs get sold to pay the man who gives him his fencing lessons. It's been like that for a while.'

'Well, I don't care, Zed. I want the eggs. Hermann's not supposed to shoot anyway while his mother is away.'

Zed shrugged. 'It's all right by me. Come on. I'll help you get them.'

'There has to be something else I can use.'

He grinned. 'Well, there are always mangel-wurzels.'

She would have liked to make soufflé omelettes, but it would have to be pancakes if there was to be enough for everyone. She had flour, eggs, milk – then right at the back of the almost empty store cupboard she found a piece of smoked ham. It was a very small piece, but chopped up to fill the pancakes it would do.

The smell brought Gudrun to the kitchen door just before lunchtime, where she hovered sadly.

'They'll be ready in a few minutes,' said Annika, busy turning the pancakes over. 'You can help me with the filling.'

'Oh, I couldn't. Mama never lets me go in the kitchen.'

Annika said nothing, just went on heaping the golden pancakes on to the plate.

'Well, if you don't tell her . . .' said Gudrun presently. 'What do you want me to do?'

Zed came back then with more wood. 'My goodness, they smell good.'

'They've come out all right,' Annika admitted. 'There's plenty for all of us.'

She got out four plates and put them round the kitchen table, only to hear Gudrun give a squeak like a terrified mouse.

'I can't eat here with the stable boy!'

'Well, then take your plate through into the dining room, and Hermann's. I'll stay here with Zed; I have to watch the stove.'

So once more Gudrun and Hermann sat at the vast oak table in the unheated dining room, while Annika and Zed ate in the warmth and comfort of the old kitchen, and he told her about Bertha.

'She won't be back till the end of the week; it's a long way, and her brother needs her. I'm hoping—' He broke off. 'Only I don't suppose he will . . .'

'What? What are you hoping?'

'I thought he might ask her to come and live with him. He's got quite a big farm and he'll be lonely.'

'But wouldn't you miss her?'

'No. Because I wouldn't be here.'

Annika stared at him.

'I meant to go after the Master died, but I knew he worried about Bertha; she'd been his nurse since he was two weeks old, and I thought I had to stay and see she was all right.'

'But where would you go? And what about Rocco – and Hector?'

'Yes. There'd be a lot to think about.'

Annika had put down her fork, feeling suddenly terribly bereft. 'I'll miss you.'

'I haven't gone yet,' he said.

But tears had come into her eyes. 'Oh, what's the matter with me,' she said, brushing them away angrily. 'I hardly ever cried in Vienna.'

'You're homesick.'

'How can I be? I'm at *home*.'

But after lunch, carrying on with the task she had set herself, she felt cheerful again. She cleaned out the bedrooms, lugging the stepladder along the landing so that she could dust high up, and polishing the mirrors. Then Zed returned with a pot of cottage cheese.

'Bertha hung up the sour milk before she went and it's ready; you can have it.'

'Good. I've found some big potatoes. I'll bake them and fill them with the cheese.'

Zed nodded. 'They'll go well with the fish.'

'What fish?'

'The fish we're going to catch this afternoon, using your Uncle Oswald's punt.'

Zed wasn't boasting. He had the punt ready in the boathouse, with Hector lying curled up as far as possible from the tackle.

'It's all right,' Zed said. 'He'll be quiet; he knows you don't retrieve fish.'

Soon they were in the middle of the lake, putting out their lines. It was lovely to be outside, seeing the house from the water, floating on the reflected clouds.

Zed caught two pike and she caught a small perch, and though she knew that Gudrun and Hermann were watching them out of the window, she didn't mind.

Later, when Zed had cleaned and filleted the fish, and they were sizzling in the frying pan, Gudrun appeared once more at the door.

'Oh, goodness, I do love fried fish,' she said.

'They're nearly ready,' said Annika. 'Tell Hermann and you can take your helpings through.'

'Perhaps Hermann would come and eat in here if I asked him. It's so nice and warm.'

But at that moment the sound of the gong pealed through the house. It was Hermann making it clear that the von Tannenbergs did not slum it in kitchens, and Gudrun scuttled away to follow her hero into the dining room.

The next day Annika got up early and went on with her tasks. When she came to think about lunch she found that Zed had shot and skinned a rabbit, and in the overgrown vegetable patch she pulled up some of last year's sprouts.

'What is that?' Gudrun asked later, helping herself to a thinly sliced white root which Annika had served as a salad.

'It's a new vegetable – I can't remember the name,' said Annika. 'It's good, isn't it?'

'Yes, it is,' said Gudrun, and took another portion of mangel-wurzel.

On the third day Annika was hardly recognizable as the quiet girl drifting through empty rooms. She was working from dawn till dusk, and as each meal approached she and Zed pitted their wits against the empty larder. That afternoon a pedlar came to the door and she bartered Professor Gertrude's manicure set for a box of gingerbread and a bag of rice.

And she made soup. She made soup of absolutely everything she could find and Zed teased her about it, pretending he could taste firewood and the bristles of her broom – but he ate it. No one trained by Ellie could fail to find *something* with which to make soup.

'Have you ever thought of marrying a Canadian settler?' Zed asked her when he found her chopping what seemed to be the last onion in Spittal.

She shook her head. 'Why a Canadian?'

'Haven't you ever wanted to go there? To the north-west – the coast is full of islands and there's forest for miles and miles and everybody's equal there.'

'No, I haven't.'

But that night she took a lamp to the library to look for an atlas. She found one too, which had not been sent to be rebound or cleaned in Bad Haxenfeld, and looked up the coast of British Columbia. Zed was right. It looked wild and beautiful, but her mother would never leave this place. If there was one thing Annika had learned, it was that there had been von Tannenbergs at Spittal for 500 years.

*

Annika had put off cleaning the library. It was never used and even colder and danker than the other rooms. But there were some beautiful old pieces of furniture there – in particular a large carved desk with numerous drawers and claw-footed legs that had belonged to the Freiherr. Nobody had used it since his death; it had been completely neglected and Annika did not feel that this was right.

She mixed a fresh consignment of beeswax, decanted a jar of silver polish, and made her way to the library.

There was a bunch of keys in one of the pigeonholes, but none of the drawers were locked. One by one she pulled them out and stacked them carefully on the floor. Then she began on the desktop, the back, the legs, dusting, polishing – and polishing again.

When she had finished she turned back to the drawers. Though they were empty they still had their lining paper – paper almost as thick as vellum with a design of fleur-de-lis. It would be a pity to throw it out; she would wipe it as best she could, and replace it.

First, though, the silver handles. Whoever had crafted them had not been troubled about the people who would have to clean them. They were elaborately wrought with a design that soaked up the polish but took longer than she would have believed to produce a shine.

By the time she got to the actual drawers, Annika was tempted just to push them back in, but at this point, as so often when she tried to take short cuts, Sigrid seemed to be leaning over her shoulder, looking pained. So she removed the paper from each of the drawers, wiped it, replaced it back . . . When she reached the bottom drawer she found something wedged right under the lining at the back.

A letter. She took it out and held it in her hand for a minute, not sure what to do. Then she heard Gudrun calling her and she put it in her apron pocket.

It was time to get lunch.

CHAPTER NINETEEN

GYPSIES

Annika was just dropping off to sleep that night when she heard the creak of her bedroom door being opened. Then footsteps – but she had no time to feel frightened before she heard Zed's voice.

'Get up and get dressed. Put on warm things and come downstairs. Don't let anyone see you.'

She fumbled her way into her clothes and found Zed in the hall, waiting.

'What is it?' she asked. 'Is anything the matter?'

'The gypsies are here. They're camped on the other side of Felsen Woods. I said I'd take you.'

She followed him out of the house and into the courtyard. It was a clear, cold night, and in the lane she could make out Rocco, packed up and waiting.

'Are we riding?'

'You are. It isn't far. I'll lead you.'

Annika followed him, her eyes gradually getting used to the darkness. 'But you can't walk all that way.'

Zed ignored this. He helped her to mount and adjusted the stirrups.

'Just grip hard with your knees.'

It was like being in a dream, except colder and more uncomfortable. The stirrup leathers pinched her legs.

'Won't they mind me?'

'No. You're my friend.'

'Do you know them then? The ones that are camped here?'

Zed shrugged. 'They're from Hungary and on the way to the Horse Fair at Stettin. They may have known my mother, she came from there. But it doesn't matter. They'll welcome us.'

They met no one on the dark road.

'Are you all right?' Annika asked after an hour.

'Don't fuss.'

They had come to the part of the wood where they had hidden from the bailiffs. Now Rocco's ears went forward. He whinnied excitedly and answering whinnies came from behind the trees. They skirted a coppice and came out at a patch of waste ground.

It was like coming suddenly to a lighted stage. Fires burned and crackled, lanterns hung between the trees. There were wagons and tethered horses – and everywhere movement and bustle and life.

Annika had thought she knew what gypsies were like. They lived in brightly painted caravans, they cooked hedgehogs in clay pots, the girls wore flounced petticoats and golden earrings. They made clothes pegs and told fortunes . . . they stole babies.

But these gypsies were not like that. Some of the wagons were brightly painted but some were ordinary wooden wagons of the kind used by tradesmen. The young girls who were busy with the cooking wore gold loops in their ears, and bangles, but most of the women looked like the village people Annika had met everywhere, with thick shawls and woollen skirts.

And they didn't look at all like people who stole babies; they looked, after days of travelling, too tired for anything like that.

Now an elderly man came forward. He wore a baggy suit and a woollen cap; his black eyes were bright and eager, and his enormous moustache curved round his face like a scimitar.

'Izidor,' he said, introducing himself, and it was clear from the way the others hung back and let him speak that he was the 'father' of the group; the man who gave the orders.

Zed bowed his head. 'Zedekiah Malakov,' he replied, giving his full name.

There was a murmur from the onlookers. Old Izidor pulled Zed closer to the light of the fire and studied his face. Then he nodded.

'You have her eyes,' he said in his own language. 'We remember her.'

Annika had dismounted and was holding Rocco, standing outside the circle of light. Now Zed turned and took the bridle and led him forward.

'Rocco,' he said, presenting his horse.

Izidor had been pleased to see Zed, but the sight of

184

Rocco overwhelmed him. He whistled through his teeth, he passed his hands over Rocco's flank . . . Carefully he removed Rocco's saddle and handed it to a man standing by so that he could run his fingers over the horse's back.

'Zverno?' he asked, recognizing the stud, and Zed nodded.

Two trusty youths were summoned and allowed to lead Rocco to the patch of grass where the other horses were tethered. Water was brought for him, and handfuls of hay . . . More and more admirers came to stroke him; girls as much as men.

After that it was Annika's turn. As Zed took her to old Izidor she was very nervous. She knew that gypsies did not approve of outsiders, of *gadjos*, and she knew that compared to a finely bred horse she did not count for much – but she gave her hand to Izidor and then, remembering her manners, she curtsied.

Then came the meal. They sat round the largest of the fires and ate some delicious meat roasted with herbs and the fiery paprika they had brought with them from the south. A girl of about Annika's own age came and sat beside her. She was cradling a small grey kitten, which she put in Annika's hand.

'Rosina,' she said, but it was not clear if she was naming the kitten or herself.

But Zed did not forget his promise. In halting Romany, mixed with Hungarian, he explained that Annika had never heard proper gypsy music.

The men were sleepy now, some had gone back into the caravans, but Annika had left her mark: not many little *gadjo* girls had curtsied to old Izidor. He clapped his hands and demanded music – and when Izidor demanded something, he got it.

Annika had seen gypsy musicians in their colourful romantic costumes in the cafes in Vienna. They had beribboned guitars and celestas and cymbalines and exotic-looking instruments of which she did not know the names.

The men who came out of the caravans were not like that. Yawning, rubbing their eyes, they came out of their wagons carrying battered fiddles, ancient cellos, accordions with worn-looking keys.

And then they started to play.

At first Annika did not like the sound they made; it was so different from the lilting Viennese waltzes she was used to. This music attacked you; it was fierce and angry . . . at least it was at first; she listened to it with clenched hands. Then suddenly one of the fiddlers stepped forward and played a melody that soared and wreathed and fastened itself round the heart – a sad tune that sounded as if it was gathering up all the unhappiness in the world – and then the other musicians joined in again and it was as though the sadness had been set free. The music was no longer about life being sad and lonely. It was about life being difficult, but also exciting and surprising and sublime.

When the players stopped, Annika shook her head, bewildered to find herself still on solid ground. She had hardly returned to the real world when something happened that frightened her badly.

Izidor was speaking to Zed and what he said was important because the others fell silent. If she did not understand all the words, Annika understood the gestures that went with them perfectly.

Izidor was asking Zed if he would go along with them. He pointed to his caravan and to the old woman who stood on the steps, nodding, agreeing with what he said. He pointed to Rocco, grazing peacefully under the trees.

Then he repeated his offer. Zed was one of them, he said. He belonged and so did his horse.

Annika held her breath.

But Zed had shaken his head. He pointed to Annika, and back in the direction of Spittal.

'Not yet,' he seemed to be saying. 'Not now.'

Izidor drove her back in a small cart to which he had hitched one of his horses, while Zed rode Rocco beside them. The little girl with the kitten came too and as they stopped at the turning to Spittal, she put the kitten firmly into Annika's lap. It was a present.

Annika's hand closed round the soft warm fur and she realized how badly she wanted something living of her own. But Zed leaned down and said something to the girl in her own language, and she looked troubled and bewildered. Then she gave a sad shake of her head and took the kitten back again.

'What did you tell her?' asked Annika after the cart had turned back.

'I told her that Spittal was not a good house for animals.'

Zed took her to the door and she got back safely to her room, but it would be a long time before she forgot the evening. Would Zed really be able to resist what his people offered: the warmth, the firelight, the freedom – and the care they would give his horse?

He had refused to go with them.

'Not now,' he had said. 'Not yet.'

But 'Not ever'?

She did not think he had said that.

CHAPTER TWENTY

THE GODFATHER

The next day, Annika was back at work, cooking, contriving, cleaning. She had been sure that when the grown-ups returned she would have time to take off her apron and become again the girl her mother wanted her to be.

But she was working in the drawing room on the other side of the house, standing on a stepladder cleaning the windows, when the carriage returned, and the first she knew of it was hearing her mother's voice.

'Annika! What on earth are you doing?'

Annika started and nearly lost her balance. Then she came slowly down; there was no point in even trying to pull off her apron. She had been caught red-handed. Behind her mother, Annika saw Hermann, smirking. He had obviously led her into the drawing room on purpose, wanting to make trouble.

'She was doing something like that all the time you were away, Mother. Scrubbing and sweeping and cooking – and she had all her meals in the kitchen. She's just a servant through and through!'

Annika waited for her mother's anger, but something had happened to Edeltraut. She was elegantly dressed in a new velvet coat and skirt and her hair was swept up in a different style which made her look younger and very beautiful.

'Oh, Annika, my darling,' she said with a rueful laugh. 'What are we going to do with you?'

And she bent down and swept Annika into her arms and hugged her.

Everything had changed, Annika saw that at once. Her mother was no longer stiff and anxious. Mathilde had stopped looking like an unhappy camel. Uncle Oswald had trimmed his beard. Whatever the business was that had taken them to Switzerland, it must have gone well.

It was decided that the family from the hunting lodge would stay the night. Uncle Oswald had bought a hamper full of good things in Zurich: tins of pâté, truffles, hothouse grapes, a smoked leg of lamb, a bottle of champagne.

'We'll have a party,' said Edeltraut. 'But first I must tell you what has happened, because we shall need to pay our respects and say a prayer.'

So the children gathered round her and Edeltraut told them why they had gone away.

'I told you there might be news which would help us

here at Spittal,' she said. 'And there has been such news. Our money troubles are over. Everything won't be settled at once, but I was able to raise enough money on my expectations to start on the things that need to be done.'

'What are expectations, Aunt Edeltraut?' asked Gudrun.

'Well, in this case they are money, which has been left to me in a will. Quite a lot of money. And this, my dears, is where the sad part comes in, because my godfather, Herr von Grotius, has died. He was a widower and we went to Zurich to make sure he had a fitting funeral. I can't tell you what a wonderful man he was and I was his favourite god-daughter.'

Edeltraut's handkerchief came out and she dabbed her eyes. It was a new one, edged with finest lace; there had been no time yet to embroider it with the von Tannenberg initials.

'Death is always sad,' she went on, 'but he was very, very old. Often in the last years he told me how tired he was; how he longed to be at rest.'

'And now he is, God bless him,' put in Mathilde.

Edeltraut raised her eyebrows at her sister. She never liked being interrupted and both the godfather and his legacy belonged to *her*. 'You can be certain,' she told the children, 'that we gave him a wonderful funeral. A dozen black horses bedecked with plumes, three carriages packed with important mourners . . . a service in the cathedral presided over by the archbishop . . . Everybody who mattered in the city was there. The Prince of Essen sent his equerry.' She dabbed her eyes once more, then put the handkerchief away. 'So tonight when you go to bed I want you to promise to kneel and say a prayer for Herr von

191

Grotius. I know you never met him, but he was a good man.'

'A very good man,' said Mathilde, who felt that she was not being allowed a fair share of the story.

'Because he begged us not to go into mourning we shall wear our ordinary clothes,' Edeltraut went on, 'except when we go out, when we shall have black armbands. There will be armbands for you also so that people know we care and I shall wear a black ribbon on my petticoat, as my mother would have done, because he was *my* godfather.'

But to Annika it seemed that the clothes the grown-ups were wearing were not very ordinary. The muff Edeltraut had thrown down was made of sable, Mathilde wore a jacket embroidered in gold thread and Uncle Oswald's shining new boots were made of finest kid.

Hermann had done his best to listen patiently, but now he got to his feet and moved to his mother's side.

'Does that mean I can go to St Xavier's?' he asked excitedly. 'Does it? *Does* it?'

Edeltraut smiled at him.

'Yes, my dear, it does. That will be our first task – to get you ready for the Easter term. The time for you to serve your Fatherland has come!'

Hermann's face flushed with joy. He pulled back his shoulders and gave a perfect military salute.

'I am ready,' he said.

For a moment no one could think of anything except the noble way that Hermann was behaving. Then Edeltraut broke the silence.

'And now you will want to see your presents.'

The boxes were piled up on the low table. Gudrun

192

opened hers to find, in nests of tissue paper, a blue velvet cloak and hood with a matching muff – and a pair of white lace gloves.

'Oh, Mama,' she said – and her long pale face lit up. She slipped on the cloak and the hood, and wouldn't take them off the whole evening.

Hermann's present took a long time to unwrap; inside the embossed paper was a leather box with the monogram Zwingli and Hammerman, goldsmiths to the president of Switzerland, stamped on the side. Inside the box were several layers of green felt, and inside that was a statuette, in pure silver, of General von Moltke on his horse.

'Be careful of it, Herman,' said his mother. 'It's really valuable.'

'Thank you, Mother.' Hermann was delighted. 'I'll be able to take it to St Xavier's and show the others.'

'And now you, Annika. This is what you wanted, isn't it?'

She handed her a box wrapped in brown paper. Annika took the first present from her mother with eager hands. Inside was a pair of rubber galoshes. Annika thanked her warmly, but she had seen at once that they were a size too small.

The next two weeks were spent in getting Herman ready for St Xavier's. This was not a simple matter. Herman had a list of the things he had to have and they were many.

'I shall need two dress uniforms and a new pair of riding boots and a hard hat with a badge and my own pistol ... and a double-breasted greatcoat with wide lapels ... and six pairs of white kid gloves ...'

It was now that a new figure entered the lives of the

family at Spittal: Herman's friend Karl-Gottlieb von Dammerfeld. Karl-Gottlieb had gone to St Xavier's at the beginning of the year and now he sent little notes to Herman telling him about the things that were not on the official list but everybody had to have if they were not to become a laughing stock, like slippers made of deerskin and silver tooth-mugs inscribed with the family crest.

Because the roof of the hunting lodge was being treated for woodworm, Gudrun and her parents were staying at Spittal until the repairs were done. But even Gudrun, who worshipped Hermann, sighed when the post brought another letter from Karl-Gottlieb.

Annika had not been allowed to help the servants, but she was definitely allowed to help Hermann. She was allowed to polish his badges and clean his buttons and iron his shirts because she did it so much better than old Bertha, who had returned from the funeral, and better even than the new maid who had been engaged.

'I don't want you to think you've been forgotten, Annika,' said her mother. 'I have a lovely surprise planned for you later, but just at the moment I know you will like to see Hermann off safely. He's waited for this so long.'

Annika didn't mind helping Hermann, but she was amazed at how much he longed to go to a place which sounded to her like a kind of prison. The boys slept forty to a dormitory on iron beds, they marched everywhere to military commands and the punishments were awesome.

'Sometimes they handcuff a boy's hand to his foot or give him ten lashes.'

'But wouldn't you be terrified?'

'No, because I won't be disobedient. I'm going to win the Sword of Honour, you'll see. And when I come out I'll be an officer in a cavalry regiment with two horses of my own, and if there's a war I'll defend the Fatherland and win the Iron Cross.'

Because Hermann had to be measured for new clothes and boots, they had to drive to Bad Haxenfeld, and since Annika had a good eye and Hermann liked having people to show off to, both she and Gudrun went with him on these shopping trips.

And it was there that Annika met the last person in the world she expected to see.

With the weather growing warmer, more and more visitors had come to the spa. There was a Lithuanian nobleman who was mad, but nicely so, and who stood on the steps of the casino handing out red roses to anybody he liked the look of, and a famous actress with an inflamed liver and a tiger cub on a lead. A band played in the park now as well as in the pump room. Men in white flannels brayed on the tennis courts, and brightly painted boats, ready for hire, appeared on the lake.

Zed had driven them in. He'd been offhand and grumpy since he took Annika to hear the gypsies, and didn't seem interested in the good fortune that had come to Spittal.

'I've never heard of any godfather in Switzerland,' he said. 'And why hasn't Bertha been paid?'

'She will be, I'm sure,' said Annika. 'Only there's so much to do. Once Hermann goes away . . .'

In Bad Haxenfeld, Zed went as usual to help the Baron and wheel him to the baths. The old man was starting on a new course of thalassotherapy, which meant that seaweed had to be brought from the Baltic and mixed with the spa water because it was rich in iodine. Seaweed is slippery stuff and the Baron liked to have Zed to lift him in and out of the squelchy fronds.

Meanwhile, Annika, with Gudrun and Frau Edeltraut, accompanied Hermann to the tailor, where his dress tunics were taking shape.

The fitting took a long time because Karl-Gottlieb had told him that in spite of what it said on the prospectus for the college, the cadets were now wearing their collars at least two centimetres higher than in the diagram. This annoyed the tailor, who said that such a collar would scratch the young gentleman's chin, but Karl-Gottlieb had already written that a sore chin was regarded at St Xavier's as a sign of manhood, and the tailor was overruled.

After that Edeltraut went to meet Mathilde in a dress shop. Her sister was spending altogether too much money on her own clothes since the visit to Switzerland and needed watching.

'You can go to Zettelmayer's for coffee and cakes,' she told the children. 'I'll meet you at the hotel.'

Zettelmayer's was the best pastry shop in Bad Haxenfeld; its cakes were famous all over the province. Everyone who could afford it came there; people taking the cure or people driving through the town. The shop overlooked the park; the tablecloths were rose-coloured, the chairs were pink velvet and gilt, and the smell wafting out – of coffee and cinnamon and chocolate and apricots – stopped people in their tracks.

Gudrun and Hermann ordered hot chocolate and went over to choose their cakes. There were iced eclairs, which were wheeled away like patients in a hospital to be injected with fresh whipped cream. There were wild strawberry tartlets, the fruit as red as drops of blood, and almond biscuits shaped like stars.

Hermann chose a nut-layer tart with confectioner's custard and Gudrun, as always, followed him and chose the same – but Annika hesitated. She knew all the cakes, she could have baked all of them except one: a small squat bun, very dark in colour, but not, she thought the darkness of chocolate. She studied it for a while and then asked the lady what it was.

'Ah – that's a local speciality. A Norrland Nussel. It's made of chestnuts and molasses and a touch of tansy. You won't find it anywhere else.'

'Can one get the recipe?' Annika asked. 'Or is it secret?'

'Bless you, no. I'll write it out for you. Are you from Vienna?'

'Yes.'

'You'll know about patisserie then.'

Annika nodded and took her bun to the table. It was unlike anything she had eaten before – a dark and serious taste, but sumptuous too – and she looked forward to sending Ellie the recipe. But Hermann, once again, was not at all pleased with her.

'Why do you always talk to waitresses and servants? It's not the thing. You're making us conspicuous.'

Their table was by the window and Annika sat watching the people outside. Children bowled hoops, nursemaids pushed prams and everywhere the patients in wheelchairs or on crutches lifted their faces to the sun.

Then suddenly she leaned forward. It couldn't be . . . except that it was. No one else's bottom stuck out like that; no one else born and bred in Vienna would wear such a violently Scottish tartan dress; no one else tugged at the

197

hand of her exhausted governess so fiercely. It was Loremarie Egghart and she was coming up the steps, pushing open the cafe door. The governess shook her head, but Annika could have told her she was wasting her time. If Loremarie wanted to eat cakes at Zettelmayer's, then that was exactly what she would do.

'I want a caramel sundae with two straws and a chocolate eclair – a round one, not a long one,' she was announcing in her loud and piercing voice, while the governess (a new one whom Annika had not seen before) tried to call her back.

'You know your mama wishes not—' she began in terrible German.

But Loremarie had caught sight of Annika sitting at her table. She stopped dead on her way to the counter. She filled her chest with air as if she was an opera singer about to launch into a tricky aria.

Then she pointed at Annika and in an accusing shriek she said, 'You're a thief! You're a dirty, disgusting thief!' Her voice rose even higher. Then, '*You stole my great-aunt Egghart's trunk!*' yelled Loremarie across the cafe floor.

CHAPTER TWENTY-ONE

THE EGGHARTS ARE
DISGUSTED

It was Leopold, the Eggharts' snooty manservant, who had brought the appalling news to his employers.

'I had it from the filing clerk in the office below the lawyers. She's engaged to the boy who cleans up for Gerhart and Funkel and he swears it's true. He carried it to the storeroom.'

'But that's outrageous. It can't be allowed. I've never heard anything so shocking!' said Herr Egghart.

'The trunk belonged to OUR great-aunt. She had no business to leave it to that little kitchen girl,' said his wife. 'No business whatsoever.'

'But, Mama, you said it was just rubbish in the trunk. You said I couldn't use it even to dress up,' said Loremarie.

'So it is rubbish. And probably full of germs too. But that has nothing to do with it.' Frau Egghart's bosom was definitely heaving. 'It was OUR great-aunt, so it is OUR trunk!'

'Actually it was MY great-aunt,' said her husband. 'All the same, it's an impertinence. How dare she leave it away from the family after all we did for her? Giving her a home.'

'Nursing her with such loving care,' said Frau Egghart.

'I'm going to get to the bottom of this,' said Herr Egghart. 'Perhaps that kitchen child blackmailed her.'

'Annika could be very cunning,' said Loremarie.

'I'm going across to the professors' house. It's an insult to the family.'

The professors were at home but not pleased to be interrupted.

But when Sigrid announced the Eggharts they gathered themselves together and came downstairs.

'What can we do for you?' asked Professor Julius politely.

'You can get your cook's adopted daughter to return our great-aunt's trunk,' roared Herr Egghart, and the professor stepped back because Herr Egghart's voice, known as the loudest in Vienna, hurt his ears.

'The trunk she stole from us by making up to the poor old lady as she lay on her deathbed,' put in Frau Egghart.

'I can think of nothing more disgusting than cheating someone out of their property when they are no longer in their right mind,' said Herr Egghart.

Professor Julius had been taught by his mother not to hit people who came to the house, but sometimes he wished that he hadn't.

'Why don't you sit down?' he said. And then, 'It is true that the lawyers told us that Fräulein Egghart had left a

200

bequest to Annika, but as you know she no longer lives with us. We gave Annika's new address to the lawyers and they said they would send the trunk to her mother – to Frau von Tannenberg – to give to the child.'

'Well, I'm not going to leave the matter there,' said Herr Egghart. 'The trunk must be returned to us.'

'The lawyers gave us to understand that the contents of the trunk only had a sentimental value – old keepsakes from her days in the theatre and so on.'

Frau Egghart gave an indignant snort. 'Are you suggesting that it would not have had a sentimental value for US?'

'She was OUR great-aunt,' roared Herr Egghart, and Emil remembered Richard the Lionheart, at the sound of whose voice horses were said to kneel.

Loremarie, meanwhile, had crept out of the drawing room and made her way to the kitchen.

'Your Annika's a thief,' she said.

Ellie was sitting in the wicker chair, shelling peas. She had lost a lot of weight and she looked tired, but her voice when she spoke to Loremarie was firm and strong.

'*Get out of my kitchen*,' she said. '*And fast!*'

That night in bed under the goose-down duvet for which so many Hungarian geese had given their lives, the Eggharts were still muttering angrily.

'I'm going to write to Frau von Tannenberg. The trunk went to her; she will make Annika give it back. And if not we'll sue.'

'I've got a better idea,' said Frau Egghart. 'You know we're going to Bad Haxenfeld at the end of the month. Well, it's only about an hour's drive from there to the Tannenberg place – remember you looked it up? If we call on her and take her by surprise she won't have time to make up any excuses.'

Herr Egghart nodded. 'Yes, that might do. Perhaps I could get leave from the office a little earlier.' He pushed his leg out of bed. 'I'll be glad to get Dr Becker on to my varicose veins. They're giving me a lot of trouble.'

'Yes, Becker's a good man, but I've never met anyone who understood my oesophageal sphincter like that young French doctor in the massage room.'

'Your what?'

'My sphincter,' said his wife patiently. 'The ring of muscle between my stomach and my gullet. I told you, it's beginning to leak.' She yawned and settled herself back on her pillow. 'They say they've got a new treatment,' she murmured. 'Something to do with seaweed . . .'

In the middle of the night Herr Egghart turned over restlessly.

'She was MY great-aunt,' he muttered angrily, and slept again.

CHAPTER TWENTY-TWO

HERMANN'S HONOUR

Annika did not like Hermann. Quite apart from what he had done to Hector, she found him snobbish, selfish and overbearing.

But in the moment after Loremarie had called her a thief, and everyone in the cafe fell silent and stared at her, Annika saw another side to him. Hermann rose to his feet. He walked up to Loremarie, he clicked his heels.

'Allow me to introduce myself,' he said. 'I am Acting Cadet Hermann von Tannenberg.' He turned to Annika. 'This lady is my sister, Fräulein Annika von Tannenberg. Anybody who calls a member of my family a thief will have to answer for the consequences. If you have a brother, it will give me great satisfaction to challenge him to a duel.'

Loremarie stood stock-still, her mouth open. The governess tugged uselessly at her arm.

'I . . . don't have . . . a brother,' she stammered.

'Then perhaps your father would care to meet me. Ask him to choose his weapons – pistols or swords.'

Everyone was still staring, their cakes forgotten.

'Oh, Hermann,' breathed Gudrun adoringly. 'How brave you are.'

'Not at all,' said Hermann carelessly. 'Any insult to those with von Tannenberg blood must be avenged.'

But Annika now tried to return to the real world. 'Loremarie, I didn't steal your great-aunt's trunk. I know nothing about her trunk. How could I steal it? I haven't seen it since she died.'

'Yes, you have. She left it to you in her will because she was mad and it isn't fair. She was OUR great-aunt, so it is OUR trunk.'

But Hermann was writing something on a piece of paper. 'If your father would care to name his seconds,' he said grandly, clicking his heels once more, 'he will find me at this address. All I require now is the name of your hotel.' And as Loremarie gaped at him, 'The hotel where you are staying.'

'It's called . . . the Haxenfeld Hydro,' she mumbled, and then the governess, with a final tug at her arm, managed to drag her to the door.

'I don't understand it,' said Annika, bewildered. 'Mitzi said they took the trunk to the cellar after the old lady died, to have it thrown away. Could someone have stolen it from the Eggharts' house?'

'What happened to the trunk is neither here nor there,' said Hermann, waving his hand. 'What matters is that a member of the von Tannenberg family has been insulted. Leave this to me.'

But Gudrun had seen a difficulty. 'If the girl's father is not ennobled, you won't be able to meet him in a duel.' And as Annika stared at her, increasingly puzzled, she explained, 'A member of the aristocracy is not permitted to fight a duel with persons of lower rank. Do you know who he is? The father?'

'He's a councillor. And he wants to be a statue.'

Both Gudrun and Hermann stared at her as though she was mad. 'Well, with a statue Hermann cannot possibly fight,' said Gudrun.

'They've run out of seaweed,' said Baron von Keppel as Zed wheeled him back from the baths. 'Well, it stands to reason, having to drive it in 200 kilometres from the coast. The smell was awful. They said it was the iodine, but I've never smelt iodine that stank like that. And little flies came off it when they put it in the water. There was a woman making a dreadful fuss this morning because there wasn't any left. Viennese by the sound of her. She wanted to try it for her sphincter. Why she should imagine seaweed would work on sphincters I don't know. Her husband's come for his veins. A common family with an awful child. They're staying at the Hydro, I believe.'

Zed made agreeing noises. He liked Edeltraut's uncle, who paid him generously and was free of the self-pity that so many invalids suffer from, but he did not always listen to every word he said.

They met a party of men coming towards them who greeted the Baron politely but did not stop to talk. 'Undertakers,' he said, sighing. 'They're here for two weeks. I still miss the dentists. Though I did overhear something quite entertaining yesterday. Apparently nearly a quarter of the coffins which are opened after a burial have scratch marks on the *inside*.'

'You mean the people had been buried alive?' said Zed. 'I expect they were making it up.'

'That's what I thought,' said Uncle Conrad. 'I suppose it must be rather a gloomy profession, you can't blame them for exaggerating a bit. Now the jewellers . . . they told some fascinating stories. There was one about a man in Paris – a famous jeweller with a crooked back who was in love with a dancer.' He broke off as Lady Georgina Fairweather came swooping towards him in one of her amazing hats.

'Have you heard that the seaweed has run out?' she said. 'It's a scandal when you think what we pay—'

Zed stopped the chair and switched off his attention.

By the time they were under way again the baron had forgotten the jewellers and was telling Zed about the man who had come the previous night and thought he was the German emperor.

'He walks through the park and clicks his fingers at a tree he doesn't like, and tells the groundsmen to cut it down. I must say, you do see life in this place.'

It was when they were buying the six pairs of white kid gloves which Hermann needed to wear with his dress uniforms that he told his mother what had happened in Zettelmayer's cake shop.

'This vulgar child came and accused Annika of stealing her luggage.'

'Her *luggage*? How could she do that?'

'Well, she didn't of course. The girl was mad. Some girl Annika knew in Vienna – Egghart, they're called. So I'm afraid I had to make it clear that if she persisted I would have to challenge her father to a duel.'

'Oh, Hermann!' Frau Edeltraut laid a proud hand on her son's shoulder. 'I'm afraid you're too young to fight a duel and you couldn't meet Herr Egghart – the family is sure to be completely common – but it's good to know that you defend your sister. What a master you will be for Spittal! In the meantime, though, these Eggharts will have to be dealt with. Poor Annika must have been very upset?'

'She was. And puzzled. Gudrun has taken her to the park.'

Uncle Conrad and Zed had just returned to the hotel when Edeltraut and her son entered his sitting room. 'Conrad, I'm leaving Hermann here with you. I have some important business to attend to.'

The Eggharts were not in their room at the Hydro, nor in any of the public rooms of the hotel. They had had a very busy morning in the treatment rooms, and now, while Loremarie was at the indoor skating rink with her governess, they were sitting on a bench in the orangery behind the hotel and admiring nature.

Actually, nature in the orangery was not very natural. The temperature was kept at twenty-five degrees by underground pipes and the plants were not really the kind that grew wild in northern Europe. Enormous fig trees, climbing bougainvilleas, breadfruit, hibiscus and of course orange and lemon trees hung with fruit. Water dripped into a fountain; the warm air was full of wonderful scents.

It was like being in a jungle without the unpleasant things that might have been found there, like jaguars or tribespeople with blowpipes, or snakes – and Frau Egghart was feeling romantic. She put a podgy hand over her husband's, but he looked so surprised that she took it away again.

'Perhaps we could go dancing in the pump room tonight?' she suggested.

'Dancing?' said Herr Egghart. It always made him nervous when his wife became romantic. 'We haven't been—'

But at that moment the door of the orangery was filled by the tall figure of a grandly dressed woman, carrying a sable muff.

The councillor rose to his feet and bowed as he recognized Frau Edeltraut von Tannenberg. The Eggharts had meant to drive to Spittal when they first came to the spa, and get back their trunk, but there was so much that needed doing, not only to their veins and their sphincters but to other parts of their bodies which the doctors had not been happy about, that they had not yet made the journey.

And here, now, was the woman they had wanted to see.

'Won't you sit down,' said Herr Egghart, pointing to the bench. He had forgotten just how tall and imposing Annika's mother was.

'Thank you, I prefer to stand. I have come to inform you that I will NOT have my daughter upset. I will not have her accused of stealing and lying. It is an outrage!'

'But we haven't—' began Herr Egghart.

'No, but your daughter has. She has accused her in a public place – MY daughter, a von Tannenberg.'

'We don't know what Loremarie has said,' began Frau

Egghart, staring at a silver brooch on Frau von Tannenberg's collar. It seemed to be the family crest. She could make out a mailed fist and the words: 'Stand Aside, Ye Vermin Who Oppose Us!'

'If you have lost your luggage it seems to me quite extraordinary that you should allow your daughter—'

'Please, please!' Herr Egghart put up a hand. He was still shouting but not so loudly as before. 'You see, we were told that our great-aunt . . . OUR great-aunt . . . had left her trunk to your daughter in her will. So naturally—'

'I'm afraid I don't know what you're talking about,' interrupted Frau Edeltraut. 'If Annika has been left anything it would have been sent to Spittal and it has not been. My son, who is devoted to his sister, wishes to fight a duel to avenge the insult. He is of course too young but my brother-in-law, who was the fencing champion of his year at university, would be willing to meet you.'

'No, no! It's a mistake. It's all a mistake. We were obviously misinformed.' Herr Egghart was sweating. 'We were told that—'

'I'm afraid I am not interested in what you were told. I'm concerned like any mother with her daughter's wounded feelings. Ever since I found Annika again I have made it my business to see that she is spared anything unpleasant or sad.'

Herr Egghart mopped his brow. 'Yes, yes. Loremarie will be made to apologize.'

'I would prefer it if you kept your daughter right away from our family. Meanwhile, I am prepared to let the matter drop, but any such insult in the future will have the gravest consequences.'

Left alone again, the Eggharts fell back against the bench.

'After all, it was probably full of germs anyway,' said Frau Egghart.

'What was?' Her husband's heart was still racing. Duels were illegal, but people fought them just the same. Frau Egghart's brother probably had a duelling scar – a great gash puckering his cheek.

'The trunk,' said his wife. 'The belongings of old people are always infected and unclean. I said so from the start.'

CHAPTER TWENTY-THREE

BEACHCOMBING

Although Annika had been very upset by Loremarie's accusations, what she felt most when she returned to Spittal was gratitude to her new family. Hermann had defended her, Gudrun had soothed her – and her mother had attacked the Eggharts like a tigress. It was time to put the past behind her and become a proper von Tannenberg – and this meant not writing so many letters to Vienna and constantly asking for writing paper and stamps, and it meant not making up recipes inside her head. She would send the instructions for making Norrland Nussel to Ellie and then she would put away her pinafores once and for all and really learn to love Spittal.

Not just the farm and Rocco and the frogs – anyone could love horses and frogs – but the house itself and the estate and all the people in it.

It was easier because it had at last stopped raining; patches of dry ground appeared, and the lake now sometimes showed glimmers of blue.

Workmen had been called in – plasterers and carpenters and roofers to repair the leaks, and new servants had been engaged – but what occupied everyone in the house was getting Hermann ready for St Xavier's. The day when he would go was getting very close, but Hermann did not seem to be nervous in the least. It was rather Gudrun who became sadder and sniffier by the hour.

'It will be like a tomb without him,' she said again and again.

It had been decided that both Edeltraut and Uncle Oswald would take Hermann to St Xavier's, which was some 200 kilometres away, in the direction of Berlin.

'But of course I shan't take him into the actual building,' said Edeltraut. 'It would shame him to be accompanied by a woman. I will wave goodbye at the gate and Oswald will take him inside.' She gave a brave smile. 'As the mother of a soldier of the Fatherland I must not allow myself the luxury of tears.'

'But he'll come home for the holidays, won't he?' asked Annika.

'Only for a few days in the year. To train a youth to become a worthy servant of the emperor takes every minute of every day.'

Annika was silent. If Hermann did not come home he would not ride Rocco. She wanted to ask what would happen to the horse, but she didn't. If Rocco was to be sent away or sold, she did not know how Zed would bear it.

*

A few days after the visit to the spa, Annika went down to the stork house to say goodbye to Bertha. As Zed had hoped, her brother had asked her to come and live with him; he was lonely without his wife and he thought they would get along well enough.

She was sitting in the carved chair and stroking Hector, who had managed to climb on to her lap and was hanging down on either side of it.

'My brother would have him, he likes dogs and he's got a big enough place, a proper farm,' she told Annika. 'He'd have Zed too, he knows he's a good worker, but Zed's in a funny mood. I can't get any sense out of him at the minute. Best to leave things as they are.'

'I'll miss you, Bertha,' said Annika.

Bertha nodded. 'And I'll miss you.'

But Annika knew whom Bertha would really miss. She and Zed had been together for four years now. They had nursed the Freiherr; Zed was almost like a son.

Annika had thought of the north Germans as dour and uncommunicative, but Bertha left sobbing. She clung to Wenzel's hand and when the time came to embrace Zed it seemed as if after all she would refuse to go with her brother.

'I've been here for more than sixty years,' she said.

But Zed helped her up into the cart, and promised to come on a visit, and, accompanied by howls from Hector, she was driven away down the lane.

'It's not far away, my brother's farm at Rachegg,' she had said to Annika before she left. 'You can drive it in a day. You'll remind Zed that there's always a place for him when I've gone, won't you?'

'Yes, I will. But would there be a place for Rocco?'

'Rocco belongs to Hermann, my dear, never forget that.'

The following week Hermann left for St Xavier's. Gudrun was so affected by the sight of her cousin in his travelling clothes – the military cape, the peaked cap with the brass insignia of the college, the little swagger stick that cadets were supposed to carry so as to get used to handling them when they were commissioned – that she gave an anguished gulp and disappeared off to her room.

Hermann had asked that the staff could be assembled in the courtyard so that he could make a proper farewell speech. He knew that this was what the master of the house was supposed to do, but the ceremony fell rather flat. Bertha had gone, Zed did not turn up, Wenzel was too deaf to hear a word that Hermann said, and the new maids hadn't been there long enough to understand what an important occasion it was.

All the same, Hermann did well, asking the staff to give his mother the loyal service they would have given him if he hadn't been going away. Then Wenzel brought the carriage round, but just before she stepped in after Hermann, Edeltraut turned round and bent down to put her mouth close to Annika's ear.

'Don't think I've forgotten your surprise, my darling,' she whispered tenderly. 'I would never do that. As soon as Oswald and I get back I shall get to work on it. You deserve no less.'

After they had driven off, Mathilde took her gulping daughter to the hunting lodge to see how the repairs were getting on and Annika made her way to the farm.

She found Zed in the paddock, schooling Rocco – except that 'schooling' did not seem to be the right word because Rocco was so obviously enjoying himself. Zed rode with a saddle but without stirrups as he took Rocco through his paces: the extended trot, the half-turn, the square halt . . . When he paused, the horse turned his head as if to say, 'Come on, what's next?'

'What you're doing, that's dressage, isn't it?' she asked.

'I suppose so. It's just making sure he understands me exactly – and I understand him.'

'Do you make him go over jumps?'

'No. I could do – he'd do anything you asked – but horses have talents, just like people . . . and his is for this . . . for becoming part of another person. But I don't teach him tricks.'

'Don't the Lipizzaners do tricks?'

Zed shook his head. 'Everything they do comes from their natural movements. If you watch colts loose in a field they rear up and show off to each other or fight. All those statues in which horses do the levade and the riders look as though they're going to slide off – in the stud at Zverno I saw them do that again and again. Rearing up is easy enough, but holding the position needs a terrible lot of strength in the back and the legs, and Rocco's only just stopped growing.'

After this came the daily grooming, which Zed never left out. Annika could have done it on her own by now. Zed trusted her to sponge Rocco's eyes and nose, to oil his hoofs . . . to comb his mane and tail. She washed the brushes and the cloths; she brought fresh drinking water and plaited new wisps of straw to burnish his bright coat.

Caring for the horse did not depend, for Annika, on being allowed to ride. It was a thing in itself.

Today, when they had finished, Zed went to fetch Hector from his kennel.

'He's still missing Bertha,' he said. 'We'll take him for a walk. There's a bittern's nest in the reeds near that clump of oaks.'

'He doesn't seem exactly heartbroken,' said Annika as Hector panted and yelped ecstatically along the shore of the lake, disappearing into the reeds and emerging again, soaking wet and covered in mud. This time of year, when the river took its share of meltwater, more and more objects were washed ashore. Hector found egg-boxes and driftwood, torn-off trouser legs, a mouse trap . . .

They had reached the clump of oaks, but the bittern's nest was empty. The shore at this point curved into a little cove, where the mud was mixed with pebbles and coarse sand. Objects that came up from the lake were stranded here; it was one of Hector's favourite places. A headless pike interested him – he picked it up in his mouth, but rejected it in favour of a derelict handbag with a strap. The strap pleased him very much; he chewed it, growled at it, and attacked it suddenly without warning.

Now, though, came the awful moment of choice.

He was an intelligent dog. At the beginning he had tried to carry several things in his mouth and take them home, but this had ended badly. Now you could see him thinking, deciding . . .

'It might be worse,' said Zed. He had made it clear to Hector that the headless pike was not in the running, and it looked as though the handbag would be the chosen object. 'It doesn't smell too bad.'

But Hector had not finished. He dropped the handbag, put his head down and, with his stump vibrating, made his way once more round the edge of the bay. He found a dead freshwater crab, but he did not trust crabs, even dead ones, and a muslin nappy, which he tried out but did not care for. There was no challenge in nappies.

Then, with a yelp of fulfilment, he pounced.

'That will be it,' said Zed. 'Thank goodness it's not too big.'

They made their way to the water's edge. Hector had found a smooth leather box about the size of a postcard. It didn't look as though it had been in the water very long; the embossed edges could still be made out, and a few faded letters in gilt. The box was old, but it was not disgusting, and Hector now swivelled his good eye in their direction, ready to defend his treasure.

'It's all right,' Zed said to the dog, 'you can keep it. Come on, we're going home.'

But as he set off with the dog at his heels he saw that Annika was standing absolutely still. The colour had drained from her face.

'Please, Zed, can you get the box from him. Please.'

'I'll try. But he won't like it.'

But Annika could only repeat the one word, 'Please.'

'What is it? What's the matter?'

Zed looked at her. Then he turned to do battle with the dog.

Annika sat on the bench in the stork house, looking down at the photograph in her hand. She had known straight away, really, only it seemed so impossible. The catch was rusty and stiff, the leather case was swollen with water and the photograph, when she took it from its wrapping, was curled with damp.

But there she was, smiling out of the picture as she stood beside her artist in the doorway of her yellow house with its wisteria-covered balcony and the weathervane shaped like a crowing cockerel.

'You look so happy,' Annika had said when she had first seen the photograph.

And the old lady, ignoring the jewels on the bed, holding the picture close to her eyes, saying softly, 'So happy . . . so very, very happy.'

Zed had put the dog back in his kennel. Getting him to give up the leather box had been difficult; not even the sock-suspender had aroused in Hector such passion and desire.

Now he sat beside Annika on the bench and waited till she was ready to explain.

'It's her – it's La Rondine,' said Annika, her voice full of bewilderment. 'It's the actual picture she showed me. It's where she went to live with her artist when she gave up the stage.' She turned to Zed. 'I don't understand. This picture was in her trunk. It was right at the bottom of the trunk, under the jewels.'

'What jewels?' said Zed sharply. 'What are you talking about?'

'Oh, they weren't real – she had this friend, a jeweller in Paris who copied her jewels when she had to sell them. Someone must have opened it and thrown the picture in the lake. But who . . . and why?'

Zed was silent.

218

'Look,' he said after a while. 'You'd better tell me all of it. About the old lady and what was in the trunk.'

For a moment she hesitated, but Zed was her friend . . . so she told him about reading to the old lady and how she had got fond of her and about the hunch-backed jeweller in Paris who had been so kind – and about swaying and strewing from her swing high over the heads of the people.

'I really loved her,' said Annika, blowing her nose. 'Only then she died.'

'And this girl Loremarie said she'd left the trunk to you?'

'Yes. But I thought she was lying – well, she was – I never heard anything about it. We thought it had got thrown out.'

She had turned away so that he couldn't see her face. Zed gave her a few minutes. Then he put a hand on her arm.

'Annika, it would be best to say nothing about the trunk or the photo to your mother when she comes back. I'd like to see if I can find out what happened first. You don't want to worry her.'

Annika looked at him with amazement.

'How can I say nothing? I can't keep things from her . . . she's my *mother*.'

'He has been given to the Fatherland,' said Frau Edeltraut. 'Hermann's great adventure has begun.'

She sat at the head of the table, magnificently dressed in crimson lace. The table had been laid with a damask cloth, crystal goblets and the best silver. The food was properly cooked; there were carafes of wine. Uncle Oswald sat at the far end, with Mathilde and Gudrun on one side and Annika at the other – but Hermann's place, beside his mother, was empty.

'He was so proud. So brave,' Edeltraut went on. 'There was never a backward glance as he walked up the drive, was there, Oswald?'

'Not one. He marched to his fate like the great soldier he will be.'

Edeltraut nodded and sighed. Now, as the new maid came through with the second course, Edeltraut instructed her to refill their glasses. 'Even the children will want to drink this toast.'

She rose to her feet. 'To Hermann von Tannenberg – my son and the heir to Spittal.'

But when everybody had sipped their wine, Edeltraut had a second toast she wanted them to drink.

'And I want you to lift your glass to my godfather, Herr von Grotius, whose generosity has enabled Spittal to rise from the ashes and take its true place as one of the great houses of Norrland.'

'To Herr von Grotius – God rest his soul,' said Uncle Oswald, and everybody sipped again.

Though the meal was grand it was not exactly cheerful. This was partly because Gudrun, whenever she looked at Hermann's empty chair, began to sniffle and partly because of the coolness that had developed between Edeltraut and her sister about the way the money from Switzerland should be spent.

Annika did her best to enjoy the meal, but since Hector had found the photograph she was filled with an anxiety and dread she could not explain. And when the supper had been cleared, she went bravely up to her mother's boudoir and knocked on the door.

Edeltraut was at her desk, with Uncle Oswald standing beside her. They seemed to be working on some figures, but when Annika asked if she could speak to her, she turned round at once, and held out her arms.

'Of course, my darling child,' she said. 'I'm never too busy to talk to you. I saw at supper that you seemed very quiet. Is it because you are missing Hermann?'

'No . . . I mean I am missing Hermann,' said Annika dutifully, 'but it isn't that.'

'Well, I hope it isn't because you think I have forgotten the surprise I promised you. I would never forget a promise to my new-found daughter. Never! Especially one that will bring you so much joy!'

'I know,' said Annika. 'I know you wouldn't.' She had reached the desk and seen a photo of Hermann, cradling a woolly puppy in his arms. 'Oh,' she said, 'is that Hector?'

Edeltraut's face had become very stern and sad. 'Yes. That was taken just after my father gave Hermann the puppy. Hermann absolutely adored it, he couldn't let it out of his sight. And then there was this tragic accident.'

'With the fireworks?'

'What? No, no – that's one of Zed's stories. The poor little thing was run over. It got tangled in the wheels of the hay-cart from a neighbouring farm. The man was going too fast, whipping up his horses . . . Bertha was there when it happened and she took him down to her hut. I was for putting the little thing down, it was in such agony and I can't bear to see animals suffering, but she and Zed managed to nurse it back to health. Only then they wouldn't let it go, they thought of it as their dog. Hermann was very good about it, I must say. That boy has a generous heart. Now, my dear, what was it you wanted to see me about?' And as Annika looked at Uncle Oswald, 'I have no secrets from your uncle; you are quite safe to speak in front of him.'

So Annika took the leather box out of the pocket of her skirt and laid it on the desk.

'What is it?' asked Edeltraut, puzzled. 'Something you have found?'

'Yes. By the edge of the lake, in that little bay by the willow trees. It must have been washed up.'

She opened the leather case, and unwrapped the picture.

Edeltraut stared at the portrait of La Rondine and her painter, and showed it to Oswald, who handed it back.

'It's a nice picture . . . but . . .' Edeltraut was clearly at a loss. 'Does it have any meaning for you?'

'Yes, it does. I saw it in Vienna. It's a picture of the Eggharts' great-aunt and the man she was in love with. And it was in her trunk. I put it back myself, and locked it, and the next day she died.'

'But that's impossible. Quite impossible. How could a picture from her trunk end up in Spittal Lake?'

'I don't know,' said Annika miserably. 'I told Loremarie I hadn't seen it and I haven't, but . . .'

Both Oswald and Edeltraut were now poring over the photo, their brows furrowed.

'You're absolutely certain this is the same picture?'

Annika nodded. 'Absolutely. I looked at it for a long time and I remember the edging. I know it's a bit smeary, but it's the same one. I'd swear to it.'

'So you're saying the trunk must have got to Spittal after all. This is a very serious business. I swore to the Eggharts on my honour as a von Tannenberg that the trunk never reached us.'

'I did too,' said Annika, though she realized that her honour was not as important as that of her mother.

'Do you know what was in the trunk, other than the photograph?'

'Old clothes that she'd had from when she was on the stage . . . garlands . . . headdresses . . . glittery things. And some fake jewels . . . copies of the ones she'd had when she was famous.'

Frau Edeltraut got to her feet. 'This must be looked into most thoroughly. Even if the contents of the trunk were worthless they are yours by right.'

Uncle Oswald nodded. 'We'll go along to the station first thing in the morning and make enquiries. Very thorough enquiries. Meanwhile, perhaps you had better leave the photograph with us as evidence.' He put out his hand, but Annika slipped the case back into her pocket.

'Please, I'd like to keep it,' she said. 'It's all I've got to remember her by.'

Annika slept little that night. Her thoughts went round and round. Who would steal a trunk full of worthless jewels and old clothes . . . and why? Loremarie hated her, she knew; had she played a trick on her by throwing the picture in the lake? But the Eggharts had been nowhere near Spittal. It was absurd. Nothing made any sense.

She was so late getting to sleep that she did not wake when Zed rode past the window, and when she came down to breakfast, her mother and Uncle Oswald had gone.

'They're off to Bad Haxenfeld on some business or other,' said Mathilde. 'They don't know when they will be back. And Gudrun wants you to play cards with her. She's in her room.'

'All right,' said Annika listlessly.

It was a long day. Her mother and Uncle Oswald did not return till late afternoon and then they went straight into the boudoir. It was only after dinner that Annika was called upstairs again, and from her mother's grave face and Uncle Oswald's frown she realized that they had unpleasant news.

'I'm afraid you were right, Annika,' said her mother. 'The trunk did come to Bad Haxenfeld. It came while we were away in Switzerland and it was fetched from the station and brought here. And now I want you to be sensible and brave.'

Annika's heart began to pound. Perhaps she was wrong. Perhaps her mother wasn't going to say what Annika thought she was. If she didn't ask the question they were waiting for, if she said nothing . . .

But she moistened her lips and said, 'Who? Who fetched it?'

'The person who runs all the errands for Spittal, who uses the carriage, whom everybody knows and to whom they would give the trunk without question even though it was addressed to me.'

'Wenzel?' said Annika with a last glimmer of hope.

'No, my dear. Not Wenzel. I think you know whom I mean.'

There was no escape then. 'Zed?'

'Yes, Zed. I suspected it at once, there have been other incidents, but we had to make absolutely certain. It would have been dreadful to accuse him unjustly.'

'But . . . why . . . why would he steal my trunk? Why would he want old clothes and jewels that aren't worth anything?'

'Annika, Zed has not had your education. It would be natural enough for him to look inside the trunk – if only to check that the contents had arrived undamaged. And then . . . well, he's a gypsy, what would he know about jewels? He would see the brightness and the sparkle . . . and it's not true that imitation jewels are worth *nothing*. Nothing to people like us, but to a gypsy boy . . . You'll probably find there are travellers all over the country now who are wearing the poor great-aunt's pathetic treasures. And when he'd sold the rest or pawned them, what would be more natural than to throw the trunk into the lake?'

Annika had turned away, trying to deal with the sudden weight in her chest. Zed. But it made sense of course. It all made sense. He had asked her not to tell her mother. He hadn't wanted it talked about.

Her mother had found one of her own handkerchiefs and was dabbing Annika's eyes.

'My poor, poor child – you're not the first person to be betrayed by a friend, but I know how dreadfully it hurts. Now I'm going to tuck you up in bed myself and let the new maid bring you a hot drink and I'll stay with you till you're asleep. And whatever you do, you mustn't go down to the farm till the police have sorted everything out. You would only shame Zed.'

Her mother was as good as her word. She took Annika to her room and sat with her, and the maid brought her a glass of hot milk and two aspirins, which her mother insisted that she swallowed. 'For I can see you have a dreadful headache. All the von Tannenbergs get headaches when they're upset.'

Annika had been awake most of the night before and so she did sleep. She slept deeply. But in the morning she woke early and dressed – and though she knew it was very wrong to disobey her mother she very quietly let herself out of the back door and made her way down to the farm.

She had to see Zed and talk to him. If he apologized and explained it would be all right. The trunk didn't matter, it was that he had lied.

But perhaps he hadn't. Perhaps he could tell her something that made it all right.

There was something funny about the stork house. At first she thought the storks had gone, there was such a feeling of emptiness and desertion. But they were still there, sitting on their eggs. She pushed the door open.

'Zed?'

But she knew already. It wasn't the storks that had gone.

Behind her the door was opened quietly and she spun round.

It was old Wenzel. 'Thought you'd be down. Zed's gone.'

'The police?'

He shook his head. 'He didn't wait for them. He went in the night.'

Then from the kennel behind the house, she heard Hector whining. 'I came to fetch the dog,' Wenzel said.

'I'm to keep him till Bertha's brother comes to take him away.'

'Do you know anything . . . about where he's gone?'

'No, I don't. And you'd better not ask too many questions – stay away from the farm, I would.'

'But what about Rocco?' Annika asked. 'What will happen to Rocco?'

Old Wenzel looked down at the ground.

'He's taken Rocco,' he said.

CHAPTER TWENTY-FOUR

ZED RIDES

When he left Spittal, close on midnight, Zed had taken two saddlebags and nothing else. One was packed with a change of clothes, a loaf of bread, such money as he had, a map, and the compass given him by the Freiherr. The other contained a halter and rope for Rocco, a supply of oats, a brush and a hoof-pick. The horse had been shod recently, but with a journey of more than 700 kilometres ahead of him, he would need to be alert.

He had ridden without stopping; all he wanted was to put as much distance between himself and Frau Edeltraut as possible. Her accusations and the threats of her brother-in-law had at first only angered him, but the anger was quickly followed by fear. He knew the power of the von Tannenbergs. They could have him imprisoned or deported and they would not hesitate to do so. No one would believe his word against theirs.

Yet at Bad Haxenfeld he had halted. His road south led past the station, it skirted the town. He was in a desperate hurry; he had certainly not stolen Annika's trunk, but he had taken Rocco. He felt no guilt about this. He could not have left the horse at Spittal at the mercy of Frau Edeltraut's whims, but in the eyes of the law he was a thief.

All the same, he had turned off into the town and ridden Rocco into the stable yard of the Majestic and now, as he left the spa behind, he was glad because he knew the truth.

He leaned forward in the saddle and urged Rocco on and the horse broke into a canter on the grassy verge. There was a thin moon in the sky and the air was still. He was free – free of the von Tannenbergs with their snobbish grandeur, free of the endless jobs on the farm . . . free to join his mother's people on the great Hungarian plain with its poplar trees and its wind-powered wells and its herds of wide-horned cattle.

And he was free of Annika and her troubles.

There was nothing he could do for her. Annika worshipped her mother. Even if he could bring himself to tell her the truth she would never believe him.

So why did he keep remembering silly and unimportant things? Annika the first day he had met her, asking if there was more mangel-wurzel . . . Annika running her fingers through Rocco's mane . . . and barrowing feed for the sheep in the rain, her pigtails turning to sodden ropes of moisture . . . He could see her trotting down the lane to the farm, pulling down a branch of witch hazel and sniffing it . . . and her streaming eyes as she chopped onions for soup.

He pushed the memories away. She was a gallant girl and he liked her, but that had nothing to do with it. He was bound for his mother's people and a new life if he escaped, and it would not be easy. Zed knew enough about the gypsies to realize that the dream of freedom and companionship had its dark side. There were thieves among them as well as people with big hearts; and women who let their children go filthy, with lice and matted hair. Old Izidor was honourable and so were his immediate kinsman, but others were not.

But they were his people now. He would throw in his lot with them, at least till he was old enough to manage on his own, and they would be good to Rocco. That was what mattered. A place where no questions were asked and the horse was safe.

Just before dawn he came to the river he would follow south towards its source. He dismounted and walked Rocco up and down before he let him drink.

There was grass by the bank and an oak tree, its branches hanging over the water. He tethered Rocco so that he could crop the turf. Then, using the saddlebag as a pillow, he lay down and slept.

Next morning the map showed him the route he had to take, across the wheat fields and orchards of central Germany and into Moravia – part of the Austro-Hungarian Empire – which he would have to cross to reach the Danube.

The distance was awe-inspiring; he only had enough money to buy oats for Rocco and a little food for himself and the horse was too young to be ridden hard.

But gradually he found himself enjoying the journey. Rocco's alert ears, his steady high-stepping gait affected

Zed. He rode him through woods, scattering herds of wild boar, and along streams where herons stood, one-legged, waiting for prey. Sometimes they had to take busy roads, jostled by donkey carts and drays, but mostly Zed found bridle paths and quiet lanes. There were bad days when the rain came down steadily and other days where there was nowhere to buy food and Zed watched Rocco graze with envy in his heart. Once a man in a loden cape stopped to question him, suspicious of a shabbily dressed boy on such a fine horse. Once they were followed by two infuriated dogs, great shaggy Komondors guarding a flock of sheep, but Rocco broke into a gallop and the dogs turned back.

But it was not the mishaps or dangers that troubled Zed; it was his thoughts. He still found it difficult to dismiss Annika from his mind. Memories of the silly Viennese song she had hummed when she polished the floors at Spittal, the look in her eyes when she first saw Hector, wouldn't leave him.

There was nothing he could do for her, he told himself again and again. He had only known her a few weeks. She would be all right; she would manage.

It was just that she had been – a *friend*.

The last week of the journey was desperately hard; both he and Rocco were getting very tired. As they stumbled over the steep hills and through the rocky gorges of Moravia there were times when Zed thought he could not let the horse go on.

Then one morning he rode down from the hills between fields and orchards coming into blossom, and saw before him the wide, slow-moving Danube, with its barges and pleasure steamers and tugs. This was the most important waterway in Europe. The towpath east led to Hungary and the plain where his gypsies were camped.

The towpath west followed the river to Vienna, where the Danube flowed through the city's heart.

Zed dismounted and stood looking at the water. He stood there so long that Rocco became impatient, gently butting Zed with his head.

'All right,' said Zed to his horse, and got back into the saddle. 'Let's go.'

CHAPTER TWENTY-FIVE

ANNIKA'S SURPRISE

In Spittal it had started to rain again. The frogs trod on each other's backs and however many the storks ate, or the cats killed, there were always more. The season for shooting ducks was over, so Uncle Oswald shot land animals instead: hares, rabbits and what he called vermin, which seemed to be anything that got in the way of his gun. Gudrun missed Hermann and mooched about, waiting till she could go back to the hunting lodge. The new servants were efficient but unfriendly.

Annika was lonely. She had been sure that the farm would be put right now that there was money again, but she was wrong. No new livestock was bought in, none of the buildings were mended. Wenzel had a boy from the village to help him, but there was less and less to do. There were rumours that Edeltraut was going to buy a motor and the carriage horses would be sold. The stork house stayed empty.

A week after Zed had run away, Bertha's brother came to collect the three-legged dog. Hector travelled in style, lying on a pile of sacking, his head resting on the sock-suspender, his eel trap by his side.

Annika ran down to say goodbye, leaning over the side of the cart to stroke Hector's woolly head.

'Is Bertha well?' she asked, and the old man said, yes, and she had sent her love.

He didn't mention Zed and nor did Annika. No one, she found, was talking about Zed.

'The poor dog is going away?' said a voice behind her, and Annika turned to find a girl with flaxen plaits wound round her head, and large blue eyes. She was carrying a pail with her lunch in it and was on her way to the village school at the head of the lake. Annika had met her often on the road and smiled at her. Her name was Frieda.

Annika sighed. 'Yes,' she said sadly. 'Everyone's going away.'

Frieda looked at her with sympathy. 'Why don't you come to our school? It's nice. We're going to make wreaths to decorate the church for Easter.'

'I'd love to come. But . . .' She shook her head. 'Perhaps I could ask again.'

It was from Frieda that Annika had learned what was to happen to the farm.

'There will be no animals, my father says. They'll all be sold and there's going to be sugar beet instead. Lots and lots of sugar beet.'

Annika had not heard this. 'Really? Are you sure?'

Frieda nodded. 'There's a lot of money in sugar beet. It

234

goes to the factory in Posen to be squeezed and sugar comes out.'

She picked up her pail again and trotted off, leaving Annika with her thoughts, which were not cheerful. She had heard a lot about sugar beet from Professor Julius, but nothing that had made her feel it would make up for living animals.

It was extraordinary how much she missed Zed. After all he had stolen her trunk and lied about it and fled in the night, taking a horse which did not belong to him. How could she miss him so badly?

But she did. It was impossible to believe that she had known him only for a few weeks. He had taught her so much; as soon as she was with him life became interesting: there was work to do and a future to think about. Sometimes she even wondered if what he had done was so terrible. If the little gypsy girl who had wanted to give her a kitten was now wearing Great-Aunt Egghart's fake earrings, was that such a crime? And then Annika would reproach herself, because theft was theft and could never be excused.

Her nights were strange now: sometimes she woke and thought she could hear Rocco's hoofs as he galloped past the window. And once, as she drifted off to sleep, she had the dream she'd had so often in Vienna: a carriage drew up outside and a woman got out, grandly dressed in furs. 'Where is she?' she said. 'Where is my long-lost daughter?'

But after that everything went wrong because when she came forward into the lamplight, she turned into a dumpy woman in a cheap woollen overcoat and a brown felt hat, and she did not smell of exotic perfume but of vanilla and green soap and freshly baked bread.

When she had this dream Annika felt guilty and ashamed, especially as her mother was being so loving to her, and seemed to understand exactly how she felt about Zed.

'My poor darling, I know so well what you are going through. I too have been betrayed by people I was fond of and trusted.'

'My father?'

'Him too – and my husband. He has written to tell me that he will never return to Spittal.'

'I'm sorry.'

Edeltraut shrugged. 'One must be brave. You must use what Zed has done to make you strong. And perhaps he is best where he belongs.'

'With the gypsies?'

'Of course. Learning to make his living in all sorts of disreputable ways. Rocco must of course be brought back – we cannot allow him to steal a valuable horse and go unpunished – but after that . . .' She sighed. 'I told my father you couldn't tame a gypsy boy, but he wouldn't listen.'

During these lonely days Annika spent more and more time wondering about the surprise her mother was planning for her. It was getting closer, Edeltraut said, very close, but there were preparations to be made which could not be hurried.

'Oh, I do hope I can bring it off,' she said. 'It will be so wonderful for you!'

Sometimes when she was alone with her mother, Annika would try and guess.

'We're going on a journey to Africa to see lions?' she

236

would suggest, and her mother would smile and shake her head.

Or: 'I'm getting a little boat with a red sail to take me over the lake?'

Or: 'My friends are coming from Vienna on a visit?'

But always her mother would shake her head and say, 'No, it's better than that!'

Then came the day when Gudrun and her parents moved back to the hunting lodge and Annika and her mother were alone.

And at dinner that night, Edeltraut raised her glass to drink a toast. Her eyes sparkled, she was flushed with excitement.

'To your surprise, my dear,' she said, stretching her hand across the table to lay it on her daughter's. And as Annika looked at her, she said, 'Yes, my darling child, I've done it! I was so afraid I'd have to disappoint you, but they've agreed. Come upstairs where we can be quite private. Oh, Annika, you're going to be so *pleased*!'

CHAPTER TWENTY-SIX

THE HARP ARRIVES

Ellie was sitting at the kitchen table, reading the black recipe book which had belonged to her mother and her mother's mother before her.

She'd got the book down because she wanted to check the quantities of sugar that were needed for some apricot preserve she was making. She had found the amounts almost at once, but now, some ten minutes later, she was still sitting with the book in front of her, and the page open at the entry that Annika had copied in on Christmas Eve.

'A pinch of nutmeg will improve the flavour of the sauce,' she read, for perhaps the hundredth time since Annika had gone.

Easter was over. On the Thursday before the holiday weekend, the emperor had given out purses to the poor and washed the feet of the twelve needy gentlemen who had been brought to him from almshouses in the city. Some of the needy gentlemen had enjoyed having their feet washed by the emperor, and some had not, but that was neither here nor there because the feet-washing was a tradition and had to be carried on.

After that, on Good Friday, the paintings and crucifixes in the churches had been shrouded in purple and the sounds of the street became muffled while the citizens mourned the death of Christ. And then on Easter Sunday the bells had pealed out joyously, there was music everywhere, the sun shone and everyone in Vienna seemed to have a new hat.

Ellie had done her best with Easter. She had not bought a new hat because her brown felt hat was only ten years old and had plenty of life in it still, but she had done all the things she had done the year before and the year before that. She had hard-boiled eggs for the little Bodek boys to paint; she had baked Easter muffins for Pauline and her grandfather, and a simnel cake for the professors, and she and Sigrid had taken flowers to the church.

But nothing gave her any joy.

'I have to get over it,' Ellie told herself. 'It's over two months since she went. Why doesn't it get better?'

But it didn't get better. If anything, missing Annika got worse.

There was a knock at the back door and Pauline came in carrying her scrapbook and a pot of glue. Since Annika had gone she came quite often to work in Ellie's kitchen.

'Have you had a letter?' she asked.

Ellie closed the book. 'No. Have you?'

'No. And Stefan hasn't either.'

'It's not so long since she wrote.'

'It's longer than it's ever been,' said Pauline. 'Perhaps her mother has sent her into the forest with a huntsman and told him to kill her and bring back her tongue, like in the stories.'

'For goodness' sake, Pauline, what's the matter with you? What have you got against Frau Edeltraut?'

'She's an aristocrat; they're always doing things like that. Look at Count Dracula. And that horrible perfume she wears, like mangled wolves.'

But Sigrid came in at that moment and told Pauline to stop upsetting Ellie. Hating people helped some people, but it only gave Ellie a stomach ache.

Pauline put down her scrapbook and the pot of glue and reached for the scissors. She had found a story she liked very much, about a little boy who had climbed into a hot-air balloon and been carried away, but a crippled lady had raced after it in her wheelchair and managed to get hold of the rope and hold on . . .

For a while there was peace as Sigrid started on the ironing and Ellie went back to the stove. Then Professor Gertrude's bell sounded from her bedroom. It was not her usual gentle ring but louder and more insistent.

'Something's the matter,' said Sigrid.

They trooped out into the hall and found Professor Gertrude, still in her dressing gown and slippers.

'It's come!' she said agitatedly. 'I saw from the window! It's come!'

No one asked what had come. Only one thing could make Professor Gertrude run round the hallway like a headless chicken, with her grey plait hanging down her back.

Her new harp. The great concert-grand harp ordered from Ernst and Kohlhart months ago; the largest and most valuable instrument of its kind in the city.

A ring on the front door was followed by a volley of thumps. Sigrid opened it to reveal an elegant delivery van with the words 'Instrument Makers to the Imperial Court' scrolled on the side, and two men wheeling an enormous wooden case towards them. It was painted a shining black, and the heavy clasps that fastened it were gold; it might have been the coffin of an exotic giraffe.

'We'll have to leave it at the door,' they said. 'We've got to take the trolley back,' and with much muttering and heaving they set their load down on the pavement, presented Professor Gertrude with the receipt to sign, and pocketed their tip.

Professor Julian and Professor Emil were both out, but Gertrude knew exactly what to do.

'Fetch Stefan,' she ordered – and Pauline ran off across the square.

Stefan was always fetched when something heavy had to be dealt with; he was by far the strongest of the Bodek boys, and he came at once. Behind him, although he had told them to stay at home, ran two of his younger brothers, Hansi and Georg.

Sigrid had already moved the hall table and the umbrella stand. Ellie took away the potted palm.

'You take the back end,' Professor Gertrude ordered Stefan, 'and I'll take the front.'

'Let me,' began Sigrid, but Professor Gertrude waved her away.

Even for Stefan the weight was enormous, but he managed to lift the case, and Professor Gertrude, walking backwards, made her way upstairs. On the third stair her bedroom slipper came off, on the sixth she became entangled with her dressing-gown cord, but she carried on, stepping bravely backwards with her bare foot.

At the landing they stopped. Gertrude's door was wedged open, but would the case go through?

'I think it would be best to unpack it here,' said Stefan, lowering the case.

On these matters Stefan was always listened to. Professor Gertrude took the keys hanging from one of the clasps and slowly, solemnly, she unlocked the case.

The inside, padded with gold-and-burgundy brocade, was unbelievably sumptuous. The harp itself was wrapped in a shawl of ivory silk, a present from the makers to those who bought this precious instrument.

Stefan lifted it out and carried it into Professor Gertrude's room. Then he came out again, the door was shut, and everyone went back downstairs, knowing that this was a time when Gertrude needed to be alone.

In the kitchen, Ellie started to brew coffee and reached for the tin of biscuits, which she kept for the little Bodek boys, but when she turned round there was no sign of them. Stefan was there, and Pauline, but not Georg – and not Hansi, and this was strange because Hansi suffered terribly from hunger and usually stationed himself by Ellie's biscuit tin as soon as he arrived.

'They must have gone home,' said Stefan. 'I'll go and see.'

He came back, looking puzzled. 'They're not there.'

They searched the downstairs rooms, the yard . . . But before they had time to become anxious, a kind of scrabbling sound came from the upstairs landing.

The harp case was where they had left it, flat on the ground. Sigrid lifted the lid. Inside the two little boys lay curled together like puppies.

'It's our house,' said Georg blissfully. 'It's the best house in the whole world. We're going to live in it forever and ever.'

The following day was a Sunday and Pauline and Stefan set off early to tidy up the hut. Even though they couldn't do plays without Annika, they still liked to use it for picnics and meetings with carefully chosen friends.

There were signs that the deserted garden was not going to be theirs for much longer. The barbed wire over the gate to the drive had been removed, perhaps to let the lorries through when the workmen came. Yet on this fine spring morning it was still very quiet and very beautiful. There was dew on the grass; a thrush sang on a branch of the cedar.

They walked past the pond, past the ruined steps . . . Then Pauline stopped dead. 'There's something behind the house. A wild animal. I can hear it snorting. I'm going home.'

But before she could turn and run, the wild animal appeared.

His rich coat was lit up by a shaft of sunlight; his black mane and tail rippled like silk. Because he was hobbled he could only walk at a measured pace, but he came on steadily, his ears twitching with curiosity and interest.

'I only like horses when they're in books,' said Pauline and backed away.

But Stefan now was staring at the door of the hut.

'I think the padlock's been—' He broke off. 'My God! Look!'

He had pushed open the door. On the floor, wrapped in the old grey blanket, and fast asleep, lay a completely unknown boy.

Three hours later, the compound behind the professors' house, which Ellie and Sigrid kept so tidy, looked like a junk yard. An old wardrobe, a washstand, a mangle and several portraits of the professors' grandparents in oils were stacked beside the wall, and on the blue bench where the servants liked to sit were the little Bodeks boys, their eyes on the door of the shed, which had been turned back into a stable. The lady in the paper shop was there too, ready with advice because she had grown up on a farm, and looking placidly over the half-door was Rocco, chewing a carrot.

But Zed was in Annika's bed in the attic, lost to the world.

'He's come from Annika,' Pauline had said excitedly, running into Ellie's kitchen.

'He's got something to tell us; he's ridden all the way from Spittal.'

Ellie had gone out and looked carefully at the boy standing in the yard, holding on to his horse. He was grey with exhaustion, and so thin that his cheekbones seemed to cut into the skin.

'Is Annika hurt?' she asked.

'No.'

'Or ill?'

Zed shook his head.

'Well, then, you'll let Stefan look after the horse; his uncle's a blacksmith, he knows what to do. As for you, you'll go straight in the bath while I get you some breakfast. Drop your clothes on the floor. Frau Bodek will find something for you to wear; her eldest is about your size. And then into bed.'

'But I have to—'

'You don't have to do anything,' said Ellie, 'except do as you're told.'

So now Zed slept, and the household waited.

It was late afternoon before he woke. Clean clothes lay on the chair beside his bed. He got up and looked out of the window at the view Annika had described to him – and suddenly he was glad that he had come to Vienna. They would not believe him when he told his story – no one would believe him – but he was glad that he had come.

First though he had to see to his horse.

He hurried down and into the yard. As soon as Rocco saw him he went into his 'Where have you been?' routine, whinnying, butting Zed with his head, stamping his hoofs . . . But the show he put on as a deserted horse was not convincing. A piece of apple hung out of his mouth; Stefan's uncle had brought straw for bedding; there were oats in his manger . . . and on the blue bench sat the Bodek boys, holding the fresh supply of carrots they had begged from Ellie in case he was overcome by hunger.

And now everyone was gathered round the kitchen table, waiting to hear Zed's story: Ellie and Sigrid, Stefan and Pauline – and the professors, who had suggested that they come downstairs, knowing how much Ellie hated the drawing room.

'I don't know if you'll believe me,' Zed began. 'Probably not, but what I'm telling you is the truth.

'When Annika came to Spittal everything was run down, the farm and the house . . . everything. There were holes in the roof, the servants had been laid off, the food was awful. The very first day I met Annika she was eating mangel-wurzels.'

Ellie made a shocked noise, but Zed went on.

'Annika thought that perhaps that was the way the aristocracy lived – toughening themselves up, not lighting fires, eating turnip jam.'

Another exclamation of horror from Ellie. 'You can't make proper jam from turnips,' she said, but Professor Julius gave her a stern look and she fell silent.

'I knew what was the matter,' Zed went on. 'Frau Edeltraut's husband was a gambler and there was absolutely no money left, but nobody explained this to Annika and it wasn't for me to tell her. Her mother didn't want Annika to get mixed up with the servants, but Annika likes to be busy and she came down to the farm to help me, and we became friends. And then Frau Edeltraut and her brother-in-law and her sister went off to Switzerland. They went on urgent business, they said – and when they came back everything was different.'

'In what way?' asked Professor Emil.

'Well, they were all wearing new clothes and they seemed to be in a very good mood and they'd brought presents. Expensive presents except for Annika's. She got galoshes that were too small for her,' said Zed, scowling for a moment as he remembered this. 'And then they started engaging servants and mending the roof and Hermann – Annika's brother – was got ready to go to a cadet school where the fees cost a fortune. And Frau Edeltraut told Annika that her godfather, who lived in

Switzerland, had died and left her all his money. A lot of money. She said he was called Herr von Grotius and they had gone to Zurich to give him a proper funeral.

'I'd never heard anyone speak of him, but I didn't think too much about it till the Egghart girl came and attacked Annika and accused her of stealing her great-aunt's trunk.'

'Loremarie attacked Annika?'

No one had heard this. The Eggharts were still away.

'Where was that?'

'At Bad Haxenfeld. She didn't attack her exactly, but she accused her in a coffee shop and Annika was very upset because she didn't know anything about it. And Annika's mother said no one at Spittal knew anything about a trunk and she defended Annika, and the Eggharts slunk off. But then . . .'

Zed had fallen silent, wondering again if anyone would believe the next part of the story. Why should they believe a boy they knew nothing about?

'Has Annika said anything about a dog . . . about Hector?' he went on.

Pauline nodded. 'He had an accident when he was a puppy and he has a leg missing. She likes him a lot.'

'Well, we were walking with the dog along the lake, Annika and I . . . and suddenly Hector pounced on a leather box, and inside was a photograph of the old lady that Annika used to read to before she died. The Eggharts' great-aunt. Annika had seen it before and she knew it was from the trunk and she was very upset because she had told Loremarie that the trunk hadn't got to Spittal. And I think it upset her altogether, remembering, because she was really fond of the great-aunt. La Rondine, she called her. It means a swallow and—'

'Yes.' Everyone round the kitchen table was nodding. 'She talked about her a lot. She thought she could stop her dying,' said Sigrid.

'Go on with your story,' said Professor Julius.

'Well, we thought it must mean that the trunk had arrived at Spittal after all and someone had thrown it into the lake. But it didn't make sense. I asked Annika to tell me what had been in it, and it didn't seem to be anything that mattered except to the old lady. And to Annika because she'd loved her. But I'd been uneasy about . . . everything really – and I told Annika not to say anything to her mother, and I would see what I could find out. But it was no good telling Annika not to tell things to her mother. She worships her,' said Zed, and heard Ellie give an enormous sigh. 'She did tell her and the next thing was that Frau Edeltraut and her brother-in-law came down late at night and said they'd made enquiries and the people at the station had sworn that I'd collected the trunk, and they were going to call the police and have me arrested.'

Zed looked up at the people gathered round the table. 'I don't know if you'll believe me, but I swear by Rocco's head that I'm telling the truth. And I was frightened because I knew Frau Edeltraut hated me because she thought her father had spoiled me and she was only waiting for a chance to get rid of me. So I decided to go and find my mother's people in Hungary; they're gypsies and I knew they'd take me in. But I'm frightened for Annika too because she ought not to be with a woman who tells lies – and worse.'

'Worse?'

'Yes. I think Frau Edeltraut stole the trunk, with the help of her brother-in-law.'

'No, no, that doesn't make sense,' said Professor Julius. 'Why should a woman in her position steal an old trunk full of worthless things? The lawyers were absolutely certain there was nothing of value there.'

'Yes,' said Zed. 'That's what puzzled me. So on the way south I stopped at Bad Haxenfeld to see the Baron von Keppel, Frau Edeltraut's uncle. He didn't really want to talk to me, but in the end he did – and then I understood.'

Zed had paused and was staring into space, remembering. It had been a raw, cold night when he fled from Spittal, and he had been shivering as he rode Rocco into the stable yard of the Hotel Majestic . . .

CHAPTER TWENTY-SEVEN

THE UNCLE'S STORY

Baron von Keppel was in bed, but though it was well past midnight, he was not asleep. His joints always hurt more at night and he had got used to reading, sometimes into the small hours.

There were many patients in Bad Haxenfeld who only slept fitfully. Lights were left on in the corridors of the hotels; porters and pageboys were on duty to check the window locks and renew carafes of drinking water.

So when he heard a knock at the door the Baron said, 'Come in,' readily enough.

But it was not one of the usual attendants who stood there.

'Good heavens, Zed! What is it? Has Edeltraut thrown you out?'

'In a way.'

Zed wore the armband he put on to work in the hotel. He was known to the staff. No one had stopped him as he rode Rocco into the stable yard of the Majestic and made his way upstairs.

'Well, I'll give you a job. My usual man is bone idle – I've been wanting to get rid of him.'

'Thank you, sir. Maybe one day, but I'm in a hurry. Only I want to ask you something. It's important.'

Now that he had broken his flight from Spittal, Zed was angry with himself. He had to get away as quickly as possible, not waste time getting mixed up in Annika's affairs.

The Baron had put down his book. 'Well, what is it?'

'It's about when the jewellers were here – three months ago.'

The Baron looked at him suspiciously. 'What about them?'

'You began to tell me something one of them had said. About a man in Paris and a dancer. Then Lady Georgina came and interrupted us and when we went on you'd forgotten what you were going to say.'

'Yes,' said the Baron sadly. 'I'm afraid that happens to me more and more often. It's dreadful getting old. This morning I forgot my grandmother's Christian name. I had to look in the family Bible. It turned out to be Serafina. You wouldn't think one would forget a name like that.'

'No. But I'd like you to try and remember the story you were going to tell me about the jeweller in Paris. The one with a crooked back.'

The Baron turned his head away. He seemed to be thinking. 'It's gone right out of my head,' he said apologetically. 'Unless it was the one about the emperor's sword stick and the doughnut?'

'No,' said Zed very quietly. 'It was the one about the jeweller in Paris. The one with the crooked back.' He paused and turned the lamp so that the light shone directly into the Baron's eyes. 'I would really like it very much if you would try to remember that.'

The Baron backed away from the light. He was remembering the other side of Zed: not the obedient bath attendant but the wild boy with Romany blood. There had been a band of gypsies in the neighbourhood a week or two ago. Perhaps they were camped outside, ready to rush upstairs and cut his throat.

'I only overheard snatches of the conversation,' he said. 'There were two men in the cubicle next to me. One was Viennese, judging by his accent, and the other one was French. It was the Frenchman who was telling the story. He'd just come back from Paris and he'd been to Fabrice's, the big jeweller in the Champs-Elysées, to do some business. It's one of the most famous firms in France and it used to belong to a man who was a bit of a legend. He had a crooked back and never married and he put all his feelings into his work. He used to make pieces for the tsar of Russia and people like that.'

Zed was listening intently. 'Go on, please, sir.'

'This man – the one with the crooked back – was in love with an actress, a chorus girl really. She used to swing high up over the stage and strew flowers . . .'

'La Rondine,' said Zed.

The Baron looked at him, startled. 'Yes. Something like that. The spotlight was on her face when she scattered the flowers and Crookback said she looked so joyous. Anyway, she went off with a painter and when she came back no one would employ her. But she still had her jewels and they were fabulous. She had the Star of Kazan and a chain of Burmese rubies and a butterfly brooch some duke had given her . . .

The Baron stopped speaking. He was frowning, staring at the curtained window. Then he sighed and went on.

'You have to remember I was next door; I didn't hear all of it. The Viennese chap he was telling the story to was a great splasher. Some people can't get into a bath without flooding the place. But it seems this actress, this Rondine, used to bring her jewels to Crookback to sell when she needed money, and he would take them and give her the price the pieces had fetched in the open market. And it was a fortune. Millions and millions of francs . . .

'But because he loved her he had the pieces he sold for her copied in paste or glass and gave them to her. Her eyesight wasn't very good by then and she used to hold the copies in her hands just as she'd done with the originals. She knew they weren't real, but she loved them just the same. She talked to them. You know what lonely people are like.'

'Yes,' said Zed. 'But that wasn't all, was it?'

'No. Apparently after Crookback died they went through his books and accounts and they couldn't find any record of the sales. And no one knew who had made the copies either, which really surprised them because everything has to be written down a hundred times for the tax people.'

The Baron stopped again, but Zed was still looking at him with those strange flecked eyes.

'The jeweller who was telling the story went out to supper with one of the partners in the firm. He was a very old man – the partner – and he didn't have much longer to live, but he'd been Crookback's apprentice all those years ago. And he swore that Crookback had never sold the jewels at all; he just gave them back to her and paid her the money out of his own pocket. Of course, you can say he was a very rich man, but I've never heard that rich men are famous for their generosity. He must have loved her very much.'

'And no one ever knew?' asked Zed.

'Only this apprentice – and he said nothing till he knew he was dying. I suppose he got tired of hearing jewellers described as greedy and money-grabbing.'

'I see. Did he say anything else – about what happened to La Rondine?'

The Baron turned his face away. 'She went back to Vienna. She came from there and one of her relatives took her in – her nephew was a councillor, a pompous and disagreeable man. She died in his house and everyone thought she died penniless; he was complaining about having to look after her. Apparently she left an old trunk with all her possessions to some orphan who had befriended her.' There was a pause. 'The jewellers were wondering how that had turned out.'

The Baron had finished.

'And you told this story to your niece? To Frau Edeltraut?'

'Yes, I did. But I swear I had no idea – even when I met Annika I didn't guess – not till the Eggharts came. But Edeltraut was desperate. She'd have done anything to save Spittal.'

Zed nodded. 'Yes. Thank you, sir.'

'You believe me, don't you?'

'Yes, I do.'

'Not that it matters. I'm too old to worry about the future. I wouldn't have told you now except for the galoshes. Annika's a nice little thing. If Edeltraut took the child's jewels she should have shared. You don't steal from your own daughter.'

Zed had finished his story.

'So you see,' he said, looking round the professors' kitchen, 'if the story is true and the jewels in the trunk were priceless, then Annika has been most cruelly robbed.'

CHAPTER TWENTY-EIGHT

COLLECTING EVIDENCE

Professor Julius now became a sleuth.

'We must get proof before we accuse Frau Edeltraut,' he said when they had finished listening to Zed. 'I believe that Zed is telling the truth, but there could be other explanations for the disappearance of the trunk.'

'What sort of explanations?' asked Professor Gertrude.

'I don't know. But Zed will agree with me, I'm sure, that we must look into this further before we confront her.'

'Yes, I do. That's partly why I came here. I don't even know whether a mother is entitled to the things that belong to her daughter. Maybe she hasn't committed a crime in the eyes of the law.'

The professors shook their heads. 'In Austrian law it is certainly a crime. The property of someone who is under age has to be kept in trust for them till they're grown up. It's twenty-one here – it may be different in Germany.'

So Professor Julius made a list of all the jewellers in Vienna and set to work, visiting them one by one to see if he could find the man who had heard the story of Fabrice and the Eggharts' great-aunt while in the baths at Bad Haxenfeld. He had some help from Professor Gertrude, but not very much. She was so shy that going into a jeweller's shop and asking peculiar questions upset her badly, and she always felt she ought to buy something to make up for wasting the jeweller's time, so that she came home with silver ashtrays and cigar-cutters and thimbles, which she did not want at all and which, when added together, turned out to be surprisingly expensive.

She was also very busy with her new harp. Harps have to ripen slowly, like fruit, and though her wonderful concert-grand had come seasoned and strung, it was a slow job keeping it at the pitch she required. Liquid 'plinks' and 'plonks' came from Gertrude's room whenever she had a spare moment, but there were times when she felt very sad because she knew that her harp would not come into its full glory till the last years of its life, by which time she herself might be dead.

As for Professor Emil, he did not help with the jewellers at all because he had been sent off to Switzerland to look for Herr von Grotius; and if possible to find his grave.

Zed had intended to remain in Vienna only as long as it took to tell Annika's story, but Professor Julius had said firmly that he would have to stay until everything was sorted out.

'We might need you to confirm anything we discover and check it with what happened at Spittal.'

Zed had tried to argue: 'I feel I should go, sir. I have hardly any money left and I need to get to Hungary.'

'The money is neither here nor there,' said Professor Julius. 'You can stay with us. It shouldn't be for long.'

'I suppose I could sleep in the hut if it's only for a few days,' Zed had suggested.

But nobody thought this a good idea. The hut was private property; and if he took Rocco it would only be a matter of time before he was discovered.

'Could he have Annika's attic?' Ellie asked, and it showed how completely she trusted Zed that she suggested this.

But Zed shook his head. 'It's hers. I wouldn't want to – it wouldn't be right.'

In the end it was Pauline who decided where Zed should sleep.

'He can come to the bookshop. There's a storeroom at the back – we can put a camp bed in there – and he can come round by the back lane to see to Rocco. Grandfather won't mind. He probably won't even notice.'

Pauline had been convinced that Zed spoke the truth the moment she saw him. 'I always knew no good would come of Annika turning into a "von",' she said, and she did her best to make Zed comfortable. Some hostesses do this by bringing their guests breakfast in bed or putting flowers in their room. Pauline did it by piling the books she thought would interest him on the upturned packing case that served as his bedside table.

She brought him a book called *The Heavenly Horses of the Emperor Wu-Ti*, who believed that his horses would carry people's souls to heaven when they died. She brought him a book by the Duke of Newcastle on how to train horses for dressage.

And she brought him one of her grandfather's most prized volumes, *On the Art of Horsemanship*, written by the famous Greek general Xenophon more than 2,000 years ago.

Zed had seen it in the Master's hands at Spittal. Now he picked it up reverently. There was a picture on the cover of Xenophon astride a black stallion on the shores of the Black Sea. His hands were thrown up as he gave thanks to the gods after a 2,400-kilometre march with his soldiers – and he rode without stirrups!

Zed opened the book.

On horses such as these even gods and heroes will appear, and men who know how to work well with them will look magnificent!

He was still reading by the light of the paraffin lamp, long after Pauline and her grandfather slept.

But when it came to looking after Rocco and admiring him, Pauline made it clear that real horses made her nervous.

'Rocco's just a person who happens to be a horse,' said Zed – but Pauline was not convinced.

To the little Bodek boys on the other hand, Rocco was a miracle of which they never tired. They burst out of their house as soon as they woke and went to the stable clutching carrots and pieces of apple which they begged from Ellie and which even Hansi only rarely ate himself. The baby, who had just learned to walk, threw up his hands and said, 'Up, up!' whenever he saw Rocco, and when Zed put him on his back he sat with his blue eyes wide with awe, and screamed horribly when he had to get down. Georg woke in the night, worrying in case Rocco, who liked to drink in the fountain, should swallow a goldfish.

Fortunately Stefan could control his younger brothers, but he did more than that. He took Zed to see his uncle, and the blacksmith shod Rocco and wouldn't take payment. When there were odd jobs to be done, Stefan shared them with Zed and divided the money he earned.

Zed had told him that Rocco did not really belong to him, and Stefan, who was usually so placid, became quite cross.

'Nonsense,' he said. 'Anyone can see he's your horse. You might as well say Annika doesn't belong to Ellie because Ellie isn't her mother. People belong to the people who care for them.'

For Zed, who had fended for himself ever since the Master died, the kindness he was receiving was overwhelming. Sigrid tore up two of the professors' old shirts and made him a new one. The lady in the paper shop gave him a rug for Rocco. Josef in the cafe saved the straw from his crates for Rocco's bedding.

And Ellie cooked him noodle soup, and schnitzels so big that they covered the plate, and sat over him while he ate.

'You're too thin,' she said. 'We've got to build you up.'

Zed mostly exercised Rocco at night, trotting down the long Prater Strasse to get to the park where the emperors of Austria had ridden for centuries, and he could let the horse go in a gallop.

But he did not always go so far as the Prater. Sometimes he rode quietly through the streets and squares of the Inner City and learned the history of Vienna from its buildings.

Here was the house where Mozart wrote *The Magic*

Flute and there the lodging where the deaf Beethoven had thumped his landlady's piano to death. Outside the university were monuments to great philosophers and famous scientists and explorers . . . and everywhere there were men on horseback carved in stone.

There was the famous statue of Prince Eugene in the Heldenplatz, the weight of his horse resting on a single hoof. The Archduke Charles, on a great charger, rode nearby, and Field Marshal Radetzky guarded the streets behind the town hall.

And often now Zed saw the real horses descended from the fabulous steeds these warriors rode. In the open-air compound beside the Hofburg Palace he saw the Lipizzaners being exercised – not dancing now, walking quietly with a groom leading one horse and riding another. Once at sunset, he met a procession of white stallions, blanketed in red and gold, returning to the Stallburg after a rehearsal in the riding school.

Rocco, when he saw them, always whinnied a greeting, but Zed would take him to task.

'Don't get ideas above your station, Rocco,' he told his horse. 'We're bound for a very different life.'

He was growing anxious. Each day he stayed in Vienna would make it harder to leave. Then, just a week after Zed came, the professors received a telegram from Emil.

The only Herr Grotius in Zurich is a shoemaker living on the north shore of the lake, who has definitely not died. No other Grotius, dead or alive, exists in the city.

'Well, that's half the evidence,' said Professor Julius. 'It seems that Frau Edeltraut was definitely lying.'

And then two days later, he walked into yet another jeweller's shop and was shown into the owner's office, where Herr Brett told him that he had indeed been to the conference in Bad Haxenfeld, and was happy to confirm that the story that the Baron had overheard was true.

None of the children could understand why the professors did not go straight to the police.

'If she invented her dead godfather and the jewels are real, she's obviously guilty,' said Pauline, who thought that Frau Edeltraut should be thrown into a dungeon straight away.

But Professor Julius said that the evidence so far was only circumstantial and Annika's mother had to be given a chance to explain, before she – and therefore Annika – was dragged through the courts.

'After all, inventing a godfather is not a crime, and though it certainly seems that the jeweller's story is true, we don't yet have absolute proof.'

So he and his brother Emil made a brave decision. They decided that they would travel to Spittal and talk to Frau Edeltraut themselves, and it was clear that they hoped she would somehow be able to clear her name. They would go at once because the university term began the following week and they would leave Professor Gertrude behind in case there was any unpleasantness.

So Sigrid packed two overnight bags for the professors in case they missed the night train back from Spittal and Ellie prepared ham rolls and bottles of lemonade because the food in the dining car disagreed with Emil.

And nearly two hours before it was necessary, because they liked to be early, the professors got into a hansom cab and were driven to the station.

They had only been gone a few minutes when Zed, who

had been cleaning Rocco's tack in the scullery, went upstairs to find Sigrid.

'Ellie's upset. She's crying into her pancake batter.'

Sigrid hurried downstairs. Ellie was not crying into her batter – she wouldn't have done a thing like that – but she was certainly crying.

'What is it, Ellie? What's the matter?'

Ellie lifted her head. 'I don't know . . . it's Annika. I don't feel right about her. If I could just see her for a few minutes to know that she's all right. I wouldn't even have to speak to her, just to see her – then I'd know.'

Sigrid looked at the clock. 'Well, why don't you go along too? The professors wouldn't mind.'

Ellie stared at her. 'I couldn't.'

'Yes, you could. Of course, you'd have to use some of your savings for the fare.'

'Oh, that's nothing. I'd use my savings a hundred times over if—'

'Well, that's all right then. Come on, I'll help you.'

Ellie's savings were not in the bank. Ellie did not trust banks. They were in a jam jar, which lived inside a tin with a picture of the emperor on it. The tin lived inside a hat-box and the hatbox lived on top of the wardrobe in her bedroom.

Because Ellie was not herself a natural climber, it was generally Sigrid who got the money down.

'There's plenty here,' Sigrid said.

'Are you sure you can manage on your own?' said Ellie in a worried voice.

'Of course I can manage. Zed'll help me, won't you?'

Zed nodded. 'Annika will be so pleased to see you, Ellie.'

And while Ellie was bundled into her coat, he ran into the Keller Strasse to fetch a cab.

The professors were travelling second class. First-class train compartments with their pink-shaded lights and starched seat covers were for special occasions – weddings and funerals.

Ellie on the other hand, like all the working people in the empire, travelled third class, which meant sitting on wooden seats and often sharing the journey with crates of chickens or baskets of rabbits on their way to market.

The third-class carriages were at the back of the train, and it was not till they reached Bad Haxenfeld that the professors caught sight of Ellie climbing down on to the platform – and then they were angry.

'Why didn't you tell us you were coming – travelling all by yourself like that? It was quite unnecessary!'

Outside the station they found a cab willing to take them to Spittal.

Professor Julius found the countryside interesting: the drainage ditches, the use of hedges as windbreaks, the rows of sugar beet – but Ellie looked round her with dismay. She had never seen such a bleak landscape.

But when they were put down by the courtyard gate, the size and grandeur of the house made them fall silent. Annika had not told them of the fortified windows, the battlements on the roof, the great iron gates, which they had to push open before they could walk across the cobbles to the front door.

Beside the door was a massive bellrope. Professor Julius pulled it and they heard the sound of the bell echo in the corridors of stone.

No one came.

The professor pulled the rope again. Still no answer. Then at an upstairs window they saw the face of a girl looking down at them before it vanished.

'There she is,' said Professor Julius.

'No,' said Ellie quietly. 'That wasn't Annika.'

They waited. Then, after the third tug at the rope, they heard footsteps and a woman in a grey linen cap and apron slowly opened the door.

'We have come to see Frau von Tannenberg,' said Professor Julius. 'She should be expecting us; we sent a telegram.'

He extracted a card from his waistcoat pocket, but the maid made no attempt to take it.

'She isn't here,' she said. 'She's gone away.'

'Well, perhaps we could wait till she comes back?'

The woman shook her head.

'She's gone on a visit; she won't be back for a week or more. She's away on business.'

'Do you know where she's gone?'

The maid looked down at her feet. 'Switzerland,' she said at last. 'And Herr Oswald too.'

'What about Annika?' asked Professor Emil. 'Could we see Annika? We're old friends from Vienna.'

Another slow shake of the head.

'Did she go to Switzerland too?'

The maid sighed. 'No. I don't know where Annika went. We weren't told. There's only me and my daughter here.'

She made no attempt to show them into the house. Short of knocking her over there was no way they could see Annika's home.

'What about Annika's cousin, Gudrun. Can we see her? We'd like to give her a message for Annika.'

Ellie had spoken for the first time, and the maid curled her lip at the Viennese accent.

'Fräulein von Seltzer and her mother are at their home.'

'And where is that?' asked Professor Julius.

'It's called Felsenheim.'

And the door was shut in their faces.

They made their way back to the road and stopped a farmer in his cart, who not only told them where Felsenheim was but gave them a lift as far as the turning into the forest.

Mathilde and Gudrun were both at home, and when she saw a group of people coming up the path, Mathilde was pleased. She was lonely and she was bored and she was very annoyed with her sister, who had taken Oswald to Switzerland yet had refused to take her. But when the professors introduced themselves, standing among the antlers and stuffed heads in the hall, she drew back. Clearly, like the maid at Spittal, she had been told to say nothing.

But now Ellie was in a relentless mood.

'Could I speak to Gudrun, please?' she said. 'We'd like to give her a message for Annika. I know they were good friends.'

Mathilde hesitated – but at that moment Gudrun came into the room. She was wearing a red scarf that Ellie instantly recognized. Ellie's heart began to pound. Had they killed Annika and buried her in the forest and taken her clothes? Nothing seemed impossible in this strange place.

Gudrun was looking pale and sad again. The supply of

beautiful clothes seemed to have dried up, her mother and her aunt had quarrelled, and she was lonely. She had written three times to Hermann and not had a single line in reply.

And she was jealous of Annika.

'They've sent her to a palace,' she told Ellie. 'I wanted to go too, but they wouldn't let me.'

'A palace?' asked Emil. 'What sort of a palace?'

'Gudrun, be quiet,' said Mathilde urgently.

But Gudrun took no notice. 'It's called Grossenfluss. It's near Potsdam and it's very grand.'

'That's enough, Gudrun,' said Mathilda, and, taking her daughter by the arm, she bundled her out of the door.

At Bad Haxenfeld the professors found they had half an hour to wait before the night train back to Vienna. It had been a most unsatisfactory visit, but there was nothing more to be done for the time being.

But it now seemed that Ellie had gone mad.

'I'm not coming back to Vienna,' she said. 'I've got to go and see for myself.'

'See what for yourself?'

'This Grossenfluss place. This palace. What's Annika doing in a palace?'

'Ellie, for goodness' sake! What on earth could you do? If Annika's in a palace she can't be having a bad time.'

But Ellie was beyond reason. 'I just have to go and see . . . I'll make up the time – I'll work all my Sundays next month. There's a train to Potsdam in the morning. I'll sleep in the waiting room.'

'Ellie, you can't stay here all night.'

'I'll be fine,' said Ellie. 'I've got plenty of money.'

But she did not look fine. Julius and Emil turned to each other. They could see how this was going to end – and they were very much displeased. They were extremely fond of Ellie, but one did not take orders from one's cook.

CHAPTER TWENTY-NINE

THE PALACE OF GROSSENFLUSS

Gudrun had not been lying. Grossenfluss was a palace. It was a very large and very grand palace, perhaps the largest and grandest palace in East Prussia. Built in 1723 by Prince Mettenburg, the front facade measured 400 metres in length. The roof was guarded by 100 lead warriors with drawn bows; the niches and ledges were crammed with warlike carvings: the heads of captured Turks, spiked helmets, crossed swords and cavalry horses with fiery nostrils. On either side of the front door stood two stone heroes, each crushing a wriggling traitor under his foot.

Inside there were vaulted stone corridors, fortified windows and a vast staircase of marble surrounding a stairwell three floors deep.

But this palace, which looked as though it had been

built for ogres or giants, was not used now for parties and pomp. It had become a school.

Not, however, an ordinary school. A school for Daughters of the Nobility and a very select and special place, as Frau Edeltraut had explained to Annika when at last she had revealed the surprise she had prepared for her.

'It's such wonderful news!' Frau Edeltraut had said, taking Annika's hand as they sat side by side on the sofa in her boudoir. 'They have accepted you!'

'Who?' Annika was bewildered. 'Who has accepted me?'

'The ladies of Grossenfluss! The committee! And you can start next week.'

Annika was still totally at sea. 'But what is . . . Grossenfluss?'

'Oh, Annika,' her mother laughed merrily, 'I always forget where you were brought up. Grossenfluss is one of the most famous schools in Germany. It only accepts daughters of the nobility and it trains them to become worthy women of the Fatherland, able to take their place anywhere in society. The principal, Fräulein von Donner, has the Order of the Closed Fist, one of the highest awards which the emperor gives, and it is very rarely awarded to a woman. I was so worried that they would not let you come because of . . . well, your father. I could not swear to the purity of his birth. But when I told them what a dear good girl you were, they relented. I cannot tell you how pleased I am for you. Your future is assured. Girls who have been to Grossenfluss can become ladies-in-waiting, or companions to high-born widows. Nothing is impossible for them.'

'But . . . do you mean I have to go away? To stay in the school all the time, like Hermann?'

'Well, yes, my dear, naturally. There will be so much for you to learn – more than children who have . . . who have been brought up in a good home from the start. But the time will fly. In seven years you will be ready to go out into the world again, and how grateful you will be to the people who have taught you so much.'

Annika had risen from the sofa, and walked over to the window, keeping her face turned away from her mother.

'I don't want to go away,' she said, trying to keep her voice steady. 'I've only just found you. I've only just come.'

'Now, my dear, you mustn't talk like a common little girl. Like a servant. In our class – the class to which you now belong – we are trained to think of the future. We are trained to achieve and to conquer and to let nothing stand in our way.'

But Annika was overwhelmed by misery. She was to go away, not back to Vienna, but to strangers, to a world she knew nothing about. And, unable to help herself, she threw herself sobbing into her mother's arms. 'Please, please, please, don't send me away,' she begged. 'I'll do anything, but please don't send me to that place.'

And she buried her head in her mother's lap, the first time she had dared to do so.

'Oh, Annika, my dearest child, you break my heart,' said Edeltraut, stroking Annika's hair. 'I was so sure you would be delighted. Think of Hermann.'

'But I'm not Hermann, I'm me, and I don't want to be a lady-in-waiting. I just want to be at home. Please, please, don't make me go. I'll do anything—'

But her mother's hands now fell away from her daugh-

271

ter's hair. She sat up very straight, and gently but firmly pushed Annika away.

'My dear, you don't want to disappoint me, do you? You don't want to make me sorry that I came to fetch you?' And in a voice of finality, 'We shall leave next week.'

But in the end it was Mathilde who took Annika to Grossenfluss. Frau Edeltraut was called away on urgent business to Switzerland to do with Herr von Grotius's will, she said, and she was taking Oswald.

'There are always so many stages to go through in these affairs,' she told Annika. 'But Mathilde will see that you get there safely.'

There was no shopping to do before Annika left. It was old Princess Mettenburg, the great-granddaughter of the man who had built the palace, who had turned it into a school where girls of good family could be trained to be a credit to the Fatherland. The uniform was provided; there were no fees to pay. The princess was very rich and this was her way of helping her country.

'Of course, the discipline is strict,' said Mathilde as they sat in the train. 'But you will quickly get used to that. Gudrun is quite jealous of you, going to live in such a splendid place.'

'Couldn't Gudrun come too?' asked Annika. 'She's much more nobly born than me.'

'Gudrun has a weak chest,' said Mathilde.

But she turned her head away, not meeting Annika's eyes.

They left the train at Potsdam and were driven to Grossenfluss in a closed carriage sent by the school. Annika could never travel long without any air and soon she felt so sick that she saw the facade of the palace, looming out of the mist, almost with relief.

'Take your dress off.'

Annika slipped her dress over her head and the lady with pins stuck all over the collar of her black overall took it away and hung it in a cupboard.

'Your number is 127 – remember that. Everything you own or wear must have that number. Now try the uniform.'

Annika had already seen the uniform on the girls walking with bent heads and folded arms down the long stone corridor. It was black with thick green stripes, worn with a starched black collar and a black apron.

She slipped it over her head and the seamstress pulled it straight.

'But it's been worn,' said Annika. 'There's a dress preserver under the arms.'

'Of course it's been worn,' said the seamstress. 'You didn't expect a new one, surely. When you outgrow it, it will go to another girl. "Thrift and Discipline" is our motto. Now come here and let me do your hair.'

'I've just brushed it.'

'It can't stay like that. It's got to be pinned back.' She took out a bundle of hairpins and began to jab them into Annika's hair and neck. 'Stand still.'

Annika stood still. She felt at that moment as though she would never move again.

'Now these are your night clothes and your underwear. Everything you brought with you has to be handed in. Books, money, letters . . . You can keep your hairbrush and

273

the Bible. And remember you are number 127. Your number is the most important thing about you.'

There was a mirror against one wall of the room. Annika, turning to go, saw a kind of female convict, a girl in stripes who could be picked off by a bullet from a warder if she tried to escape. Prisoner 127.

A pale, dark-eyed girl called Olga von Seefeld was put in charge of Annika. She explained the rules. No talking in the corridors, no running ever, only the back stairs to be used by the pupils; the main stairs were for the staff. A full curtsy whenever she met one of the teachers, a half-curtsy for older girls.

'Can we write letters?' asked Annika. 'Would they let us have stamps?'

'We're allowed one letter a month, but the teachers have to read them first. If we put anything in about being home-sick or the food being bad or anything like that, it isn't sent and we get punished. You can't write the first one till you've been here a month, and you can't get any letters till then either. It's so you settle down.'

'Do you . . . are you happy here?' Annika plucked up the courage to ask the question.

Olga's dark eyes rested for a moment on Annika's face.

'It is a privilege to be here and learn to be a credit to the Fatherland,' she said in a flat voice.

She took Annika to join the line of girls waiting to go in to supper. A bell shrilled and they shuffled forward into a bare, vaulted room with green linoleum on the tables. In front of each girl was a plate of stew, mostly consisting of potatoes, but the girl standing opposite Annika was looking down at something different: a bowl of congealed rice speckled with a few pieces of dried mushroom.

'That's Minna,' Olga whispered. 'She didn't finish her food at lunch – she can't bear mushrooms – so she has to eat it now for supper. And if she doesn't eat it for supper she gets it again at breakfast. It's the rule, food mustn't be wasted.'

The bell shrilled again and the girls said grace and sat down. As Annika swallowed her tasteless stew, she smiled at Minna. But Minna did not smile back. She had picked up her spoon and two huge tears were rolling down her cheeks.

'Once a girl had her breakfast served up for two whole days,' Olga went on. 'She was sick over it in the end – they had to stop then.'

After supper there were prayers in the hall, then another bell summoning them to their dormitories. In Annika's were thirty iron beds, each covered in a single grey blanket. There were no curtains between the beds, only bare lockers. A bell rang, and the girls filed in wearing their regulation-flannel nightdresses, and knelt down. Another bell, and they rose and got between the scratchy sheets.

The light went out.

It was the old Princess Mettenburg who had turned Grossenfluss into a school, but she no longer lived in the palace herself. Once a month she came to inspect both the pupils and the staff. Once a fortnight she sent some of her musicians to give concerts of patriotic music to the pupils. It was the headmistress, Fräulein von Donner, who ran the school.

No one who met Fräulein von Donner was surprised

that she was the only woman in Germany with the Order of the Closed Fist. She was a terrifying figure with a moustache, grey hair pulled relentlessly into a bun and rimless pince-nez on a metal chain. One of her hips had been displaced as a child and she walked with the aid of a stick. The thump, thump, thump of this stick along the stone passages was like the bell of the old plague bearers announcing another death.

Annika was taken to see her on the second day.

The headmistress was sitting at her desk. Behind her hovered her assistant, Mademoiselle Vincent, a thin white-faced woman who moved like an eel, gliding along in a wave-like motion, her head thrust forward.

'You know our motto, "Thrift and Discipline"?'

'Yes, Fräulein von Donner.'

'For you it will be necessary to be particularly careful in view of your early life. Lapses in your case would be particularily serious.'

'Yes, Fräulein von Donner.'

'We shall do our best to train you to be a worthy daughter of the Fatherland.'

'Yes. Only Germany isn't my Fatherland. I'm Austrian. At least I used to be.'

Fräulein von Donner looked at her as though she couldn't believe her ears. She fingered the three keys round her neck: the big key for the front door, a smaller key for the isolation room where troublesome girls were kept, and the smallest key of all which was also the most important. It was the key to the cubbyhole where the recently installed telephone lived.

Then, 'That is something I would advise you not to

mention. Or even to *think*,' she said – and Annika was dismissed.

For the first week Annika still hoped. She hoped that her mother meant well by her and that something good could be made out of her new life. Perhaps there would be one teacher who could make her subject interesting; one girl who would show her friendship.

She set herself to work hard. She learned to walk downstairs with wooden blocks on her head so as to aquire an iron-straight back, and to recite the family tree of Europe's noble families from the *Almanach de Gotha*. She learned poems about the glory of war, and who should be placed above a field marshal at the dinner table. There were even a few proper lessons, but not many because the teachers were as cowed and miserable as the pupils and the sound of the headmistress's stick along the corridor sent all ideas of grammar or arithmetic out of their heads.

In the afternoon, if it did not rain, they were taken for a walk, lining up in pairs, but not allowed to choose their partners in case they formed special friendships. The walk took forty minutes exactly, marching down the avenue, turning left at the gate along the road to the village, then back to the drive behind the house. At all other times it was forbidden to go out of doors.

Annika's mother had told her that it was difficult to get into the school, but it seemed to her that all the girls were there because they were not really wanted. Olga's mother was dead and her stepmother did not like her. Ilse had a club foot and was teased by her sisters. Hedwig had been brought up by grandparents who found the care of a young girl too much for them.

'Don't let anyone tell you different,' she said to Annika. 'We're here to be out of the way and because we don't have to pay. The Fatherland could manage without us very well.'

The food was worse than Annika could have believed and the punishments were endless: being shut in a dark cupboard, kneeling on dried peas . . . Minna was served her breakfast four times then sent to the isolation room for a week.

Annika lost weight. She found it difficult to sleep. One day she asked Olga what had happened to pupil 126.

'Hedwig is 125 and I'm 127, but who is 126?'

Olga looked down at her feet.

'We are not allowed to talk about her.'

But Annika found that she already knew. 'She's dead, isn't she?' she said. 'She died in the school?'

'Don't ask me any more,' said Olga. 'I'll get into trouble.'

But Annika was not so easy to shake off. 'What was she like?'

'She had nice hair,' said Olga, and walked away.

All the same, some part of Annika would not give in to total despair. She forced herself to remember details of her life when it had been good; when she was busy and fufilled. So, lying in bed at night, Annika recalled her time in Ellie's kitchen – and when she felt misery engulfing her completely she cooked the Christmas carp. She didn't leave anything out. The part at the beginning where she washed the fish four times in cold water. Then the marinade: chopped onions, herbs, lemons and white wine. Not any old white wine but Chablis, which was the best and which Sigrid had fetched for her from the cellar.

Lying in her cold and narrow bed, Annika took herself

through all the stages and when she reached the moment when Ellie had taken down the black book and told her to write 'A pinch of nutmeg will improve the flavour of the sauce', she could usually drop off to sleep.

But then came the night when she was going through the ingredients for the stuffing: truffles and chopped celery . . . grated honey cake and lemon rind and chestnut purée . . . but there was one other thing. One thing that was really important. Not chopped prunes – the lady in the paper shop had suggested chopped prunes, but Annika hadn't used them. But it was something like prunes . . . Oh God, what was it? If she forgot that, if she forgot how to cook, everything was lost.

She sat up in bed in the dormitory where the girls snored and snuffled and whimpered in their sleep – but she could not remember.

And at that moment she was defeated, and she sank down into a dark place where nobody could reach her.

CHAPTER THIRTY

SWITZERLAND

'I think Herr Zwingli is right,' said Edeltraut, sipping her coffee. 'We'll sell the butterfly brooch next. That should bring in enough to finish the repairs at Spittal and enable us to live in comfort for two or three years.'

'And at Felsenheim,' put in Oswald. 'The repairs at Felsenheim aren't finished and Mathilde wants a new carriage.'

Edeltraut put her cup down with a clatter.

'Oswald, how many times do I have to tell you that Annika is *my* daughter, not Mathilde's. When Annika signed away her belongings, she signed them over to me, not to you or your wife.'

'Yes. Yes, of course. But Mathilde feels—'

'I'm not interested in what Mathilde feels. I shall do exactly what Zwingli suggests and sell the pieces at intervals so as not to attract attention. After the butterfly brooch the emeralds, and then the earrings. And I think he's right – the Star of Kazan should wait till the end: it's such a showy piece. Questions might be asked.'

They were sitting at a table in one of Zurich's most luxurious cafes overlooking the river. A chestnut tree beside them was just coming into blossom; there were flowers in tubs on the pavement; everything sparkled with cleanliness: the streets, the buildings, the people . . .

Getting hold of the trunk had been ridiculously easy. As soon as she received the note from the stationmaster that a trunk addressed to her was waiting at Bad Haxenfeld, Edeltraut had driven in with Oswald.

They had loaded the trunk into the carriage, driven to a remote shed on the Spittal estate and transferred the jewels to Oswald's locked leather shooting bag. Then they waited till dark, returned to Spittal and threw the trunk into the lake.

That, of course, was only half the battle. They had to find out if the story that the Baron had overheard at Bad Haxenfeld was true and the jewels were real, and to do this they had gone to Zurich.

Zurich is the biggest town in Switzerland and it is a beautiful place, built on either side of a fast green river which flows into a wide lake ringed by mountains. The streets of Zurich are elegant, the shops are sumptuous and the hotels are as comfortable as palaces.

But what makes Zurich important in the eyes of the world is its banking houses. Many of the best-known banks in the world have their headquarters there and they are famous for being discreet and reliable, with underground safes where people can keep their money or their gold bars or their jewels in numbered boxes, and no one asks any questions about what is stored there or for how long.

And along with the banks, the city had the best jewellers and lawyers and accountants in Europe.

It was to the firm of Zwingli and Hammerman, the best-known jewellers in Zurich, that Edeltraut, with Oswald and Mathilde, had taken the jewels from Annika's trunk, and as they unpacked them and laid them on the green baize table in Herr Zwingli's strongroom their hearts were beating very fast.

'I can't give you an opinion on these straight away,' he said. 'I shall have to get my experts to look at them.'

So he gave them a receipt and looked at their documents of entitlement and they waited for two days in their hotel for what the experts would say. They were the longest two days of their lives, but when they returned they knew by Herr Zwingli's beaming smile that their troubles were over.

'Yes, all the pieces are genuine, and I have to say I have not seen such a collection for a long time.'

And he suggested it would be wise to sell the pieces one at a time, with intervals in between, and keep the rest in the vaults of the Landesbank, in a strong box.

'You should have enough to live on for the rest of your life in comfort,' he had said.

So Edeltraut had arranged for the sale of the Burmese rubies, and it was the money from these that they had spent on the repairs and changes to Spittal, and on Hermann's fees.

Now, though, they needed more money and they had

come back to Zurich to arrange the sale of the butterfly brooch. Herr Zwingli had sent a description of the brooch to a customer in America who was willing to pay a fortune for it.

When they had finished the business, they walked down the main street, stopping again and again at the windows of the shops, each one as beautifully arranged as a room in a museum.

'Mathilde asked me to look out for a mink coat,' said Oswald.

'Oh really?' said Edeltraut. 'Might I point out that when I brought Mathilde here last time I allowed her to spend a fortune on clothes for herself and Gudrun – but enough is enough.'

Oswald shrugged. He was completely under Edeltraut's thumb. But he looked greedily at a pearl-handled pistol in the window of a gun shop and went on looking so long that at last Edeltraut bought it for him. She did not need her sister, but she needed him.

Later, as they sat having dinner in a glamorous restaurant which overlooked the town, Oswald brought up the question of Annika.

'Do you think Grossenfluss is quite the place for her?'

'Most certainly I do, otherwise I wouldn't have sent here there. You know she had to be sent away quickly after that wretched dog found the photograph. She went on asking me about Zed almost every day – wondering if it had to be him who took the trunk. We can't take that kind of risk.'

'No, she had to go, but I wondered about Grossenfluss. They say the discipline is—'

'Oswald, please don't interfere between me and my

daughter. She will get an excellent education there. And, as I have told you, the school is free. I should have thought you would be glad of that, considering how good your wife is at spending my money.'

'Well, well, I'm sure you know best,' said Oswald. In spite of his duelling scar and his passion for killing animals, he was a weak man. 'I think I'll have another glass of this excellent wine.'

CHAPTER THIRTY-ONE

PUPIL NUMBER 126

Two kilometres from the Palace of Grossenfluss, which housed the Institute for Daughters of the Nobility, stood an inn called the Fox and Feathers.

It was the kind of country inn one could find all over the north German countryside, with carved shutters, heavy wooden tables, big pitchers of beer and ample helpings of roast pork with sauerkraut.

As well as serving food and drink, and stabling horses, the Fox and Feathers had four bedrooms that it let out to travellers, and it was in one of these that Professor Julius woke the morning after the visit to Spittal.

He was not in a good temper. He'd been kept awake by a group of drunken guests singing sad songs about their lost youth, and a cockerel had disturbed him at dawn. His first thought as he woke was that he and Emil must have been raving mad to let their cook drag them to this place, and his second was that the sooner they saw Annika and returned to Vienna, the better.

He got out of bed and went along the corridor to find his brother.

Emil too was in a bad state; he had had a second helping of onions fried in lard at supper and his stomach had not taken it well.

'I think you'd better go along by yourself and find out when we can see Annika. I don't feel it would be wise for me to go out just yet,' he said.

Professor Julius washed and made his way downstairs. There was no sign of Ellie in the dining room, but out of the window he could see her talking to the maid she had made friends with the night before. She was helping her to hang up the washing. He drank a cup of coffee, put on his hat, took up his walking stick, and set off up the long drive that led to the school.

The closer he got the more certain he became that they had been ridiculous to come. The building became larger and grander the nearer he got. The Emperor Franz Joseph's palace in Vienna did not have half as many statues and pediments and curlicues and towers.

Professor Julius was not in the least overawed but he did feel that he was wasting his time. Grossenfluss was the sort of building that any young girl must long to live in.

He mounted the flight of steps to the front door, stopped for a moment to examine a patch of feldspar on the heel of a statue – and rang the bell.

'What's the matter?' asked Emil, who was still in his pyjamas. The maid had brought him a hot-water bottle, which he was resting on his stomach, and Ellie had asked permission from the girl in the kitchen to make him some gruel. 'You look upset.'

'I am not so much upset,' said Julius, laying down his walking stick, 'as angry. Very, very angry. I told them who I was, I showed them my card – and I was turned away.'

'Turned away. What do you mean?'

'I mean what I say,' said Julius. 'I was not admitted. I told them that I had come from Vienna with friends to arrange for a time to visit Annika and they said that none of the pupils were allowed visitors in the first month, and then only with written permission from the girl's mother. And they left me,' said Professor Julius, beginning to glare again as he remembered, 'they left me standing outside the door. I was not even taken into the office. I can't remember ever having been treated with such rudeness. One wonders just who these people think they are.'

'Well, it looks as though there's nothing we can do at the moment. We'd better pack up and go home,' said Emil.

A sound from the doorway made both professors turn. Ellie was standing there with the bowl of gruel and as soon as they saw her face they knew there was going to be trouble.

'I'm going to see Annika,' said Ellie. 'I'm going to see her if I have to stand there all day and all night. The maid says they take the girls for a walk most days; they come out of the side door and go down the avenue and back. I'll wait, and I'll see her and when I see her I'll know.'

So she left them, walking down the dusty village road in her stout shoes, her felt hat pulled over her forehead.

When she got to the junction of the road and the avenue she stopped and she waited.

She did not sit down – there was nowhere to sit. She stood and she waited all morning, and at lunchtime the maid from the inn brought her a bread roll, but she shook her head. If Annika came past she did not want to be eating, she wanted to *see*.

In the early afernoon, it began to rain. Ellie had no umbrella but she did not notice her discomfort. All she thought about was whether they would take the girls out in spite of the weather.

She stood there till dark, but Annika did not come. When there was no hope she went back to the inn and allowed the maid to bring her hot soup. She had expected that the professors would have returned to Vienna but they were still there.

In the morning she took up her vigil again. No one came in the morning, and no one came in the early afternoon and Ellie went on standing there.

Then at three o'clock on the second day of Ellie's watch, the side door of the palace was opened and a line of girls in black cloaks and black bonnets came slowly down the avenue . . .

Since she had given up hope, Annika had only one aim: not to be noticed. So she shuffled through her day, from the moment the bell shrilled at six in the morning and the girls lined up in the washroom for their turn with the jug of cold water and the cake of slimy soap, to the same bell shrilling them into bed at night.

All the same, she was noticed.

'Number 127 isn't settling too well,' said the matron to Annika's form mistress. 'She's very thin and pale.'

'Give her some cod liver oil and malt,' said the form

mistress. 'Force it down her throat if she won't take it – she's probably anaemic.'

There was no need to force it down Annika's throat – she didn't want to end up like Minna, who still sometimes had last night's supper served up to her at breakfast and then again at lunch. She obediently gulped the vile stuff down – but it made no difference. Each day she became more listless and quieter.

But it wasn't till the school went for a walk one afternoon that she became really frightened.

She was walking with a girl called Flosshilde, who hardly ever spoke. Annika's hands were folded, as were the hands of all the girls; she walked with a straight back.

At the front of the line was Fräulein Heller, who had flat feet; at the back was Fräulein Zeebrugge, who wheezed.

It was a misty day. Yesterday's rain had passed but the air was moist.

They reached the end of the avenue and prepared to turn to the left. There was a tree by the gate and somebody was standing under it. Standing very still, just looking . . .

Annika stopped dead – and from behind her Fräulein Zeebrugge shouted, 'What are you doing, girl? Keep moving, you've upset the line!'

So Annika moved on, and passed the woman who stood there – and it was then that she realized she was going mad.

Because she had seen Ellie. She was absolutely sure she had. And Ellie was 1,000 kilometres away in a city she herself would probably never see again.

Ellie was in Vienna.

'She can't stay there,' said Ellie. 'She can't stay in that place a day longer.'

Professor Julius and Professor Emil looked at each other in dismay. They had packed their suitcases and asked the innkeeper for the bill. The summer term at the university began the following week.

And now Ellie wasn't just being difficult. She was being impossible.

'She's ill,' said Ellie. 'She's ill inside her head.'

'Ellie, you only saw her for a few moments, muffled up in a cape on a foggy day. You said so yourself. How can you tell that she's ill?'

'I can tell,' said Ellie. 'If her mother won't take her away then we'll have to.'

'I suppose we could inform her mother and—'

'There's no time for that,' said Ellie, who had never before interrupted her employer. 'And her mother thinks it's a fine place; Gudrun said so.'

'Look, we have to get back to Vienna,' said Professor Julius. 'We can return later—'

'I'm not moving from here without Annika,' said Ellie.

The professors stared at her, baffled. When your cook turns into a kind of tigress it is not easy to know what to do for the best.

'I'll rescue her myself if I have to,' said Ellie. 'I'll get a ladder.'

The professors shook their heads and went into the parlour to discuss what to do.

'It's not going to be easy leaving her here,' said Julius. The thought of Ellie on top of a ladder climbing through a window at Grossenfluss was not a calming one. 'But I don't see what else we can do.'

Emil nodded. 'I imagine she'll see sense soon. But I think we should definitely write to Frau von Tannenberg and ask her to find out if Annika is happy. This is an entirely different matter to that of the jewels, which can be left to the police.'

The maid with whom Ellie had made friends came in to wipe down the tables and straighten the chairs.

'Would you want any help with your luggage, sirs?' she asked the professors.

'No, no; we've only our overnight things. Will you make sure that the cab is ordered to take us to the station?'

'Yes, sir. Frau Ellie's staying on, she says.'

'Yes. She's worried about a child at the school.'

The maid pushed another chair straight. 'Well, you can't be surprised after what happened last winter.'

Both professors looked up sharply. 'What did happen?'

'Didn't you know?' The maid's kind face was troubled. 'One of the pupils killed herself. Number 126, they called her. Climbed over the balustrade at the top of the staircase and jumped. They tried to say it was an accident, but everybody knew it wasn't.'

Professor Julius put down his pipe.

'Why? Did anyone find out why she'd done it?'

The maid shrugged. 'She was just unhappy. Homesick, they said. She was a nice little thing . . . such pretty hair, she had.'

CHAPTER THIRTY-TWO

RAGNAR HAIRYBREEKS

The professors and Ellie had been away for three days. The only telephone in the square was in the Eggharts' house, and the Eggharts were still on holiday. Sigrid and Gertrude told each other that it was nothing to worry about, and became more and more worried. What could have happened at Spittal? What had kept them away so long?

Zed had his own anxieties, which he tried to keep to himself. He knew he could not stay in Vienna much longer however much he wanted to – yet he felt he could not leave till he knew what was happening to Annika.

Whatever troubles the humans had, Rocco did not share them. Life in Vienna suited him and he was making more and more friends. An old mare between the shafts of one of the cabs in the Keller Strasse seemed to think he was her long-lost son; the man who sold newspapers in the square behind the opera saved sugar lumps for him. Traffic did not trouble Rocco; he trotted serenely past honking motors and swaying trams. Children began to point him out.

'Look, there's Rocco,' they told each other. 'Rocco and Zed.'

Even the Lipizzaners, stepping proudly out of their princely stable, would often now return Rocco's greetings, as though they knew that he was beginning to belong.

Then something happened which made Zed realize that he must leave the city and leave it fast. It was his own fault, he told himself. He had grown careless, taking Rocco out by daylight instead of waiting for the cover of night – but he'd been helping Pauline's grandfather unpack books all morning and longed to be outside. So he shook off a handful of little Bodeks, saddled Rocco – and set off for the Prater.

This was not the funfair part of the Prater but the Royal Park, with its ancient trees and meadows, which had once belonged only to the emperor but which the people of the city were now allowed to use.

And on this fine spring afternoon, the people were certainly using it. Soldiers on leave walked with their girl-friends on their arms; old people whizzed along in bath chairs, propelled by their relatives; groups of pretty girls in their new Easter hats giggled together on the grass – and everywhere there were children. Children in prams, children pulling toys on wheels, children bowling hoops . . .

Two men in sober dark-brown uniforms stood out from the crowd. One was very tall and thin and wore his cap pulled down over his head; the other was small, with a ginger moustache.

There was a stretch where the cinder track for the horses ran beside the turf path on which the people walked. It was permitted to gallop in the Prater, but with so many people about, Zed kept Rocco to a canter.

On the path beside the track, a tired woman pushed her baby in a basketwork pram. With her free hand she pulled along a tiny, plump boy in a sailor suit.

'Keep hold, Fritzi,' she said. 'Hang on to the pram.'

But Fritzi was bored. He let go of the handle and ran forward. Another child came towards him kicking a large red ball. They met head on.

'My ball,' said Fritzi, trying to grab it. 'Mine.'

'No, mine!' said the other child – and he kicked the ball hard on to the cinders.

'Stop, Fritzi,' screamed his mother. 'Stop, STOP!'

But Fritzi did not stop.

'Ball,' he cried passionately – and trotted on his fat little legs right across Rocco's path – and fell.

Zed didn't have time to think. Rocco gave a shrill whinny of fear, and then he reared up . . . and up on his hindquarters with his hoofs pulled under him . . .

The child's mother screamed again, there were cries from the bystanders, a soldier let go of the girl on his arm and moved forward.

Rocco's hoofs were poised over the little boy's body as he lay tumbled in the earth. But they did not come down. Rocco still held his levade and Zed gave no command, only adjusted the weight of his body imperceptibly to help the horse to stay as he was.

A levade can only be held for seconds, even by the strongest and most experienced horse, but these were long seconds. When Rocco came down again, slowly, carefully, the soldier had run out and snatched the little boy to safety.

After that there was pandemonium. People shouted and cheered; there were cries of 'Did you see that?' and Fritzi's mother burst into tears of relief.

But Zed was watching two men only: the tall man in his dark-brown uniform and the man beside him with the ginger moustache. They were staring intently at the horse, but not in an excited way like the people in the crowd. The tall man had taken the other's arm and they looked serious and businesslike.

'We'll have to look into this,' Zed heard him say, and his companion nodded and took out a notebook and pencil. 'A bay stallion. It all fits.'

'I've seen him before,' said the other man.

Zed heard no more. He urged Rocco into a canter – but as he made his way back to the square he realized that time was running very short. The two officers had looked like policemen. Not ordinary ones, they were too smart for that, but officers perhaps in one of the special units which flushed out people who had no right to be in the city: spies for one of the Balkan countries intent on destroying the empire, anarchists wanting to blow up members of parliament . . . and thieves . . . Horse thieves in particular. Frau Edeltraut must have issued a description of Rocco . . . he was distinctive enough with his single white star.

When he had stabled Rocco and rubbed him down, he made his way into the kitchen

'Sigrid, I have to go soon. Tomorrow . . . I'm sure I saw two men in the park who guessed that Rocco wasn't really mine. They looked like special police.'

But Sigrid was too preoccupied to worry about Rocco.

'Professor Gertrude's had a telegram from her brothers,' she told Zed. 'She's in a dreadful state. Stefan's up there now trying to calm her down; you go up too while I make some coffee.'

Gertrude was sitting in a chair holding the telegram in her hand. It was a long telegram and obviously very upsetting.

'They want me to come to this place called Grossenfluss and give a harp recital. On my concert grand – the new one. They say I must come quickly; it's urgent. There's something about a child known to us all.'

'Annika,' said Zed instantly, and Stefan nodded.

'Yes, but why do I have to go and play the new harp? It isn't ready yet. And why do I have to play military music? I never play military music: it isn't what I play,' said poor Gertrude. She looked at the telegram again. 'And there's something about a man called Ragnar Hairybreeks. It all seems to be in code.'

But Pauline, hurrying in from the bookshop with *The Dictionary of Myths and Legends* under her arm, solved this particular problem.

'I've found it,' she said. 'It's in the Saga of the Nibelungen. Ragnar Hairybreeks was a Viking warrior whose wife was hidden in a harp. There's a lot more, but that's the bit that matters.'

The children looked at each other. They were beginning to understand.

But Professor Gertrude was desperate. 'I can't go all that way with the instrument. I can't carry it by myself.'

'I'll come with you,' said Stefan quietly.

Sigrid came in then with a tray of coffee, and a second

telegram, which had just been delivered. Gertrude tore it open eagerly. Perhaps her brothers had seen sense and she did not need to go.

But the message was simple.

'Bring Emil's stomach powders,' it said.

CHAPTER THIRTY-THREE

THE RESCUE

It was Olga who found out that there was to be a harp recital in the school on Sunday evening.

Annika lifted her head from the handkerchief she was hemming.

'A harp? Are you sure?'

For a moment the cloud in which she lived rolled away and a door opened on the past. Professor Gertrude was carrying her harp downstairs; she was wearing the black skirt from which Sigrid was always removing small pieces of food, and both she and the harp smelled overpoweringly of lavender water.

'She's French, she's called Madame La Cruise. A friend of the princess sent her to show us that you can play patriotic things on the harp.'

Annika bent her head again over her sewing. It was strange how hope could die even if you hadn't *had* any hope. Aunt Gertrude seldom left Vienna and it was impossible to imagine her playing patriotic songs on the harp.

It was the patriotic songs that were particularly worrying Gertrude as she sat in the parlour of the inn going through the plans for Annika's rescue.

She had transposed a song called 'Slay and Smite if God Demands It' and another one about a soldier's death on the battlefield with a refrain about the red-soaked earth renewed by the warrior's spilt blood.

'I can't do any more,' she said miserably to her brothers. 'They're nasty.'

'It doesn't matter. The girls won't know what you play,' said Professor Julius. 'School concerts aren't about music; they're about not having to do homework while they're going on.'

Stefan thought that the songs Gertrude was going to play would be the least of their worries. The plan, which had been explained to him when he arrived, seemed to be full of holes.

He and Gertrude were to unload the harp from the carriage and wheel it into the school. In the hall they would take the harp out of its case, leave the case in the cloakroom and ask for help in carrying the instrument up the stairs.

In the interval of the concert, Annika would say she felt sick and hurry to the toilet in the downstairs cloakroom. Stefan, who was guarding the harp case, would help her into it and, when the concert resumed and everybody was out of the way, he would carry her out to a closed carriage in which Ellie was waiting with a change of clothes. Annika would be let out and driven away to the station, Stefan would take the harp case back to the cloakroom and, at the end of the concert, he and Professor Gertrude would go home with the harp in the usual way.

'I'll have to have a reason for taking the case out in the interval,' said Stefan. He was not a boy who worried easily but he was worried now. 'In case anyone sees me. Maybe I would need to fix a new wheel on the base.'

'We'll just have to improvise,' said Professor Julius grandly. Since he was to wait for them at the station he could afford to be relaxed. 'After all it will be dark.'

Both the professors had been determined to return to Vienna and leave Ellie where she was. However much Annika disliked her school, she had been put there by her mother, and they were not the sort of people who planned cloak-and-dagger rescues, and interfered with authority.

But what they had learned from the maid at the inn about pupil 126 would not go out of their minds.

'Such pretty hair, she had,' the maid had said . . . and Annika too had pretty hair. The professors began to be haunted by the image of Annika lying on the stone flags in pools of her own blood.

Once they had decided to stay, the professors became very forceful. There was an old encyclopedia in the smoking room of the inn, and when Emil turned to the page about Ragnar Hairybreeks he found that his memory had not been faulty. A beautiful maiden, the daughter of a king, escaping a cruel war, had been carried to safety hidden in a harp.

Professor Julius had already been to the school when he went to enquire about visiting Annika. It was Emil therefore who called late that afternoon and asked to see the principal, Fräulein von Donner.

He wore a black beret pulled down over his forehead and a pair of thick-rimmed glasses and introduced himself as Henri de Malarme, a concert impresario who had been sent by the music master of the Duchess of Cerise.

'The duchess, as you know, is a close friend of your patron the Princess Mettenburg.'

Fräulein von Donner was impressed. She did not usually see people who came to the door, but a messenger from a duchess, especially one who knew their own princess, had to be listened to.

'Her Grace's concert master has a harpist whom he values greatly – a Frenchwoman. She has transposed the patriotic songs of the Fatherland for the harp. There is one song, "Let Our Enemies Tremble", which has already become famous in aristocratic circles. It is in the key of E flat minor,' said Professor Emil.

'And how does this concern us here at Grossenfluss?' asked Fräulein von Donner, bending forward so that the three keys on her chest – the one for the front door, the one for the isolation room and the one for the cubbyhole, which housed the telephone – all clanked together.

'Her Grace has suggested that this harpist visits a few specially chosen schools to give a concert. Free of charge, of course – the concert is free. It seems important for the pupils to know that an instrument that is often played by women can also be used to hearten men for heroic deeds. Even for war.'

'Well, that is true. We are always concerned that the girls in our care are trained to serve the Fatherland in any way – and music of course has often been used as a battle call. Though not,' she went on, 'on the harp.'

'No. And that is what interests the duchess. That is why she is sending Madame La Cruise to give recitals to young people. And it so happens that Madame is going to Schloss Bernstein to play there, and she could stop here on the way. I take it that you have a suitable hall?'

'Yes, of course. Our round room on the first floor is traditionally used for concerts.'

'And all your pupils attend?'

'Of course. Unless they are being punished.'

'Then may I take it that you will receive Madame La Cruise at six p.m. on Sunday?'

'So soon?'

'That is the only day she has available, I'm afraid. I will let you have all the arrangements in writing. Now, if I could just see the recital room? Madame La Cruise is particular about the acoustics – and about draughts. Draughts are very bad for harps, as you know.'

'Our acoustics are excellent,' said Fräulein von Donner. 'And a draught would not be permitted here.'

But she beckoned to her eel-like assistant, Mademoiselle Vincent, who took Emil to the round room on the first floor, which was reached by the wide flight of stone steps leading up from the main hall.

He did not catch so much as a glimpse of a single pupil in the silent building.

'I expect they keep them underground,' said Ellie when he told her this.

Which left the problem of getting a message through to Annika. 'She's got to know exactly what to do,' said Professor Emil.

There was a long silence. Grossenfluss seemed as impenetrable as a castle full of ogres.

But even ogres need someone to cook and clean and shop for them, and the maid who was Ellie's special friend had a sister who worked in the school.

'I'm seeing her this afternoon,' she said, 'it's her day off. I'll ask her if she can help. But it's no good giving her a note – they're all terrified of Fräulein von Donner. You'll have to tell me what she's to say to Annika, and keep it very short. I'm sure she'll do her best, but it can't be a promise.'

But the chambermaid managed it. The message she gave Annika in a hurried whisper as she was turning down the beds was not very clear, but when she had received it, Annika realized she would not need to pretend to be sick. She felt sick already: with excitement, dread – and something she had not felt since she came to Grossenfluss. Hope.

They had managed to unload the harp case and trundle it towards the door. Professor Gertrude was trembling with nerves, but Stefan was dogged and calm. He had no faith in Professor Emil's plan and could wish that Ragnar Hairybreeks was at the bottom of the sea, but he was going to get Annika out somehow.

He pulled the bell rope and the porter who came said that they were expected. Stefan looked carefully round the cold, dimly lit entrance hall. The big flight of steps leading up to the concert room was straight ahead: he could just make out the murmur of the girls' voices through the open door. The cloakrooms were on the right, and to the left was an unlit corridor leading to the back of the building.

It was from the corridor that there now came the tap tap of a walking stick and Fräulein von Donner came towards them out of the dark. The glinting keys, the steel-tipped stick and the badge of the Order of the Closed Fist on the headmistress's collar all filled Stefan with an instant loathing. This was an evil place run by an evil woman, and he realized that he would stop at nothing to rescue Annika.

Fräuelein von Donner greeted Professor Gertrude, and ignored Stefan.

'The girls are ready,' she said.

But before they could unpack the harp, the principal's assistant appeared from behind her employer and asked Professor Gertrude if she would care to follow her to the staffroom to take off her coat and freshen herself up.

Mademoiselle Vincent not only spoke French, she *was* French – and since she had been told that the harpist was a fellow countrywoman, it was in her own language that she addressed poor Professor Gertrude.

The professor had learned French at school, but that was a long time ago. However, there was nothing for it and she allowed Mademoiselle Vincent to lead her away, leaving Stefan to look after the harp in its case.

Upstairs in the concert room the girls waited.

Annika was sitting near the big double doors, which were folded back to allow the entrance of the harp, and she was sitting next to Fräulein Heller. Normally Annika would do anything not to sit next to a teacher, but if she

304

was to feel sick in the interval and ask to be excused it would be easier to get permission if she was close by.

The maid who had given Annika the hurried message had said only that someone Annika knew was coming to give a concert, but she had mentioned one name to which Annika clung now like a drowning person clutching a lifebelt.

Stefan. The maid had mentioned Stefan's name.

Annika closed her eyes, summoning up memories of her childhood friend. Stefan carrying his brothers on his shoulder; Stefan reaching a hand out to help her up when she fell; Stefan climbing a tree to bring down a screaming, panic-stricken child . . . Stefan was strong, he was true – if there was safety anywhere it lay with him.

Down in the hall, Professor Gertrude returned with Mademoiselle Vincent, looking very shaken. Emil had had some stupid ideas in his time, but why had he told them she was French? Why not Portuguese or Finnish or South African? Mademoiselle Vincent had spoken to her incessantly and rapidly in the kind of French that is never taught at school, and Gertrude did not feel that she had given a convincing performance as Madame La Cruise.

'Shall I take the case to the cloakroom now?' asked Stefan, and Professor Gertrude nodded and followed him into a tiled alcove with five doors discreetly closed. Like everything else at Grossenfluss, the cloakroom and the lavatories would have housed a tribe of giants.

Stefan opened the harp case, and Gertrude lifted the instrument out, and tenderly removed the silken shawl which covered it.

'We shall need help,' she said to Fräulein von Donner. 'Two strong girls, reliable ones.'

305

'Go and fetch the Messerschmidt twins – Brunnhilde and Waaltraut,' ordered the principal.

But Mademoiselle Vincent, usually so humble and obedient, did not go upstairs at once. She had been hovering round the headmistress and now she leaned forward urgently and whispered something in her ear.

Fräulein von Donner frowned. 'Well, that should be easy to check,' she said. She detached the smallest of the keys from the chain round her neck and stumped off down the corridor, while Mademoiselle Vincent went upstairs and returned with the Messerschmidt twins: large, solid-looking girls who curtsied and asked what they should do.

Gertrude handed the shawl and a sheaf of music to Brunnhilde and told Waaltraut to help hold the pillar of the harp in front. Stefan, at the back, steadied the instrument and prepared to take most of the weight.

Slowly, they made their way across the hall and began to ascend the stairs.

In the concert room, Annika took a deep breath and then another. She wasn't imagining it: the smell was real, stealing into her nostrils. Lavender water. Professor Gertrude was here – and it was all she could do not to get up and rush out of the room. At the same time she felt that if anything went wrong now and she had to stay in Grossenfluss then she would quite simply die.

On the stairs, the harp carriers climbed steadily.

'Careful – oh, careful,' said Professor Gertrude on every other step. 'You've no idea how valuable it is. Gently. Slowly.'

There was no choice about the slowness. The harp was not only weighty but cumbersome and top-heavy. Just keeping it balanced took all Stefan's skill and he was noting every obstacle in their path, alert for anything that could damage the instrument.

But when danger came, it came from below.

'Stop, stop!' cried Fräulein von Donner, hurrying to the bottom of the staircase. 'Stop at once! These people are impostors. I have telephoned the princess and she knows nothing about them or about the Duchess of Cerise!'

'They are anarchists,' shrieked Mademoiselle Vincent, emerging from behind the headmistress. 'Assassins! Murderers. Stop them, STOP!'

The harp was now two stairs from the top and from the landing in front of the concert room. The cries from below caused utter confusion. Stefan said, 'Go on, keep going,' and the twins said, 'No no, we must stop.'

Brunnhilde dropped the pile of sheet music she was carrying and Gertrude's foot slipped on 'Slay and Smite if God Demands It'.

'Go on, go on,' urged Professor Gertrude.

'Stop them!' came Fräulein von Donner's shriek from below. Her foot was on the bottom stair. She heaved herself up and began on the next one.

In the concert room Annika's heart seemed to stop. It wasn't going to work. They were going to be turned back.

Stefan and Professor Gertrude were alone now in carrying the harp. The twins, terrified by Fräulein von Donner's shrieks, had let go, but there was only one stair left to climb. At least whatever happened they could carry the harp to safety.

They had reached the top. Stefan steadied the instrument, setting it on its pedestal. It was poised at the top of the stairs like a great golden swan with its curved neck.

'Let me,' said Stefan, coming round to stand beside

Professor Gertrude. He took hold of the pillar of the instrument and gratefully she relinquished the weight to her trusted helper.

'They must be stopped!' yelled the headmistress from down below.

Stefan and the harp now blocked the top of the staircase.

The principal took one more step.

No one knew exactly what happened next. It seemed as though Stefan was trying to pull the harp backwards on to the safety of the landing.

But the harp did not obey him. Rather it seemed to move the other way – forward – to the very edge of the flight of stairs.

Stefan lunged out to save it – and missed. For a terrifying instant the instrument seemed to hesitate as if it was a living creature fearful of the descent.

Then it toppled . . . and fell.

It fell slowly at first . . . then faster and faster still . . . and as it fell it cried out – a tragic glissando of sound . . . There was a series of explosions as the base of the pillar struck the tread of the marble stair and the sounding board began to break. The wooden frame started to crunch and the strings stretched and sprang free, shrieking their outrage . . . and all the time the harp thundered and rushed and hurtled on . . .

Fräulein von Donner stood at the bottom of the stairs. She was rooted to the spot, staring upwards at the great juggernaut as it came down. Her pince-nez glittered in the light of the chandelier and she raised her stick like the prophet Moses willing back the waves.

But Fräulein von Donner was not Moses. Suddenly it

was too late. The harp crashed down the last few steps and, in its death throes, it let out a final reverberating growl of pain . . .

The principal tried to step back, and stumbled.

The next minute she lay felled and quite unconscious beneath the splintered instrument.

In the concert room the girls heard the crash and jumped to their feet. A terrible cry came from Mademoiselle Vincent down in the hall.

'She is dead – *Mon Dieu*, she is dead!'

'Come back – come back at once,' the teachers ordered the girls who were streaming from the room. No one took any notice. The landing and the stairs filled up with excited girls.

Now Professor Gertrude's hysterical sobbing was added to the pandemonium.

'My harp! My harp – I cannot bear it!'

The teachers had abandoned the girls and joined the throng staring in horror at the headmistress, buried beneath wire and splintered wood. The harp had pushed her down the last two stairs – she lay spreadeagled on the stone flags of the hall. One foot stuck out between the strings. It was very still.

'A doctor, a doctor,' cried Mademoiselle Vincent. 'Quick, quick. A doctor . . .'

'Yes, yes, a doctor,' wheezed Fräulein Zeebrugge. She bent over the headmistress, saw the blood on her forehead – and fainted.

The porter came.

'If I'm to telephone for the doctor I'll have to get the key from round her neck,' he said.

'I'll get it,' said Fräulein Heller. She began to move aside pieces of splintered harp.

'No, no – don't touch her,' someone shouted. 'She mustn't be moved.'

'Is she really dead?' the girls asked each other, their faces full of hope.

'I'll have to go for the doctor in the carriage,' said the porter, and made his way to the front door.

Annika had surged out of the concert hall with the others girls. She passed Professor Gertrude sobbing on the stairs, but the professor did not see her and she ran on down.

She had to find Stefan. If she could find Stefan there was still hope. But there was no sign of him in the milling crowd.

'Smelling salts – we must have smelling salts.'

'No, burnt feathers are better.'

'Iodine,' shouted a tall girl, 'there's some in matron's room.'

The servants came hurrying out from the back.

'God be praised, the harp has eaten her,' cried one of the scullery maids.

'Oh, the *blood*,' moaned Mademoiselle Vincent. 'There is so much blood!'

The headmistress's foot was still pointing upwards. It had not moved.

'We must go to the chapel and pray for her soul,' said one of the girls, and she ran off down the corridor, followed by two of her friends.

In the confusion and noise there were two people who only sought each other. Annika looked for Stefan, Stefan looked for her.

There was no sign of him in the hall, but the front door was open. Girls were beginning to run out into the dark and none of the teachers attempted to bring them back. They stood as if hypnotized over the remains of their headmistress. The golden pillar of the harp had fallen on her chest. Could she still be breathing?

'Oh, where is the doctor?' cried Mademoiselle Vincent.

Fräulein Zeebrugge groaned, coming round from her faint, and was pulled out of the way by her legs.

Annika was getting desperate. If Stefan had gone . . . if he had already been turned away . . . Then she remembered that she was supposed to say she felt sick and make her way to the cloakroom, but when she reached it, there were girls ahead of her, gulping cold water from the tap, talking excitedly.

But now a figure stepped out from behind a pillar.

'Oh, Stefan!' she sobbed.

And he put his arms round her and said, 'It's all right, Annika, it's all right.'

The harp case was where he had left it, but Stefan ignored it. Ragnar Hairybreeks's day was done. For what was happening in Grossenfluss was a riot, a break-out, as more and more of the girls rushed out into the night, shouting, dancing, vanishing between the trees – and were not pursued. As surely as the walls of Jericho had fallen to Joshua's trumpet, so the gates of Grossenfluss had fallen to the death cries of Professor Gertrude's harp.

'Come on,' said Stefan, and he took Annika's hand and ran out with her to the carriage where Ellie waited.

CHAPTER THIRTY-FOUR

STEFAN CONFESSES

'She's back,' said the lady in the paper shop, handing a copy of the *Vienna News* to the cab driver who had come in from the rank for his morning paper.

'Annika's back,' said Josef, bringing a jug of coffee to Father Anselm, who always had his breakfast in the cafe.

'Have you heard? Annika's come home,' said the old flower seller, tying up bunches of sweet peas.

The postman knew; so did the milkman. The stall-holders in the market had sent a basket of fresh fruit. The little Bodek boys trotted back and forth with messages of goodwill. Though the Eggharts were still away, their maid Mitzi called in daily for bulletins.

But Annika slept. She lay under the white duvet in her attic, and slept as deeply as if she had been enchanted and the professors' house was ringed by a hedge of thorns.

It was the old family doctor, called out to Annika after she had been carried up to her bed, who had come up with a phrase which was a godsend to those who were protecting Annika.

'She has nervous exhaustion,' he had said. 'She's to be kept absolutely quiet. Don't tell her anything; just let her rest.'

The phrase 'nervous exhaustion' travelled round the square. No one knew what it was, but it sounded serious and kept visitors at bay.

It was three days since Annika had been rescued from Grossenfluss. The first time she woke she sat up, terrified, thinking she was still back at the school. Then she felt the warmth of her duvet and saw the familiar bars of light through her shutters.

She was safe; she was home – and she let her head fall back on to the pillow.

When she woke again, she knew where she was in an instant and remembered everything. She had run away and defied her mother. Soon now she would have to face the consequences.

But just as she began to be anxious, Ellie came in with a tray. A croissant warm from the oven, fresh raspberry juice, a poached egg in a glass.

'You're to stay quiet,' she said. 'You're not to get up yet.'

And all that day, and the next, whenever Annika started to fret, Ellie appeared as if by magic with chicken soup, a ripe peach or a piece of milk-bread spread with butter.

'Go to sleep,' she'd say, whenever Annika started to ask questions – and Annika did. She had not been told yet that Zed was in Vienna; she knew nothing about the suspicions surrounding her mother or that the jewels in Fräulein Egghart's trunk were real.

And while she slept, her friends waited.

For Zed, the waiting was hard. He was still sleeping in the bookshop and working in the professors' house, but he was anxious to be on his way. The image of the two men in their brown uniforms haunted him. He only took out Rocco at night, and he was packed and ready to leave at a moment's notice. Yet he could not bring himself to go without saying goodbye to Annika.

Pauline too found waiting difficult. She had looked up 'nervous exhaustion' in the medical dictionary and she did not think much of it.

'I don't really want to have a friend to whom one has to bring soup,' she said to Ellie when she met her going upstairs with yet another tray. 'Soup is for old ladies.'

Though he too was waiting for Annika to wake, Stefan kept away from the professors' house. The journey back from Grossenfluss with Professor Gertrude and the shattered, bloodstained remnants of her golden harp had not been happy, and since her return she had stayed in her room and brooded.

The harp was not insured, and the men who had made it for her said it could not possibly be mended. In any case, who would want to play a harp to which pieces of the headmistress's unpleasant skin and hair had stuck? Because of Stefan's clumsiness Professor Gertrude – who had owned the most exotic and expensive harp in Vienna – was back to playing the old pedal harp she had had for fifteen years.

It was true that the tone of her old harp was very beautiful – after all this time, the sounding board had curved gently so as to give the special resonance that old instruments acquire. And it was true, too, that her old harp was easier to take to concerts and made it possible for her to move more freely round her room. All the same, she could not bring herself to speak to Stefan and he was banished from the house.

Then on the third day after her return from Grossenfluss, Professor Gertrude crept up to Annika's attic and opened the door. As she tiptoed over to the bed, Annika woke and suddenly sat up.

'It was dark plum jam,' she said – and her voice was full of joy. 'That's what I couldn't remember, for the stuffing!'

Then her head fell back and in an instant she was asleep again.

That afternoon Professor Gertrude sent for Stefan.

'I wondered if you had anything to tell me about the . . . accident,' she said to the boy who stood before her.

Stefan cleared his throat. 'Yes,' he said, summoning up his courage. 'It wasn't an accident. I did it on purpose.'

The professor nodded. 'I know,' she said.

'You know? How? When?' Stefan could not believe his ears. 'When did you . . . ?'

'Not at first. I was too distressed – but soon afterwards. I have known you since you were a few weeks old and you have never been a clumsy boy.' She stopped for a moment, looking him up and down. 'There are children who don't know – "push" from "pull", but you're not one of them. I understand you have been troubled in your mind, so I wanted to tell you that you did right.'

'It was because of Annika,' he stammered. 'I thought once they knew we weren't meant to be there we'd be turned out without a chance to get to her. The only thing

315

seemed to be to make a diversion and hope—' He broke off. 'I'd have done anything to get Annika out.'

'Yes,' said the professor. 'You did right. It was the most expensive instrument I've ever owned and it can't be mended – but you did right to push it down the stairs.'

In the end it was Rocco who got Annika out of bed.

'I keep hearing Rocco whinnying,' she said restlessly to Ellie. 'Even in my sleep I hear him. They say all horses sound the same, but it isn't true.'

Ellie made up her mind. 'It is Rocco,' she said.

And she told Annika about Zed's journey and that they were sure he hadn't taken her trunk, but she said nothing about Frau von Tannenberg.

'Well, if he didn't, I don't care who did,' said Annika. 'Who cares about a trunk of old clothes?'

Ten minutes later she was dressed and out in the stable yard.

'He remembers you,' said Zed, as Rocco rubbed his head against Annika's arm.

'I certainly remember him,' said Annika. 'Oh, I can't believe you're here and Rocco's here; it's like magic, finding you in Vienna.'

She had forgotten her fears, and her fatigue. Seeing Zed when she thought he was gone forever made everything right. Now she said, 'You're staying here, aren't you, Zed? You're staying in Vienna? Ellie says you can find plenty of odd jobs to do and the professors don't mind stabling Rocco.'

'Annika, I can't.' Zed had turned his face away so that she did not see how much he minded the thought of leaving. 'I have to go and find the gypsies. We could be in trouble here, Rocco and I, if I stay.'

'But why? What sort of trouble?'

'There were two men – special police I think, or informers. They saw me when I was riding Rocco in the Prater and they kept staring at me and they wrote things down in their notebooks. And I saw one of them again; when I was teaching Rocco to do a collected trot on that piece of waste ground behind the museum, and I was sure he was going to come up to me, but someone came and talked to him and I got away.' He paused, rubbing Rocco's neck. 'You've got to remember, Annika, I stole Rocco. The Master bought him for Hermann, not for me. The police must have been told to look out for me – and if Rocco is taken back to Spittal he'll be sold to anyone who wants him, and I've got to see that doesn't happen. I chose Rocco when he was a foal – and I suppose I chose him again when I took him away. Maybe stealing is a kind of choosing.' He shrugged. 'Anyway, I don't want to go to prison.'

'Yes, I see. But couldn't you just stay a little longer? I want to know about your journey. And I want to show you Vienna. You have to go on the Giant Wheel in the Prater, and down the Danube in a paddle boat – Oh, a lot of things.' And as Zed remained silent. 'Please, Zed?'

'I wanted to see that you were all right and you are, but now I must go.'

'Just for a few more days?' she pleaded. 'No one will find Rocco in our backyard.'

'It isn't that I want to go, Annika. Everyone has been so kind – everyone. I haven't had a home since the Master died . . . Well, never mind all that. I'll stay till the end of the week but no longer than that. And all right, we'll all go on the Giant Wheel. I suppose no one is allowed to leave Vienna without going on *that*!'

CHAPTER THIRTY-FIVE

THE EMPTYING SCHOOL

The headmistress's bedroom on the first floor of Grossenfluss had been turned into a hospital. The lower legs of the four-poster bed rested on two upended iron cauldrons so that the blood, when it reached the principal's feet, would be sure to return to her head. Large bronze cylinders of oxygen were propped up against the walls, rubber tubes and kidney bowls and syringes were piled on the bedside table. Fräulein von Donner's leg was in plaster and hung from a pulley on the ceiling; there was a splint on her broken nose, one arm was bandaged.

She had pinned the Order of the Closed Fist to the collar of her flannel nightdress, and she was eating a pork chop.

The pork chop was slightly burnt and this was because it had been cooked by the principal's faithful secretary, the eel-like Mademoiselle Vincent, and the reason for this was simple. There had been twenty maids in the kitchens and sculleries of Grossenfluss and now there were only two.

Nor was it necessary to tell the girls to be quiet outside the door of the sickroom because the corridor was almost empty of pupils, and every hour or so a carriage drew up and yet another nobly born lady or gentleman came to fetch their daughter home.

For Stefan, when he let the harp fall on to the headmistress, had started something which was not yet finished. Single-handedly, he had brought about the downfall of the school. It had begun slowly, like the fall of the harp itself, but now, a week later, it was almost complete.

Annika was not the only girl who had escaped that night. In the uproar and pandemonium three other girls had run away. The mushroom-hating Minna and the silent Flosshilde reached their homes safely and were not returned. A big, good-natured girl called Marta was hidden by a farmer, fell in love with his son and decided to stay.

But even the girls who did not escape had suddenly gone mad. The sight of the headmistress enmeshed in the strings and splintered woodwork of the harp seemed to undo years of fear. Some of the girls, herded into the chapel to pray for the principal's recovery, stood up and burst into a hymn of praise to God for smiting her. Olga slid down the banisters, whooping with joy, followed by her friends, and none of the teachers stopped them. In fact the day after the accident two of the teachers left suddenly, and the day after that, three more.

Perhaps it was the servants who did most to end the tyranny of Grossenfluss. They came out of the kitchens and gave out food to the girls who had been hungry for so long: loaves of bread were tossed into dormitories; bags of dried fruit were emptied into outstretched hands.

Then the police were called in, but for those wishing to restore the old order this was a mistake. The police had notes on the case of pupil 126. They had not been allowed to investigate the girl's death properly; they had been told it was an accident and sent away, but they had not believed it. Now, with Fräulein von Donner out of the way, they took statements from the maids and from the pupils who were left. The old princess received a visit from a government minister. By the end of the week no one doubted that the school would have to close.

And all the time, Fräulein von Donner lay helplessly in her bed and raged. The pork chops poor Mademoiselle Vincent brought became smaller and more burnt; the corridors became increasingly empty. Only the sound of the carriages on the gravel as the parents came for their daughters broke the silence.

'I can't see anyone,' Fräulein von Donner said as the days passed and the storm clouds gathered. 'Don't let anyone in. I'm too ill . . . I'm in pain.'

But there was one parent who took no notice of the principal's bleats or the shooing-away movements of Mademoiselle Vincent. Frau Edeltraut von Tannenberg's knock on the door was brief, she entered the room like a battleship with all flags flying – and behind her, his duelling scar throbbing with unease, came Oswald.

The news that Annika was missing from Grossenfluss was waiting for Edeltraut when she and Oswald returned from Switzerland. It caused them great distress.

'We must get her back at once, Oswald. This could be very serious. If the Vienna people get hold of her we could be in trouble. I don't think Annika went on believing that Zed took the trunk – if she should start asking questions again, or those wretched professors. The place is full of lawyers . . . and those ghastly Eggharts.'

'I wonder how she did it,' mused Oswald. 'Got out, I mean. Grossenfluss is supposed to be like a fortress.'

'It doesn't matter how she did it,' snapped Edeltraut. 'She must be brought back and we must keep her close all the time. Remember how that jeweller looked at us in Switzerland? Not Zwingli, the other one. The one who said it was unusual for a child to sign away her rights like that.'

So now, storming into the principal's room, she went on the attack at once.

'Do I understand that my daughter – *my* daughter – whom I entrusted to your care, has run away?'

'We don't know if she has run away,' said the head-mistress. 'She seemed very happy here and she was settling in well.'

'Well, what do you suggest happened?' demanded Frau von Tannenberg.

The principal lifted herself higher on her pillow. 'We think she may have been kidnapped,' she said. 'Perhaps by someone who knew of the good fortune that has come to your family of late.'

'What good fortune?' said Edeltraut angrily. 'I hope nobody has been gossiping about the affairs of Spittal. And in any case we would have received a ransom note and we have heard nothing. Nothing at all. We returned from

Switzerland to get your letter and that was the first we heard that Annika was not safe and sound.'

She took out her handkerchief and dabbed her eyes.

'What exactly happened?' asked Oswald.

'We would like to know precisely when she disappeared, and how,' said Edeltraut. 'Every detail of that tragic day.'

'Well, it was the day of my accident. I was seriously injured, and needless to say the staff and the girls were very concerned. For a few hours they were running about, fetching doctors, carrying me to my room . . . nobody had time to think of anything else. I was very nearly killed.'

She waited for sympathy, but what came from Edeltraut was more in the nature of a snort.

'How were you injured?'

'A harp fell on me from the top of the stairs. A very large harp, a most dangerous instrument.'

'A harp! How on earth—'

'A woman came with a harp and said she was sent by the Duchess of Cerise to give a concert to the girls. But I became suspicious – I am always concerned with the safety of the girls – and sure enough she was an impostor. So I ran out to stop her . . .'

She described the horrible events of that day in detail. When she had finished she leaned back on the pillows, overcome by the memory, but both her visitors were unimpressed.

'What was the harpist like?'

'A middle-aged woman with a bun of hair. She looked perfectly respectable. So did the boy who was with her, a peasant boy but well spoken. I didn't suspect until—'

'Wait,' interrupted Edeltraut. 'This peasant boy, what was he like?'

'He had fair hair and blue eyes. He was just the servant who helped to carry the instrument. I'm afraid you must ask my secretary to come to me – I'm feeling faint.'

But Frau von Tannenberg was already on the way to the door.

Outside she turned to Oswald. 'Professor Gertrude was a harpist. And the boy fits the description of the washer-woman's child whom Annika befriended. Could they have had anything to do with this? If Annika wrote a letter to Vienna and said she wasn't happy?'

'How would she get the letter out? All the post is read.'

'She might have got one of the maids to post it for her. You know how she always clung to servants. Unless Gudrun told them where Annika was, but she swears she didn't.'

'Gudrun is my daughter; she wouldn't lie.'

Edeltraut ignored this. 'There can't be any other explanation. She's either in Vienna or running round the countryside and I don't know which is worse.'

When they returned to Spittal she found a letter from Profesor Julius explaining that they had taken Annika away from Grossenfluss and she was safe with them.

'How *dare* he?' raged Edeltraut. 'Annika is my daughter and I am her legal guardian. These professors are going to be very sorry for this. Very sorry indeed!'

CHAPTER THIRTY-SIX

IS SHE COMING?

It was as though the city knew that Zed was leaving and that everything had to be as beautiful as possible. The sun shone, the lilacs and laburnums were in full bloom, the cafe tables were out on the pavement . . .

Annika behaved as though she had arranged all this for the benefit of her friend. She wanted to show Zed everything and take him everywhere. The professors had given her some pocket money and Zed had saved some of his earnings, so they began by exchanging presents in the marzipan shop in the Karntner Strasse: a spotted ladybird for Annika, a bushy-tailed fox for Zed.

'We have to eat them at once,' said Annika, 'otherwise we won't have the courage.'

They went to the fruit market, where the stallholders all knew her and made remarks about her handsome friend.

She took him to the cathedral, with its solemn paintings and the pile of skulls in the crypt from the days of the great plague. She led him behind the scenes in the art museum, where Uncle Emil's friends were cleaning a picture of John the Baptist's head, and past the statue of St Boniface under which Sigrid's uncle, the one who had eaten twenty-seven potato dumplings, had hidden on his wedding night.

And as they walked, they talked. Annika still knew nothing of what her mother had done, she never mentioned Spittal. These few days in Vienna had to exist without a future or a past.

They stood on the big State Bridge and watched the Danube, which flowed wide and deep and rather murkily grey, down to Budapest in Hungary, and on through the plains of Eastern Europe.

'You could put a message in a bottle if you wanted me, and throw it in the river,' Zed suggested. 'Then I'd find it when I was out riding and I'd come. Messages in bottles are important; I wouldn't ignore it.'

'Yes, I could do that . . . if I was here,' said Annika, and this was the closest she came to saying how uncertain she felt about the future. 'Perhaps by that time you'll be married to Rosina.'

'Rosina?' Zed looked at her, puzzled, and she was glad he had forgotten the name of the girl who had tried to give her a kitten. And, 'No, I won't,' he said firmly when she had explained, and he looked at her in a way that made her feel absurdly happy.

'Still, we might never see each other again,' she said.

'Yes, we will,' said Zed. 'We will.' And he put his hand over hers for a moment as it rested on the parapet.

They took the tram back to the Inner City and walked

past the arcaded Stallburg, where the Lipizzaners lived, towards the Imperial Palace. When they came to St Michael's Gate, Annika stopped suddenly and took hold of Zed's arm.

'Look, there he is!'

And it really was the Emperor Franz Joseph, driving out in a carriage with golden wheels to inspect the Razumovsky Guards, and putting up a white-gloved hand to wave, even to this one schoolgirl and her friend.

Zed followed the carriage with his eyes. 'I'm glad I've seen him. It's like seeing a piece of history.'

'You would stay if you could, wouldn't you, Zed? Stay in Vienna?'

She had annoyed him. He stopped dead and turned to face her.

'What do you think?' he said angrily. 'There's everything I've ever wanted here: books to read and a chance to learn things, and Ellie and Sigrid treating me as though I was their son . . . and friends. I've not had friends before – I was always on my own. You think life with the gypsies is roman- tic because you saw them one night round the campfire, but it isn't. It's hard and rough – and it can be cruel.' He broke off. 'Oh, never mind, you wouldn't understand.'

'Perhaps I would,' she said very quietly. 'Perhaps I do. I've had to leave here once and probably—'

'No.' He interrupted her, and then remembered that she knew nothing of the suspicions surrounding her mother, or of the plan the professors had made.

In the afternoon, when Pauline and Stefan returned from school, all four of them took Rocco to the deserted garden and let him graze.

Stefan was resigned now to following his father as a groundsman in the Prater.

'What's the point of making oneself miserable?' said Stefan. 'There's no money to train as an engineer and that's the end of it. And at least you'll have someone to take you round the fair and get you in half-price.' He turned to Zed. 'You'll see tomorrow when we go on the Giant Wheel. It really is something. There isn't a higher one in Europe.'

Tomorrow was Zed's last day but one, and they were going to spend it in the Prater. But when the morning came it turned out to be a very different sort of day, because, as soon as they had finished their breakfast, the professors sent for Annika.

'We have something to tell you,' they said.

It was not a nice 'something', Annika could see that at once. All three professors were looking grim – indeed they had only just stopped arguing about whether what they were about to do was right. Professor Gertrude was against it: 'There's no need to tell her, it'll only make her miserable.'

But both Julius and Emil said she should know. 'Truth is important,' they said, 'even for children. Particularly for children.'

All the same, they did not find it easy to begin.

'It's about your mother,' said Professor Julius.

Annika's heart began to beat wildly. 'Is she coming?'

'Yes, she is coming. She is staying at the Hotel Riverside and she will be here tomorrow afternoon to fetch you. We wrote to tell her that you were safe with us, and that we took you away from Grossenfluss because you were unhappy there, and that we think you should not return. Dr Flass has given you a medical certificate to say it would be bad for your health.'

'Thank you.'

'But there is something . . . Perhaps we should explain why Zed came to Vienna. He had found out that the jewels in the trunk which the Eggharts' great-aunt showed you were real.'

Annika looked at him in amazement. 'But they can't have been. She told me all about them . . . how the jeweller in Paris had them copied.'

'Nevertheless, they are real.' He told her the story of Fabrice's deception. 'He was very fond of the old lady, so he played a trick on her.'

'A kind trick,' said Annika. 'I wish she'd known. Or perhaps it was best as it was.'

'And it seems,' the professor went on, 'that the jewels are worth a fortune – and that they were left to you. Fräulein Egghart left you the trunk and all it contained; the lawyers have confirmed this.'

Annika was bewildered.

'But where is it then? My mother thought that Zed had taken it and at first . . . But I'm sure he didn't. I'm absolutely sure.'

'We are sure too.'

'But then who did?' Annika was completely at a loss.

'When Fräulein Egghart showed you the jewels,' the professor went on, 'did you see a brooch shaped like a butterfly?'

'Yes, I did. Blue sapphires for the wings and filigree gold for the antennae with rubies for the eyes. I suppose I

328

should have known the stones were real, they were so beautiful.'

Professor Julius picked up a letter on his desk. 'Yes. That is an exact description. We asked a friend in Switzerland to make some enquiries and his letter came this morning. Your butterfly brooch has just been sold by Zwingli and Hammerman for two million Swiss francs.'

'I don't understand. How did the brooch—'

Professor Julius put a hand on her shoulder. 'We think your mother may have taken it. That your mother and your Uncle Oswald took the trunk. The description of the woman who brought the brooch to the jeweller fits your mother perfectly.'

'NO!' Annika pulled away from him. 'It isn't true. I don't believe it. My mother wouldn't steal from me – why should she? Anything that belongs to me I'd have given her. She knows that.'

'It would have to be proved, and since it is you who have been robbed it is you would have to bring the case against her. If she was convicted and sent to prison we would ask the courts if you could come back to us, at any rate for the length of the sentence. This would mean that you could stay in Vienna and—'

But Annika couldn't take in another word.

'NO!' she said again. 'It isn't true. You're lying!' And she turned and ran from the room.

CHAPTER THIRTY-SEVEN

THE RIVERSIDE HOTEL

Frau Edeltraut sat at the dressing table of her room at the Riverside Hotel, brushing her hair. Bottles of scent and ointments, her silver combs, her powder puffs were spread out in front of her; sunlight filtered in from her private veranda with its deckchairs and pots of hanging carnations. Oswald was in an adjoining room, gazing at the paddle steamer and the colourful pleasure boats on the river through his binoculars.

Mathilde had been difficult, before they left for Vienna.

'I don't see why you should use Oswald all the time to fetch and carry for you,' she had said, glaring at her sister. 'Oswald is *my* husband; he doesn't belong to you.'

'I never said he did. If it's of any interest to you, I find Oswald extremely dreary. He has no breadth – no vision,' said Edeltraut. 'But I need him for this last journey to

Vienna. Once we have Annika back at Spittal I will find a person to be with her at all times and see that there's no more nonsense. If necessary . . .' But this was a sentence she did not finish, since Mathilde was weak and dithery and had been fond of Annika. 'And I have to point out that you were pleased enough to come to Zurich and spend my money.'

'Your daughter's money, you mean.'

Edeltraut ignored this. 'If the truth came out you'd be in quite as much trouble as Oswald and myself.'

'No, I wouldn't. I didn't steal the trunk. And Gudrun knows nothing about it, nothing at all.'

'Well, of course not. Nor does Hermann. One would hardly bring children into something in which secrecy is essential. But I tell you, if we don't get Annika away from Vienna, and quickly, and make sure she cannot escape again, everything we have worked for could fall to the ground.'

'Well, all right,' said Mathilde sulkily. 'But this is the last time – and I shall expect you to bring back a present for Gudrun. I suppose you won't go back to the Hotel Bristol.'

'You know perfectly well that I can't go back to the Bristol,' said Edeltraut, who had left without paying her bill.

'Well, in that case why don't you stay near the river instead? There's a good hotel by the Danube – the Riverside. Oswald thinks we need a new boat for the lake and there's a boat-builder near there.'

'Oh, Oswald wants me to buy him a boat now, does he?'

But she did in fact book two rooms at the Riverside Hotel on the edge of the city, and when she and Oswald arrived in Vienna she was glad she had done so, because the weather was fine and warm and the hotel, with its verandas over the water and its riverside walks and its view of the landing stage where the steamer unloaded its cargo of passengers, was a very pleasant place to be.

'I have business to attend to in the morning, as I told you,' Edeltraut told her brother-in-law when they arrived. 'I shan't need you for that. But in the afternoon I want you to come with me to fetch Annika. I have full legal rights as her mother, but I don't trust these professors.'

'You don't think they suspect something?'

'Don't be silly, how could they? Zed's with the gypsies in Hungary and no one else knows anything.'

So now she was busy creating herself in readiness for another day. Her morning dress of coral silk was protected by a chiffon peignoir; her coral earrings and matching necklace were waiting on the jewellery stand. She had powdered her face and darkened her eyelashes. Her long hair, washed the night before by the hotel hairdresser, hung loose down her back and she was brushing it. One could never brush hair hard enough, or for too long.

She was interrupted by a knock at the door and a hotel page announced that there was a young lady to see her.

'Did she give her name?'

'No, madam. She's very young; just a child. Shall I send her up.'

'Yes, you had better do that.'

Annika had been awake the whole night. The professors' accusations went round and round in her head, and every time she pushed them away they came back again.

The professors were lying; they had to be. They may not

have meant to lie but they had lied just the same. It was not possible that her mother was a thief. If she was guilty, she had not only stolen the trunk but blamed Zed for the theft – and that was impossible.

Annika remembered the joy of that first meal in the Hotel Bristol, the excitement and pride of finding that she belonged to such a beautiful woman. The hope with which she had travelled to Spittal . . .

Perhaps Uncle Oswald had done it? He was always doing things for her mother; yes, it could be that. And her mother hadn't known till it was over.

Oh God, she had to believe that her mother was good. How did people live if they thought their mother was dishonest?

As soon as it was light Annika had got dressed and crept out of the house. She had to see her mother at once and she had to see her alone and find out the truth. Nothing mattered except that.

The journey to the Riverside Hotel was long and wearisome: the tram to the terminus, then the little train which steamed along the Danube, and a dusty walk from the station to the hotel.

But as she came up to the front entrance with its flowering trees and its awnings and verandas, her mood lifted. This was a place for summer and happiness, not for lies and intrigue. In ten minutes, in five, the nightmare would be over.

Her mother would put her arms round her and tell her the truth. And the truth would set her free!

'Come in,' called Edeltraut. She sprayed herself with scent once more and shook out her hair so that it mantled her shoulders. Then, her brush still in her hand, she rose quickly and went to the door.

'Annika, my dearest child! My own darling! What is it – you look so pale?'

Annika had not come forward. She was still standing, very straight, her back against the door.

'What has upset you so, my child? What have they been telling you to make you look like that?

'They told me that it was you who stole La Rondine's trunk,' Annika said steadily. 'You and Uncle Oswald – because the jewels in it were real.'

Her mother's hand went to her throat.

'How *dare* they? How dare they tell you such dreadful lies! No wonder you look so upset.'

'Zed came – he's in Vienna. He heard the story from Baron von Keppel and—'

'Zed! Zed is in Vienna?'

'Yes.'

For a moment there was complete silence. Annika had not moved from the door, nor had her eyes left her mother's face. When she spoke again her voice was very low, but each word was absolutely clear.

'Could you please tell me the truth,' said Annika. 'Just the truth, Mama. Nothing else.'

Edeltraut had slipped off her peignoir; in her coral silk dress, her wonderful hair mantling her shoulders, she was dazzling. Her scent was different; not strange and exotic but light and summery. Beautiful people always surprise one afresh, but Annika stood her ground.

'Please, Mama.'

Then something extraordinary happened. The tall proud woman in her silken dress seemed suddenly to

334

crumple. She took a few faltering steps – and then she dropped on to her knees in front of Annika.

'You shall have the truth,' she said brokenly. 'Yes, I did it. I made Oswald fetch the trunk – it was addressed to me, remember? I took the jewels and took them to Switzerland. But before you call the police, would you try to understand? Not to forgive, that would be asking too much, but to understand.'

'I shan't call the police,' said Annika. 'Not ever. You're my mother. But I'd certainly like to understand.'

'Of course, of course . . .' Edeltraut rose from her knees and fell back into a low chair. She stretched her hands out to her daughter, trying to conceal the relief she felt. Annika took them, but her eyes were still fixed steadily on Edeltraut's face.

'If you could try to imagine,' said Edeltraut, 'I was only twenty when I married – far too young to be a judge of character – and when I realized that my husband was a compulsive gambler I was very much afraid. There was no one to turn to, no one to help me. Week by week, month by month, I saw the house stripped of all its treasures; the paintings, the books, my own jewels, and my sister's. Well, you know all that – but remember, my darling, I was a von Tannenberg. We're a proud family. The shame of being beggars . . . of people turning their faces away when they met me – people I'd known all my life . . . oh, it was dreadful!

'Then my husband fled to America and I was quite alone at Spittal, with a young son to care for. I didn't know what to do; I saw Spittal becoming a ruin . . . and there have always been von Tannenbergs at Spittal. And then my father died and I had an idea, which lifted my spirits; no, more than that – it made me wonderfully happy. Can you guess what it was?'

Annika shook her head.

'I would find my little daughter, the one I had been forced to abandon when she was only a few days old. And suddenly life seemed to have a meaning and a purpose once again.'

Edeltraut had soaked a handkerchief. She crumpled it into a ball and picked up another.

But still Annika did not speak.

'It was hard to find you. I went to Pettelsdorf and there I learned that you'd been adopted and taken to Vienna, and then I tramped the streets, trying to find out where you were. I found a lawyer, a famous man – Herr Pumpelmann-Schlissinger – and he helped me . . . and then at last I found you. Oh, Annika, when you came in through that door in the professors' house and I saw you there before me with your father's eyes and hair and that look of trust . . . I think it was my first happy day for many years.'

'Yes. I was happy too,' said Annika quietly.

'But of course I was worried about bringing you to Spittal. We were living . . . well, like peasants, with no money at all.'

No, Annika wanted to say. Peasants don't live like that. They cook and clean and chop wood and make do – but she did not speak.

Edeltraut got up and walked to the window.

'But you see, Annika, the lawyer had found out something else about you. An old lady who lived in the square had left you a trunk full of keepsakes; the will was still being proved and you knew nothing about it. Then, when I went back to Spittal to get ready for your arrival, my uncle told me the story about La Rondine's jewels and that they were real but nobody knew it.

'Of course I should have told you – but I didn't know if the story was true; the jewels might have been fakes, as everyone believed. And I had this dream, Annika – the dream of making Spittal great again and you and Hermann living there in comfort. I have made a will, you know, leaving you a share of Spittal. Not just Hermann, you. Oh, Annika, I have been so very foolish.'

'I would have given you the jewels for Spittal. I would have given you everything I had,' said Annika quietly.

'I know – oh, I know now, my darling. But remember, I hardly knew you then. I could see that you were sweet and pretty, but a little girl can have her head turned by sudden wealth. I should have trusted my own daughter – my own flesh and blood – but I had been hurt so much.'

Annika was very tired. Something seemed not to fit, but she was too weary to work it out.

And Edeltraut's eyes had filled with tears again. She put a hand on Annika's shoulder. 'We could start a new life together, you and I. We could make my dream for Spittal come true together. There is a lot of money left, and you shall decide how it is spent. Without Hermann I am so very much alone. Say it isn't too late. Say you'll come, my darling. I need you so very much.'

'I won't go back to Grossenfluss. Not ever.' In spite of her exhaustion, Annika's voice was firm.

'No, no, of course not. It was wrong of me to think that you might be happy there. I thought you needed companionship of your own age, but the school has changed completely in the last few years. I should have taken you there and seen for myself instead of letting you go with

Mathilde; I have been guilty there too – dreadfully guilty. You shall never go back there, I swear it.' She had found another handkerchief and managed to smile through her tears. 'My poor, pale darling, don't stand there by the door. Let the sun warm your face, come out on to the balcony.'

Annika let herself be led out of the French window. In front of her was the dazzling water with its gaily painted boats. Tulip trees were in flower along the bank; children splashed in the shallows. The world was still there and it was very beautiful.

'Look, there's the steamer just going off to Regensburg.'

Annika nodded. 'It's the *Princess Stephanie*.'

Her mother had put her arm round her and her scent stole into Annika's nostrils.

'There's so much to see, so much to do. Couldn't we do it together?'

Still Annika was silent. She did not think that she had ever been so tired.

'I've had such an idea,' said Edeltraut eagerly. 'We could go back home on the steamer. Go back by river. The boat goes quite a long way into Germany, we'd have days on the water before we had to change to a train. You'd like that, wouldn't you? You like travelling by boat.'

'Yes.'

'You'll come then, my darling? You'll forgive me?' She stretched out her hands imploringly and looked deep into Annika's eyes. 'Because if I don't have your forgiveness I don't know . . . how I shall live.'

CHAPTER THIRTY-EIGHT

THE LETTER

Nobody could believe it.

'You're not going to do anything about the jewels? You're going to let her have them and say nothing?'

Everybody was amazed and distressed, but Pauline was furious.

'You must be completely mad,' she said.

They had all gathered in the courtyard to find out where Annika had been.

'Would you give your mother up to the police?' asked Annika. 'Would you, Ellie?' She turned to the professors. 'Would you?'

For a moment she had silenced them. Ellie remembered her mother, who had once taken a small wilted sprig of parsley hanging down from the side of a market stall because the stallholder was busy serving a queue of customers and she was in a hurry. The following day she had sent Ellie to walk five kilometres in the heat down a dusty road to find the woman and pay her.

'You see,' said Annika, 'you wouldn't. Not your own mother.'

But what they minded – what was almost impossible to understand – was that Annika was going back of her own free will to Spittal. She wasn't even going to try and stay in Vienna.

'She asked me to forgive her; she went down on her knees to me.'

Pauline snorted and the professors frowned at her, but it was true that they too were very much upset. They had given Annika a way out and she had not even tried to take it.

'It's just snobbishness,' said Pauline. 'You really like being a "von" and having people bow and scrape to you. You must like it or you wouldn't be so feeble.'

'No.' Annika's wretchedness was beyond tears. 'I don't like it.'

The boredom of life at Spittal came back to her. The long empty days, not being allowed to help . . . and she would go back without Zed, without Rocco's whinny of greeting when she went down to the farm. Without the farm . . .

She set her teeth. She had given her word and she could see no other way. Perhaps people who had always had mothers felt differently, but to her, her mother's arrival after the years of daydreaming about her had been a miracle. She could not now turn her back on the person who had given her life.

'It's in the Bible,' Annika said wearily. 'It's where Ruth says, "Whither thou goest, I will go; and where thou

340

lodgest, I will lodge: thy people shall be my people, and thy God my God.'"

But it was not wise to quote things to Pauline, who had always read more than anybody else. 'Ruth didn't say it to her mother, she said it to her mother-in-law, and that's completely different.'

But Annika had fought her battle on the way back from the Riverside; no one could shake her decision. If people did not forgive those closest to them, how could the world go on?

'It's in the pictures too, everywhere.' She turned to Uncle Emil. 'The whole museum is full of mothers holding their children.'

Emil, however, could see no connection between Frau von Tannenberg and the Holy Mother of God, and said so.

The person who said the least and perhaps understood the most was Ellie – but her hurt was absolute. She knew that Annika was not a snob and that she was unimpressed by riches. Annika was a person who was interested in doing things, not in having them. Only an overwhelming love for her mother could make her behave as she had done.

Up to now Ellie had hoped that her foster child still remembered her old life with affection. Now she faced the truth, but she did not know how she was going to endure a separation for the second time.

'I think I'll go back to my people,' she said to Sigrid. 'They'll be glad of some extra help. They'd take you in too.'

Ellie's cousins ran a little hotel high in the Alps.

'I'm sure it'll be better up there,' she went on. 'The mountain air's so thin it makes you see things differently.'

But the air would have to be very thin indeed, thought Sigrid, to make either of them forget the girl they had brought up.

Annika had asked for two days more in Vienna. She wanted to say goodbye to Zed – and she wanted, for the last time, to cook a meal.

'I shan't try and help or interfere at Spittal,' she said to Ellie. 'They've got servants and there would be no point. But I'd like to make one meal for all of you tonight. If the professors don't mind we could all eat in the dining room. And I'd like to ask Frau Bodek.'

She began the preparations for the farewell meal at once, writing the menu down and assembling the ingredients.

'Would you like me to help you or do you want to work alone?' said Ellie.

'I would like it if you helped me, Ellie. Please. And Sigrid. It's not a difficult meal, but I'll need lots of ice . . . and somehow I've got to get hold of molasses.'

'Molasses?'

'You'll see. I want to make those Norrland Nussel – at least I do if you've kept the recipe I sent you.'

'Of course I've kept it. It's on the back of the envelope it came on. I put it in the black book.'

'You haven't tried them yet?'

'No. I wasn't sure if I could get tansy, but Sigrid says she's seen some in the market.'

'Good.' Annika had finished scribbling. 'I'm going to start with beef broth with very small dumplings; they'll be light for Uncle Emil's stomach. Then roast saddle of venison with peas and celeriac and potato puffs . . . then a

342

strawberry bombe – and with the coffee, the Norrland Nussel. How does that sound?'

'It sounds just fine,' said Ellie. 'Now you just tell us what you want us to do.'

They cooked together all afternoon. Cooking is hard physical work, and while they were busy pounding and stirring and chopping and sieving, the grief of the parting that was to come could be pushed to the back of their minds, and be endured.

'Now for the Nussel,' said Annika. 'I do hope I can get them right. I can't see how they can help being heavy with the molasses and the chestnuts . . . but the ones I had in Bad Haxenfeld were really light. And she was such a nice woman, the one who gave me the recipe.'

Ellie was reaching up for the black book, looking at the envelope she had placed between its pages. Annika's hand-writing sprawled over the back. 'It's the egg white that will keep them light,' she said. 'Twelve eggs, it says here; we'll have some beating to do.'

'You can get egg-beaters that work mechanically,' said Annika. 'I saw one in a shop.'

'Over my dead body,' said Ellie. 'No egg is going to be touched by that new-fangled machinery in my kitchen.'

But Annika was looking at the envelope. 'What an idiot – I sent it on the back of the letter I found in the desk at Spittal. I suppose I'd better take it back with me when I go.'

And suddenly the lull in which the three of them had worked together, as so often before, was over.

The farewell meal had been cleared away. The food had been a triumph, but no one felt very cheerful and Pauline

actually lost her temper and stormed out before the strawberry bombe, though this was her favourite dessert. It
happened when Frau Bodek asked Annika if she really had
to go back to Spittal and Annika said, 'She is my mother,'
in a way that made Pauline, she said, feel sick.

'Did you like the Norrland Nussel?' Annika asked Ellie.
'What did you think?'

'They were good,' said Ellie, who did not feel like saying that the whole meal had tasted to her like sawdust.
And, looking at Annika's anxious face, 'I think you ought
to copy the recipe into the book.'

'Really?' Annika was pleased. 'Then you can cook them
when I've gone.'

And Ellie nodded, though she thought that nothing was
less likely than that she would swallow a Nussel ever again.

'I'll do it in my room,' said Annika, and she took the
black book and the envelope and kissed Ellie and Sigrid
rather quickly, because this was not a night for lingering
over anything emotional.

The house was very quiet. Zed had gone to say goodbye
to Stefan's uncle. He had already packed up his belongings
in the bookshop and set up his camp bed in Sigrid's ironing room, ready for an early start.

The cathedral clock struck eleven. This time the day
after tomorrow she would be gone. No, that was silly, she
wouldn't think like that. There might be an earthquake.
She might die in her sleep.

She reached for the black book and for her pen and
inkwell.

'Twelve egg whites, 200 grams of chestnut purée, six
tablespoons of molasses . . .' wrote Annika.

The letter was still there inside the envelope – probably

it was just an old bill, in which case there was no point in taking it back to Spittal.

She finished copying in the recipe, and slit open the envelope.

Annika read the letter once, peering at the old-fashioned, looped handwriting. Then she read it again.

It was definitely not a bill.

CHAPTER THIRTY-NINE

ROCCO

Zed had not forgotten the police officers who had stared at him so hard in the Prater, but as the time to leave came closer he was sure that he would get away.

So when the bell rang early in the morning as he was packing his saddlebags he did not think it had anything to do with him. Then Sigrid came and said there were two uniformed men at the door, asking for the boy with the bay horse.

Zed's first instinct was to go into the backyard and ride Rocco away down the lane. But it was already too late. The front door was open, the tall man with the bushy eyebrows was standing in the hall. He did not look like someone with whom one could play cat-and-mouse for long.

'I'll show them into the sitting room,' said Sigrid.

Zed squared his shoulders. It had come then. Prison for him for stealing a horse – and for Rocco, what?

The two men were standing beside the porcelain stove: the very tall one and the smaller, tubby one with the gingery moustache.

At least they were polite. They said good morning, shook hands, asked his name.

But then came the words Zed had heard so often in his head.

'We would like you to come with us. You and the horse. Just halter him – no need to bring his tack.'

So they weren't just going to charge him. They were going to confiscate the horse.

'Come along, boy; we have a lot to do.'

There was nothing for it. Zed led them out of the house and into the courtyard.

Rocco was not a vicious animal, but he could bare his teeth as threateningly as the next horse when he wanted to. Now, however, he let Zed down badly, rubbing his face against the uniformed sleeve of the tall man as though he was meeting his oldest friend.

Zed slipped on the halter. His hands were clumsy; misery engulfed him. It was over then, everything was over.

What happened to horses who were taken away by the police? Did they get sold on or spend their days in some wretched compound, a sort of dumping ground for equine down-and-outs?

Or did they simply get shot?

He led the horse round by the back lane and into the square. Rocco was stepping out as if to a party, his feet high, his neck arched, as though impressing the policemen who walked beside him was the most important thing on

347

earth. So much for the instinct of animals, thought Zed bitterly.

They began to cross the square, making their way towards the chestnut trees and the Keller Strasse.

How long did one stay in prison for stealing a horse? Two years, three . . . no, more probably. Much, much more. Would they put him in a dungeon, or in a cell with murderers and drunks?

'Stop. STOP, Zed. Wait!'

He turned round and so did the two men who were taking him away.

'Good heavens!' said the taller one.

A girl with streaming corn-coloured hair was running across the cobbles towards them. She was barefoot, and still in her dressing gown, but even without shoes she ran like the wind.

'Stop, stop,' she cried again – and Rocco too turned his head and recognized someone he knew, and came firmly to a halt.

Annika came panting up to them.

'I found this last night. Read it, Zed, quickly.' And to the two men, 'Please let him read it. Please?'

Zed took the sheet of paper she held out to him.

'Go on then,' said the tall man, and took the halter rope from Zed. 'But remember, we are busy people.'

Zed opened the letter. He recognized the handwriting at once and his heart beat faster. It was from the Freiherr von Tannenburg to the head of the stud at Zverno, asking him to find a horse suitable for his grandson, Hermann. 'Something very steady and quiet,' he wrote, 'as the boy is not a natural horseman. I'm giving Rocco to Zed; I think together they will go far.'

The rest of the letter was about the price he was willing to pay for Hermann's horse and the details of how he wanted it to be sent.

The letter was dated the sixteenth of March 1906 and had never been posted because the following day the old man had his stroke and neither wrote nor spoke again.

For a moment Zed could not speak. It was as though the man he had loved so much was there beside him. Then he felt an incredible relief and joy. He was not a thief. Rocco was his.

'He's my horse,' he said in a dazed voice, looking up at the two men. 'I haven't stolen him. He belongs to me.'

'Well, of course he belongs to you,' said the tall man. 'Anyone can see that. Now please don't keep us waiting any longer.'

'Why?' Zed was suddenly very angry. 'Why should I come along? I haven't done anything. I suppose it's because my mother was a gypsy. You're going to find something you can use against me and arrest me – my people have always been persecuted.'

The tall man sighed. 'What's the matter with you, boy? We're not from the police.'

'Well, where are you from then?'

The tall man was displeased. He had thought that everyone in Vienna knew who he was; certainly everyone who owned a horse.

'Here is my card,' he said.

Zed looked at it and read: 'Herr Kapitan Muller, Deputy Director, Imperial Spanish Riding School'.

At the gates of the Stallburg a groom came and led Rocco away into the stables he had passed so often. He went reluctantly, looking back at Zed again and again, but the groom who led him soothed his fears and took him forward.

Zed followed Captain Muller into his office, on the other side of the street. It was a big room, filled with pictures and statuettes of horses and silver cups. On the walls was a tapestry of trophies and rosettes, citations from the emperor and signed portraits.

The captain sat down behind his desk and the man with the ginger moustache got out his pen, ready to take notes.

'I want to ask you a few questions about your stallion. What is his name?'

My stallion, thought Zed dazedly. Mine!

'Rocco. His full name is Rococo Florian Devanya.'

The captain exchanged glances with his assistant.

'Do you know anything about his pedigree? Where was he foaled?'

'He comes from the stud at Zverno, in Hungary. My father was the manager there till . . . he was killed.'

'What was your father's name?'

'Tibor Malakov.'

The two men exchanged glances. 'It begins to become clear,' the captain said. 'I met your father once or twice. A man who knew his job. He died trying to stop a fight, I believe?'

'Yes.'

'And Rocco was foaled there. Do you know his dam?'

'She was a mare we got from a man called Count Halvan. He used to get horses from the stud at Lipizza and cross them with Arabs he bought from a breeder at Cadiz. They'll have the papers at Zverno.'

'So one could be certain of some Lipizzaner blood. A

quarter.' The captain was speaking in a low voice to his assistant. 'That might be enough to get it past the committee.' He turned back to Zed. 'Now tell us how you came by him. Tell us everything you know about the horse.'

So Zed told them about the visit of the Freiherr to the stud and the finding of the foal. Now that he was no longer afraid of being branded a thief, he told them everything: about his efforts to stop Hermann riding him, about the Freiherr's death.

'But you yourself have been riding him? And training him?'

'I had to ride him up to a point. I rode him to Vienna. But he's very young – just four – and I didn't want him to do unnecessary tricks. The things he does were mostly the things he wanted to do. He likes learning things.'

Captain Muller nodded.

'And the levade he performed in the Prater? The one that saved the life of that little boy? Did you teach him that?'

Zed flushed. 'Not really. He likes to rear up and . . . well, I suppose I moved my weight a bit and showed him how to hold it . . . but I know horses have to be trained very carefully and that's a movement that needs their muscles to be mature. With the boy in the Prater it was mostly his instinct.'

'Hmm. It's true horses don't trample people if they can possibly avoid it, but I think there was rather more than instinct at work there.'

There was a knock at the door and a messenger in a brown uniform with brass buttons put his head round the door. 'Here's the report from the stable, sir.'

The captain took it, and read it in silence. Then he said, 'This is only the result of the first quick examination. But it confirms what you said – the horse is just four years old, and in good shape physically. And they've found the Zverno brand on his withers.' The captain leaned back in his chair. 'I wonder,' he said slowly, 'if you know the story of the Emperor's Horse?'

'No, sir.'

'I don't know if it's a true story. Nothing is written down about it, but it's part of the heritage of the Imperial Spanish Riding School.' He folded his hands. 'As you're aware, it is only the white stallions that are trained to become performers and to learn the "airs above the ground". And even then, of all the stallions bred at Lipizza, only a very few are suitable for the training. The work is incredibly hard, for both the horse and the rider, and it takes years of patience. A horse who doesn't enjoy the work is not suitable. Such horses are sent back to Lipizza or to our farm near Piber, and either sold as riding horses or kept for stud.

'So you will see then that the horses we have here are all greys . . . the "white horses of Vienna", that is our trademark, you might say.

'But in every performance now there is just one horse that is not white. A horse that performs along with the rest: a bay horse. And it is known as the Emperor's Horse because having it in the troupe is supposed to bring luck to the Imperial House of Hapsburg and to the city.

'Apparently many, many years ago there was an epidemic at Lipizza and a great many of the horses died. It was impossible to send all the greys they needed in Vienna, so the manager sent along one bay. He was called Siglovy Rondina. He was a Lipizzaner all right, but he didn't turn white. As you know, Lipizzaners start dark and turn light gradually – but not all of them do. Some stay dark and sometimes among them you get a bay. This particular bay turned out to be a wonderful horse to train and they put him into a performance just once, with apologies to the audience. That's him over there.' He pointed to a picture on the wall behind him. 'But he was a great success, and that year none of the horses at Lipizza died; the epidemic was over. And the stable men said the bay had brought luck to the Imperial Spanish Riding School and it came to be called the Emperor's Horse. One year they couldn't find a bay, all the horses they used were white, and that was the year that the empress was assassinated . . . And another year when they didn't use a bay the crown prince died. Since then we've always tried to find a bay to work along with the rest – and that horse, whatever his real name, is known as the Emperor's Horse. So that's how the story came into being. We don't advertise it because everyone knows the Lipizzaners are white, but for the people who work with the horses it's important.' He leaned back in his chair. 'Now do you see what I'm trying to tell you?'

Zed shook his head.

'Come, boy . . . We have a bay now, but he's old and the bay we tried out as a replacement has not proved suitable. We think . . . it is possible . . . only possible, not even probable, let alone certain . . . that your horse . . . that Rocco could be trained to become part of our team. That he could become the Emperor's Horse. There are many difficulties. We only use horses that have Lipizzaner blood, usually pure, so that is one hurdle. There are always sticklers for the letter of the law. And he might prove to be quite unsuitable after further training. But the question I

353

brought you here to answer is this. Would you be prepared to give Rocco to the Imperial Spanish Riding School? You know how we work – it would take several years to train him, and he would have only one rider always, so it is a decision for life.'

Zed was silent. He imagined Rocco disappearing through the great gates of the Stallburg forever. Imagined him turning his head reproachfully as Zed allowed him to go to strangers, heard his whicker of reproach. Tears stung his eyes, and he bent his head. But he knew what he had to say. He had owned Rocco knowingly only for a few hours, and now he must let him go. 'Rocco is a person who happens to be a horse,' he had said to Pauline. How could he deny him his chance?

He swallowed the lump in his throat.

'Would I be able to see him sometimes . . . to talk to his rider . . . or is it not allowed?'

The captain looked at him impatiently. 'Don't be silly, boy. His rider of course would be – you.'

CHAPTER FORTY

PAULINE'S SCRAPBOOK

After she had stormed out of Annika's farewell supper, Pauline shut herself up in the bookshop.

Her grandfather was away at a book sale; Zed had dismantled his camp bed and taken his things next door to pack.

'I am alone,' said Pauline to herself in a hollow voice. 'I shall always be alone. My friend is going back to her man-eating mother because she's a snob and doesn't like me enough to stay in Vienna. Very well. I shall manage. I have my books. I have my dreams.'

All this sounded so tragic that she cheered up a little and took out her scrapbook. Since Annika had been brought back from Grossenfluss, Pauline had had no time to paste in her cuttings. Now she got down the bottle of glue, and set to work.

The story about the boy with whooping cough who had waded right through the sewers beneath the city to find his terrapin did not take long to paste in. Nor did the one about the woman who had thrown herself over her twin daughters during a sudden sandstorm and shielded them with her body, even though she was completely covered in boils at the time.

But the third cutting was longer. It was an article about a man who was 102 years old and had had twelve operations and was on his deathbed when he heard the mewing of a trapped kitten on a ledge outside his house. All his relatives were standing round the bed and he asked them one by one in a failing voice to rescue the little animal. But none of them would, so he rose from his deathbed and climbed out on to the ledge in his nightshirt and brought the kitten safely down – and then he died.

Pauline read through the story once again; then she turned it over and picked up the bottle of glue and the brush.

But the brush stayed in mid-air, because she was looking at a smudgy picture of a dapper man in evening clothes and a top hat.

Underneath the picture were the words: 'Eminent Viennese lawyer faces prison. Pumpelmann-Schlissinger accused of fraud and illegal practices.'

Pauline read the piece once, then read it again.

There are things you can forget and things you can't – and even if she hadn't known quite a lot about Herr Pumpelmann-Schlissinger she would not have forgotten his name.

He was the lawyer who had witnessed the document that Amelia Plotz, the midwife at Pettlelsdorf, had signed.

The document in which she had sworn that on the sixth of June 1897 she had attended Frau Edeltraut von Tannenberg and delivered a baby girl.

Pauline had seen the document in the professors' sitting room, with Amelia Plotz's sprawling signature counter-signed by the neat, spiky signature of the dapper laywer, and all of it stamped with red sealing wax bearing the double-headed eagle of the House of Austria.

Fraud and illegal practices. What exactly did that mean? As far as Pauline could see, it meant that Pumpelmann-Schlissinger was a cheat. Which meant . . . But as Pauline saw what it might mean she felt fear rise inside her. Her stomach churned, her heart began to thump and she closed her eyes because the room had begin to spin.

It meant that she, Pauline, would have to leave the shop – and set out alone because her friends were not there to help her.

It meant getting on a tram by herself, and after the tram reached the Southern Railway Station it meant buying a ticket to Pettelsdorf, and when she reached Pettelsdorf it meant asking to see Amelia Plotz the midwife. Pauline knew about midwives – after all, her mother was a nurse. Midwives often had to bring babies into the world without the help of a doctor or anyone else, and in the middle of the night. They had huge strong arms to pull out babies, and they boiled kettles of water and tore up sheets . . .

'I can't,' said Pauline aloud. 'I absolutely can't.'

She put the cutting away and went to bed. But the following morning she was up at dawn, writing a note to her grandfather.

'I have robbed the till,' she wrote, 'because I had to have

money for something important. I will pay you back from my wages when you pay me some.'

Then she locked the shop, put the key under the mat and walked across the square and through the chestnut trees to catch the tram.

There is a name for what it was that troubled Pauline. It is called agoraphobia, which means fear of open spaces and strangers. People who suffer from it are perfectly all right indoors or if they go out with friends they know and trust. But when they're alone in unfamiliar places they suffer from panic and dread. They tell themselves not to be silly, but it doesn't help any more than it helps people who are terrified of snakes or spiders to tell themselves that they are being silly. A phobia is a silliness you can't control and it is a very frightening thing to have.

So Pauline's stomach went on lurching and her heart went on hammering as she sat on the tram, and again as she walked through the vaulted railway station and bought a ticket for the lakeside halt that served Pettelsdorf.

Inside the compartment she felt better; compartments are closed and cosy, like rooms, but as the train chugged up into the mountains the thought of what she had set herself to do was terrifying. She imagined Amelia Plotz with her huge arms and her face covered in sweat and the water boiling away behind her and tried to think what she would do to a girl who came from nowhere and asked her impertinent questions.

The train went no faster than it had done when Ellie and Sigrid had taken it to the mountains all those years ago. Pauline had been with them often since then, on Annika's Found Days, but never alone. Still, she set off on the familiar walk to the village and everything was there:

the cows with flowers hanging out of their mouths, the goat bells up in the high pasture, the pine-scented breeze.

In the village she stopped at the post office and asked if she could be directed to the house of the midwife.

'I've got a message from someone in Vienna who wants to thank her for delivering her baby,' she said.

The postmistress was helpful. 'It's the little house at the end of the street on the right. There's a carving of a donkey on the gate, and a peach tree in the garden.'

The house was nice; there was a little boy playing on the grass who reminded her of the Bodek boys. The midwife was preparing lunch for her family, but she invited Pauline into her kitchen and poured her a glass of milk.

But it seemed quite quickly that something was wrong. She did not remember a baby she had delivered twelve years ago because she had only been working in Pettelsdorf for four years.

'And the nurse who worked here before me has gone to Canada,' said the midwife.

Pauline tried to fight down her disappointment. The trail had gone completely cold.

'That would be Amelia Plotz then?' she said. 'It's Amelia Plotz I'm looking for.'

The midwife put down her spoon. 'Amelia Plotz? Are you sure?'

'Yes.'

'Well, well . . . she's here – she lives about half an hour's walk away up the hill. But I don't know—'

'Will she see me?' asked Pauline.

'Yes and no . . . I can't really explain.'

She gave her instructions, and a doughnut, and Pauline set off up the hill. The empty road leading to nowhere gave

Pauline another panic attack: she felt as though she had been cut off forever from the safety of her home. But she sat down on a kerbstone and took some deep breaths and then she could go on again.

Amelia Plotz's house was rather a sad little one. It stood on the edge of a river which had cut its way deep into the hill. The windows were dirty and the cat that slunk past her as she knocked on the door was thin and wild.

But that was nothing to what she found when the door opened and an old woman with a tufty grey moustache and rheumy eyes asked her what she wanted.

'I wondered if I could see Amelia Plotz? Are you—?'

The old woman cackled. 'No, I'm not Amelia, the Lord be thanked,' she said. 'What do you want with her?'

'I have a message from someone in Vienna.'

The woman with the moustache gave her a sharp look. 'Well, you can talk to her if you like. She doesn't get many visitors.'

Pauline followed her up a narrow flight of stairs. There was a smell of cat, and of other things that Pauline was careful not to give words to.

'A visitor for you, Amelia,' shouted the old woman.

She could have saved her breath. Amelia was propped against soiled cushions on a vast armchair which only just accommodated her bulk. Her white hair was loose; her eyes stared into space. She took absolutely no notice of Pauline or of the woman who had spoken to her.

'She's got a message for you,' shouted the moustached lady.

Amelia Plotz's vacant eyes continued to stare at nothing. A drop of spittle came from her mouth.

'What happened to her?' asked Pauline.

'She's been like that for twenty years or more,' said her carer. 'Had a stroke and never recovered. She can't speak, can't hear . . . Looking after her is a nightmare, I tell you, but what can you do, she's my sister.'

Pauline stared at the wrecked figure in the chair. So when Annika was born, she had already been like this.

'Can she write?' asked Pauline. 'Could she write her name.'

The old woman stared at her. 'Funny you should ask that. There were some people who came a few months ago – said they'd a few bits for her left by a patient years back and she had to sign a paper. They helped her to write her name. Well, they held the pen really and wrote for her. The poor old thing didn't have an idea what she was writing. We're still waiting for the things.'

'Was it a tall, very stately woman with a German accent?'

'Yes. And a man with her, very smartly dressed. Looked like a frog, but you could see he was a gentleman. A lawyer, he said he was. He wouldn't let me into the room to see the paper – said it was private. You might as well get a dog to sign a paper, but I didn't tell him that.'

CHAPTER FORTY-ONE

THE DANUBE STEAMER

The river boats that carried passengers up and down the Danube were named after members of the Austrian royal family. The boat Annika was due to travel on was the *Empress Elisabeth*, and it was the newest and smartest of the river fleet. The steamer was bedecked with flags, her funnel was striped in the black and red and white of the House of Austria. The cabins were roomy; there was a sun lounge and a restaurant on the foredeck.

The band of of the Danube Valley Fire Brigade was playing rousing music on the quayside to send the passengers on their way.

It was a beautiful day. The river sparkled; there was just enough of a breeze to cool the travellers as they looked over the rails at the Riverside Hotel and the row of flowering tulip trees. Annika and her mother and uncle had boarded the boat early, and while the adults went below to find their cabins, Annika stayed on deck, leaning over the rails and trying to fix her mind on what she saw: a mother coming up the gangway holding a pair of identical twins, one in each hand: little boys in leather trousers and loden hats . . . A man with a rucksack, a woman in a striped dress, carrying a parasol . . .

If she looked hard enough at the people as they came aboard she might be able to blot out her thoughts. Or even free her mind of any thoughts at all.

Thoughts of goodbye, thoughts that she might never see Vienna again, thoughts of her future at Spittal . . . Memories of Ellie's face as she stood in the door of the professors' house, memories of Stefan explaining to his little brothers that Annika was going away again. And she had quarrelled with Pauline; her friend had not been there to say goodbye.

She mustn't mind that; all that was in the past. And she mustn't be jealous of Zed, who was staying in Vienna with work he loved – staying in the city from which she was banished.

Why was it so difficult to do what was right? She thought of all the people she had learned about at school who had stuck to their beliefs: there was St Margaret, who had been pressed to death under a door, St Cecilia, who had been smothered in her bath, and St Catherine, who had been broken on the wheel.

Whereas she was just going back to live with her mother. There was no need to feel this utter, black despair.

'There you are, my dear. I've put your things in our cabin. You'd like the top bunk, I expect.'

'Yes. Thank you.'

Her mother smiled at her. 'Oh, Annika, I'm so happy to

be going home with you. My own daughter beside me for-ever more.'

The *Empress Elisabeth's* boiler was lit. She let off a burst of steam. The band of the Fire Brigade broke into an old folk song.

Must I then, must I then,
leave the city that I love . . .
the city that I love . . .
while you my friends stay here . . .

Annika bit her lip. Music could be horribly unfair.

'You're happy too, aren't you, my darling?' came her mother's voice.

'Of course.'

Pauline returned to Vienna after dark. She was utterly exhausted but she was triumphant. She had the evidence she needed and she'd been right all along.

In the bookshop she found her grandfather waiting up for her. He was not pleased.

'How dare you go off like that? Anything might have happened to you.'

'But it didn't,' said Pauline. And she told him what she had discovered at Pettelsdorf. 'I'm going over now to tell them.'

'No, you're not. Everyone will be asleep. You can go first thing in the morning.'

'But I must catch Annika – you've no idea how impor-tant it is.'

'You'll catch her in the morning. She isn't leaving till midday.'

So Pauline, still arguing, was persuaded to go to bed, where she fell at once into a deep sleep.

But at six-thirty the next morning she was knocking at the door of the professors' house.

Sigrid came after a while, still in her dressing gown.

'What on earth?'

'I've found out something terribly important. I have to see Annika and the professors and—'

'You can't see Annika; she's gone.'

Pauline stared at her. 'But she wasn't going till noon today.'

Sigrid shrugged. Her face was grey; she looked as though she had scarcely slept.

'They sent a carriage for her last night. They're taking an earlier boat.'

'What boat? When?'

'The *Empress Elisabeth*. It leaves from the Riverside quay at nine o'clock.'

'Sigrid, listen to what I've found out – and then please wake everybody up. We have to stop Annika going on that boat. We have to. She's in danger, she really is.'

Zed had come out of the back, pulling on his jersey. He ran at once to fetch Stefan, and now the professors appeared in various stages of disarray.

'What is it?' they wanted to know. 'What's the matter?'

'Listen,' said Pauline, 'please listen,' and she told her story once again.

There was no need for her to persuade or argue. It was as though deep down they had all expected something like this.

'We've got to stop her going.'

But how? The boat sailed in less than two hours' time,

and not from the Danube Quay in the town but from the landing stage above the Riverside Hotel, several kilometres out of the city.

Everyone had different ideas of how they might get there.

'If we take the number nineteen tram from the Praterstern and then go over the bridge and change to a number twenty-three . . .'

'The twenty-three only runs every quarter of an hour. We'd do better to take a cab. If we choose—'

'Those nags will never do it. The train to Kasselberg would be faster, and then a cab along the river.'

But even as they argued, pulling on their clothes in all sorts of strange ways, they knew they would never get to the quay in time.

'The police?' suggested Gertrude.

The police had the fastest horses, but persuading them to act instantly would be almost impossible.

It was then that they heard it: the strident pooping of Herr Egghart's motor horn. Then came the cloud of dust, the roar of the engine as he drove into the square, and the squeal of brakes as the great yellow machine drew up in front of his house.

Herr Egghart got out and stretched. He was in his goggles and leather gauntlets, his cap and floor-length duster coat. His wife in her motoring veil followed, then Loremarie.

Up to this moment every single person in the square only had to hear the pooping of the Eggharts' motor and they went back into their houses and shut the windows and the door. Nobody had ever been known to run towards him and his machine. Now, without looking at each other, the child did just that – and threw themselves on Herr Egghart just as he was following his wife and child into the house.

'Please, please, you must help us,' Pauline cried. 'It's desperately important.'

'We have to rescue Annika; it's a matter of life and death,' said Zed. 'You have to drive us to the Riverside Quay.'

Herr Egghart looked at them as though they were insane.

'Drive you to the Riverside Quay – after the journey I've had? You must be out of your mind. Now please get out of my way.'

Professor Julius had caught up with the children. 'It really is important, Herr Egghart. We have reason to believe that Annika is—'

'I'm afraid I'm not interested,' said Herr Egghart.

He was almost inside his house.

It was Stefan who found the magic words.

'It's about your great-aunt's trunk, sir. We think we know who stole it and—'

Herr Egghart turned. 'The trunk? Well, why didn't you say so?'

'Faster – oh, faster,' begged Pauline. She was in the back with Stefan and Zed. Professor Julius sat beside the driver.

But Herr Egghart was already driving very fast. He roared down the Karntner Strasse, rounded the Praterstern, sent a donkey cart into the kerb. His horn blew incessantly, clouds of dust rose in the children's faces.

There was a line of carts waiting to cross the bridge over the canal but Egghart's horn sent them to the side and he drove on.

An old lady leaped to safety in the Schwartzer Strasse. A stallholder stared open-mouthed.

The dial shot up to thirty-two kilometres per hour, then to forty: a record even for a custom-built Piccard-Pictet.

They were driving beside the Danube now, but there were several kilometres still to go. Past warehouses, past a boatyard . . . past a municipal park – and then they were at the Riverside.

'Oh no. No!'

They were too late; the gangway had been pulled up; steam poured from the *Empress*'s funnel. On the boat and on the shore there was a flurry of waving handkerchiefs.

Herr Egghart stopped with a squeal of brakes. The children rushed out of the car. They could see Annika in her red kerchief standing by the rail, but she hadn't seen them.

On the bandstand the conductor raised his baton to play the steamer out – and Zed ran to him like a streak of lightning and pulled at his arm.

The last of the ropes had been thrown on to the quay. The *Empress* was free.

Pauline rushed to the water's edge and cupped her hands and shouted the words which would save Annika.

Annika saw her now – but she could not hear her.

Pauline shouted again – and then Stefan came. His voice was stronger and he too shouted the same words, but he too could not make his voice carry across the water.

Herr Egghart got out of the car and made his way to the edge of the quay. He pushed Pauline and Stefan aside and removed his gauntlets. Then he too cupped his hands and shouted the all-important words as they had done.

But this was Egghart, whose voice as he yelled at his

wife and child could make the pigeons fly up from the rooftops. The man whose shout could make horses kneel.

And Annika heard them.

She heard the words. And as she did so, a great weight fell from her and she understood everything that had happened.

She shrugged off her cloak and let it fall on to the deck. Then, without a moment of hesitation, she climbed on to the rails, steadied herself – and jumped.

CHAPTER FORTY-TWO

FOUND DAY

Annika woke in her attic and stretched and opened the shutters.

In the square everything was as it should be. The pigeons flew up from General Brenner's head, the cathedral bells rang for morning mass . . . Stefan came out of the Bodeks' house with a pail to fetch the milk, and waved to her.

But after all everything was not quite the same as before, because they had decided that from now on they would have to be nice to Herr Egghart.

'We might not even mind if he becomes a statue,' Pauline said.

'As long as the statue was somewhere else,' said Stefan.

For it was this unpleasant, conceited man, with his foghorn voice and his ridiculous motor car, who had brought Annika safely home. The words which Pauline and Stefan had not been able to make her hear had reached her easily when Herr Egghart yelled them.

'*She is not your mother!*'

And as soon as she had heard them, Annika had known.

'I must have known all along, in a way,' she said. 'I tried too hard.'

When she came home they had all watched Annika for signs of shock or grief or disbelief – but there were none. The waters of the Danube, as she swam to the shore, had woken her completely from her spell. Forgiving a mother who had robbed her would have been a hard task – but what of a woman so greedy for wealth that she pretended to have a daughter, took her away from those who loved her, fed her with lies . . . ?

A woman like that could be banished from one's mind completely and forever. It would take time, for Annika's love had been real and it had been deep, but she knew that in the end she would succeed.

'You're not nobly born, then,' Loremarie had taunted her the day after Annika returned. 'You're not a "von" after all.'

And she had stepped back at the happiness in Annika's face.

'No,' said Annika. 'I'm completely ordinary. I'm me! And I have the most marvellously ordinary mother in the world. I have Ellie!'

Annika washed and dressed and came downstairs. In the kitchen the water was boiling for coffee, the rolls were warming in the oven – but there was no sign of Ellie.

The door to the courtyard was open. On the bench sat Ellie, and across her lap, though there was plenty of room for him on either side, lay the three-legged dog.

'You'll have to make the coffee,' said Ellie.

Annika turned away to hide her smile.

'Couldn't you just tell him to get off?'

Ellie looked at her reproachfully.

'He's tired,' she said.

There had been a nasty row when Bertha had written that she was going into hospital for an operation and asked if they could take Hector.

'Couldn't we have him?' Annika had begged. 'I've always wanted a dog.'

'Over my dead body does a dog come near my kitchen,' had been Ellie's reply.

'He's not *a* dog. If it wasn't for Hector finding the photograph I'd still be at Spittal.'

'All the same, he's a dog,' Ellie had said. 'Germs and hairs on everything and dirt.'

But Hector by this time had been on his way.

Zed came in just as they were clearing breakfast. He was still sleeping in the bookshop and working by day in the professors' house, but in September, when the Lipizzaners returned from the mountains, he and Rocco would join the riding school. Apprentice riders lived in the school; they learned to do everything not only for their horses but for all the horses. But once a fortnight they were allowed home for a whole Sunday – and home for Zed was now the professors' house.

'Are you ready?'

Annika nodded. 'I finished it last night. Professor Julius

let me use his typewriter, but I kept spelling "agoraphobia" wrong.'

She took down a large sheet of paper and Zed looked at it.

'That's fine,' he said. 'They're meeting us at the hut.'

Pauline and Stefan were there before them. They had tidied up and put a bunch of daisies on the table and laid out the mugs and a bottle of lemonade. There were even paper napkins because this was not an ordinary meeting, it was a presentation.

'We've got something for you,' Stefan told Pauline. 'A cutting for your scrapbook. Take care how you paste it in; it's a good one.'

Zed took the folded paper in its heavy envelope and handed it to Pauline.

Amazing Courage of Bookshop Worker, she read. *A young girl who suffers from the rare and serious disease of agoraphobia undertook a terrifying journey from the Inner City to the mountain fortress of Pettelsdorf in the High Alps. Not only did she brave the long walk across open streets and the journey alone by train, but she confronted a hostile old woman who could neither hear nor speak. There is no doubt that her conduct saved the life of her friend, who was in considerable danger. In particular, the speed with which she acted on her discovery . . .*

There was a lot more; it was a long article, and as Pauline read it she flushed to the roots of her hair.

'I can't put that in,' she said.

'Oh yes, you can,' said Annika. 'You were quite as brave as the man with the bee stings, and the lady who chased the hot-air balloon.'

'And the boy who hung on to the cow under the ice – if he existed,' said Stefan.

'Of course he existed,' said Pauline.

But for once she was in no mood to argue with her friends, and they lifted up their mugs and drank her health.

Pauline's discovery at Pettelsdorf had been the key that enabled the professors to untangle the story.

Frau Edeltraut had heard about the jewels in the trunk far earlier than anyone had realized, before she even knew who Annika was, and the story would not go out of her head. The idea of a fortune going begging when she was at her wit's end was more than she could bear. So she had gone to the old lady's lawyers in Vienna, veiled and grieving, and under a false name, pretending to be a friend of La Rondine's, and begged for a keepsake out of the old lady's trunk.

Only the lawyer's young clerk was on duty. He was very sorry, but it was out of the question – the trunk had been left to a little foundling girl. It was under lock and key, in the lawyer's basement; there were still legal matters to sort out.

'If you were a relative of the girl it might be possible to arrange something,' said the clerk, who was sorry for the grieving woman in her veil. 'A close relative. Even so you would have to get permission. The child does not even know of her legacy yet.'

Frau Edeltraut got Annika's name from him and went away to think. A relative? A close relative. Why not a very close relative? Why not her mother? She was desperate enough to try anything.

It was only then that she consulted Pumpelmann-Schlissenger, who was known to do 'unusual' jobs, and promised him a share of the fortune if he would help her to trace the details of Annika's birth and adoption and provide her with the necessary papers.

When she arrived at the professors' house, two weeks later, it was as a woman who, against all odds, had found her long-lost child.

It had been difficult to interest Annika in what was to happen to the money for the jewels which Frau von Tannenberg had not yet sold.

She had started by saying that she didn't want the money. 'I don't need it for anything,' she had said. 'And I don't want to punish her. She may not have been my mother but I thought she was.'

But Pauline said that that was nonsense. 'You need it to pay for Stefan's training as an engineer for a start.'

They were all in the kitchen, as they so often were these days.

'I wouldn't take money from Annika,' said Stefan.

'Yes, you would. If it was a loan. And you need it to pay back Ellie's savings,' Pauline went on.

'And there's Professor Gertrude's harp,' said Stefan.

'Isn't there anything you want for yourself?' asked Zed.

Annika grinned and looked sideways at Ellie.

'Maybe a mechanical egg-beater?' she suggested.

And waited while Ellie's eyebrows drew together in a frown and she said, 'Over my dead body.'

All the same, it seemed as though Annika would get some money in the end whether she wanted it or not, because the Eggharts were now on the warpath. As the truth came out about Frau von Tannenberg's activites, they were once again making it clear that the famous trunk had belonged to *their* great-aunt.

'She was OUR great-aunt so it was OUR trunk,' they pointed out in case anybody had not heard this yet.

They also threatened to dispute the will on the grounds that the old lady had not been right in her head before she died.

'One of the maids said she spoke about a rose garden in the sky,' said Frau Egghart, 'which *shows* she was wandering.'

'No, it doesn't,' said Pauline. 'There is a rose garden in the sky above Merano. It's a glacier, very high, which turns a rose colour in the evenings and that's what they call it. It's in the guidebook.'

But the Eggharts were not easy to shake off.

'If Annika won't take the matter any further we will take steps ourselves. It is outrageous that the woman should get away with her crime,' they told the professors.

The professors felt the same, so in the end it was agreed that while Frau von Tannenberg should keep what she already had – 'because of Spittal,' said Annika. 'It would be awful if everything fell down again' – the rest of the jewels should be sold and the money divided between Annika and the Eggharts.

Pauline of course thought this was monstrous, but it was the Eggharts who were going to consult the lawyers and brief them and take all the steps that would be necessary to keep the police out of the investigation, and everyone knew that if it was left to Annika she would do nothing. Annika was to get a small allowance each month

376

and a lump sum for the loan to Stefan, and the rest would be put in a trust for her till she was twenty-one.

'Actually,' said Annika. 'If there's enough money in the end maybe we could buy the house in Merano with the weathervane shaped like a crowing cock and Ellie and Sigrid could live there when they're old. All of us could. It would be nice to have a rose garden in the sky.'

Found Day had come round again, and with it the Found Day treat.

Annika knew exactly what she wanted to do. She wanted to take everybody on the Giant Wheel in the Prater for a celebratory lunch high above the city.

And there was something she wanted to do when she got up there, but she didn't mention this to anyone in case it didn't work, or people thought she was silly, or both.

Everyone was to come who had been to see the Lipizzaners the year before, and of course Zed. The treat needed a lot of preparation because they had to rent the special carriage used for wedding parties, which was bright red and had a crown painted on the outside. Unlike the other carriages, which only had wooden benches and sealed windows, the wedding carriage was furnished with a long table screwed to the floor, benches covered in velvet, and velvet curtains – and it had one window, high up, which could be opened.

By paying extra – by paying quite a lot of extra – the carriage could be stopped at the highest point – sometimes for a few moments, sometimes for much longer. If the full price was paid it would stay suspended at the highest point for a whole hour, and the other passengers had to wait down below. Stefan's father had arranged everything for them.

Annika and Ellie and Sigrid were up at dawn on the day, packing cold pheasant in aspic and ham strudels and salads of cucumber and radish. They piled chocolate mousse and vanilla puffs into boxes, and made lemonade, and wedged the professors' champagne into a silver bucket filled with ice.

And Annika bought two big bunches of summer flowers from the old flower seller in the square, because there could be no proper celebration without flowers on the table, and found two heavy vases that would not fall over as the wheel went up into the sky.

They piled into three hansom cabs and drove to the Prater, and Stefan and Zed unloaded the hampers and then Annika and Ellie and Sigrid set the long table with a white damask cloth and put the flowers in the vases and slowly, very slowly, in regular jerks, the famous wheel rose up, and then up again, and up once more.

The food on the table held steady, the professors walked from side to side pointing out places that mattered to them, and Annika remembered the last time she had been on the wheel by herself, and thought how fortunate she was to grow up in this place.

At the highest point the carriage stopped with a little click and they hung suspended in space.

Ellie, however, did not permit long sightseeing sessions.

'The meal is ready,' she said firmly, and at these important words the professors left the window and everybody seated themselves at the long table – and ate.

But after the last of the chocolate mousse had been scraped from the dishes, and the last sip of wine had disappeared down the professors' throats, Annika got to her feet.

'There's something I wanted to do when I was up here last time,' she said. 'Only I couldn't. So I'm going to do it now. Would you please pass me the vases – both of them?'

So Professor Gertrude pushed down the vase opposite her, and Zed pushed over the one which was next to him – and everybody watched as she took all the flowers out of both vases and patted the stems dry with her napkin.

Then she gathered up the blooms and walked over to the side of the carriage with the one small, high-up window which could be opened – and asked Stefan to open it.

'I think I can reach.' she said. 'Yes. Just. Could you hand me the flowers one by one please? I don't want to knock anybody out.'

So they passed her the flowers they had brought, and Annika stood on tiptoe and strewed them – the blue irises, the pink tulips, the marigolds and larkspur and zinnias, the delphiniums and the sweet-scented stock . . . strewed them and scattered them over the golden city which was her home once more.

The wind had dropped; the flowers fell gently. Some swirled away on air currents to the city's edge, but most fell down over the roofs and booths of the funfair, and the people who saw them looked up for a moment and then went back to their work as though this kind of thing was no more than they deserved. And one – a large red tulip – fell on the turf path of the Prater where Rocco had reared up to save the life of a small fat boy in a sailor suit.

And it so happened that Fritzi, in the same sailor suit, was walking with his mother and his sister in her pram, as he walked each afternoon along the path that he had walked along that day, when a large red tulip descended and fell at his feet.

Fritzi had learned not to let go of his mother, but he picked the tulip up with his free hand and examined it.

'Mine,' he said – as he had said that day when he found the big red ball.

But this time no thief came running towards him to deprive him of his spoils.

Fritzi was pleased. There is a lot you can do with a tulip – fill the flower cup with sand, hold it aloft by the stem like a sword, put it over your shoulder like a rifle . . .

'Mine,' he said again, and his mother nodded, for it did not seem to her at all surprising that the heavens had opened and thrown a flower at the feet of her magnificent son.

This, after all, was Vienna.

CHAPTER FORTY-THREE

HERMANN CHANGES HIS MIND

Edeltraut was standing by the window of her drawing room, looking out at her estate. Though it was summer now, the lake was still grey; a cold wind rippled its surface.

She was alone. Uncle Conrad was leaving Bad Haxenfeld, to follow the dentists to a newer, more fashionable spa in the south. The dentists had convinced him that the waters were hotter there, and smelt stronger, and the treatment was more up to date.

At least that was what the Baron had told her, but she knew he was angry with her for having pretended that Annika was her daughter, for having deceived the family about Annika's birth.

Mathilde too was angry. She had been fond of Annika, she said. It was all right to 'borrow' the belongings of a true daughter, but not to pretend to have a daughter and take her away from those who loved her.

Edeltraut thought this was nonsense. She had so nearly succeeded in her plan. If only she'd had that wretched dog put down when Hermann had first tied a firecracker to his tail ... And if she'd succeeded, everyone would have grovelled at her feet.

But it was no good thinking about the past. Only the future mattered now, and the future was Hermann and Spittal, and the great inheritance of the von Tannenbergs. There had always been von Tannenbergs at Spittal. Always. Since the first Ritter von Tannenberg had conquered this marshy corner of Norrland and built his great fortified house and dug his moats and put iron studs on his doors, there had been von Tannenbergs with their proud flag fluttering in the wind.

And there always would be von Tannenbergs. Everything she had done, she had done for Hermann. In five years he would ride in at his gates, a fully commissioned officer, and she would hand him the keys of his kingdom. Lieutenant Hermann von Tannenberg, her son, Master of Spittal and its villages and forests and fields.

And after Hermann would come his sons and his son's sons – and then she could die content.

She put on a shawl and went out of doors to stand on the terrace. The pike plopped in the water, the storks were wading in the ditch, picking off the last of the frogs. At least she had made the roof sound, and repaired the stonework. Spittal would be safe now for many years.

She was still standing there, lost in her dream, when she heard a carriage turn into the courtyard and went to see who could be calling at this time of day.

The carriage was unfamiliar but the letters on the side made her heart pound. *St Xavier's Military Academy for the Sons of the Nobility.*

The carriage stopped and two men in uniform got out: a captain with a weather-beaten face and the ribbon of the Iron Cross on his chest, and a young lieutenant who turned and spoke to someone huddled on the back seat.

The huddled figure straightened itself and stepped out on to the cobbles.

It was Hermann.

Not in his St Xavier uniform with the cap and the swagger stick and the shiny boots . . . Hermann in a cloth jacket and trousers, with a woollen cap pulled over his forehead. He looked pale and ill, and when his mother went towards him, he turned away.

'Hermann!' she cried. 'What has happened? Why are you here?'

The boy did not answer, and she saw that he was trembling.

'May we have a few words with you in private?' said the captain.

Frau Edeltraut led them into the drawing room. 'What is it?' she cried again. 'Is he ill?'

The captain bent his head. 'Yes, you could say that. It would be the kindest way of putting it. We have had to expel him, Frau von Tannenberg. He is not suitable for St Xavier's.'

'Not suitable! What are you saying? He has thought of nothing but the army all his life.'

'Nevertheless he is quite unsuited to army life. I'm afraid the boy is a coward and a weakling. There will be a report from the principal which we will send to you. But there are no circumstances under which we would allow him to return to St Xavier's.'

She went on anxiously questioning them, but they would say no more and left again without saying goodbye to Hermann.

'I knew the Freiherr,' said the captain as he climbed into the coach. 'This would have been a sad day for him.'

She found Hermann on the terrace, staring sightlessly at the lake.

'Hermann, I can't believe this. You wanted nothing except to be a soldier, all your life.'

Hermann turned his head. There were dark circles under his eyes and he was very thin. 'I've changed my mind,' he said.

'But, Hermann . . . do you mean you want to stay at home and look after the estate? If you do, maybe we could—'

'No, I don't want to do that. I want to be a painter.'

Edeltraut was completely at a loss. 'You want to paint houses?'

Hermann sighed. 'No, Mother. I want to paint pictures. I want to go to Paris and study to be a great painter. Karl-Gottlieb is going to live there. You remember Karl-Gottlieb? He wrote and told me what kind of tooth mugs I had to bring to St Xavier's. He was the only one who tried to help me.' Hermann faltered, then went on in a low voice. 'When I first came the other boys pushed me on to the ledge outside the dormitory window and shut me out. It was very narrow and very high up – three floors. You had to stand there all night and not make a sound. It was a test . . . an initiation. But after a few hours I got giddy and I was sure I was going to fall . . . and I called out and shouted, and a teacher came and let me in again. After that none of the boys would speak to me. Except for Karl-Gottlieb. Then he ran away. Even though his father's a field marshal and very high up. When he'd gone they used to hang me from the hooks on the cloakroom wall and pretend to charge me with their bayonets.' Hermann's voice shook.-

Edeltraut tried to take this in. She had thought of anything except that her son would turn out to be a coward. 'You're being quite ridiculous, Hermann. No von Tannenberg has ever been a painter.'

'Then I will be the first. Karl-Gottlieb has a sister who has a studio in Paris – she's very modern – and she would help us. We think we could find some more people to join us and then we could become a famous group of artists.'

'Hermann, you're mad. There have always been von Tannenbergs at Spittal. Always.'

'Yes, I know. But if you sold Spitall there would be enough money to pay for our painting lessons, and you could come and have a flat near us. We'd let you attend our exhibitions and everything.'

Edletraut tried to gather herself together. 'My poor boy, you have lost your reason. There have been von Tannenbergs at Spittal since—'

Hermann put a hand on her arm. 'I know, Mother,' he said patiently, and she saw that a little colour had returned to his face. 'I know, Mother,' he said patiently and she saw that a little colour had returned to his face. 'I know there have always been von Tannenbergs at Spittal. But that doesn't mean that there have to go *on* being von Tannenbergs at Spittal. You must see that. Karl-Gottlieb

385

says there have been von Tannenbergs at Spittal for long enough, and I *entirely* agree with him.'

Three weeks later, Annika came downstairs to find a letter from Gudrun, who wanted Annika to send her some more kerchiefs like the one she'd give her at Felsenheim and a snood for her hair.

There has been a terrible row here, she wrote. *Hermann came home – he's been expelled and he's going to Paris and Aunt Edeltraut is going with him. She tried to make my father come too, but he said there was nothing to shoot in Paris except people so he's staying with us. Mama won't speak to Aunt Edeltraut ever again, she says, because of trying to take away her husband and also because she thought you really were her niece and she had got fond of you, though I can't see how Aunt Edeltraut could have known that they gave her the wrong birth certificate.*

Spittal has been sold to a man who makes saucepans. He made Aunt Edeltraut sell him the family crest too, the one about 'Stand Aside, Ye Vermin Who Oppose Us', because there are people who pretend to make better saucepans than him and they are vermin, he said.

He's very rich and has a son who is a bit older than me. Of course I couldn't ever marry anybody who is lowly born – at least I don't think I could – but he is very handsome. I suppose you couldn't send me a lace collar like the one you had on your brown velvet dress as well? We don't seem to have any money for clothes again, but Papa says we won't have to dig a bear pit, at least not yet.

With best wishes,
Gudrun.

CHAPTER FORTY-FOUR

THE EMPEROR'S HORSE

The arcaded palace of a prince, now the royal stables, was lit by pools of light from the gas lamps on the walls. From the chapel further down the road came the sound of the Vienna choirboys singing vespers.

There was the smell of straw, of saddle soap . . .

A lone dark horse was walking down the well-worn path towards the great double door, which opened now from the inside. The boy leading the horse walked steadily on, but just before he reached the door he turned and waved.

The people clustered on the pavement waved back. They waved back hard. A row of little boys, silent for once because the occasion was so important. A girl with frizzy hair who was frowning because it had all become rather solemn and after all a horse is just a horse. A lady to whose long black skirt there clung the fragments of a buttered roll.

Annika had been pushed forward to the place of honour, closest by the gate. Her eyes followed every step that Zed took, but in some other part of her mind she was waking up on that first morning in Spittal when an unknown boy had ridden past her window, and she had known that both the boy and his horse would become part of her life.

Inside the stables a horse whinnied his welcome and Rocco replied. Then Zed led him forward over the threshold – and the great door closed on them both.

For a moment there was no sound except the singing of the boys in the little church.

Then, 'I'm hungry,' said Hansi – and Ellie nodded, and they all went home.

Journey to the River Sea won the Smarties Book Prize Gold Award, was the runner-up for the Whitbread Children's Book of the Year Award and the Guardian Children's Fiction Award, and was shortlisted for the Carnegie Medal.

Praise for *Journey to the River Sea*

'Enchanting and inspiring. Any reader presented with this book will be enriched for life'
Anne Fine, Children's Laureate

'The most perfect children's book of the year . . . captivatingly told, funny and moving'
Nicolette Jones, *Sunday Times*

'A plot too exciting to put down. Sheer pleasure'
Sarah Johnson, *The Times*

'Journey to the River Sea is pretty much perfect. A richly satisfying, superbly written adventure'
Dinah Hall, *Sunday Telegraph*

'A warm-hearted, well-written and absorbing adventure'
Independent on Sunday

'*Journey to the River Sea* is funny, wise and true'
Philip Pullman

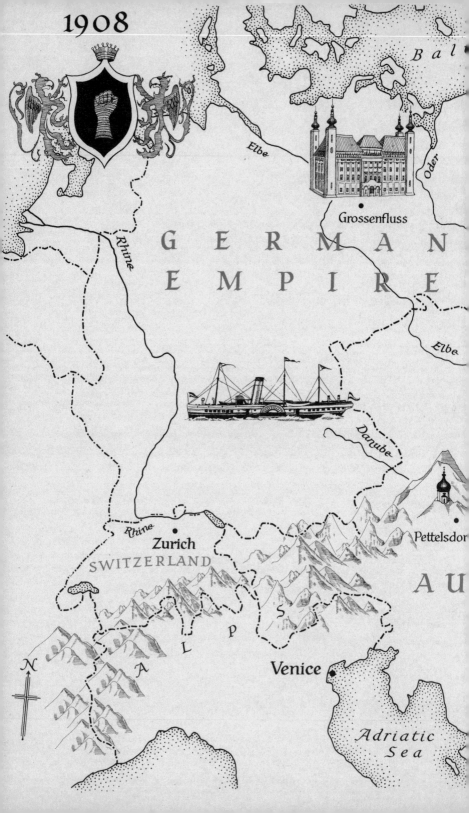